COUNTRY TALES

Also available in 'Country Classics'

Adventures Among Birds by W.H. Hudson
A Cotswold Village by J. Arthur Gibbs
The Country House-Wife's Garden by William Lawson
The Essential Gilbert White of Selborne
Gypsy Folk Tales edited by John Sampson
Life in a Devon Village by Henry Williamson
Memoirs of a Surrey Labourer by George Bourne
The Old Farm by Thomas Hennell
Sweet Thames Run Softly by Robert Gibbings
Tales of Old Ireland by James Berry

COUNTRY TALES

H. E. Bates

R

ROBINSON PUBLISHING

LONDON

Robinson Publishing
11 Shepherd House
5 Shepherd Street
London W1Y 7LD

First published 1938
Published by Robinson Publishing 1985
Copyright © The Estate of H.E. Bates
Series Design: Lawrence & Gerry Design Group

British Library Cataloguing
in Publication Data

Bates, H.E.
    Country tales.
    I. Title
    823′.912[F]   PR 6003.A965
    ISBN 1-85004-026-5

Printed in England by Richard Clay (The Chaucer Press) Ltd.

CONTENTS

THE WRITER EXPLAINS

I HAVE selected these thirty stories from five volumes of my published work: *Day's End* (1928), *The Black Boxer* (1932), *The Woman Who Had Imagination* (1934), *Cut and Come Again* (1935), and *Something Short and Sweet* (1937). They represent something like a quarter of my output in short story form over the past ten years. Except in the ordinary way of proof reading I have not revised them at all. I have done this not through laziness, but deliberately, and for a reason: because I feel that once a story is written, printed and published it should have reached, in a sense, a state of finality. The author should then resist impulses to tamper with it, to superimpose on it the touches of a maturer experience and technique. Painters do not, as far as I know, visit the galleries in which their pictures are hung and retouch them there; nor do sculptors hack at their monuments after they have been erected in public places. What is true of them should be also true, I feel, of authors. The finished work of an artist, in a sense, no longer belongs to him.

I first began writing short stories, with any pretence of seriousness, when I was nineteen. I was then working eight hours a day in a warehouse. From that time until I was twenty-three I must have written between thirty and forty stories, of which twenty-five made up the volume *Day's End*. From these stories I got the reputation of being rather a delicate writer with a carefully polished style — which was a mistake. My style was not polished and I wrote with what Edward Garnett once called a 'facile devil inside you'. Stories like 'Fear', 'Fishing', 'Blossoms', 'The Idiot' and 'Harvest', none of which are included here, were written easily, quickly and light-heartedly, often between breakfast and lunch. Later stories, such as 'The Gleaner', 'Time', 'Little Fish', 'Harvest Moon' and 'Italian Haircut', which are included here, were written in the same way, quickly and happily, but with a difference. In the first stories I was groping my way towards becoming a conscious writer; in

7

the later stories I had become one. Again, in the early stories, and stories like them, I showed a dangerous appetite for sucking the significance out of trivialities — dangerous because it came to me so easily and naturally that it threatened to become a habit. This eager interest in trivialities, though it was precisely what made me a short story writer, threatened about the time of *Day's End* to make me a writer of very limited scope. I became aware of this, my mind going back to the warning given by Edward Garnett in the preface to my first novel — 'there is the path of art endlessly difficult' and I saw that I had the choice either of repeating myself in a series of charming episodes which I could produce as easily as breathing or of consciously trying to widen my range of sympathy and develop myself. This process of development from the dreamy world of the subjective, seen in such stories as 'The Birthday' and 'Two Candles', in which mood was more important than character, to a wider, harder, more objective world in which character was of greater importance, was very difficult for me. It was a transition accomplished primarily by two stories, 'Charlotte Esmond' and 'The Black Boxer'. Both of these stories, drawn directly from life and not from imagination, were not written by the facile devil inside me; they were hard work; but they were both, in a sense, a triumph. They marked the end of a struggle; they projected me, confidently, into a new world. Without having written them I probably could not have written 'The Mill', 'The Station', 'The Kimono' or 'I Am Not Myself', which I reckon as being among the first half-dozen of my stories to date.

'The Kimono' brings up another question. I have never from the first had the slightest interest in plots, and no one who reads these thirty stories will need to be told that the idea of plots is something completely foreign to my whole conception of the short story. Not only do I doubt whether I could evolve a formula for writing a short story to save my life, but I have never in my life written a story even to illustrate an idea. But there was an occasion when I was invited to write a story round an idea, and the result, astonishing though it may seem, is 'The Kimono'. This story is one of a dozen others, all similarly commissioned and all written round the same idea. The only difference between 'The Kimono' and the rest of the stories, all contained in one volume, is that 'The Kimono' is not written round the idea but in defiance of the idea. It is a straightforward story in which character and atmosphere are predominant and the idea almost completely subservient. The characters, as living characters should, have swallowed up the plot. 'The Kimono', in fact, written out of genuine and not artificial impulses, was intended to be a story that could stand by its own strength. One result of this, at least, was interesting. When 'The Kimono' and its companion stories later came to be serialized in a Sunday newspaper 'The Kimono' was banned. This brings me to another and more important point. As I write this preface it seems to me that the short story, which I regard as being not by any means the least of this generation's contribution to literature, stands a fair chance, as near as matters, of being starved out of existence. In England, at the moment, there is not one reputable magazine devoted entirely to the short story, and the periodicals which take any interest in it at all can be numbered on the fingers of one hand. And outside of one or two periodicals the rates paid for short stories are pitiful. There is no magazine in this country to compare, for standards of taste and remuneration, with *The Atlantic Monthly*, *Harpers*, *Scribners*, or *Esquire* in America. Here in England, by a nice irony, it is the newspapers which have saved the short story from complete oblivion and many short story writers from starvation. I say by a nice irony deliberately, for though newspapers have the lowest possible standards of taste regarding rape, homosexuality, murder, perversion, cruelty, suicide, divorce, public indecency and sexual behaviour in general so long as such things are related in terms of fact, they have the severest and most impeccable standards of taste when these same things are related in terms of fiction. Don't ask me why. I treasure greatly a letter of refusal from the editor of a leading newspaper: 'Sorry. Don't you know that Mrs. Grundy is co-editor of every English newspaper?' Nor is this true exclusively of newspapers. I could name half a dozen English magazines where Mrs. Grundy appears to have a seat on the editorial board.

The existence of the short story seems to depend largely therefore on its survival in volume form: in anthologies and in volumes such as this. That it is the most fascinating of all prose forms I myself have never had any doubt. Its lack of appeal to a wide public completely defeats me. Its flexibility, almost unlimited range of subject and sympathy, and its very brevity, make it as perfectly suited to the expression and mood of this age as the heroic couplet was to the age of Pope. To my mind it is in every way a finer means of expression of our age of unrest, disbelief and distrust than either the novel or poetry. For that reason alone, in spite of petticoat editors and a prejudiced public, I have no doubt as to its future. As we know it, it is still an art in its infancy.

Of my own stories there is nothing to say in explanation for the simple reason that I hope, and think, they do not need explanation. Those who are interested will be able, from these thirty stories, to see quite plainly what forces have influenced me. They can work out, if they so care, the stages of my development, from 'The Easter Blessing' to 'The Mill'. But they are not asked to do that. They are similarly not asked to accept a philosophy, a point of view, a creed, a moral, a sermon on good or evil. The best I can hope is that they will read these stories with something of the spirit in which they were written: for pleasure, and out of a passionate interest in human lives.

H. E. BATES

COUNTRY TALES

THE EASTER BLESSING

SUDDENLY, across the empty seats of the church, the two women caught sight of each other. One of them, Helena, the young doctor's wife, crouched on the altar steps in the middle of a little sea of wood-anemones and daffodils, for it was Easter Sunday, and in an hour the service would begin. The other, an older woman with a grey scarf tied over her head, sat far back in great shadows which made her features indistinguishable. It was just possible to tell she was staring at Helena, nothing more.

Having allowed herself what seemed a hasty glimpse, Helena bent her head away again and began putting anemones with daffodils in artistic bunches. On her moving the flowers the altar became full of spring scents; sunlight fell in a great beam across the floor, and from the stones a sweet coolness rose up through her limbs.

All at once she shivered. Why was it the woman was so early for the service, which did not begin for an hour? She shifted her position a little and was able to take other looks at the dark figure, which sat with a sort of desperation about the hang of the head, as if trying not to faint or fall asleep. She was quite motionless. Soon afterwards a pinkish glow from one of the windows fell on her, and lighting up her face, made her look like a picture of one of the saints.

Under some unconquerable impulse Helena went down and along the nave to where the woman sat sunk in thought. In silence the two faced each other, until, half-ashamed of her erectness, Helena sat suddenly on the seat in front and blinked in an ashamed way.

'Is it the service you've come for?' she asked.

'They don't have services in the morning, do they?' The voice had no spirit.

'Yes, that is, to-day,' she quietly replied. 'It's Easter.'

'Is it?' came in faint tones. 'Well — '

They sat in silence until Helena said:

'There's a service in an hour.'

Then in a whispering voice that seemed to run in among the stone pillars as if afraid, she was asked in return:

'Have you got anything to eat?'

She had the foolishness to ask in reply:

'Are you hungry, then?'

As the woman stared a pair of white slits in her sombre eyes seemed to imply, 'Has it been so long since you saw anyone hungry that you've forgotten what it looks like?'

And with a pale forefinger and thumb she began picking at the dark material of her dress above the wrist; the joints stood out like very thin flints and the wrist-bone like a stone knob.

'Who are you?' asked Helena.

In reply she received a look which suggested: 'I expect you've forgotten that words don't feed folk,' but otherwise the question went unanswered.

Under the tyrannical looks which the woman sent out, Helena began a stream of questionings.

'Who are you? What have you come into the church for?' — these were uppermost.

To all of them she received one answer.

'I'm hungry and beat.'

She had an idea that at that point it was dutiful to do something kind and illuminating, and not ask other questions or sit drumming her fingers on the head of the seat. She had even an inclination to prayer, which was strange enough, such as, 'Lord God, open Thy heart to Thy servant ... have mercy upon us, have mercy upon us. Let the words of my mouth ... glory everlasting ... Jesus Christ ...' She felt herself babble after the manner of the priests. But it wouldn't do. Something of a simple, earnest nature was necessary: 'Thou who art God of all flesh, let not Thy children suffer ... suffer iniquities and hardship,' she tried again in desperation, 'Christ our — '

But 'Christ our Lord' went unfinished as if she had been caught in an immoral act.

'Haven't you got anything?'

'I'll get something — Yes — ' The words flowed torrentially. 'In a minute — tell me who you are? Promise you won't move till I come back? Who are you?'

The woman looked up. A shaft of cordial yellow light fell on her hands, and her lips moved once or twice: 'I'll tell you when you come back.'

As she moved away Helena saw scraps of straw on the woman's back, and thinking instinctively of barns and ditches and that there was some coincidence in the woman coming into the church on Easter Sunday, opened the door and began to run.

Her husband, meeting her on the steps of the house, tried to prevent her brushing past him, and even attempted to kiss her, but she cried out: 'Let me go! You don't understand what a hurry I'm in!'

'The service isn't due to begin yet,' he whispered as a reminder. 'Have you decorated the church? You smell of daffodils.'

She looked at him sharply and because she felt unclean would have been less surprised had he said: 'You smell of dirt and straw.'

'The spring's in your head,' she suggested and tried to run. 'You must let me go. You don't understand. Don't keep me! There's a heap of flowers still lying on the altar; the service will begin and I'm late!'

'I'll help you bunch them!'

'No, no!'

'What's the matter?'

She replied 'nothing' and began wondering first if the woman would stay in the church, then if the strips of straw would drop from her back when she got up, and lastly what made her look so adamant and chastising. With fresh shades of meaning the words 'I'm hungry and beat' kept rising up, then the moments when the women had first become aware of each other, when the other had looked like a picture of one of the saints, when the sun had fallen on her wrists and she had looked reproachfully up and said: 'Haven't you got anything?'

'Let me go in! Let me go in!'

'Not so much hurry! Not so much —'

'But you don't understand what a state I've left it all in,' she half-yelled at him. Fiercely struggling she ran into the house at last.

But it was already late, and in the foremost seats of the church one or two children and an old woman had gathered, whispering in low tones, when she returned. Beams of sunlight lay on the altar-brasses and seats of the south side. Up and down the altarsteps the figure of the verger, already cassocked, moved busily and noiselessly, clearing away wood-anemones and daffodils.

All this she saw as she crossed the threshold and went quickly to the seat where she had left the woman. But there, except for sunlight and strips of straw, the seat was dark and empty.

She sat down, hid the basket with her dress and feet, and while watching the first stragglers come in for the service thought of the woman and of where she might be. But no conjecture seemed strong enough, and little by little she gave herself up to the contemplation of the woman's face as she had first seen it. As she did so the church half-filled and the bell began to ring harshly. Those who came in sat looking stupidly at the flowers, and fidgeting impatiently seemed glad when the bell ceased and chants upset the stillness.

She babbled with the rest: 'Therefore let us keep the feast; not with the old leaven ... but with the unleavened bread of sincerity. ...'

And she sat still and was silent as if stupefied in the prayers. On occasions she could not bear the darkness, but opened her eyes and stared at the scraps of straw visible as dull-yellow dashes in the shadows. Gloom hung through the church and reminded her of the gloom of the woman's face under the grey scarf. She fancied she heard a sound close to her face and started violently, then saw the offertory box beneath her nose. It passed on. To-day the offerings were for the priests, she remembered. The service seemed interminable and dull. The hymns were many and tedious, the wood-anemones drooped and the sun did not come out again.

'And the Holy Ghost, Amen!'

Clouds piled on top of each other and patients kept her husband away all the afternoon. Of the woman she saw nothing and in the solitude thought of her face, then of her wrist-bones and hands and dirty back, and was revolted. In

16

a mood of self-reproach she vexatiously tapped her hands together and fancied she heard someone demanding things to eat. Although it was strange and even ironical that she should shed tears for a woman whose eyes had never for one moment been anything but dry, she felt she must weep. And she did so, and Easter Sunday wore on. At evening, in the church, candles were lit. She saw them and a monotone of voices at prayer seemed to fall oppressively on her head from the bluish sky.

When she was seated at the supper-table, eating nothing, the gardener came in and said it was hailing, and listening she heard the stones on the window. Then, foolishly, she tried to pray, but the hail fell sharply, drowning the sound of the prayer in the beginning.

Her husband came home at last, looking tired, and she noticed traces of the storm in the shape of hail-stones lying in the brim of his hat. While he sat at the table, grunting and eating, she stirred the fire and sat looking into its heart.

'A most unfortunate thing,' her husband soon afterwards began. 'A suicide in Low Pond. Imagine how annoyed I was to be dragged from one end of the town to the other and then be quite useless.'

'Yes.' The voice had no spirit.

'Yes, it was really not only annoying, but quite nauseating. A woman — starved. Nothing on under her dress and only a bit of a scarf over her head.'

She listened hardest, it seemed, when he paused.

'We brought her home in the hail. The hail bounced on her face.'

He continued to eat. Helena rose and going to the window gazed out at the hail reposing in uneven lines of white on the dark paths and lawn. Now, however, no more was falling and through the clear air were plainly visible the lighted church-windows, the casts of light on the ground, and the coloured figures of the saints on the glass. She remembered the moment when she had seen the woman in a pinkish glow, and with a sudden flash of horror recollected that while looking like one of the saints she must have been hungry too.

Her husband ate stolidly and for a long time. 'A nice

thing,' he would declare. 'A suicide and a hail-storm on Easter Sunday.'

When Helena looked out again the hail still lay over the earth in thin unmelted streaks which were lit to a dazzling purity where the shafts of light fell. The night was frigidly calm and spiritual and suddenly it seemed that the air about the white and yellow lights gave up the soul of the woman and let it soar and disappear soundlessly into the dark sky.

In a minute it was all over, and murmuring 'Thank God!' she sank into a chair, and sighed twice.

'Didn't you say something to me?' inquired her husband. 'Nothing.'

'I thought you said "Good God". But that's not like you.'

She felt sick and harassed and selfish.

'It's nothing,' she falteringly told him. 'But in the church this morning, in one of the seats — '

'You're crying!' he exclaimed.

'In the church this morning,' she tried again, 'and now you come with this story — '

'The service has made you tired,' he said. 'In the morning it will be all right again. You mustn't go again this week. I agree, it's a nauseating thing, and on Easter Sunday, too.'

But seeing that she still cried he turned away, ate something with one hand and with the other patted her neck.

'I understand. I understand,' he whispered as she cried again. 'Now confess and tell me what you've been doing all day and that it's been lonely without me.'

NEVER

IT was afternoon: great clouds stumbled across the sky. In the drowsy, half-dark room the young girl sat in a heap near the window, scarcely moving herself, as if she expected a certain timed happening, such as a visit, sunset, a command. Slowly she would draw the fingers of one hand across the back of the other, in the little hollows between the guides, and move her lips in the same sad, vexed way in which her brows came together. And like this too, her eyes would shift about, from the near, shadowed fields, to the west hills, where the sun had dropped a strip of light, and to the woods between looking like black scars one minute, and like friendly sanctuaries the next. It was all confused. There was the room, too. The white keys of the piano would now and then exercise a fascination over her which would keep her whole body perfectly still for perhaps a minute. But when this passed, full of hesitation, her fingers would recommence the slow exploration of her hands, and the restlessness took her again.

It was all confused. She was going away: already she had said a hundred times during the afternoon — 'I am going away, I am going away. I can't stand it any longer.' But she had made no attempt to go. In this same position, hour after hour had passed her and all she could think was: 'To-day I'm going away. I'm tired here. I never do anything. It's dead, rotten.'

She said, or thought it all without the slightest trace of exultation and was sometimes even methodical when she began to consider: 'What shall I take? The blue dress with the rosette? Yes. What else? What else?' And then it would all begin again: 'To-day I'm going away. I never do anything.'

It was true: she never did anything. In the mornings she got up late, was slow over her breakfast, over everything — her reading, her mending, her eating, her playing the piano, cards in the evening, going to bed. It was all slow —

purposely done, to fill up the day. And it was true, day succeeded day and she never did anything different.

But to-day something was about to happen: no more cards in the evening, every evening the same, with her father declaring: 'I never have a decent hand, I thought the ace of trumps had gone! It's too bad!!' and no more. 'Nellie, it's ten o'clock — Bed!' and the slow unimaginative climb of the stairs. To-day she was going away: no one knew, but it was so. She was catching the evening train to London.

'I'm going away. What shall I take? The blue dress with the rosette? What else?'

She crept upstairs with difficulty, her body stiff after sitting. The years she must have sat, figuratively speaking, and grown stiff! And as if in order to secure some violent reaction against it all she threw herself into the packing of her things with a nervous vigour, throwing in the blue dress first and after it a score of things she had just remembered. She fastened her bag: it was not heavy. She counted her money a dozen times. It was all right! It was all right! She was going away!

She descended into the now dark room for the last time. In the dining-room someone was rattling teacups, an unbearable, horribly domestic sound! She wasn't hungry: she would be in London by eight — eating now meant making her sick. It was easy to wait. The train went at 6.18. She looked it up again: 'Elden 6.13, Olde 6.18, London 7.53.'

She began to play a waltz. It was a slow, dreamy tune, ta-tum, tum, ta-tum, tum, ta-tum, tum, of which the notes slipped out in mournful, sentimental succession. The room was quite dark, she could scarcely see the keys, and into the tune itself kept insinuating: 'Elden 6.13, Olde 6.18,' impossible to mistake or forget.

As she played on she thought: 'I'll never play this waltz again. It has the atmosphere of this room. It's the last time!' The waltz slid dreamily to an end: for a minute she sat in utter silence, the room dark and mysterious, the air of the waltz quite dead, then the tea-cups rattled again and the thought came back to her: 'I'm going away!'

She rose and went out quietly. The grass on the roadside

moved under the evening wind, sounding like many pairs of hands rubbed softly together. But there was no other sound, her feet were light, no one heard her, and as she went down the road she told herself: 'It's going to happen! It's come at last!'

'Elden 6.13. Olde 6.18.'

Should she go to Elden or Olde? At the crossroads she stood to consider, thinking that if she went to Elden no one would know her. But at Olde someone would doubtless notice her and prattle about it. To Elden, then, not that it mattered. Nothing mattered now. She was going, was as good as gone!

Her breast, tremulously warm, began to rise and fall as her excitement increased. She tried to run over the things in her bag and could remember only 'the blue dress with the rosette', which she had thrown in first and had since covered over. But it didn't matter. Her money was safe, everything was safe, and with that thought she dropped into a strange quietness, deepening as she went on, in which she had a hundred emotions and convictions. She was never going to strum that waltz again, she had played cards for the last, horrible time, the loneliness, the slowness, the oppression were ended, all ended.

'I'm going away!'

She felt warm, her body tingled with a light delicious thrill that was like the caress of a soft night wind. There were no fears now. A certain indignation, approaching fury even, sprang up instead, as she thought: 'No one will believe I've gone. But it's true — I'm going at last.'

Her bag grew heavy. Setting it down in the grass she sat on it for a brief while, in something like her attitude in the dark room during the afternoon, and indeed actually began to rub her gloved fingers over the backs of her hands. A phrase or two of the waltz came back to her. . . . That silly piano! Its bottom G was flat, had always been flat! How ridiculous! She tried to conjure up some sort of vision of London, but it was difficult and in the end she gave way again to the old cry: 'I'm going away.' And she was pleased more than ever deeply.

21

NEVER

On the station a single lamp burned, radiating a fitful yellowness that only increased the gloom. And worse, she saw no one and in the cold emptiness traced and retraced her footsteps without the friendly assurance of another sound. In the black distance all the signals showed hard circles of red, looking as if they could never change. But she nevertheless told herself over and over again: 'I'm going away — I'm going away.' And later: 'I hate every one. I've changed until I hardly know myself.'

Impatiently she looked for the train. It was strange. For the first time it occurred to her to know the time and she pulled back the sleeve of her coat. Nearly six-thirty! She felt cold. Up the line every signal displayed its red ring, mocking her. 'Six-thirty, of course, of course.' She tried to be careless. 'Of course, it's late, the train is late,' but the coldness, in reality her fear, increased rapidly, until she could no longer believe those words. . . .

Great clouds, lower and more than ever depressing, floated above her head as she walked back. The wind had a deep note that was sad too. These things had not troubled her before, now they, also, spoke failure and foretold misery and dejection. She had no spirit, it was cold, and she was too tired even to shudder.

In the absolutely dark, drowsy room she sat down, telling herself: 'This isn't the only day. Some day I shall go. Some day.'

She was silent. In the next room they were playing cards and her father suddenly moaned: 'I thought the ace had gone.' Somebody laughed. Her father's voice came again: 'I never have a decent hand! I never have a decent hand! Never!'

It was too horrible! She couldn't stand it! She must do something to stop it! It was too much. She began to play the waltz again and the dreamy, sentimental arrangement made her cry.

'This isn't the only day,' she reassured herself. 'I shall go. Some day!'

And again and again as she played the waltz, bent her head and cried, she would tell herself that same thing:

'Some day! Some day!'

22

THE BLACK BOXER

THE morning sun was beating hot over Peterson's fair-
ground. The big coloured awnings shrouding the shows and
roundabouts hung heavy and still, and the rings of little gay
triangular flags on the roofs of the roundabouts and on the
helter-skelter tower flapped senselessly in the summer air.

Perched on a ladder outside the entrance to Sullivan's
boxing show a figure in blue dungarees was polishing the
big copper bell hanging before the gold and scarlet curtains.
In the intervals between polishing the bell and staring lazily
over the fair he sometimes spat and dreamily watched the
spittle make its arc in the bright sunlight and settle in the hot
dust below. Sometimes he seemed to take languid aim at the
specks of confetti scattered in the dusty grass like handfuls of
gay coloured seeds.

He was a small, sharp-faced man, like a little terrier. His
yellowish face was peppered with pock-marks and he was
slightly deformed in his left shoulder so that he looked by
turns pathetic and sinister. His name was Waite but
Sullivan's boxers called him Dutchy. He helped to clean up
the show and he often towelled the sweat off the boxers and
rubbed them over with the flesh-gloves after the fights.

He gave the bell a final polish and descended the ladder
and lit the fag-end of a cigarette and slouched off across the
fair-ground. Men in dungarees and red check shirts and
woollen jerseys were busy polishing the brass spirals of the
roundabouts and women were hurrying to and fro with pails
of water. The smoke of cooking-fires was rising in soft
bluish-white clouds from behind the caravans. A workman
kneeling high up on the roof of the highest roundabout was
hammering and screwing behind a figure of Venus, naked
and shining gold in the sunlight. At every tap of his hammer
the Venus trembled in all her limbs.

Dutchy stopped and looked up at the man and whistled
him softly.

'Seen Zeke?' he called.

The man raised his oily face and looked over the fairground and called down.

'Some chaps round at the back of Cappo's.'

'See Zeke?'

'Can I see through a bloody shooting-gallery?'

He bent down again and tapped behind the Venus, so that she trembled again. Dutchy threw away his cigarette and flashed out a remark about the Venus and the man.

'Aw, go to bed!' the other bawled. He put his arm about the naked Venus in order to steady the figure. Dutchy flashed another remark and walked away.

He slouched lazily through the fair towards Cappo's shooting-gallery. On reaching the shooting-gallery he slipped through a gangway between the awnings and walked across a space of grass and skirted a group of caravans. Beyond the caravans a line of Peterson's great yellow-and-scarlet trailing vans was drawn up, making a little secluded space of clean grass out of reach of the black and white ponies grazing in the field beyond them. He saw at once that something was happening: a group of show-hands had formed in a ring and were laughing and clapping their hands and shouting noisily. Dutchy slouched from behind the caravans and leaned against the wheel of a water-cart and looked at them.

In the middle of the ring a big negro was dancing a curious dance, alone. He was dressed in a pair of old grey flapping trousers and a grey sweater tucked in at the top of his trousers, which he kept up with a big bandanna handkerchief printed with great spots of yellow. He was six feet tall, powerful, with magnificent shoulders; the arch of his massive chest looked formidable and superb. He was dancing with a curious flowing negro rhythm, swaying his big hips with an arrogant invitation, brandishing his long arms above his head and letting them droop and swing senselessly with the rhythm of his body. Sometimes he clapped his black hands above his head and on his thighs and his big haunches, and sometimes he let them rest with light grace on the folds of the bandanna handkerchief. He bent his knees and twisted his feet and slithered backward over the grass and then worked forward again, comically slipping and pitching head-first like a man on a sheet of ice. He arched his whole body backward and began to work his feet furiously, as though the grass were moving from beneath him. The show-hands roared at him. He curled and twisted himself and worked the patter of his feet to a mad crescendo and let them fall as suddenly into a solemn, melancholy step again. As his big arms dropped to his side and the dance died down he suddenly began to fling wild cartwheels, scattering the show-hands in all directions. His wild calls mingled with the shouts and laughter of the show-hands, who all applauded. At the noise a young girl came to the door of a green-and-gold caravan carrying a copper jug which flashed in the sunshine. She set down the jug on the topmost step of the van and clapped her hands. Dutchy spat in the grass and grinned at her and applauded too.

When the dance had finished and the applause had died away the show-hands closed in about the negro again and he began explaining the steps of the dance. He danced each step slowly again, talking above the murmurs of the men in a clear bass voice. There was something fine and superior about the quality of his deep voice, his perfect accent and the slow, meditative choice of his words. He had a habit of throwing back his head and smiling richly as he talked. His head was massive, the nose flat and broad and the left ear was wrinkled like a cauliflower. The skin of his face was a deep gleaming black, but it was softened by a strange blush of rose. His thick hair was black and dull as soot, and his eyes were bright and sharp as jet against the whites. He looked invincibly strong and as though he gloried in his strength, and at moments there was something about his face solemnly noble, marvellously dignified and sad.

Someone came up behind Dutchy and tapped him on the shoulder and whispered:

'Zeke busy?'

Dutchy jerked back his head and discovered O'Brien, a young light-weight of Sullivan's.

'See for yourself,' he said.

25

'He's wanted,' O'Brien said.

'Who wants him?'

'Sullivan. He's down at the booth with Sandy.'

Dutchy took his hands out of his pockets and spat.

'I'll go over and tell him. I want to see him myself,' he said.

He walked across the grass and broke the ring of showmen and touched the negro on the shoulder and whispered something to him.

'I'll come,' said the negro.

Dutchy waited aside. The negro slowly put on his jacket. The show-hands were dancing about the grass, practising the steps he had shown them. The negro kept smiling broadly. Finally he walked away with Dutchy past the caravans and by the shooting-gallery and across the fair-ground. 'You know what Sullivan wants,' said Dutchy, as they walked along.

The negro did not speak. They passed beneath the work-man tapping at the gilded Venus.

'It's about this training,' said Dutchy.

'There's nothing wrong with me,' said the negro.

'But you're going to fight this Harrison boy Friday and I ain't seen you doing a skip or a bit of shadow for a hell of a while.'

'When you've done as much shadow-boxing as I have,' said the negro, 'you won't be in a travelling-show.'

He suddenly thrust out his arm as they walked along. 'Feel that,' he said.

Dutchy pinched the flesh of the negro's forearm: it seemed as hard as the foreleg of a horse. He nodded and was silent.

'If I train too much I go stale,' said the negro. 'You know that.'

'Tell that to Sullivan,' said Dutchy.

'I hate Sullivan,' said the negro.

They came within sight of the long scarlet, gold-tasselled tent of Sullivan's boxing-show. The ladder was standing at the head of the entrance-steps where Dutchy had left it, and in the hot sunshine the copper bell flashed brightly against the red curtains behind. The sun-baked awnings, the painted yellow pay-box and the immense pictures of the world's boxing champions painted crudely across the whole width of the show all looked cheap and tawdry.

Dutchy and the negro stopped before the steps of the show. The air was hot and breathless and the negro's skin gleamed like rose-black silk in the sunshine.

'Go in and tell him you're doing a bit with the ball this afternoon,' said Dutchy. 'We can play pontoon for a bit when you're done.'

The negro shook his head.

'I'm going to sleep this afternoon.'

He turned abruptly on his heel and walked away behind the long red show-tent. He walked without haste, gracefully and lightly.

Coming to the rear of the tent he turned the corner. Sullivan's vans were drawn up behind the tent and outside Sullivan's own van stood a young red-haired boxer talking to Sullivan himself. Sullivan was resting one foot on the steps of the van. His elbow was crooked on his knee and he was fingering his black chin with his hand. He was a small, thin-faced, unshaven, dirty man with narrow eyes and weedy black hair. His mother had been a dancer from Belfast and his father, a Pole, had been a conjurer in a travelling-show. Sullivan had inherited his mother's name and her dirty tongue. From his father he had learned inexhaustible trickeries. He had been in the show-business for longer than he could remember and had run the boxing-show for twenty years.

He looked up at the negro quickly and searchingly. There was something mean and shifty and subtle about the continual flickering of his small black eyes.

'Hello, Zeke,' he said.

The negro nodded.

'Been training, I see,' said Sullivan. 'Yes?'

The negro shook his head.

'Ain't it time you trained a bit?' said Sullivan.

The negro showed his white teeth and said, 'I'm all right. I don't want to go stale.'

Sullivan sprang off the steps of the van and in a flash of

angry temper thrust his face up towards the negro's. 'Stale? By Christ! You know the rules of this bloody show as well as I do.'

The negro looked down at his quivering face impassively, without a word.

'You know the rules of this show!' shouted Sullivan. 'You train and keep yourself in proper nick. I've run this show for twenty years and if you can tell me anything I don't know about boxing I'd be bloody glad to hear it. Bloody glad. You never fought a round last week — not a damn round! And you talk to me about going stale. While I keep you in this show you keep yourself fit like any other man.'

The red-haired boxer walked quietly away. Sullivan's hands were quivering with temper. The negro held out his right arm and said with perfect calm:

'Feel that. I am as fit as any man you ever had in your show.'

Sullivan knocked the arm aside impatiently.

'You know as well as I do you don't need to worry about your arms!' he half shouted. 'Nor your head. It's here, my old cock' — he pressed his two hands on the negro's stomach and screwed up his eyes ominously and lovered his voice — 'You niggers are all alike. Your guts are like a sponge.'

The negro, impassive and tolerant and composed, did not speak.

'Ain't forgot you're fighting this Harrison boy Friday?' said Sullivan quickly.

'I know.'

'I want you to beat him. If you beat him he'll want to come back before the show goes and fight you again. See that? That means another house — means money. I'm putting up ten pounds in this bout — seven and three. That's money. Ain't that worth training for? Ain't it? I want to see you win, Zeke, I want to see you win this fight. Christ, I do.' Sullivan spat. 'You ain't been winning so many fights lately,' he added slowly.

'I have won plenty of fights for you,' said the negro.

'Not lately — you're getting soft — I don't like it!' Sullivan paused and scratched his unshaven chin and squinted up into the negro's face. His eyes were narrow and inquisitive.

28

'How old are you, Zeke?' he said.

For the first time uneasiness came into the negro's face. He hesitated.

'I am thirty-four,' he said.

Sullivan whistled very softly.

'Good age for a boxer,' he said.

'For a white man.'

'It's a good age for any boxer — I don't care who he is,' said Sullivan. 'If a boxer ain't careful that's when he begins to lay the fat on. And that's what you'll do — that's what I don't like. Look at your guts. You better do a bit with the ball before the sun gets too hot.'

'I will train this afternoon,' said the negro.

'You'll train now! Christ! do I run this show or do you?'

'I don't feel the heat so much.'

'You'll do it now!' shouted Sullivan. 'You'll do it now or get out of this show!'

They stood looking at each other for one moment antagonistically, in perfect silence. Sullivan's little eyes, bloodshot in the whites, were dilating with anger and his hands were unsteady with temper. The negro gave one long look at him and then without a word or a change of expression he turned and strode away, imperturbable, solemn and dignified, and vanished into the boxing caravan, a long red vehicle painted with Sullivan's name in big yellow letters across the sides, before Sullivan himself could move or speak again.

II

On Friday evening Sullivan and his four boxers were displaying themselves in the blazing light of the big electric lamps hanging over the platform outside the show. The fair was flashing and whirling and quivering with light. Between the shows moved a dark flock of people. There was an air of gaiety and great excitement in the shrieking and laughing and shouting of voices, the brassy music of the big roundabout, the crack of rifle shots and the thunder of switchback cars, which never seemed to rest. The night was sultry, without wind, and above the electric lights the summer darkness, freckled with tiny stars, was coming down a soft dark blue.

The four boxers, in dressing-gowns, stood in an imposing line, their arms folded, facing the crowd. Sullivan stood before them in his shirt-sleeves, shouting and gesticulating with a megaphone. His voice was thin and hoarse and he kept striking his fist with the palm of his hand, like an orator.

'The greatest array of real fighters any generation ever saw in any one show at any time! I'm telling you. I ain't asking you if these men look like fighters. Look at 'em! You know what a boxer looks like. You don't want me to tell you that these men ain't milk-sops! You're sportsmen! You come here because you're sportsmen. Now take a look at that young feller in the blue dressing-gown. Take a look at him! Dan O'Brien — nine stone ten — nineteen years old — and he'll fight a six-round exhibition bout with any jack-man in this crowd, any jack-man two stone above his own weight. Any jack-man you like to name!'

Sullivan seized a pair of boxing gloves and flourished them before the crowd and searched it fiercely. A hand went up among the white faces and Sullivan tossed the gloves among the crowd.

'There's a sportsman!' he yelled. 'Now another? Where's another? Any man like a six-round exhibition bout with Sandy Hack, from Dunkirk, twenty-three years old, eleven stone six? Hack will fight any man in the fourteen stone class! Thank you!'

Sullivan leapt nimbly across the platform and stood before a huge, sardonic-faced heavy-weight, dark and glowering as a Russian, and yelled:

'Dado Flowers! Twelve stone ten! Flowers has fought in America, and it would be an honour for any boy to beat him in a six-round bout! An honour! What will he give away? He'll fight an elephant!'

Someone at the back of the crowd threw up his hand and Sullivan tossed the gloves away and clapped his hands. 'And now, gentlemen.' He leaned forward confidentially and spread out his hands in caricature of a Jew, and spoke in a harsh deliberate whisper.

'Half a crown. See!'

There was a flash of silver in his dirty fingers, he smiled, and the coin vanished. He stepped across the platform and twisted the ear of the huge sardonic heavy-weight and the coin dropped neatly into his hands from the boxer's nose. He tossed the coin in the air and caught it again and washed his hands of it. It reappeared in Hack's red hair. Sullivan made a joke about the Scottish people. It was an old joke. The spectators laughed, and then Sullivan pointed his fingers at them and whispered dramatically: 'Wait!' The crowd, fascinated, watched him without a murmur as he crossed the platform and stood by the huge, impassive figure of the negro.

There was a moment's pause. Suddenly the negro opened his mouth and the coin flashed bright against his black skin and seemed to disappear between his red lips. When his mouth closed he stood immobile, staring over the crowd without a change in his expression of superb dignity, as though nothing had happened.

Dramatically Sullivan waved his arms and sent his fingers rippling through the negro's thick black hair and disentangled the coin. He grinned cleverly at the crowd and shouted hoarsely:

'Zeke Pinto! The coloured man! The American coloured boxer! Pinto will fight a special ten-round bout for a purse of ten pound with Dan Harrison, your own man!'

The faded red curtains behind the boxers parted and Harrison himself, not yet stripped for boxing, slouched forward on the platform for the crowd to applaud him. His thick, loose body, his half-crouching walk and the heavy-browed, glowering expression of his blond, small-eyed face contrasted strangely with the perfect repose, the superb pride and the blackness of the negro. While Sullivan continued to shout hoarsely the details of the contest between them, they stood side by side without moving or looking at each other, incongruous and indifferent to one another to the point of contempt.

The crowd were beginning to throng towards the pay-boxes and vanish through the openings in the red curtains on either side of the booth. Sullivan seized the megaphone and began to yell a frenzy of speech over the crowd, cajoling and demanding vociferously like some desperate orator. Between his more impassioned speeches O'Brien clanged arresting notes on the copper bell. The big Russian-looking heavy-weight began working on the punch-ball hanging up outside the curtains, fisting it grimly with light fascinating punches and watching it perpetually with a sardonic, half-smiling grin. Harrison slouched through the curtains and disappeared.

The negro did not change his expression of impassive dignity, and suddenly, as though incensed by it, Sullivan took the megaphone from his lips and whispered to him in a voice of sneering impatience:

'For Christ's sake wake up. Do something. Get round to the van and get Dutchy to give you a rub-down. You look as if you're having a bad dream.'

The negro turned and vanished through the curtains without a word. He elbowed his way through the waiting crowd inside the booth and walked out of the booth across the grass between the show-vans towards the boxers' dressing-van. He hated Sullivan. He had hated him bitterly since morning for his meanness, his bad temper, his sneers, the insult of the word nigger. He had ached to knock Sullivan senseless. He had hated so much the craftiness in his sudden question 'How old are you, Zeke?' that it had given him a curious sense of pleasure to tell him that he was only thirty-four. But the pleasure had quickly vanished again. During the hot afternoon, sitting gambling with Dutchy in the shade of one of Peterson's vans, he had often reminded himself that he was older than Sullivan dreamed. He was past forty. At forty a boxer was an old man. Until lately it had been easy to deceive Sullivan; but lately he had begun to feel slower in the ring and had lost fights which he ought to have won. When he lost the money went out of the show, so that Sullivan also lost. That was bad business. He saw the significance of Sullivan's question: he was growing old and he was bad business. There were younger boxers. He knew already what to expect if he lost the fight with Harrison.

He walked across the dark grass and up the steps of the dressing-van slowly, realizing for one moment what it all meant to him. He opened the door of the van. A paraffin-lamp was burning, there was a powerful smell of liniment, and he saw Dutchy sitting on a box, smoking a cigarette and reading a pink comic-newspaper. He stepped into the van and shut the door with his back. It seemed every moment more than ever imperative that he should win the fight with Harrison.

At the sound of the door Dutchy dropped the pink newspaper as though startled and jumped to his feet.

'All right?' he said quickly.

'Sullivan sent me to you for a rub-down.'

'You don't want a rub-down before you fight, do you?'

The negro sat down on the box.

'In this show you do what Sullivan tells you.'

Dutchy spat a shred of tobacco from his mouth with a sound of disgust and took a penny from his pocket and spun it in the air. He caught it deftly on the back of his left hand and covered it with his right. He had a passion for gambling. The smoke of his cigarette burned straight upward into his eyes, so that his face was wrinkled and squinting as he turned it to the negro.

'Heads,' said Pinto.

Dutchy looked at the coin and put it back into his pocket.

'Again,' said the negro. 'What I lose I'll square up later.'

Dutchy tossed the coin and the negro called 'Heads' again, wrongly. Too lazy to take the cigarette from his mouth Dutchy blew away the ash with a snort of his nose. The negro, dreamily watching the grey ash float in the air and settle again, seemed oblivious for a moment of Dutchy and the toss of the coin. He murmured 'Heads' again.

'Your luck's out,' said Dutchy.

They went on alternately tossing and calling the coin for what seemed to the negro a long time. The repeated spin of the coin became like the everlasting revolution of the thought

33

that he must win the fight with Harrison. He felt himself filled by an oppressive gloomy determination to win.

Dutchy was in the act of tossing the coin when footsteps ran up the ladder of the van and Sullivan burst in. He immediately began to speak to the negro.

'I want you to win this fight, Zeke,' he said. 'And I want you to win it fair — straight — no monkey business. See that?'

'What sort of a house?' drawled Dutchy.

'Packed. D'ye hear me, Zeke?'

The negro was staring at the photographs of boxers pinned everywhere on the walls of the van.

'D'ye hear me, Zeke? I want you to win this fight — and clean. This boy can box. But you beat him clean and it'll be credit to you. Box him and beat him clean. You hear me?'

'Don't I always fight clean?' said the negro.

'I know, I know you do. Don't get your rag out. I want you to win, that's all. I'll treat you square. Trust me. I'll get back now and watch Dado finishing, and you can come over and show yourself in a minute or two. I'll treat you square.'

He left the van quickly, but before Dutchy or the negro could move the door opened again and Sullivan thrust in his head. He delivered an urgent last whisper:

'Box him and beat him clean, that's all. That's all. I'll treat you square. Trust me.'

He vanished.

There was a moment of silence. The negro slowly unloosened his dressing-gown and stood on the box on which he had been sitting. Dutchy spat out his cigarette in disgust. 'Trust me,' he sneered softly. 'Trust a bloody snake.'

With quick light fingers he began loosening the negro's muscles, first on the calves, then the thighs, and finally on the body. The black skin was supple and fine as satin in his fingers. The air was sultry and little yellow balls of sweat stood on his face before he had finished.

'You'll win,' he kept saying to the negro between little panting noises. 'Any money. Easy.'

The negro stood utterly immobile, not speaking, staring

34

at the rows of boxing photographs with something sceptical and philosophical in his eyes. Dutchy worked over the muscles just above the belt-line, kneading them gently. The muscles yielded, flabbier than the rest of his body.

'You'll win,' said Dutchy. 'Keep him off your guts, that's all.'

The negro nodded. Presently he knotted up his dressing-gown and they walked together out of the van and across the grass among the show-vans and entered the boxing-booth. The tent, brilliantly lighted, was thronged with spectators surging backwards and forwards about the ropes of the ring like a flock of sheep penned between the ropes and the red canvas. There was a low, continuous murmur of voices. The white light of electric lamps poured down on Flowers and a bony young boxer in red drawers, sparring out their last round. Flowers was ambling carelessly about the ring, flickering and tapping his man with sardonic friendliness. Sometimes the young boxer would aim fierce unhappy blows at Flowers, making the loose boards creak under his clumsy feet, and the crowd would break into laughter. Flowers was smiling and there was a smear of blood across the young boxer's mouth as the round ended and the crowd applauded the men.

The negro elbowed his way through the crowd and the ring had been empty a second or two when he climbed over the ropes and sat down in the corner. Almost at the same moment Harrison climbed into the ring too, and sat in the corner opposite him. The crowd cat-called and applauded and broke into a hum of conversation at the sight of Harrison, who sat staring across the ring from under his blond surly brows. The negro looked at the crowd calmly. It was a big house. Two of Sullivan's men climbed a ladder and rolled back a sheet of the canvas roof and let in a current of fresh air. Dutchy climbed into the ring and began to put on the negro's gloves.

'Keep him off your guts,' he whispered. 'Let him wear hisself out. He's a madhead. Let him gallop for three rounds and you'll have him taped.'

Without speaking or even nodding in answer the negro

35

leaned back his head and let it rest against the ropes. Staring upward he could see through the gap in the roof a sprinkle of stars shining against the darkness of the summer sky.

Dutchy was putting on his second glove when Sullivan crawled into the ring under the bottom rope. Standing in the centre of the ring he held up his hand and called for order. The negro did not look at him and he heard only vaguely the speech he began to bawl at the crowd. He felt tired and he did not want to fight.

Sullivan was repeating the old formula. 'You come to this show to see a fight! You come to see fair play! And you shall have 'em! If you have any remarks to pass I ask you to pass them afterwards — not while the rounds are in progress. Be fair to these boys and they will give you a good fight. A good, honest fight! That's straight, ain't it? No love-tapping! You know what I mean by no love-tapping! The boys are out to win. I tell you on my oath, my solid oath, and God strike me dead if I tell a lie — there never has been a squared fight in this show — and never will be!'

His voice rose to a shout and the crowd applauded vigorously.

'Now I shall present a ten-round contest between Dan Harrison — '

Harrison stood up and the crowd began to cheer for him.

'Dan Harrison, of your own town, and Zeke Pinto, the American coloured boxer. A ten-round fight for a purse of ten pounds!' The negro stood up and nodded his head, and Sullivan appealed to the spectators:

'Give the coloured man a clap. A man's a man and a boxer a boxer, whether he's coloured or not. Pinto will fight fair and clean, and if he wins I hope you will acknowledge him like the sportsmen I know you are. Give the coloured man a clap, gentlemen, give the coloured man a clap.'

The negro half rose to his feet again, making a slight bow. He was conscious vaguely of the noise of applause, the quivering of the many white pairs of hands under the bright lights, and of Harrison arching back his thick neck, drinking something from a dark wine bottle and spitting it over the side of the ring again.

THE BLACK BOXER

A moment later Sullivan, who was to referee the fight himself, took off his jacket and called the two boxers to the centre of the ring and spoke with them. Conscious merely of the harsh voice repeating the old formula again, the negro did not listen. By turns there would come over him the strange feeling that he did not want to fight, and the gloomy oppressive thought that he must fight and win. 'And keep your tempers,' said Sullivan. 'Like good boys. That's all.'

The negro returned to his corner. He took off his dressing-gown and putting his hands on the ropes, worked his body to and fro, loosening his muscles. Against his bright yellow drawers his naked skin gleamed very black, the fine lights suffused with rose, as though the blackness had been smeared with a soft pink oil. He took one long deep breath; Dutchy whispered something to him; and he heard the stroke of the gong.

He stood upright, turned about, walked towards the centre of the ring and touched gloves with Harrison. His pose was quiet, unstooping and unexaggerated. His huge black form was splendid and intimidating in its dignity. His face was marvellously calm. Harrison came forward with a low crouch of his shoulders, his surly blond head thrust forward aggressively, his guard very close. They worked away and round each other for a second or two, watchfully. The crowd was silent.

Suddenly Harrison made a lead with his left to the negro's face and followed up swiftly. The negro took the punches on his gloves. Harrison led again and the negro fought back, grazing Harrison's face. They closed with each other, and Harrison began peppering the negro's body with short jabs which fell on his ribs and the soft flesh just above the belt. The negro tried to cover himself and step away but the blows were unexpected and quick and he took the punishment of them unguarded. When he finally broke away he was panting and there was a dull throbbing in his body where the punches had fallen. As he stepped away Harrison forced him to the ropes and attacked him viciously, hooking his right. The negro saw the blow coming and waited for what seemed a complete second, and then side-stepped swiftly. It was a beautiful movement. He heard the crowd murmur in admiration. Experiencing a moment of satisfaction and feeling fresh and cool again he worked away from the corner before Harrison could recover. Harrison followed and they began fighting close in again, and again a shower of quick jabbing blows fell on the negro's body. The punches were short, stinging and powerful. The negro felt shaken and winded. He covered his body with his arms and ducked his head, taking the blows on his arms and shoulders until he had recovered his breath. Harrison came to a clinch at last and Sullivan broke them away. A little excited, Harrison left his hands loose after the clinch had been broken and the negro stepped across and found his jaw with a quick hook of his right. Harrison went down, panting and resting on his elbow while Sullivan counted to nine, bawling the counts in order to make himself heard above the babble of the crowd. At nine Harrison was on his feet again. He rushed straight for the negro, his head low and aggressive. They closed, and they were chest to chest, struggling for an opening, as the gong rang.

In the interval the negro sat with his arms limp on the ropes, his head back and his eyes closed. The fanning of the towel sent waves of cooler air on his face. He nodded when Dutchy gave him the old advice: 'Keep him off your guts,' and sometimes he felt the muscles of his body flutter just above the belt, where Harrison had jabbed him. He knew that Harrison had found his weakness.

The second round began as though Harrison had conceived a violent hatred for the negro. He was younger than the negro by twenty years. He had a fast, powerful, fearless style, and he was warm with resentment at having taken a count of nine. He led quickly for the negro's face but Pinto stepped aside and struck his left ear with the heel of the glove. It was as though the punch had released a whirlwind: the short jabbing blows began to rain on the negro's body before he could cover up again. Crooking his arms and lowering his head, he staggered against Harrison and tried to fend him off, but the punches had sickened him. He had backed away to the ropes, and this time when Harrison attacked again he was too slow to duck away. He took a fresh onslaught of body blows that sickened him from his knees upward. He felt strange and stunned and the shouts of the crowd were like a great drumming in his head. The crowd was shouting for Harrison. He staggered drunkenly and recovered and then crouched and staggered against Harrison, keeping his head low. For the rest of the round he did nothing but try desperately to keep out of Harrison's reach and he was lying on the boards when the gong rang.

During the interval Dutchy worked on his stomach and freshened him with the towel and urged the old advice upon him. He nodded vaguely. The whole pandemonium of the fair seemed to clamour in his head, the shouting of the crowd, the tunes of the hurdy-gurdy, the snap of rifle-shots, the thunder of switchbacks and the silly shrieking of young girls. He could not gather his thoughts.

During the third round and again in the fourth Harrison knocked him down. Each time he took a count of nine, resting on his elbow. At every count the crowd shouted wildly. He knew that he was losing, and he knew that no one wanted him to win. After every punch he felt slower, and behind Harrison's big menacing face the white faces of the crowd seemed to surge up to him and ebb away in a babbling tide.

In the intervals his arms felt leaden, his legs fluttered with sickness, and his body felt old and sore. He knew that he was looked upon as beaten already. He could see the unpleasant-ness in Sullivan's face as he leaned in the corner and noted the points on a scrap of paper.

When the gong rang for the fifth round Harrison rushed across the ring and met him with a wild attack on his body. He was flushed and sweating, and his eyes were glowing with an eagerness to finish off the negro. He hooked wildly but the blow missed and the negro, full of a sudden despairing calmness, gathered himself and swung heavily at Harrison's jaw. The punch connected, Harrison went down, and then leapt to his feet again before Sullivan had time to count. The crowd cheered him. He rushed at the negro madly again, without success. The negro felt strangely calm, his fears lessened. Harrison seemed suddenly baffled and angry. He repeated his attack and the crowd clamoured madly for the knockout. He came and attacked again, angry and distressed by his failure to hit the negro. The negro, for the first time impassive and unharassed, struck Harrison's jaw with a short, straight punch. Harrison tottered and fell on one knee, hanging to the rope with his left hand. The booth was like a madhouse, the crowd yelling for Harrison to stand up. He rose slowly, holding to the ropes, panting heavily. The ropes were very loose and as he trusted his weight to them they sagged and he pitched forward drunkenly. The negro followed up with his right. Harrison gloved off the blow but staggered and pitched forward again, like a boomerang. Something like a primitive frenzy came over the negro. He leapt forward and hit Harrison madly as he was falling. The blow struck hard below the belt and Harrison quivered and pitched upward through the ropes and dropped heavily into the crowd.

The negro stood utterly still in the ring. It was all over. He was conscious vaguely of Harrison being counted out and of the crowd yelling angrily for a foul. He knew that he had fouled Harrison, and he knew that the crowd hated him.

Sullivan finished the count and seizing the negro's arm held it above his head and shouted:

'Pinto!'

The crowd hooted the negro, who stood statuesque and bewildered, as though not understanding what had happened. His arm dropped listlessly. Dutchy came into the ring and flung the dressing-gown over his shoulders. Sullivan walked round the ring holding up his hands and trying to quieten the pandemonium, but the crowd called derisely 'Go to Hell! Shut your bloody mouth!' Harrison crawled back through the ropes, holding his stomach, dazed and reeling. The crowd cheered and clamoured for him. His seconds began a furious altercation with Sullivan, thrusting their faces close up to him, livid with temper. Flowers and Hack leapt into the ring and pushed away the seconds, elbowing them away like policemen. The booth was full of a shouting, quarrelling pandemonium.

Dutchy kept close to the negro. 'All right,' he kept repeating. 'All right. Didn't I tell you you'd win?'

The negro, dazed and despondent, never moved. He looked like a solemn black statue. He stared apathetically from the crowd to Harrison and from Harrison to Sullivan. He saw Sullivan waving some paper money in his hand and he saw Harrison take the money and count it. There were three pounds. After that he vaguely understood that Sullivan was appealing to the crowd, who were beginning to listen to his hoarse insinuating voice.

'You know that in this show or any other show the referee's word must stand. Ain't that so? If the referee gives way to the crowd what happens? You know what happens! He's no more good! He's finished. He's done. Napoo! I've refereed more fights than any man in this show has ever seen. And if any other man will come up here in my place I shall welcome him gladly! Gladly! Harrison's a good fighter — a game feller — and when he was knocked out he was leading on points, let me tell you that. He's a game feller.'

The crowd began to cheer again.

'But he was knocked out! Knocked out! And fair. And no man in this crowd will make me change my opinion that he was knocked out! But to show that I think he's a game feller and a good fighter — '

The negro saw Sullivan flourish another pound note in the air. He saw Harrison come forward and accept the money while Sullivan patted his back. The crowd cheered and clapped and stamped its feet for Harrison.

Sullivan held up his hands and quietened the crowd.

'And now give the coloured man a clap,' he shouted; 'and now give the coloured man a clap!'

The crowd gave the negro a round of applause.

The negro knotted the cord of his dressing-gown. He saw Sullivan looking at him closely, his shifty eyes filled with impatience and contempt. He felt humiliated and dazed, and he hated Sullivan bitterly for awarding him the fight. He climbed under the ropes and leapt softly down on the grass and began to elbow his way through the crowd, back to the dressing-room. Dutchy, following him, threw a towel about his neck. The crowd murmured a little as it parted to let him through.

He went into the dressing-van and sat down on a box. There was an odour of sweat and liniment and the oil from the lamp burning on the table. He stared vaguely at the flame burning steady and yellow behind the smoky lamp-glass, and then at the rows of boxing photographs lit up by the orange light of the lamp. His legs were unsteady and fluttering, as though he had been running very hard and for a long time. His stomach and his ribs were bruised and sore. His arms seemed heavy and wooden and his whole body felt old and feeble and empty, like the husk of something.

'Christ! You won,' said Dutchy. 'Didn't I tell you you'd win?'

The negro lifted his hands listlessly for Dutchy to take off the gloves. He was thinking of Sullivan, the foul, and the way the crowd had hooted him. The mad frenzy in which he had fouled Harrison had left him tired and stupefied and ashamed.

Dutchy slipped off first one glove and then the other. The negro opened his hot damp hands and was too listless to shut them again.

Dutchy unknotted the cord of his dressing-gown and threw the gown back over the black shoulders, warm and shining dark with sweat, and began to rub the shoulders gently. The negro slowly stood up. His dressing-gown slipped to the floor and he stood motionless, solemn and mute, staring straight at the boxing pictures pinned on the wall before him.

'Feeling all right?' Dutchy asked. 'Didn't I tell you you'd win? You'll be all right. Didn't I tell you? Easy! You'll be all right.'

He threw the towel aside and drew the flesh gloves on his hands. The negro slowly bent his back. There was a strange expression of sadness on his face and an air of weariness about his whole body, and he was not listening to Dutchy's words.

'Easy,' said Dutchy. 'You'll be all right. Didn't I tell you?'

DEATH IN SPRING

WE had walked up the wood for the second time to look at the young foxes. It was lovely April weather, windless and sunny in the wood under the leafless oak trees and the slender black ashlings. The old hazels were yellow with catkins and the primroses made drifty yellow distances wherever we turned to look; the bluebells were darkly budded and the first purple orchids had unfolded and the first oxlips. The riding ran through the wood from east to west, smooth and green and wide enough for ten horses to canter abreast; it was flooded with sunlight and out of the shelter of the trees we could feel the west wind very soft on our faces, blowing straight from the corner of the wood where the foxes were.

At the end of the riding we stood still and listened. We had walked up slowly and quietly, without speaking. To the right of us stood an old shooting-hut built of straw and hurdles, and on the left was a long mound of earth burrowed with fox-holes, and bare except for young nettles and a clump or two of elder. On the far side of the mound was a pond, the trees growing down to the edge of it, making the water black with the motionless reflections of their thick trunks and branches. A day or two before I had come upon ten or twelve fox-cubs playing in and out of the bushes of elder. An east wind had been blowing and they had not scented me. They were pretty, amusing, impish things, a little lighter in colour than earth, their soft hair ruffled in the wind like the feathers of birds. Sometimes they trotted down to the edge of the pool and looked at the water and sometimes they roamed off into the wood itself, through the dark green stretches of dog's-mercury to where the tide of primroses began. Wherever they went they moved quite soundlessly, with a fine, foxlike assurance and a grace of movement more beautiful than in all other young woodland creatures.

A rabbit scuttled away noisily among the dead wood and undergrowth as we came to a standstill. I stooped and

43

looked between the undergrowth at the fox-burrows: the
wind was blowing our scent towards them and the mound
was deserted. Irene moved her feet and cracked an ash-twig
and a young rabbit made off wildly from under a tangle of
old honeysuckle wood. I looked at her quickly and she
smiled. She had never yet seen a fox-cub or even an old fox;
she had gathered anemones, as we had come up through the
wood, and her hands were full of them and she had put a
dark violet in her mouth. She smiled with her lips closed,
sucking the sweetness of the violet-stem at the same time.
The air was elusively fragrant with the scent of the flowers
she was holding and of the thousands of primroses lying
everywhere like pools of yellow and green.

I moved cautiously forward for a pace or two until I was
level with the shooting-hut. A young fox came suddenly up
from a burrow and gazed at me as though puzzled, head
sideways and ears cocked, and another trotted noiselessly
over the brow of the mound towards the pool.

Irene came up behind me and I pointed out the cub,
drawing down her head so that her line of sight should be
level with mine. Her hair brushed my cheek. We stood
motionless and the fox was motionless too, his eyes impish
and bright and filled with a wise mistrust of us. He watched
us for a minute and then without haste turned tail and
vanished down the burrow again.

'You saw him?' I whispered.

She nodded.

'You see they are timid,' I said. 'If we could skirt the wood
and come up on the far side of the pond we should see them
better.'

'Shall we go then?' she whispered.

There was a gate at the end of the riding, and we had only
to climb it and walk across a piece of pasture land and skirt a
corner of the wood. I was moving towards the gate when
suddenly I heard a faint cough and a second later a voice
saying:

'I should hardly do that if I were you. You were quite
right. They are very timid to-day.'

We turned at once and looked towards the shooting-hut.

The voice was very quiet and dignified, and had about it also something tremulous and faded, as though it belonged to someone very old. We stood still for one moment. I could see nothing and suddenly the voice spoke again.

'Come in, won't you? There's plenty of room. I shan't eat you.'

We walked towards the shooting-hut, glancing at each other rapidly every second or two, until we stood in the door-way. The sunlight made an angle of light across the dry earth floor, and beyond the sunlight — on a rough seat of split hazel sticks running along the back of the hut — an old man was sitting, with a double-barrel sporting gun across his knees. It was difficult to believe that he had ever spoken to us. He seemed at once voiceless and spiritless. He looked incredibly old and he sat as immobile as a mountain, the skin of his long, sunken face the colour of a dead corn-husk and more transparent, so that the veins shone softly through it like a fragile network of lavender threads, so faint in colour that the dead shining yellowness of the flesh itself was hardly broken. He was dressed in an old pepper-and-salt sporting jacket with breeches to match and coarse green stockings that hung loosely on his thin legs, like moss on an old stick; he looked as if he had long ago lost even the strength to dress himself; his knee-buttons were half undone and his jacket hung open, showing underneath it a waistcoat of faded canary yellow with the ends of a thick green silk neckerchief drooping across it and tucked away into the armpits. His hat was an old square grey bowler; he wore it at a slight angle towards his right ear, showing a wisp, like a mere silver petal, of his thin hair. The jaunty poise of the hat and the eyes looking at us from underneath it were both symbols of life. The eyes were wonderful. His body was like an aged tree, and his eyes were like two miraculous young leaves. They looked at us as we came to the door of the hut with a vivid expression almost naive in its intense brightness; they did not move, except to lift themselves the finest fraction in order to watch our faces; the light falling upon them redoubled their life, illuminating their colour until it shone like melting ice, infinitely blue and more beautifully vivid; they were like the eyes of a child or of a young girl, full of unquenchable life and curiosity and wonder.

He looked at us in silence for perhaps ten seconds or more; it seemed a long time; and then he made a slight gesture with one hand, lifting two or three fingers from the stock of his gun.

'Come inside, come inside,' he repeated.

His voice and his simple gesture of the upraised fingers were full of a profound courtesy. We walked into the hut. His eyes rested on us steadily and attentively, and then he moved a fraction along the seat. We had been his guests from the moment of entering.

'Sit down, won't you? Sit down. You can look straight across at the foxes from here — good view of 'em,' he went on. 'Sit one on each side of me. That's right, that's right,' he murmured. 'It's a clear view if they come. But I doubt if they will — I doubt it. Wrong wind. They're getting older too.'

He spoke very slowly, pausing between the phrases, his wet, strengthless red lips quivering in the act of finding his words. He stared into the wood while talking; the sunshine as it fell through the half-leaved branches was broken up into endless flakes of quivering yellow light; he seemed to be watching their inexhaustible dance on the dark earth covered with flowers and bright green flower-leaves. He was not lost however, and he never forgot that we were there; the extreme courtesy of his voice made us feel that there was nothing in all the world he would rather do than sit and talk to us.

Suddenly he ceased gazing into the wood and turned to Irene and remarked, reflecting:

'Anemones and foxes,' repeating the words two or three times. 'Anemones and foxes, anemones and foxes.' Finally he put out his hand towards the anemones and said: 'Excuse me; may I take one?'

His hand faltered weakly among the bunch and a few anemones were loosened and some fell to the ground. I bent down at once but he was already stooping and saying, 'I insist, I insist.' His body was as dry and stiff as old leather. He picked up the anemones one by one, breathing with little distressful gasps and bending as though his joints had been locked together. At last he straightened himself with the anemones quivering in his fingers. His face was colourless and his eyes were moist with tears of exhaustion, which began to creep down his cheeks like drops of thin oil. His breath was dry and dead and he sat for a long time with his hands resting heavily on the gun across his knees, with the bluish, sagging lids of his eyes closed, his whole frame struggling to be calm again.

Finally he opened his eyes and made a gesture of beautiful tired courtesy towards Irene and said:

'You must forgive me.'

She smiled. He smiled also, and then as though it were simply the natural excuse for his clumsiness he said quietly:

'I'm afraid I'm dying. Damn it.'

He spoke as though he bitterly hated the thought of dying and there was a kind of defiant life in his words. I did not look at him. I sat looking instead at the gun lying across his knees; it resembled him — old, worn, polished, aristocratic, and I wondered why he had brought it up there, out of season, with the wood full of mating birds and animals and their young.

He saw me looking at the gun. He glanced at me for a second and his bright eyes seemed to take in all my thoughts.

'You are wondering what makes me carry a gun in spring,' he said. He looked slightly ashamed of himself, as though he were a boy and we suspected him of hiding eggs in his cap.

'I wanted a shot,' he confessed. 'I've been a sportsman all my life. You know how it is — something you've always done — can't leave it alone. I had to come up. I've been in bed for a God-forsaken month. I had a room overlooking the orchard and they let me sit up in bed and shoot sparrows through the open window with an air-gun. I used to wait until they settled on the plum-bloom. Kill about a bird a day if I was lucky. I got bored to death. I like the open country and something worth shooting, like snipe, you understand.' He turned his head and looked at us in turn. There was a gay light in his eyes — that light which always comes into the eyes of old men when they talk to children. I dare say you think it's wrong to shoot?' he asked. 'What's wrong in it?

47

All sentimentality — nonsense, a great deal of nonsense. It's only a law — the strong preying on the weak. Yes, it's nonsense — a lot of talk by people who probably wouldn't know a tit from a hawk, and who wouldn't care if they did. Life won't stop because I shoot a pigeon.'

He broke off, a little exhausted by talking, and leaned back his head against the wall of the hut and let his gaze rest again on the bright green wood and the flakes of trembling sunlight. It was warm and sheltered in the hut, and the breeze came in at the doorway full of the sweetness of the wood breaking into life again.

There was a silence. I looked over towards the fox-holes; the mound was still deserted. I heard a sigh. And suddenly, out of his meditation, the old man was saying:

'When I look at this wood I have immortal longings in me.'

A moment later he went on, muttering to himself, as though he had forgotten we were there:

'The stroke of death is as a lover's pinch which hurts and is desired.'

He broke off and lifted his hand from the stock of his gun and said with a tremor of excitement in his voice:

'I used to know it all. A long time ago — sixty years ago. A young girl I knew was Cleopatra. I didn't act, but I knew the part. I used to shut myself up and learn it.'

A young fox suddenly trotted over the mound, sniffing among the elder-bushes, and I watched him until he disappeared by the pool. The old man went on talking again, telling us of the girl who had taken the part of Cleopatra. He talked of her gently and meditatively, half to himself, sometimes quite absently, and then a little shyly when he recalled suddenly that we were there. She had been a dark, brilliant, capricious creature, with all the eager, passionate, irresponsible gaiety of a young girl just opening her eyes to life. He talked of her for a long time, breaking off, forgetting, meditating — his voice by turns dreamy and tremulous with the effort of remembrance; sometimes he repeated a line or two of a speech, and sometimes he moved his hands and tried to describe to us how beautifully she had acted. There were things he remembered perfectly, such as a yellow silk dress she

48

had worn, a certain way in which she would stand and click
her fingers when angry or perplexed; a winter afternoon
when he had stood on his head in the snow again and again,
just in order to amuse her. He had forgotten how long the
play had run, but at the end of it they had run away to the
Continent together. There had been days of sweet, hectic
happiness. He spoke of her always as Cleopatra, as though
too shy to mention her name, and he went on for a long time
unfolding his tale, losing the thread and picking it up again
uncertainly, until it was like some old picture, sewn in silk,
of another century.

His voice trailed off at last; he traced over the pattern of
the gun-breach with his long, bony forefinger. The girl was
dead; he did not want to talk of her again. We sat silent,
listening to the silence of the wood broken now and then by
the crack of a twig, a blackbird singing, the soft, halting coo
of a pigeon — almost a summer sound.

The old man sat sunk in meditation, his chin dropping
towards the anemone he had threaded in his buttonhole.
He suddenly looked older than ever, an immemorial figure,
overburdened by the weight of a thousand years, the wrinkles
of his face eternal. Suddenly he turned and looked at me
wonderfully, his blue eyes alert and twinkling, as though his
whole being had come to life in them.

'You find it difficult to believe I was once a young man?'
he said.

I had been trying to make myself believe. Before I could
answer he said:

'An old man looks permanent — inevitable — as though
he had been born an old man, isn't that it?'

'I think that's it.'

'Are you glad you are not old?'

'Yes.'

'You'd like to remain young? No? You want to go on
growing, but whatever happens you want to keep life, don't
you? I know, I know. One of these days I shall snap in half
like a damn twig, but I still want life. I'd like time for another
shot or two. I want to hang on a bit longer — a bit longer.
It's nice to think of summer coming on. I see the oaks are

breaking bud. I've great faith in that. But I haven't heard the cuckoo yet, have you? It seems late this year.'

He went on talking again, talking of the past, his youth, his shooting days — a time when he had shot a hundred snipe; he had been a gay bird; he had lived joyously and he wanted to go on living; he knew that he was dying and he hated the thought of death. He made long pauses and rested and breathed carefully as he spoke, as though trying to sustain the life in him a little longer. A young fox came over the mound and trotted away in the shadow and sunlight under the trees; he saw it and pointed it out with his thin white forefinger, and we watched it vanish by the pool.

'I should like as many more years to live as foxes I've helped to kill,' he said. 'You're young. I envy you.'

He talked a little longer; he seemed to grow tired and presently we rose to go. He rose also. He stood amazingly straight and tall, only bending his head a little, like a great hollyhock. He shook hands, holding our hands in his bone-cold fingers for a long time.

'It has been a great pleasure,' he said.

'It has been charming,' I said. 'I hope you will get a shot.'

'Thank you. I shall probably miss in any case.'

We said good-bye.

'Good-bye.' He gave us a slight bow, leaning on his gun. He smiled at Irene with his wonderful entrancingly bright eyes, full of gallantry and life. Finally, just as we were going, he said:

'I hope you don't mind if I say something to you — a little advice. If you wish to do anything, do it. Do what you feel you must do. Don't listen to other people. You're young. Let them go to the devil. It's your life, not theirs. If I listened to other people I shouldn't be up here this afternoon. I should be in bed. Good-bye.'

He took off his hat; his thin, silver-yellow hair shone beautifully; he came to the doorway of the hut to watch us depart. We walked down the riding, and once we turned and saw him still standing there, still hatless, but when we turned a second time he had vanished into the hut again. We said a few words about him, and I thought again of his

intense blue eyes, his perfect courtesy, the story of the girl
who had been Cleopatra, the way he had learned her lines by
heart, and the way he still longed for summer to come. I
thought of him lying in bed shooting sparrows through
the open window, and of how he could not bear to lie there
and had dragged himself up into the wood for another shot
before he died.

We struck away from the riding and walked diagonally
through the wood along a narrow path. We came upon the
shell of a sucked blackbird's egg, and Irene picked up it and
walked with it in her hand, admiring its colours.

There was suddenly the report of a shot in the wood. We
stopped. The shot went racing through the trees and rattled
the air. A blackbird screamed, and we heard the rabbits
scuttling away to hiding, rustling the dry leaves. The shot
spent itself at last and the wood was calm with a silence that
was like death.

We listened for the sound of the second barrel, but it never
came. We walked on again and came out of the wood, and
crossing a field of young wheat we heard the cuckoo calling
for the first time that spring.

I wondered if the old man had heard it too and how often
he would hear it again.

THE STORY WITHOUT AN END

I

The Restaurant Rosset, which had once been painted a prosperous white, was now dingy and cheap; so thickly freckled were its windows with the black dust of London that from the outside nothing within was visible except the ghostly white circles that were the tables and the even more ghostly white blobs which were the shirt-fronts of the waiters. It looked like the kind of place into which unhappy lovers would go to talk over some misfortune and come to a decision about their lives. On the second floor were rooms which other lovers, having a different purpose, might have used also. Pierre Moreau had been learning to be a waiter there all winter.

He was fifteen: a thin, gawky boy with long black hair, heavy southern lips that he hardly ever opened and dark mute eyes that stood out with sombre dreaminess from his sallow face. He had been growing paler and thinner throughout the winter and he now looked like a plant that had been tied up in darkness and blanched. When there was nothing to do in the restaurant, when no one wanted wine or coffee, which it was his duty to pour out, he stood with his back to the wall and stared at the opposite wall as though he were staring at something beyond it — and beyond it hopelessly.

It was April, and spring was late. He had come over from France the previous November, alone, with his belongings in a black glacé bag and enough money to bring him to London; he knew no English: but he would learn it from Rosset and his wife, who were distant relations, and from the other waiters; it was part of the bargain his mother had made with Rosset.

From the first he had been wretched. At the very beginning he had also been frightened. He had arrived on a Sunday and he had been troubled by the bleakness of London, his loneliness, the sensation of being in a strange country,

52

the walk with Madame Rosset through the rainy darkness to the restaurant, and then by Rosset himself.

His first sight of Rosset sent him sick; the hard lump of fear in his chest was shaken suddenly by an acute convulsion, a spasm that seemed to turn it to water, filling him with a cold nausea. Rosset was a gross figure, a man of appalling physique. Like some old boxer, he had degenerated to fat without losing his air of brutality; his greasy face, a strange yellowish-grey colour, had a loose red slit of a mouth and little black eyes that quivered under depraved loose lids that would close slowly and open again with incredible quickness, leeringly suspicious; his whole body was like that of some ponderous ape, latent with brutality and anger waiting beneath the skin to be stung into life. Continually he worked his brows up and down, as though itching to fly into a rage at something. When he smiled there was something loosely and suavely cynical about it; it was a potential leer. He moved about heavily, rolling from side to side, his hands clasped behind him with a kind of meditative cunning. He spoke with guttural rapidity, with a mean, sneering, brutish, domineering voice, uttering also queer noises of disgust or satisfaction.

But it was not only this. He took an instant dislike to the boy. 'Pierre, eh? Ha! Pierre?' he muttered. 'Pierre, eh?'

A spasmodic terror shot through the boy at the sound of the voice, speaking with a dark sneer of significance, as though Rosset had been waiting all his life for that moment. Rosset leered, looked him up and down. They were in the restaurant, in the long alley between the empty white tables. It was five o'clock and since it was Sunday the place was not yet open. Madame Rosset had vanished to take off her wet coat, so that Rosset and the boy were alone.

'Sit down!' roared Rosset suddenly.

And the boy, before he had realized it, sat down. It was a miracle wrought by fear. Rosset smiled with wet loose lips and grunted. The boy sat sick and white; he could feel his strength oozing from his finger tips.

'Stand up!' roared Rosset.

And the boy, again by that miracle wrought through fear,

53

stood up, sick and weak. He could not look at Rosset and in desperation he stared at the opposite wall.

'Look at me!' ordered Rosset.

Pierre's eyes fixed themselves on Rosset's face at once. There had not yet been a word of French from Rosset, yet the boy had obeyed. Rosset was leeringly triumphant. The boy stood staring, mute, mystified, at a loss to understand.

'You see!' said Rosset suddenly. 'That zow you learn English — that zow. You see!'

Then, as though remembering that the boy could not understand a word, he began speaking for the first time in French. His thick glistening lips moved with repulsive rapidity; he seemed to suck and taste the words of his own language greedily, his lips protruding and sucking back again like those of a man gorging on a ripe fruit, and his voice took on a thick lusciousness of tone, almost sensual. His features were amazingly flexible and in a way that bewildered the boy he worked his lips and cheeks and brows incessantly, every movement exaggerating the grossness of his face, its lines of cruelty, its perpetual sneer of insidious suspicion.

He spoke for ten minutes, rapidly, yet coldly, with that sensual ripeness of tone, yet with intense calculation. 'So he had come to be a waiter, eh? To learn to be a waiter? Did he know how long it took to learn that? How long did he think? How long?' The boy listened mechanically, his sense numbed by Rosset's voice, as Rosset told him his duties, how he must take the orders for wine and coffee, pour the wine and coffee, lay the knives and forks, clean the knives and forks, how he would be subordinate to everyone, Rosset, Madame Rosset, the waiters, the chef, even to the girl at the counter, how he must wash up the dishes in the afternoon and again in the morning. By a curious cynically playful tone of voice, Rosset implied that there was little to do. Only to pour the wine and the coffee, only to wash up, that was all: only a little — a little, but so important.

Rosset talked on without ever pausing for answer. All the time the boy stood stiff, half-stupid, his big mute eyes bulging. At the end of it all he understood only two things: that it took a lifetime to learn to be a waiter and that the only way to learn English was Rosset's way, to speak nothing but English, to be addressed in nothing but English. He was wondering how, since he knew not a single word of English, he was to do this when Rosset suddenly shouted again:

'Sit down!'

He sat down, as before through fear, and again Rosset leered in triumph. A moment later he sucked in his thick lips and became almost menacingly serious. That was the way! Did he understand that? He was to speak French to no one but Rosset; to the rest, the diners, the waiters, the girl at the counter, he was to speak English. And so he would learn.

He gave the boy one single look, a queer look of insinuation, his dribbling lips curled and one eyelid sagging, and then was finished.

'Madame!' he called. 'Madame!' Without waiting he rolled off, grunting, between the rows of tables and vanished as Madame Rosset appeared in the restaurant to take the boy to his room.

Pierre followed Madame upstairs, to a little room under the roof, four stories up. Madame was fat and glum but there was no strength in her bulk and nothing to fear in her silence: she had weak grey eyes that blinked continually as though at a strong light and a little red cupid mouth whose colourlessness she painted over with some dark red colour, like that of cheap red wine; her hair was black and frizzy, half hiding her little tumbling black ear-rings. She was like some round, naive, mindless doll. Perhaps Rosset had forbidden her to talk, for when she spoke she kept glancing back, with little apprehensive uneasy smiles, towards the stairs. She seemed glad when she had told the boy to change into the waiter's suit that lay on the little iron bed and be down in the restaurant by six. She left him a candle, flickering on the wooden washstand under the roof-window. He would rather have been in darkness. He changed his suit; the trousers struck damp against his legs, his hands were cold and he could not manipulate the shirt studs. Only these things kept him from blowing out the candle, from plunging himself into a darkness in which he could feel safe from Rosset, in which he could even hide from Rosset if necessary.

He did not realize until he began to go downstairs the full depth of his weakness and terror; his legs would scarcely support his body, weighed down by its flood of sickness and dread, a sickness which he felt might at any moment make him swoon and a dread which was already half-turned to terror. He groped his way heavily and slowly, as though ill, downstairs. At moments only his body seemed to be in existence; the rest of him became annihilated, dead even to terror. At last the smell of cooking reached him, awoke the deadness in him and gave him a little comfort. He went into the restaurant with a queer, forced, half-paralysed step.

To his relief Rosset was not back. A waiter was just drawing back the bolts of the street-door to open the place for the evening. Pierre stood still, watching. The waiter switched on the lights, fingered the dark leaves of the aspidistra in the window, peered into the dark street. The lights of other restaurants shone out across the street. The waiter stood still, his napkin on his arm, his thin sallow face negative, blank, thoughtless, his weak round-shouldered body broken and servile.

Turning, he saw the boy. He came from the window, hobbling badly. 'Bon soir, Pierre.' His voice was hollow, and spiritless. The boy nodded, formed some words on his lips, heard them in his mind and felt that they had been spoken. In reality he knew he was afraid to speak. He expected Rosset at any moment: the waiter also had fear in his eyes, an unconscious fear, an emotion bred of years of just such waiting.

But Rosset did not arrive; and they held a brief whispered conversation, the man giving the boy hoarse scraps of advice, little tips to remember. He was not to be afraid, he was not to be afraid, he kept whispering. It was all right.

The only other waiter appeared and stared also with that fixed blankness into the dark street. How long had they been there, these waiters? The boy kept wondering. Had they also come, as boys, to learn? Would he too go on serving for years and years and become like them? Would he also, in time, stare out into the dark street with that fixed emptiness of expression, his body crushed and servile, waiting for

something? Was that what Rosset meant when he said that
it took years to become a waiter? He caught himself staring,
too, with a curious static gaze, as he wondered.

A moment later he was standing alone; the waiter beside
him was hurriedly flicking at the tables with his napkin, the
waiter at the window was nervously busy over a cruet. He
turned in sudden alarm at their sudden fearful activity.
Rosset had entered.

He had come in silently, and in the same silent way he
moved to the window. He did not look at the boy, who stood
stiff and contracted with fear. After a moment, rubbing his
hands together, he turned from the window and came back.
Fear seized the boy like a paralysis; he held himself rigid as
though against a blow, contracted, sick. And again Rosset
did nothing, neither looked nor spoke.

Diners began to drift in by twos and threes, Rosset greeting
them with obese affability, rubbing his hands or hiding them
behind his back. The place became animated: there was a
clatter of conversation and crockery together, the shouting
of waiters and the answering echo from the kitchen below.
Rosset walked up and down. And the boy, all the time, might
not have existed.

From taking the wine-list to each table the boy returned
always to the same place: an opening between two empty
tables, at the edge of the gangway. There he stood, his fingers
gripping the wine-list, enduring over and over again the
same piercing fear of Rosset each time he passed him. He felt
always weak, cold, dazed; he hardly saw anything except
Rosset. It would have been a relief to do something, to pour
out some wine: but no one had yet asked for wine. He was to
discover later that it was an event when anyone did.

Finally he almost conquered his fear of Rosset. He could
do it by staring at the opposite wall, by staring so intensely as
to see beyond it and there lose himself. He would stare in
this desperate way for minutes on end, while Rosset passed
and repassed, saying and doing nothing to him.

He was aroused from one of these stares by a sudden blow
on his chest, a blow which made him stagger back against
the wall, and by Rosset's voice in a fierce whisper:

'Always against the wall — always against the wall.' The words came first in English and then in French. 'Always against the wall. You see? Always against the wall.'

The boy pressed himself back against the wall. His head, cracked against the wall, ached and throbbed. He shut his eyes, groped in a cold swooning darkness and came to life again. Rosset had gone.

He stared at the opposite wall. A long time seemed to pass. Finding that someone wished for coffee he roused himself, took it, poured it into the cups, came back to the wall again. 'Always against the wall,' he kept thinking. A little later, realizing that someone was staring at him in return, he let his eyes flicker back to a conscious gaze. This brought back a consciousness of mind also. He looked down the restaurant towards the door.

There, on a table, stood the cash-desk, at which Madame Rosset had sat all evening. Now Madame Rosset had gone and her place had been taken by a girl of perhaps twenty-eight or nine, a dark, sallow-skinned girl with a mass of luxuriant black hair, and warm liquid eyes. He did not understand her sudden presence. Perhaps the Rossets had gone for their evening meal. His mind seemed stupid, drugged. He tried to force into his eyes some expression of understanding, or response. It was futile. Something in him had been crushed, annihilated, by that blow of Rosset's sending him back against the wall.

Nevertheless the girl continued to look at him. With her big, fluid dark eyes she coaxed him back gradually to a belief in his own existence. He felt inexpressibly soothed. Finally she shrugged her shoulders, smiled and made a droll face in the direction where Rosset must have gone. In spite of himself he smiled. She repeated it all, with a momentary flash of mimicry, mocking Rosset's twitching brows, his fierce eyes and loose drooping lips. As, in spite of himself, he smiled again, she looked round, saw an imaginary Rosset approaching, bent her head hastily over the accounts and then looked up again, grinning with eyes that were bright and mischievous.

As the evening went on she would repeat all this. It saved him from complete despair, took him away from himself.

Her dumb-show was delicious. Normally he would have abandoned himself to absurd laughter. But he still felt sick; he was still apprehensive about Rosset's sudden return; and he gave her back quick little smiles which simply flickered across his face and fled.

The clatter of the restaurant died down. On Sundays it shut down at eleven, and long before then he was utterly weary by that prolonged standing against the wall. His head ached, the sickness in his heart persisted, and only the smiling mimicry of the girl saved him, again and again, from desolation.

Once, just before eleven, Rosset returned, on drunken legs, took a lugubrious look round the empty restaurant and then disappeared.

Soon afterwards a waiter bolted the door. The girl came from behind the cash-desk, straight to the boy. She spoke to him quickly in the flexible, sweet tones of his own language.

'Go up to bed, quickly,' she told him. 'Quickly. We'll clear up. Go along and sleep. We'll talk to-morrow.'

She put her arm softly about his shoulders, gave him a brief squeeze, and took him to the door. 'There you go — sleep well.' He caught the comfortable odour of her dress and the thick warm fragrance of her body.

As he dragged himself upstairs he burst into tears, silently, and he lay on his bed choking with deep sobs of agony, holding his hands desperately to his mouth, afraid that Rosset would hear and come up and knock the life out of him.

II

It was Sunday again, Easter Sunday. He stood there, against the wall, pressed back, as he had done every day of the winter. It was midday: in April the sun, at noon, could just clear the high roof of the buildings opposite Rosset's; it was fitful windy April weather, with stumbling white clouds which hid the sun, and snow-cold air. There was no sign of spring: not even a daffodil on the tables of the empty restaurant. The two waiters stood at the window, gazing into the street, waiting for something to turn up, and the girl, Yvette, sat at the cash-desk, scratching her head with a pencil, licking her lips, and exchanging occasional glances with the boy, her eyes sparkling and mischievous. Sometimes she hugged herself against the cold and at last she got up and walked about the restaurant, stamping her feet. She walked to the far end of the empty room and turned, and it occurred to her then to retrace her steps like Rosset and she came back with his heavy rolling gait, twitching her brows up and down, her hands clasped behind her back, her full red lips loosely drooping. 'Ah! bon jour, m'sieu, bon jour! You like to sit 'ere? No? Over there? Nize table, ver' nize. The Preence of Wales sit sometimes there — sometimes. Oh yes. Sometimes. You sit 'ere? As you wish, m'sieu.'

She had come down to the door and was bowing and rubbing her hands to that imaginary customer, while the waiters rolled against themselves and laughed and the boy smiled with delight by the wall, and now suddenly she flung up her hands and turned back by a series of quick rhythmical turns up the room, like a dancer, her black skirts flowing out wider and wider like an opening sunshade, showing her plump legs and the mauve garters on her black stockings just above her knees. Laughing with delight, she kept snapping her fingers, and performing little seductive wriggles of her body for sheer joy.

'Ach! Rosset! Who cares anything about Rosset now? Who cares anything? Pouf!'

It was a great day, for Rosset and his wife had gone away for Easter Sunday, on a visit to some relations, so that Pierre, the girl and the waiters would be free after three o'clock until the place opened again at six in the evening.

Almost intoxicated by the mere thought of freedom, the girl bantered with the waiters, satirically. Where were they going for their long holiday? Ah! but she knew. They didn't need to tell her. She knew! She walked up and down the restaurant, hobbling a little, talking to the imaginary image of a girl on her arm, smiling. 'Where do I work? Tut, tut!

Don't you know, I'm the *maître d'hôtel* at the Restaurant Rosset? Fifty waiters! You didn't know it? Ah, ah! Let us sit down, shall we? My feet ache.'

Without Rosset the place was transformed; and since no one had yet come in to eat it was strangely quiet in the intervals of the girl's foolery. Yet the boy, by the wall, was weary, almost afraid. Without consciously knowing it, he kept looking at the door, expecting to see at any moment the fat shadow of Rosset on the white curtain. It was something which no mere gaiety could dispel, this fear of Rosset. It was something cancerous, unseen but deep, gnawing at the tissues of mind, never letting him rest, blackening his brain. His heart still bounded to his throat, flooding him with its sickening nausea, at the mere approach of Rosset, and alone again, even though Rosset had said nothing to him, he would feel weak and swooning, drained white by his own fear. It might have been different, he sometimes reasoned, if Rosset's own antagonism had lessened; but that too increased. He seemed to hate the faintest sight of the boy's mute face, with its dark bulging eyes, and its shrinking mouth. It was a hatred that had no limits; it rose from the mere cold despising sneer when the boy dropped a spoon to the fanatical heat of fury that poured out savagely as when he spilled the wine, as he had once done, at the table of a party of suburban fools, half-drunk, who had come in late one night to play a kind of Bohemian pantomime which they found amusing. But it could go beyond this, to be more petty or more diabolical, so that the boy feared not only its outward manifestations, but its inward strength, its terrible potentiality. One day Rosset would kill him; not by a blow or by deliberation, but by the mere persistency of his hatred, of a long cruel sucking at his life. When there was no more pleasure in cruelty he would throw the boy out perhaps, but as long as there was a response from him, that sudden awful light of fear in his eyes, he would torture him, like an animal, for the mere pleasure of seeing him suffer. The boy hoped for dismissal, praying to be sent back: but there was no hope of it. He was as necessary to Rosset's life, though he did not know it, as Rosset was to his.

He could speak a little English now, but his words were

mere repetitions of words, made into quaint phrases, that he had picked up surreptitiously from the girl and the waiters. Except that he was whiter, more strained, it was the only outward sign of change in him. Underneath he had the big yellow-black bruises where Rosset had kicked him, on the legs and thighs, but he said nothing of them. He limped sometimes, but to questions he said that he had slipped on the brass-shod stairs. But the girl knew, and from the look of strained pity in her eyes he was made aware of it.

They had become intimate. With her gaiety she made friends easily: her moods were elastic and the current of her joy would sometimes transmit itself to him. There were things that they must do together, the washing-up, the cleaning of the silver, down in the basement. They sat at the table or stood over the sink for hours together, the girl keeping up her tireless pantomime, mocking Rosset, Madame Rosset, the two waiters, the regular diners. They talked in whispers, learned the art of laughing silently, and could read each other's eyes.

She was twenty-nine, a Breton, one of a big family; there were always letters for her, from sisters and brothers and her mother, long letters which she read to the boy, mimicking the writer, as they cleaned the cutlery together. He was from the South, the Mediterranean; he had wanted to go to sea, but his mother, blindly worshipping, had only one dream for him. She saw him as a kind of heavenly *maître d'hôtel*, the archangel of all waiters, and with joy and pride she had made this bargain with her cousin Rosset. She kept a little wine-shop overlooking the sea, and sailors came in to bring her fish in exchange for a bit of bread and some wine. There was a fisherman named Anton, a very old man with a little red woollen tasselled cap, who had taken him fishing in the bay in summer afternoons. His heart began to ache whenever he thought of it. Quick to catch at his moods, the girl would see this and make him tell what troubled him and when he told her she would laugh it off, with gentle carelessness.

'Fishing? For what? Shrimps? What else could you and an old man hope to catch, eh?'

'We'd row out, a long way out.'

'Who? — who rowed? Not that old man! No? Then you? — ach! with arms like that — with those drumsticks?'

'I used to be fatter.'

'I wish I could say that!'

She would shrug her shoulders, spread out her hands in a ballooning curve. 'Soon I shall be like that.' And sometimes she would seize his head impulsively and draw it down and rest it on her plump shoulder, tangling his hair, patting his cheeks, kissing him, all to comfort him, to make him forget himself and Rosset.

To-day, Easter Sunday, they were going out together, alone, for a joy ride, and since they could not hope for more than two free hours they had decided to ride on a bus to Hyde Park. It was Yvette's idea: simply to walk on the grass, to see the daffodils swaying and fluttering in the cold April wind, like fluffy yellow birds, to have tea somewhere, to know the joy of being waited upon for once in their lives, to come back. The boy had no money and knew nothing of London. It was to be a treat for him, said the girl, at her expense. But within himself it had already become something more; he felt his heart pulling against his body, wild at his chance of escape.

He was afraid almost to think it: but he might even not come back to Rosset's.

It was nearly two o'clock. A thin young man, a regular customer, had been in, eaten his *hors d'œuvres* and cutlet, shaken his head at coffee and had gone. There remained only a middle-aged man, alone in one corner, masticating a steak and fried potatoes. When he had gone the waiters would shut the place, and Pierre and the girl would go too.

At last they were in the basement, washing up, bantering, almost free. Yvette washed the dishes and the boy dried them. The cook had already departed and soon the waiters came down, overcoats on, to say good-bye.

'I do so hope you have a nice holiday,' said the girl. 'You will write, won't you? You will be away so long!'

The waiters hobbled off, there was a sound of the restaurant door shutting, and they were alone.

'Now you go,' she said, 'and change your clothes and make yourself look pretty. Quick! Be ready in ten minutes.'

And as he bounded upstairs, almost frightened by the thought of even temporary freedom, she called after him:

'Pierre, Pierre!' and when he halted, wondering sickly: 'Don't forget to wash your ears! Ach!'

He was ready quickly and stood at the window as he put on his collar, looking at the low clouds which had begun to gather sombrely, an ugly goose-grey, over the roofs of the city. Suddenly he saw the sky and the roofs pencilled with rain and heard the quick April clatter of it on the slates above his head. As it came faster and persisted, darkening the roofs with its flood, he felt depressed to wretchedness.

He ran down a flight of stairs to the next landing and tapped at the girl's door.

'It's raining,' he said. 'It's raining.'

'You know what they say in our part?' she called from the bedroom. 'Let it!'

'Shall we go?'

'We'll swim.'

He stood still outside the door, listening to the rain beating heavily on a skylight above, the sound depressing him again.

'Are you still there?' she called.

'Yes.'

'You can come in.'

He opened the door slowly and went in. She was sitting half-dressed before a mirror by the window, combing her hair. 'It will soon leave off,' she said. She spoke to his reflection in the glass and watched him standing awkwardly by the door, his dark eyes seeking her and her image in the mirror diffidently, and as though she knew what his feelings must be she tilted the mirror so that he could see only a black half-moon of her hair in the glass and she saw a quick start of light in his eyes as she did so. Her hair was long, so that it took a long time to comb it straight, brush it and coil it back into the intricate knot which must rest low on her neck. Newly brushed, the hair was fine and sleek as satin. Outside the rain smashed in the window. 'Well, if it must rain,' she

said, 'you must row me there in a boat. I will be that old
man, that Anton you talk about, and we will catch fish in the
Serpentine. I see you rowing — you, with those drumsticks!'
Laughing, she bent her arms and began to row an imaginary
boat, pulling strongly, so that her bare shoulders rippled and
her breasts swelled richly upward.

As he watched the rich movement of her body he felt a
sudden hot spasm in his blood, an electric start of surprised
delight. In the mirror she saw his face, and half-wishing
she had not asked him to come in, she rose and began to
search about for her dress and stockings, the old dark
mischievous look no longer in her eyes, which she kept
averted, hardly daring to meet the passionate watchfulness
in his own.

Finding her stockings she sat on the side of the bed farthest
from him and rippled them quickly on, looking at the rain
lashing at the windows, carelessly, white and hard as a storm
of hail. Once she shrugged her shoulders, fatalistically, as if
to say 'If it rains, it rains,' and the ripple of her bare shoulders,
though she did not know it, made him start excitedly again.
Yet he stood near the door every moment, with the curious
half-eager look of youthful passion in his eyes, and something
keeping him back from her.

At last there came a moment when they must decide
whether to wait or go. The rain was lashing down in a flood;
the light of the afternoon had been washed out.

'Well?' she shrugged her shoulders.

He made no answer. Downstairs a clock chimed and struck
three. It was a heavy black marble clock which stood in a
private room, one of those rooms which Rosset kept for the
convenience of special customers, on the floor below. Rosset
wound it up himself every Sunday at three, timing it carefully
and was insistent about it, though the room was hardly ever
used.

Suddenly the girl sprang into activity. 'Ach! What of a
little shower? Let's go now quickly. We must wind the clock
as we go downstairs.'

She slipped into her dress. 'Pierre, come and button me!'
she cried, and then:

65

'Ah! no, I'll manage. Go down and wind the clock. I'll come down in a moment.'

He went down reluctantly, his heart beating with excitement, his limbs curiously heavy. In the little private room he found that his hand trembled as he searched behind the clock for the key. He was opening the round glass face of the clock when the girl came down.

'Wind the clock with one hand,' she cried out to him, 'and do up these buttons with the other. Only two — at the top. I've done the rest.'

She was laughing and the dark mischievous flash was back in her eyes.

As he tried to obey her, fiddling with the clock-key with one hand and the clasp of her black dress with the other, something came over him, a flush of passionate longing to touch her, and he suddenly forgot the clock and unfastened her dress instead of fastening it and ran his hands falteringly over her breasts, touching them at first very shyly, through the fine stuff of her dress, and then, because she offered no word or sign of resistance, in their warm fragrant nakedness. She could feel the shy trembling of his hands, almost in agony, as they brushed her, and later in the afternoon the gasp of ecstatic pain from him as she loved him. And knowing only too well the pain of that first love to him she put her mouth hard against his head and ran it backwards and forwards, with little caressing murmurs, to comfort him. At times he looked at her almost in fear, but with a fear which she had never seen on his face before, the fear not of Rosset but of the strength of his own emotions.

The rain kept on all afternoon and they gave up the thought of going out unconsciously, but they remembered that they had intended to eat and they went downstairs at last and made themselves coffee in the kitchen and ate fresh bread with it. All the time she saw in his face the flash of new emotions; and there was a fresh bright strength about him, almost swaggering, which banished the old mute fear. Her love had emancipated him, renewed him. There was a tumultuous joy in her own breast, a joy both at the giving of her love and the vanquishing of his fear.

The rain went steadily on, but they were hardly conscious of it. In the little private room Rosset's clock stood open and still unwound and they made it an excuse to go up again. While they remained there she could feel him all the time rising above his old dumbness and fear and she felt blissfully happy.

Suddenly she sprang up, hearing something down below, the noise of a door being opened, and then both she and the boy leapt to their feet at the sound of Rosset's voice.

'Who is 'ere? Where are you? Who is it who 'as made coffee? Where are you? Where are you?'

The voice, at first subdued, rose to a yell as Rosset came to the stairs. They heard him begin to come up, shouting:

'Who is it? Where are you? Where are you? Come out!'

Like a blundering animal, he came bellowing upstairs, throwing open doors, shouting more loudly than ever into the silence of the top story. Pierre and the girl stood absolutely still, staring and listening.

'Who is it? Where are you?' he kept shouting, more and more angry as the silence of the house met him.

Stamping and cursing he passed the door of the little room and was hastening downstairs when the marble clock struck a quarter. He turned back at once like a furious beast and burst into the room. Pierre and the girl stood there transfixed, never having moved since his first shout, and he came upon them with an exclamation of guttural joyous anger. The girl had not even buttoned her dress.

He stood for one moment glaring at them, his brows working up and down in anger, his body grunting for breath. His lips trembled violently and his little eyes fixed themselves with fury on the girl's unbuttoned frock.

'Get out of this room!' he roared at last. 'Get out!'

The boy, so used to obeying that voice even when he did not understand its language, came forward involuntarily. With a grunt of fury Rosset knocked him aside, pointing to the girl instead.

'You!' he shouted. 'You, I mean. Get out of this room — this house. And don't come back — don't come back.'

As she moved forward and past him and out of the room

and went upstairs he hurled after her a spout of abusive fury until he was exhausted and had no strength even to look at the boy, standing in readiness to be abused and he hoped also, like the girl, dismissed.

Half-way downstairs Rosset remembered and there came a shout:

'And you — down in the restaurant. I will see you.'

At the words the old sickening terror ran through the boy, sapping away completely the strength and joy the girl had given him. He stumbled downstairs, conscious only in a dazed way of what was happening.

In the evening he stood in the restaurant by the table, mutely waiting and watching the waiters peer into the dark street and Rosset marching up and down in agitation. As Rosset passed him he shrank into himself, half-swooning with fear, always expecting a torrent of abuse such as that he had flung at the girl. It did not come but, knowing it would come, in time, he fell into the old trick of staring at the opposite wall and losing himself beyond it.

Suddenly he felt again that blow at his chest, flinging him backwards.

'Always against the wall!' Rosset's voice whispered fiercely with anger. 'Always against the wall!'

The boy pressed himself back to the wall, so hard that there was a pain where his head touched it.

In his eyes lay an expression not only of fear and sickness. They had a queer furtive, sideways look, that half-desperate, half-hopeless look, almost criminal, that dwells in the eyes of the oppressed and persecuted, of those who cannot escape.

THE GLEANER

She is very old, a little sprig of a woman, spare and twisted.
The sun is hardly past its noon. She has climbed uphill out
of the town, up the hot, white road, with curious fretting
footsteps, half-running, half-walking, as though afraid that
some other gleaner will have come up before her. But as far
as she can see, into a distance of mellow light under a sky as
mild and wonderfully blue as the stray chicory-stars still
blooming among the stiff yellow grasses by the roadside, the
world is empty. She is alone, high up, insignificantly solitary
in a world of pure untrembling light that pours straight
down, washing away the summer-green gloom from the tops
of the still trees. There is not even the stirring of a sheep
over the land or the flickering of a bird in the sky; nothing to
alarm or rival or distract her. Yet she goes on always with
that fretting eagerness, as though afraid, not resting or
satisfied until she sees the wheatfield before her, empty like
the rest of the earth except for that downpour and flood of
golden light upon its stubbled slope.

She pushes open the gate, clicks it shut behind her, flaps
open her sack, takes one swift and comprehensive glance at
the field, and bends her back. Her fingers are rustling like
quick mice over the stubble, and the red wheat ears are
rustling together in her hands before she has taken another
step forward. There is no time for looking or listening or
resting. To glean, to fill her sack, to travel over that field
before the light is lost; she has no other purpose than that
and could understand none.

Long ago, in another century, she also came up to this
same field, on just such still, light-flooded afternoons, for
this same eternal and unchanging purpose. But not alone;
they would glean then, in families, occasionally in villages,
with handcarts and barrows, from early morning until evening, from one gleaning-bell to another. Since it meant so
much, since corn was life — that law was as old as time itself
— they gleaned incessantly, desperately. Every ear on the

face of every field had to be gathered up, and she can remember her mother's fist in her back harrying her to glean faster, and how, in turn, she also urged her children to go on and on, never to rest until the field was clear and the light had died.

She is already away from the gate, moving quickly out into the field away from the ruts that the wagons have cut and the ears they have smashed into the sun-baked soil. She moves with incredible quickness, fretfully, almost as fearfully as she came up the hill. In her black skirt and blouse, and with her sharp white head for ever near the earth, she looks like a hungry bird, always pecking and nipping at something, never resting, never satisfied.

Her sleeves are rolled up, showing her thin, corn-coloured arms, with the veins knotty and stiff about her bony wrists. Her hands seem to be still young in their quickness and vitality, like the young tips of an old tree, and the intent yet tranquil look on her face is eternal. It is a little, sharp, fleshless, million-wrinkled face; it is like a piece of wood, worn down by time, carved down pitilessly and relentlessly, the softness of the cheeks and mouth and eyes scooped out to make deep hollows, the bone of the cheeks and chin and forehead left high and sharp as knots in the wood. As though years of sun-flooded days in gleaning fields had stained it, the flesh is a soft, shining corn colour. Even the blue dimness of her eyes has become touched by the faintest drop of this corn-coloured radiance — the colour of age, of autumn, of dying, almost of death itself.

In the open field the sun is very hot. Beating down from an autumn angle the force of its light and heat falls full on her back or into her eyes as she zigzags up and down or across the stubble-rows. She appears to move carelessly, without method, gleaning chance ears as she sees them; she moves, in reality, by instinct, to some ancient and inborn system, unconsciously, but surely as a bird. Miraculously she misses scarcely an ear. She moves incessantly, she looks tireless. Sometimes she glances quickly over her shoulders, across the field, into the sky, with brief unconscious anxiety about something, but the world is empty.

It is as though there is no one in the world except herself
who gleans any longer. She is not merely alone: she is the
last of the gleaners, the last survivor of an ancient race.
Nevertheless, moving across the field under the mellow sun,
nipping up the ears in her quick hands, shaking her sack,
dragging it over the stubble, she looks eternal. She is doing
something that has been done since the beginning of time
and is not conscious of it; she is concerned only with the ears,
the straws, the length of the stubble, the way she must go.
She scarcely notices even the flowers, ground blooming and
creeping flowers that the binder cannot touch, little mouse-
carpets of periwinkle and speedwell, purple coronets of
knapweed, trumpets of milk-coloured and pink convolvulus,
a scabious bursting a mauve bud, bits of starry camomile.
Occasionally she is impatient at something — at the straggling length of the stubble, the riot of thistle and coltsfoot that
chokes the rows. Nowadays the binder leaves the straw so
long and shaggy. Nobody hoes any longer, nobody gleans,
nobody troubles. The crop is poor and uneven, and she
comes across wastes of thin straw and much green rank twitch
where the earth is barren of corn and she scarcely picks an
ear, though she never straightens her back and never ceases
that mouse-quick searching with her brown hands.

But later, in the heat of the afternoon, with her sack filling
up and the sun-heat and bright light playing unbrokenly
upon her, she begins unconsciously to move more slowly, a
little tired, like a child that has played too long. She will not
cover the field, and as she moves there, always solitary, up
and down the stubble, empty except for herself and a rook or
two, she begins to look smaller and the field larger and larger
about her.

At last she straightens her back. It is her first conscious
sign of weariness. She justifies it by looking into the sky and
over the autumn-coloured land sloping away to the town;
briefly she takes in the whole soft-lighted world, the effulgence
of wine-yellow light on the trees and the dove-coloured roofs
below and a straggling of rooks lifting heavily off the stubble
and settling farther on again.

She stoops and goes on once more; and then soon, another

rest, another glance into the sky, and then another beginning. Very soon there is a thistle pricking her hand, and she is glad to stop and pull it out and suck the place with her thin lips.

Ahead of her there is a hedge of hawthorn and blackberry, with great oaks that throw balloons of shadow across the field. She moves into the oak shade with relief; it is cool, like a drink of water, like a clean white sheet; and the coolness fills her with a new vitality, so that she goes on gleaning for a long time without needing to rest.

By and by she is working along the hedge. Straws have been plaited and twisted by wind among the hawthorn and blackberry and wild clematis and sloe, and she goes along picking them off, twisting them together and dropping them into her sack, her body upright. It is easier. She can smell the darkening blackberries, the first dying odour of leaves. She stops to gather and eat a dewberry, squeezing it against her palate like a dark grape; to rub the misty purple-green bloom off a sloe with her fingers.

There are many straws on the hedge. The sack is heavy. She walks very slowly, dragging it, wondering all the time why she does not lift it to her shoulder and start for home, but something stronger than herself keeps her picking and gleaning, missing nothing.

It is not until the light begins to fail that she thinks of departing. She has begun to carry the sack in her arms, hugging it to her chest, setting it down at intervals and gleaning the stubble about it. There is no need to go on, but some inherent, unconscious, eternal impulse keeps her moving perpetually. But still she glances up sometimes with the old fear, wondering if some other gleaner will come.

She has worked towards the gate and there she sets down the sack and rests a moment. It is late afternoon; dark crowds of starlings are flying over and gathering in invisible trees, making a great murmuration in the late quietness. Before she can depart she must lift the sack to her back or lift it to the gate and bend her back beneath it. She is very tired. She might leave the sack under the hedge; she might come again to-morrow; but she suddenly catches the sack in her arms, hoists it to the gate with an immense effort as though her life depended upon it.

Her strength is not enough. The sack, very full, half falls back upon her, but in a moment she makes a tremendous effort and, as she makes it, lifting the sack slowly upright again, she feels her eyes, for some reason, fill with the stupid tears of age and weakness.

In a moment it is all over, forgotten. She makes a great effort to lift up the sack. She succeeds. The sack falls across her back, bearing her down, and she catches at its mouth, holds it and staggers away.

Her tears have stopped and she has not thought of wiping them away, and as she staggers off down the road towards the sunset they roll down among her million wrinkles and find their way to her mouth. She goes on without resting. She looks more than ever eternal, an earth-figure, as old and ageless and primitive as the corn she carries.

As she goes on, the light dies rapidly until there is only an orange glow in the western sky like the murky light of a candle. The air is cool, still, autumnal. Her tears have dried on her cheeks, and now and then she can taste the salt of them still on her lips: the salt of her own body, the salt of the earth.

THE WOMAN WHO HAD
IMAGINATION

I

THE yellow brake climbed slowly uphill out of the town,
leaving behind it the last ugly red houses; the two white
horses broke into an abrupt trot along the level road, the
brasses tinkling softly and winking brilliantly in the noon
sunshine, and all the passengers who had leaned forward up
the hill to ease the strain on the horses leaned back with relief
and then lurched forward again with the sudden onward jerk
of the brake, the men's straw boaters knocking against the
wide sunshades and the big flowered hats of the giggling
women. There were many shouts of mock alarm and
laughter: 'Whoops! What ho, she bumps! Whoa! mare!
Want to throw us out? Whoa! Get off my lap! Stop the
brake, me voice's slipped down me trousers' leg! What's the
matter? Horses going to a fire or something? Oh Lord, me
bandeau's slipped! Get off my lap I tell you! Whoops!
Steady! How d'ye think we're going to sing after this? Stop
'em, me voice's crawling up me other leg! Oh, ain't he a
case? Oh dear! Ain't he a caution? What ho! Now we're
off! Oh, don't he say some bits? Now we're off! Altogether!
Whoops! Dearie! Altogether!'

Gradually the parasols became still and circumspect,
the women gave their hatpins little tidying pushes and
smoothed their dresses, and the horses fell automatically into
a smoother pace, the sound of running wheels and the click-
clocking of hoofs becoming an unchanged and sleepy rhythm
in the still midsummer air.

At the rear of the brake, wedged closely in between a
hawking fishmonger who still gave off an odour of red herrings,
and a balloon of a woman who was sucking rosebud cachous
and wheezing for breath as though she had swallowed a
button-whistle, sat a youth of twenty. At the height of the
giggling and banting and shouting he sat in unsmiling silence.

He looked proud and bored. The brake was filled with the Orpheus Male Voice Glee Singers and their wives and sweethearts. That afternoon and again in the evening they were to sing on the lawns of a big house, in competition with a score of other choirs, ten miles on in the heart of the country. Aloof and sensitive, the youth had made up his mind that he was above such things.

'Like a cachou, 'Enry?' said the stout woman.

'No thanks,' he said.

'Real rose. Make your breath smell beautiful.'

'No thanks.'

He had come on the outing against his will. And now — cachous! He looked about him with a kind of bored disgust in which there was also something unhappy. The whole brake was tittering and chattering with a gaiety that seemed to him puerile and maddening. The strong odours of violet and lavender perfumes and the stout woman's rose-scented cachous mingled with the hot smell of horses and sun-scorched varnish and men's cheap hair-oil. He caught now and then a breath of some dark carnation from a button-hole, but the clove-sweetness would become mixed with the odour of stale red herrings. At the front of the brake he could see his father, a little man dressed in a straw hat cocked on the back of his head and a dapper grey suit with the jacket thrown wide open in order to show off a pale yellow waist-coat with pearl buttons. Opposite his father sat his mother, plump, double-chinned, with big adoring brown eyes, dressed in a lavender-grey dress and hat to match his father's suit. Round her neck she wore a thin band of black velvet. The very latest! No other woman in the brake sported a band of black velvet. Yet he thought his mother looked hot and uncomfortable, as though the black velvet were strangling her, and his father sat as though she never existed, bobbing constantly up and down to call to someone in the rear of the brake, talking excitedly to anyone and everyone but her.

It was solely because of his father that Henry Solly had come on the outing. Solly! What a name! His father was conductor of the choir, a sort of musical Napoleon, very small and absurdly vain, who wanted to conquer the world with the sound of his own voice. Stout, excitable, electric, he was like a little Napoleonic Jack-in-the-box, with tiny cocksure blue eyes, a fair, sharp-waxed moustache, and a kind of clockwork chattering voice that changed as though by a miracle, when he sang, into a bass of magnificent tone, warm, rich and strong. By profession he was a draper, but the shop was gloomily unattractive and poorly patronized, so that Alfred found a good deal of time to sit in the back living-room and practise hymns and oratorio and part-songs on the American organ while Henry attended the shop. It was a boring, passionless, depressing existence. 'When you grow up, Henry,' his father had been fond of saying, 'you'll have to wait in the shop.' He often wondered and sometimes still continued to wonder what it was he must wait for? Already he had now been seven years in the shop, waiting. And he had begun to feel now that he would go on for another twenty, thirty, perhaps even fifty years, still waiting and still wondering what he was waiting for. There he would be, fifty years hence, still dusting and re-arranging the thick flannel shirts, pants, waistcoats, corduroy trousers, body-belts, patent collar fasteners, stiff cuffs and starched white dickies; still writing the little white cards to pin on the frowzy articles in the window, *Solly for Style — Solly for Smartness — Solly for Shirts — Socks — Suits — Studs and Suspenders — Solly for Everything*; still dusting and setting out the window every Monday morning, carrying in the absurd naked dummies, dressing them and pinning on them, as he did now, a card saying *The Latest for* 1902, only changing the style of the dresses and the date as he grew older. He saw himself as some fatuous patriarchal draper grown half-idiotic from years behind a counter, his mind starved and enfeebled by lack of the commonest pleasures of the world. And there he would be, still waiting, with the certainty of achieving nothing but death. He felt sometimes as if he could hurl a dummy through the shop window on some dead and empty Monday morning and then walk out and never come back again. Or if only one of those grey, naked ladies' dummies would come to life!

At the same smooth and now monotonous pace the brake went on into the heart of the country. All the time he sat silent and contemplative. He was fair-haired, with a pale, almost nervously sensitive face that had something attractive in its very pallor and in the intensity of the blue eyes and the small mobile mouth. His body, slight and undeveloped from years of waiting in the ill-ventilated and gloomy shop, had something restless and almost anxious about it even as he sat still and stared from the faces in the brake to the fields and woods, quivering and bright in the noon heat, that travelled smoothly past like some slowly unwound sun-golden panorama. It had about it also something stiff and unsatisfied and unhappy. His straw hat was fastened with a black silk guard to the lapel of his coat; it was his mother's idea: as though on that windless, burning day his straw hat would blow off! And just as his straw hat was tied to him he felt tied to the brake, the absurd giggling passengers and the monotony of his own thoughts. As he sat there, unhappily wishing he had never come, he thought dismally of the after-noon ahead — singing, tea in a noisy marquee, more singing on the lawns in the summer twilight, refreshments, more singing, the ride home, and more singing again. Singing! It would have been different if the word had meant any-thing to him. But he couldn't sing a single note correctly or in tune. How often had his father offered him half a crown if he could sing, without going sharp or flat, one verse of 'The Day Thou Gavest, Lord, is Ended.' He had never succeeded.

'Can you 'itch up a bit?' said the fishmonger suddenly.

Henry moved along the plush seat a fraction, but without speaking.

'That's better. Ain't it hot? If this weather holds I'm a dunner. Fish won't keep, y'know. I had a case o' fresh whiting in yesterday and the missus fainted. Went clean off. That's the fish-trade. See y'money go bad under your eyes.'

The fishmonger's coarse red skin oozed little yellow streams of sweat, which he kept wiping off with his hand-kerchief, puffing heavily as he took off his bowler hat and mopped his red bald head. He was renowned for his voice, a light sweet tenor, and for his moving and passionate interpretation of 'Come into the Garden, Maud'.

'Blimey,' he kept saying. 'I'm done like a dinner.'

The road, after climbing up a little, had begun to drop down again towards a wooded valley. The country stretched out infinitely green and yellow under the pure intensity of noon light. In the near distance the road shimmered under the heat like quivering water. Cattle had gathered under the shade of trees, unmoving except for the clockwork flicking of their tails as they stared at the passing brake with its crowd of laughing passengers. By a woodside there was a murmur of doves invisible in the thick-leaved trees, warm, liquid, sleepy, and no other bird-sound except the occasional cry of a jay disturbed by the noise of wheels and voices. The brief cool wood-shade was like a draught of water; the shrill voices and clocking hoofs made cool empty echoes in the deep sun-flickered shadowy silence. Someone in the brake reached up and shook a low-hanging bough that in swishing back again seemed to set all the leaves in the wood rustling with a soft, dry, endless whispering. The scent of honeysuckle was suddenly very strong and exquisite, pouring out from the wood in a sweet invisible mist that seemed to disperse as soon as the brake was out in the sunshine again. After the dark coolness of the overhanging trees the day was blinding and burning. And out in the full glare of sunlight the world was steeped in other scents, the smell of drying hay, the thick vanilla odour of meadow-sweet, the exotic heavenliness of lime trees.

The road went down to a village. There, at a white-washed public-house with red geraniums blazing vividly in the window-boxes, the brake pulled up to a concert of cries and laughter.

'Whoa! What's the matter with you, old horses? Whoa there! Are they teetotallers? Whoa?'

Shouting and laughing, the passengers began to alight and vanish into the public-house. Those who did not drink walked about to stretch their legs or stood in the shade of the inn wall. Men reappeared from the public-house doorway with glasses of golden beer, their mouths ringed with beads of foam. From the tap-room a bass voice boomed and pom-pommed deep impromptu notes of noisy pleasure.

Henry got down from the brake and walked about moodily. His father and mother stood in the shade, each drinking a small lemonade.

'Get yourself a lemon, 'Enry, my boy,' said his father.

'No thanks.'

'Feel dicky?'

'I'm all right.'

'Liven yourself up then. Haven't lost nothing, have you?'

'I'm all right,' said Henry.

He refused a sip of his mother's lemonade and walked away. He felt bored, morose, out of touch with everyone.

With relief he saw the passengers emerge from the public-house and begin to climb back into the brake. He climbed up also and found himself sitting, this time, between a tall scraggy man with a peg-leg who gave off the mustily dry odour of leather, and a girl of his own age who was dressed as if she were going to a baptism, in a white silk dress, white straw hat, long white gloves that reached to her elbows, white cotton stockings, white shoes and a white sunshade which she carried elegantly over her left shoulder.

'Oh! It's going to be marvellous,' she said.

'What is?' he said. 'Don't poke me in the eye with that sunshade.'

'The choir, the house, everything.'

'Glad you think so,' he said.

The brake had begun to move again, the shouting and excited laughter of the passengers half drowning the girl's voice and his own. And above the din of the brake's departure there arose the sound of insistent argument.

'I tell you it's right! Seen it times with my own eyes.'

'You dreamt it.'

'Dreamt it! I *seen* it. Plain as a pikestaff.'

'In a churchyard? Tell your grandmother.'

'Well, if you don't believe me, will you bet on it? You're so cocky.'

'Ah, I'll bet you. Any money. Anything you like.

'All right. You'll bet as what I've told you ain't on that tombstone in Polwick churchyard? You'll bet on that?'

'Ah! I'll bet you. And I *know* it ain't.'

'Well, go on. How much?'

'Tanner.'

There were shouts of ironical laughter and reckless encouragement. A little black frizzy-haired man was bobbing excitedly up and down on the brake seat urging a large blond man wearing a cream tea-rose in his buttonhole to increase the bet. 'Go on. Make it sixpence ha'penny. You're so cocky. How can you lose? You know it ain't there, don't you? Go on.'

'Sixpence,' said the blond man. 'I said sixpence and I mean sixpence.'

'You'll go to ruin fast.'

'I dare say. But I said sixpence and I mean sixpence. And here's me money.'

'All right! Let the driver hold it.'

The blond man handed his money to the fishmonger, who had climbed up to sit by the driver, and then began to urge the little man:

'Give him your money. Go on. And say good-bye to it while you're at it. Go on, say good-bye to it. Ah, it's no use spitting on it. It's the last you'll ever see o' that tanner.'

'You're so cocky. Why didn't you bet a quid?'

'Ah, why didn't I?'

Up on the driving-seat the driver and the fishmonger rolled against each other in sudden storms of laughter. Women giggled and men called out to each other, making dark insinuations, urging the driver to stop at the churchyard.

Opposite Henry and the girl a handsome man with a dark moustache and wearing a straw hat at a devilish angle had rested his hand with a sort of stealthy nonchalance on the knee of a school teacher in pink. She in turn averted her eyes, trying to appear as though she were thinking profound, far-off, earnest thoughts.

'What's the matter?' he said.

'It's so hot,' she murmured.

'So are you,' he whispered.

The school teacher's neck flushed crimson and the blood surged up into her face.

And as if to cover up her own embarrassment the girl at Henry's side began to talk in a rather louder voice to him, but her prim banal voice became lost for him in the giggling and talking of the other passengers, the loud-voiced arguments about the bet, the everlasting sound of wheels and hoofs on the rough, sun-baked road. Down in the valley the sun seemed hotter than ever. The brake passed a group of haymakers resting and sleeping in the noon-heat under the shade of a great elm tree. They waved and called with sleepy greetings. A woman sitting among them suckling a baby looked up with sun-tired eyes. Further on a group of naked boys bathing in a sloe-fringed pond jumped up and down in the sun-silvered water and about the grass pond-bank, waving their wet arms and flagging their towels. In the brake there was a thin ripple of giggling, the women suddenly ducking their heads together and whispering with suppressed excitement. The blond man and the frizzy-haired dark man argued and taunted each other with unending but friendly vehemence. And under the intense sunshine and the dazzling fierce July light the slowness of the brake was intolerable. Up the hills it crawled as though the horses were sick. Down hill the brakes hissed and checked the wheels into the deathly pace of a funeral. Henry sat drugged by the heat and the wearisome pace of progress. Faintly, through the sun-heavy air, came the strokes of one o'clock from a church tower. Already it was as if the brake had travelled all day. And now, with the strokes of the clock dying away and leaving the air limitlessly silent beyond the little noises of the brake it seemed suddenly as if the journey might last for ever.

Twenty minutes later the brake went down hill through an avenue of elms towards a square church tower rising like a small sturdy grey fortress out of a village that seemed asleep except for a batch of black hens dust-bathing in the hot road. The sudden coming of the brake sent the fowls squawking and cluttering away in panic-feathered half-flight.

'Ah! Your old horses are too slow for a funeral. Might have had a Sunday dinner for nothing if you'd been sharper.

81

What d'ye feed 'em on? Too slow to run over an old hen. Gee there! Tickle 'em up a bit.' And mingled with these shouts the repeated cry:

'And don't forget to stop at the churchyard.'

The frizzy-haired man began to stand up and wave his arms. He became ironically tender towards the blond man. 'I feel sorry for you. It's like taking money from a kid. Pity your mother ever let you come out.' The blond man kept shaking his head with silent wisdom. The brake crawled slowly by the churchyard wall. 'A bit farther,' cried the dark man with excitement. 'T'other side o' that yew-tree. Gee up a bit.' The passengers were craning their necks, laughing, standing up, bantering remarks. With mock sadness the frizzy-haired man patted the blond man on the back, shaking his head. 'Feel sorry for you,' he said in a wickedly dismal voice. The blond man airily waved his hand with a gesture of pity. 'Not half so sorry as you'll feel for yourself in a minute,' he said.

The frizzy-haired man did not listen. He was beginning to survey the tombstones with great excitement, craning his neck. Suddenly the blond man seized him and held him aloft like a child.

'Now can you see, ducky?' he cried.

'A bit farther! Farther! Steady now. Whoa there! Whoa!' The brake stopped. The small man wriggled down from the blond man's arms. There arose a pandemonium of laughter and shouts in the brake. The driver stood up and chinked the money in his hand. The small man spoke with twinkling irony.

'Oh! No, it ain't there, is it? It ain't there? It's melted. Well, well, I must be boss-eyed. The sun's so hot it's melted. Would you believe it? Fancy that. Just fancy that. It ain't there.'

The blond man was staring with dumb gloom at a gravestone.

'What are you looking at?' began the small man mercilessly. 'What? — If it ain't a tombstone I'll never —. Well, well!'

'I'll be damned,' the blond man was saying slowly. 'I'll be damned.'

'Read it!' yelled the little man in triumph.

'I've read it.'

'Read it out loud.'

'Ah, what d'ye take me for? Three pen'worth o' tripe? You read it.'

'All right. It's worth it.' Solemnly the small man read out the rhyme on the tombstone:

> *'Let wind go free where'er you be!*
> *In chapel or in church.*
> *For wind it was the death of me.'*

Suddenly the driver clicked at the horses and the brake jerked violently on. The women shrieked, the blond man sat disconsolate, the small man piped in triumph above the bubbling and spluttering of laughter.

Henry sat with a little smile on his lips, faintly aloof, his thoughts lofty and cool. He felt wonderfully above and detached from the puerile jokes and empty laughter of the rest of the brake, his brain manufacturing little self-conscious philosophies which seemed very clever, and when the mood seemed to be dying at last it was suddenly revived by the spectacle of his father standing up in the brake, signalling the driver to halt for a moment and delivering his final words of advice and admonition to the choir.

'Well, we shall be there in a few more minutes. And I just want to remind you of a few things. We've had our little jokes. And now I want to be serious for ten seconds. This is a serious business. We are down to start singing at four o'clock. All hear that? Four o'clock. Four o'clock on the big lawn in front of the house. We shall start off with "Calm was the Sea"; and then after that it will be "On the Banks of Allan Water", and then last of all "My Love is Like a Red, Red Rose". We shall sing these three in the afternoon. And then in the evening, at seven o'clock, we shall sing a test piece chosen from one of these and three others. It might be one of these three. It might not. It might be anything. We don't know. We've got to stand ready to sing anything at a moment's notice.' He waved his arms up and down constantly in his excitement. His voice was like that of a little chattering ventriloquist's doll. 'And one more thing. Remember the words. When it says "Calm was the Sea" don't sing it as if it were "The Wreck of the Hesperus", but sing it as if it were calm — calm and soft. Imagine it. Lovely day. Boats hardly moving. Softly, softly, does it, softly. Imagine it. Imagine you're on Yarmouth pier if you like, looking at the sea. Water hardly moves. And then "the wandering breezes". Soft again, very soft. Let them wander. Let them flow from you. And breezes — remember it's breezes. Not a thunderstorm. Still soft — you'll see in the copy it's marked *dulce*. Italian word — means sweet, soft, gentle. Remember dulcimer. Close your eyes if you like. Sing it as if you was dreaming.' He closed his fair-lashed eyes and put on a wrapt dreamy expression of soft ecstasy. 'Dah — dah-dah — daaah-dah!' he sang in a soft falsetto. 'Wand'ring bre-e-e-zes.' He opened his eyes. 'Feeling — that's it — feeling. Expression. That's everything. Anybody can bellow like a bull. But that's not singing. That's not interpretation. Not feeling. And don't be afraid of how you look. The judges aren't looking to see how pretty you are. They're *listening*. Well, make them listen, soft, softly does it, remember, softly.'

His voice trailed off to a fine whisper and he sat down. Henry smiled and the brake went on, the passengers in a changed mood after his father's words, the women tidying their hats and smoothing their stiff puff-sleeves and long dresses, the men fingering their buttonholes, clearing their throats and sitting in silence as though suddenly musingly nervous of the thought of the singing.

The country began to change also. The yellowing wheat-fields, the dark fields of roots shining and drooping in the hot sun, the parched hayfields and woods were replaced by an immense park of old dark trees under which the grass was still spring green and sweet. Far off, timid and startled, groups of young deer, palest brown against the dark tree-shadows, with an occasional dark antlered, resentful stag, stood and watched the brake go past with glassy, wondering eyes. Soon, through wider spaces between the trees, there was the big house itself, a square, stone tall-windowed place, with a carved stone balustrade round the lead roof and immense black cedars encircling the lawns. It looked cold and sepulchral even against the rich darkness of the trees in the hot sunlight.

The brake turned into the park through high iron gates on which the family crest blazed in scarlet and gold. It was as if it had driven into a churchyard. The passengers were suddenly transformed, sitting with a stiff, self-conscious silence upon them. As the brake drove along under a great avenue of elms extending like a sombre nave up to the lawns of the house, the horses fell into a walk. The fishmonger sat very upright on the driver's seat, preening his buttonhole, and the fat woman, sucking her last cachou quickly, wiped her lips clean with her handkerchief. The handsome young man in a rakish straw hat, taking his hand away from the school teacher's knee, ceased his seductive whispers. The carriage-drive emerged in an immense sweep from under the dark avenue into the sunlight and curved on between the lawns and the house. The brake pulled up behind a row of other brakes standing empty by a tall yew-hedge and the choir began to alight, the men handing down the ladies from the awkward back-step and the ladies giving little delicate shrieks and pretending to stumble. Henry's father dragged out from under the brake seat an immense portmanteau of music. From over the lawn, gay with parasols and flowing frocks, there came a scent of new-mown grass and women's dresses, the swooning breath of lime trees and a hum of human voices like the sound of bees.

Across the lawn also came a man in an old panama hat, a yellowish alpaca suit and a faded green bow, beaming with smiles and gestures of aristocratic idiocy.

'Oh, pardon, pardon me!' he cried. 'But 'oo are you? Oh! Orpheus choir! Yes! Orpheus! Marvellous! T'ank you a t'ousand times for coming. Yes! And if you desire anyt'ing please come to me. Anyt'ing you like. Anyt'ing. And T'ank you a t'ousand times for coming! T'ank you a t'ousand times! And ezz it not ze most marvellous day? Most marvellous!'

II

In the full heat of the afternoon, tired from walking about
the crowded lawns in the fierce sunshine and even more bored
than he had been in the brake, Henry saw people passing in
and out of the house through a side door on the terrace.
Following them, he found himself in a wide lofty entrance hall
that had about it the queer half-scented coolness of a church
and the same hollow silence broken at intervals by the sound
of voices and strange receding and returning echoes. He
took off his straw hat and wiped his sweaty forehead with his
handkerchief. The air felt as cool as a leaf on his hot face. In
answer to his question a negative-faced manservant standing
at ease like a tired soldier at the foot of a wide stone staircase
told him that the house was open to visitors till five o'clock.
He walked quietly up the stairs, his feet soundless on the
heavy carpet, staring at the magnificence of gilded ceilings,
dim tapestries, old dark portraits, immense sparkling chandeliers, touching the flower-smoothness of old chests and chairs
with his finger-tips as he passed. Upstairs he went in and out
of innumerable rooms, staring at vast canopied bedsteads,
lacquered cabinets filled with never-opened books and fragile
china, dim painted screens and ornate fireplaces of cold blue-
veined marble. He wondered all the time who had ever
lived and slept there, contrasting it all unconsciously with the
room behind the shop at home, with the cheap German silk-
fronted piano, the brass gas-brackets, the cane music-rack,
the broken revolving piano stool, the flashy green jars con-
taining aspidistras whose leaves his mother counted and
sponged religiously every Saturday. The place had an air of
unreality. The yellow blinds, drawn to keep out the sun,
threw down a strange shadowy apricot light. Here and there
rents in the blinds let in streaks of dusty sunlight. When he
put his hand on the walls they struck cold and damp. Across
the floors he noticed trails of candle-grease dropped perhaps
by some servant coming in to lower the blinds at night or let
them up again in the morning. How long ago? he wondered.
There was a melancholy air of the past, of vague, dead,

forgotten things. There was also a curious feeling of poverty about it all in spite of that rich magnificence. The blinds were old and stained, the paint was cracked and dirty, and here and there a ceiling had crumbled away, revealing naked laths draped with black skeins of cobweb.

Going slowly up the second flight of stairs, he stopped now and then to look at the prints on the walls. A clock in the house struck four, the notes very soft and delicate, a silver water-sound. Some visitors passed him, coming down, their voices dying away down the two flights of stairs like a vague chant. Going up, he found himself in a bare corridor.

Walking into a room by one door and out by another he turned along a narrow corridor in order to return to the stairs, but the passage seemed contained within itself, to lead nowhere. And in a moment he was lost. Trying to go back to the room through which he had come he tried a door, but it was locked. He began to try other doors, which were also locked. It was some minutes before he found a door which opened.

Relieved, he hurried through the room. But half-way across the floor, thinking of nothing but escaping by the opposite door, he was startled into a fresh panic by a voice:

'But unfortunately, in bestowing these embraces, a pin in her ladyship's headdress slightly scratching the child's neck, produced from this pattern of gentleness, such violent screams as could hardly be outdone by any creature professedly noisy. The mother's consternation was excessive; but it could not surpass the alarm. . . .'

At the word alarm he stopped. The voice stopped too. He felt himself break out into a prickling sweat. Across the room, with his thin fingers outstretched to a low wood fire, sat an old man in a torn red dressing-gown. He was sunk into a kind of sick trance. By his side there was a woman, a young woman. Arrested in the act of reading, she sat with her averted head still and intense, looking across the room with the blackest eyes he had ever seen, black not only with their own richness of colour but with an illimitable darkness of sheer melancholy.

'I'm lost,' Henry said.

87

'Lost?'

She stood upright as she echoed the word, rubbing the fingers of her left hand up and down the yellow leather binding of the book. Trying to face her he was sick with confusion. The old man turned stiffly and stared at him also. The old eyes were pale and vacuous.

Suddenly the woman smiled.

'It's all right,' she said.

For some reason or other Henry could not answer her. He stood half-foolishly hypnotized by her figure, tall and wonderfully slender, her very long maroon-coloured dress, her unspeakably brilliant eyes. Her voice had in it a kind of mournful sweetness which held him fascinated.

At last he attempted to explain himself. He had no sooner begun than she cut him short:

'I'll show you the way,' she said.

He still could not answer. She turned to the old man:

'Sit still. I'll come back.'

'Where are you going?' he muttered querulously. 'Who's that young man?'

In one swift movement she turned from the old man to Henry and then back to the old man again, smiling at the youth with half-grave, half-vivacious eyes. And there was the same mischievous solemnity in her voice.

'He's the new gardener,' she said.

'Eh?'

'The new gardener. Here, take the book. Read a little till I come back. From the top of the page there. You see?'

'What? I'd like some tea.'

'All right.'

'It's not so frightfully warm in here either,' he said pettishly.

'Keep your dressing-gown buttoned. You're not likely to be warm. See, button it up.'

She fingered the buttons of his dressing-gown, quickly, impatiently. And then, while he still protested and complained, she walked swiftly across the room, opened the far door and vanished into the passage outside. In bewilderment Henry followed her. She shut the door quickly behind him.

'Well, now I'll see you out,' she said.

She began to walk away along the passage and he followed her, a step or two behind. She walked quickly with long, impatient steps, so that he had difficulty in keeping up.

They walked along in silence except for the sound of her dress swishing along the carpet until he recognized the window at which he had stood and looked down on the choir.

'I'm all right now,' he said. He began to utter dim thanks and apologies.

'Go and enjoy yourself,' she said. 'Have you seen the lake?'

'No.'

'Go and see it. Across the park and through the rhododendron plantation. You'll find it. It's lovely.'

Before he could speak again she had turned away. There was a brief flash of maroon in the passage, the sound of her feet running quickly after she had vanished. He waited a moment. But nothing happened, there was only a curious, almost audible hush everywhere. Outside the singing had ceased. He moved towards the stairs in a state of dejected and tense astonishment.

III

The singing was over for the afternoon. There was nothing to do but wander about the lawns and terraces or take tea in the large flagged tea-tent. Privileged ladies were playing croquet on a small lawn under the main terrace, giggling nervously as they struck the bright-coloured balls. Gentlemen in straw boaters and pin-striped cream flannel trousers with wide silk waist-bands applauded their shots delicately. There was an oppressive feeling of summer languor, a parade of gay hats and parasols and sweeping dresses. Henry went into the tea-tent for a cup of tea to escape the boredom of it all. Coming out again he met the fishmonger.

'Cheer up,' said the fishmonger.

'Oh! I'm all right.' He put on a casual air. 'I was wondering which was the way to the lake.'

'The lake?' said the fishmonger. His eyes began to dance

like little bubbling peas as soon as he heard the word. The lake? What did he want with the lake? Becoming quite excited, he took hold of Henry's coat-sleeve confidentially and led him across the lawn. So he wanted to know the way to the lake? Well! Very strange. He wondered what he wanted with the lake? Not for fish by any chance? Oh! no, not for fish. Perhaps he didn't even know there were fish in the lake? Henry protested. He cut him short:

'Ah, you're dark, you're dark.'

Finally, losing a little of his excitement, he began to tell him of the days when, as a young man, he had fished in the lake. Fish! They hadn't breathing room. They were the days. But now there hadn't been fish, not a solitary fish, not a stickleback, pulled out of that lake for twenty years. 'Not since old Antonio came.' It was a shame, wickedness. He began to talk with lugubrious regret. Who was Antonio? Henry asked. The fishmonger echoed the words with tenor astonishment, his voice squeaking. Antonio? Hadn't he seen him running about all over the place — 'T'ank you a t'ousand times! T'ank you a t'ousand times!' So that was Antonio? Yes, Antonio Serelli. It was he who was mad on singing and had the choirs come every summer. It was he who hadn't allowed a line in the lake for twenty years. 'In the old days you could give a keeper a drink and fish all day.' But not now. Antonio wouldn't allow it. The police had instructions to keep their eyes open for anyone carrying anything that looked like a rod. And Antonio would go mad if he heard a fish had been hooked. But then he was mad. They were all mad, the whole family, always had been. The girl and all.

'The girl?' Henry repeated. 'Who is she?'

'Maddalena?' The fishmonger shook his head. He didn't know anything about Maddalena. He'd never seen her. She never came out. He only knew old Antonio.

'And what's their name?'

'Serelli.'

'Which must be Italian.'

'Half and half. Don't do to inquire too much into the ins and outs of the aristocracy.'

Finally he pointed out the path going down through a

plantation of rhododendrons to the lake and Henry climbed over the high iron fence of the park.

'Keep your eyes open,' the fishmonger whispered. 'They say he's down there every night. Singing the fish to sleep, I shouldn't wonder.'

Henry left him and walked down through the rhododrendrons to the lake. It was larger than he had imagined, a wide oval of water, stretching for a quarter of a mile before him and on either hand. A thick wood came down on the opposite shore to the fringe of reeds and wild iris fronds. The water was still and smooth until a pair of wild duck, frightened by his coming, shot up and flew high and swift over the alders darkening the bank, their feet dripping silver, their long necks craned to the sun, their alarmed quack-quacking splitting the warm silence. The water-rings, undulating gently away, struck islands of water lilies with a soft flopping sound. Under the sun-shot water countless lily-buds were pushing up like dim magnolias and on the surface wide-open flowers floated like saucers of white and yellow china.

As he walked along the lakeside he could still hear the faint cries that rose from the crowded lawns, and now and then the clock of croquet balls. Hearing them he thought of how he had wandered about the lawns and gardens trying to find courage enough to go into the house again in the hope of seeing for a second time the girl who had been reading to the old man. He could not forget the melancholy intensity of her face. But when finally he had hurried along the terrace the door had been locked.

He walked along by the lake. The grass was spongy and noiseless to walk on, the air very still and warm under the shelter of the rhododendrons, and pigeons made a soft complaint in the silence.

Abruptly he was aware of something moving on the opposite bank. He half stopped and looked. It seemed like a group of yellow irises fluttered by a little deliberate wind. Then he saw that it was someone in a yellow dress. The sleeve was waving. He stopped quite still. The sleeve seemed to be making signals for him to go on.

He began to walk slowly along the bank and the woman

on the opposite bank began to walk along in the same direction, hurrying. At the end of the lake, where the water sluiced in, was a wooden bridge. The woman began to run as she approached it. Her dress was very long and hampered her movements and she paused on the bridge to straighten her skirt and then hurried on again to meet him.

'You shouldn't come along here, you know,' she began to say, as she approached him.

She seemed to be very agitated. Henry stopped. He felt that she had not recognized him.

'I am very sorry,' he said.

And then, perhaps because of his voice, she recognized him. Her face broke into a half smile, but the agitation remained:

'But you shouldn't, you shouldn't,' she kept saying.

'But it was you who told me to come.'

'It makes no difference.'

He did not speak. All this time they had stood at a distance from each other, four or five yards between them. Now she came nearer. In the house he had thought of her as very young, a girl. Now, as she came nearer, she seemed much older. He took her now for twenty-seven or eight. And perhaps because of the yellow dress she seemed darker too. Her eyes were utterly black, not merely dark, and brilliant without the faintest mistiness, like black glass. And she seemed taller also and her body finer in shape, again perhaps because of the yellow dress, and her skin had a kind of creamy duskiness, soft, very smooth, a rich duskiness that had covered also her heavy southern lips and her straight black hair.

Staring at her, he was still at a loss for something to say. She had begun to bite her lower lip, hard, making little white teeth-prints on the dusky flesh, as though in agitation or perplexity. And it occurred to him suddenly why she did not want him there. She had come down not to meet him, but someone else. And she was angry and troubled at finding him there.

'I'm very sorry,' he said again. 'But I'll go at once.'

He put his hand to his straw hat. She startled him by saying instantly:

'I'll walk back with you.' And then added: 'I'm going back the same way.'

It looked as if she didn't trust him. But he said nothing. A path slanted up the slope through the rhododendrons and they began to walk up it. The rhododendrons, old wild misshapen bushes, were full of withered seed-heads. He said something about their having looked wonderful in early summer. She did not answer. He thought she seemed preoccupied. Once, without stopping, she glanced back at the lake as though looking for someone, and as she turned back he remarked:

'It's been a wonderful day.'

'Yes,' she said. She said it unthinkingly, the word meant nothing. And suddenly she added:

'You think so?'

And, as she spoke, she was smiling, an extraordinary smile, vivacious, dark, allusive. It had in it something both tender and mocking.

'You don't think so?' she said.

'No, perhaps not.'

She seemed to feel instinctively that he was bored. He felt it. And he felt that she might have triumphed over him for knowing, but she said nothing, and they walked slowly on up the path.

All the time he wondered why she had been so agitated at finding him by the lake. And finally he asked.

'I didn't recognize you,' she said.

That was all. He didn't believe her. And she sensed his unbelief at once. She looked quickly at him and he smiled. She smiled in return, the same vivacious tender smile as before, and in a moment they were intimate. She said then:

'I didn't want you to get into any unpleasantness, that's all.'

'What unpleasantness?'

'Well, the lake is private. The fish are preserved and there are keepers and so on.'

He said nothing, but at heart he was disappointed at leaving the lake.

'You're not disappointed?' she said at once.

'Yes,' he said.

And then she did an extraordinary thing. She suddenly lifted her arms with a gesture of almost mocking abandonment and declared:

'All right. We'll go back.'

He protested. But she turned and began to walk back down the path to the lake, not heeding him. He turned and followed her, a yard or two behind, protesting again. And suddenly she let out a laugh and began to run. For a moment he stood still with astonishment and then he ran after her.

At the bottom of the path she paused and waited for him. She was still laughing.

'What shall we do?' she said recklessly. 'There's a punt. We could go out on the lake.'

'All right.' He was ready for anything.

And then, as suddenly as she had turned and run down the path, she was saying:

'No, I mustn't. You must excuse me. I must go back.'

'Don't go,' he said.

She caught the tone of entreaty in his voice. And it seemed to hurt her. Her eyes filled with pain, then abruptly with swimming wetness, and he stood still, too astounded to speak, while she bent her head and let the tears fall helplessly down her face. She began to cry with the helplessness of utter dejection, like someone worn out, not even lifting her hands to her face to hide it, but letting them hang spiritlessly at her side, not moving. She hardly made a sound, as though her tears were flooding away her strength. And when gradually she ceased crying and at last lifted her head she never uttered a word of apology or excuse or regret. But she gave him one amazing look, her black eyes swimming with many conflicting emotions; anger, helplessness, dejection, bitterness, fear and pain.

A moment later they were walking back up the path again. He could not speak. She dried her eyes with the sleeve of her dress, making a little yellow handkerchief of it. He felt that there was something unforgettably strange and touching about her, about her beauty, her amazing changes of mood, her tears and her silence.

And just as he had given up the idea of her ever speaking

94

again, she made a sort of excuse, half for her tears, half for her behaviour on first seeing him:

'My brother might be very angry if he knew people had been down by the lake. And that might mean the end of the singing contests.'

That was all. It was very lame, very unconvincing, but he said:

'I understand.'

She must have felt that the excuse was poor and that he didn't understand, for a moment later she began to tell him, half apologetically, something about her brother: of how he was passionately fond of music, of singing especially. Twenty years before, her father had brought her mother to live there. Her father had been an English doctor and her mother Italian, an opera singer, a very gay woman, but a little irresponsible. Now that her father and mother were dead the brother and sister lived alone in the place and the brother devoted himself to music.

'He lives for nothing else,' she concluded.

She told him all this quietly, a little disjointedly, offering it as an excuse. But there was a curious bitterness in her voice, sharpest when she said 'He lives for nothing else'. He said nothing at all and by the time she had finished speaking they had reached the crest of the path.

There they paused. Across the park, through the thick summer trees, they could see the tent with its flags, the fluttering panorama of dresses across the lawns, the flowers on the terraces. And as they stood there the evening singing began, the harmony of male voices low and soft but very clear on the still evening air. They listened a moment; the choir was singing 'Calm was the Sea', and the voices, falling, crooned away almost to silence. There was a gate in the iron fence beyond the rhododendrons. The woman put her hand on the latch and he pushed it open and she slipped through and before he could say anything she smiled and was going away in the direction of the trees.

Just before she disappeared she turned as if to wave her hand and then, as though remembering something, she let it fall loosely to her side.

IV

It was nearly midnight, the sky was clear and dark, a pattern of blue and starlight. Down the avenue of elms the line of conveyances gave departing winks of light. The horses' hoofs made hollow clock-clocking echoes under the roof of thick leaves. The air was still warm. There was a scent of limes, an odour of horses, an acrid whiff of candles from the carriage lamps. Above the noises of departure a thin emasculate voice kept piping continually:

'T'ank you a t'ousand times! T'ank you a t'ousand times. T'ank you so much.'

It was all over. Henry was in the brake, squeezed between the fishmonger and the school teacher who sat half lost already in a pair of dark entwining arms; the brake was moving away, the lamplight was shining down the avenue, the lawn with its web of fairy-lights, azure and red and emerald and gold, was receding, fading, vanishing at last.

'Well, it's been a grand day. And if you ask me we done well. Yes, it's been grand. I'm satisfied. I shan't be sorry when I'm going up wooden hill, now. I like my rest.' The voices of the women were tired, disjointed, the words broken by yawns. A mutter of dissatisfaction ran among the men. They had won the second prize, there has been some unfairness, they had expected the first, they were sure of it, they had sung beautifully. The judges were too old, they were finicky, they had been prejudiced. The voices of the men, discussing it, were petty, regretful. 'A day wasted, I call it.' Little arguments flamed up in the darkness. 'Ah! not so strong. It's been grand.' Jokes cracked out, someone made the sweet wet sound of a kiss, laughter flickered and died, the petty arguments were renewed. A woman suddenly complained: 'There! and I forgot my honeysuckle,' and a voice quietened her from the darkness: 'Come here and I'll give you something sweeter'n honeysuckle.'

The brake went slowly on into dark vague country. The night was warm and soundless, the houses were little grey haystacks clustered together, the woods were blacker and

96

deeper. It was like a tranquil dream: the lovely glitter of summer starlight, the restfulness of the dark sky after the glare of sunshine.

Henry sat silent, only half-conscious of what the voices about him said. He was thinking of the woman: he could see her in the room with the old man, he could see her crying by the lake and half-waving her hand. He could see her clearly and could hear her voice unmistakably; yet he felt at times that she had never existed.

The fishmonger broke in upon his thoughts, his breath sweetish with wine, his voice a little thick and excited:

'Remember I was tellin' you about old Fiddlesticks, Antonio? I been havin' a glass o' wine with him.'

Henry only nodded.

'Would make me have it. Dragged me into the house. Drawing-room. Kept shaking hands wimme. Nice fellow, old Antonio. You'd like him. Nice wine an' all — beautiful — like spring water. Made your heart sing, fair made your heart sing.'

His voice trailed off and he sat silent, as though overawed by these memories. Thinking of the woman, Henry said nothing. His mind puzzled over her with tender perplexity. Who was she? Why had she wept? What was she doing now?

The fishmonger broke in again, a little garrulously:

'Did I tell you the old man came in? No? Came in about half-way through the second glass. Dirty old dressing-gown, all gravy and slobber down the front. I tell you, nobody knows how the rich live only those who do know. Had the girl with him. In a yellow dress. Know who I mean? The girl who never comes out, never goes nowhere.'

Henry was listening now. He listened a little incredulously, but gradually there crept into the fishmonger's voice a quality of earnestness, of sober truth:

'I know now why that girl never goes out. Do you know — she didn't drink. That was funny. She just sat looking at the old man. I should like you to have seen her looking at him.'

'How did she look at him?'

'Just as if she hated him. Every time he slopped his wine down his dressing-gown she looked just as if she would shriek. And then another funny thing happened. She went out. Just as if she couldn't bear it no longer.'

'Went out?' His heart was beginning to beat with a curious excitement.

'Yes — and then, perhaps you won't believe me, the old man went mad. Raving mad, all because she'd gone. Jealousy! That's all. Mad with jealousy. In the end he went clean off — sort of fit, and Antonio and me had to rub his hands and get him round. Old Antonio was very upset. Kept apologizing to me. "Excuse," he kept saying. "Excuse. He is so jealous about her. He never wants her out of his sight. And she is so young. And then she is a woman of great imagination." What did he mean by that? — a woman of great imagination?' The fishmonger broke out in answer to himself, in a little burst of disgusted fury:

'Imagination! It needed a bit of imagination to marry that old cock.'

The brake had reached the crest of the hill and had begun to descend on the other side. The dew, falling softly, was turning the air a little cooler. The figures in the brake were silent, the lovers enfolded each other. A clock chimed its quarters over the still fields, the fishmonger took out his watch and verified it and dropped it back into his pocket.

'Half-past one,' he murmured.

Henry was silent and as the brake drove steadily on there was a sense of morning in the air in spite of the stars, the silence and the darkness.

THE WATERFALL

I

THE only sound in the air as Rose Vaughan hurried across the park was the thin glassy sound of the waterfall emptying itself into the half-frozen lake. The snow that had fallen a few days after Christmas had thawed and half vanished already, leaving little snow islands dotted about the sere flattened grass among the wintry elms. It was freezing hard, the air silently brittle and bitter, the goose-grey sky threatening and even dropping at intervals new falls of snow, little handfuls of pure white dust that never settled. Now and then the black trees and the tall yellow reed-feathers and the dead plumes of pampas grass fringing the lake would stir and quiver, but with hardly a sound. The winter afternoon darkness gave the new skin of ice across the lake a leaden polish in which the shadows of a few wild duck were reflected dimly. The duck, silent and dark, stood motionless on the ice as though frozen there, but as the woman came down the path and crossed the wooden bridge over the lake-stream they rose up frightened, soaring swiftly and with wild quackings flying round and round, their outstretched necks dark against the wintry sky.

The woman, hurrying over the bridge and up the path under the trees, hardly noticed them. She walked with strange, long half-running strides, as though walking were not quick enough for her and running too undignified. As the path ascended sharply from the lake she began to pant a little, breathing the icy air in gasps through her mouth. There was the desperation of fear in her haste. Her father, the Reverend Ezekiel Vaughan, lay very ill at the rectory, which stood at the far end of the park, where she herself had been born and had lived for forty years and where she expected to go on living until she died; and she was hurrying to get across the park to the big house in order to telephone from there for the doctor. Her father was a man who had grown old before his time, and she had lived alone with him for so long that as she panted up the path, with her mouth a little open and her feet slipping backwards on the half-frozen path, she also looked prematurely middle-aged, her face joyless and negative, her pale grey eyes devoid of alertness and light.

She met no one coming down the path, and in her desperate hurry might not have seen them if she had. Until lately the path had been public, a right of way going far back in time, but at Christmas some deer in the park had been molested and the path closed. She and her father alone had been granted the special privilege of it. There had been a putting up and a breaking down of fences which had distressed her. She was distressed also because her father had said nothing, not a word, on the side of the people. 'My silence,' he said, 'will be ample evidence of my impartiality.' But it was clear enough, and to her painfully clear, that his sympathies were with Abrahams, the owner, whom he could not afford to offend. She had found herself despising for the first time the old liaison of church and property. It had struck her so forcibly that she had been angry, her anger breeding a kind of timid horror at the mere realization of that emotion. Alone, as she hurried up the path, it was difficult to realize that she had ever cherished emotions, sinful emotions, like hatred and anger. And she felt ashamed, the pain of her conscience mingling with the pain of her fears.

Where the path divided into two she took the left-hand turn to the house. The right-hand path, formerly a way to the vicarage, had been cut off by a new snake-fence. She saw that the fence had been smashed down again. It had happened since the snow. She could see the scars and fractures made by the axes on the new skinned chestnut stakes and the black footprints in the islands of snow.

She felt at once distressed again and as she hurried on she half resolved to speak to Abrahams. She would reason with him; she would make him see the pettiness of it all. He must see it. And she would make him see it, not for her own sake nor for her own satisfaction, but for his own sake and the sake of his fellow men. Words of entreaty and reason came easily to her mind: 'What you give comes back to you. It comes back a thousand fold. Surely you don't need me to tell you?' softened and quickened by her fears and agitations about her father.

But suddenly the house appeared from behind its dark barricade of yew and pine. The sight of it, huge and red, with its weather-green cupola high on the grey roof, made her suddenly and inexplicably nervous, and her footsteps on the gravel drive and their echo among the trees seemed painfully loud to her in the frost-silent air.

She hurried up the steps leading to the terrace and the house. Along the terrace formal rows of flower-beds lay bleak and empty, the earth snow-flattened and lifeless. She rang the big brass door-bell and waited, apprehensive. A servant came, she murmured a request about the telephone, and a moment later she was in the entrance-hall, the door shut behind her.

The telephone stood on a large mahogany table in the hall. She sat down in a chair by the table, picked up the receiver and gave her number. She spoke very low, so that Abrahams, if he were about, should not hear her; but the operator could not catch what she said and asked her once, twice and then even a third time, to repeat the number. She repeated it, her face growing hot and scarlet, her voice in her own ears so loud that she felt she was shouting and that Abrahams would hear and come into the hall. Her fears were multiplied into panic, all her resolutions to speak to Abrahams driven away. She gave her message for the doctor quickly, too quickly, so that again she had to repeat the words, and again louder.

In the middle of this confusion she became conscious of another voice. It was Abrahams, saying:

'Let me see what I can do, Miss Vaughan.'

In another moment he was standing by her, had the telephone from her hands and was half-shouting: 'A message for the doctor. Yes, yes. Put a jerk in it, do. Ask him to come at once, for the Reverend. Yes, he's very bad. It's urgent. For the Reverend at once, please.'

She stood apart half-nervous, half-affronted, until he had finished speaking. His way of speaking about her father, offhandedly as it were, as the Reverend, offended her. Yet when he put down the receiver she was bound to murmur her thanks.

'And now I must go,' she added quickly.

'Oh, stop an' have a cup o' tea,' he began.

'Oh no, I must get back,' she said. 'I'm urgently needed. I must get back.'

'Ah, you can swallow a cup o' tea in a jiff,' he insisted. 'It'll help to keep the cold out.'

But she was at the door, rigid, drawing on her thin kid gloves. Against her prim nervous voice Abrahams' seemed aggressively loud, almost coarsely self-confident. He himself was big-framed, getting to stoutness, his hair very grey above the red temples. He cultivated the prosperous country air, with loose check tweeds, a gold watch chain, and brown boots as polished as a chestnut. But his butterfly-collar, stiff and white, and his black necktie upset the effect. He had made his money quickly, out of boots and shoes, during the war period, rising from nothing. The tightness, the struggle of the early years had left its mark ineffaceably on his features, his lips compressing narrowly and his eyes hardening, at unexpected moments, with unconscious avarice. Coming out into the country, to enjoy his money, he had lost his wife within a year, and had presented the church with a window of stained glass in her memory. He had still about him the hardness, the bluster and the coarseness of the factory. And it was this about him which intimidated her and made her draw on her gloves, more rigidly and hastily, by the door.

Seeing that she would not stay he stood with his hand on the big iron door-latch.

'And how is the Reverend?' he asked.

'He's very ill,' she said, 'very ill.'

'I'm sorry to hear it, I am that, very sorry.'

It seemed an unconscionable time before he began to lift the door latch. In the interval, remembering her resolution to speak about the fence, she half-reproached herself:

it was her duty, now that her father could no longer speak, to say something. It was clearly her duty. But still she said nothing. The words she had formed so clearly and easily in her mind had been driven away by her foolish panic and fear.

'Ah, well, if you must go,' said Abrahams, lifting the door latch.

'I *must* go,' she said. Her voice was strangely distant with its prim, polite emphasis.

'Anything I can do? Can I have anything sent down?' he said.

'Nothing,' she said. 'Thank you. Nothing at all.'

She fled, buttoning her coat collar against the freezing air, not glancing back, knowing by the long interval before the sound of the door clanging, that he was watching her.

Down by the lake the waterfall fell with an even sharper, thinner sound in the ice-covered lake. The duck had not returned and the ice was empty of all life, growing darker every moment. Little patches of new black ice and frozen snow cracked under her feet as she panted up the path, beyond the lake, towards the rectory. The house, its grey stone drabbened but unsoftened by time and rain, stood half-hidden by a line of elms, a gaunt solitary place, walled in, with half its windows plastered over long ago, a squat stone belfry in the roof of the disused stables, a light burning in a single upstairs window. She hurried on, apprehensive, fearing the worst intuitively, falling into the old half-running, half-walking pace, hardly pausing to shut the gate in the stone wall of the garden.

Before she could reach the house the front door opened and the white figure of the servant-girl appeared and stood there ready to meet her. With tears in her voice she began to tell Rose Vaughan what she already half-knew, that her father was dead.

II

She spent the first days of the New Year putting things in order, on wet days indoors, arranging her father's papers, packing his sermons into neat piles, which she tied together with tape, rejecting old letters, reading through them and sometimes weeping a little and then reproaching herself both for reading and weeping. On fine days she and the servant-girl carried the rejected papers out to the garden, in clothes-baskets, and set fire to them under the elms, but the earth and the dead elm leaves were never dry and the papers burnt sluggishly, with thick harsh smoke that hung under the wet trees and stung the women's eyes. At last rain set in, dismally and as though it would last the year, and a south-west wind that cried in the house and howled in the black dripping elms. The burnt and half-burnt scraps of paper were blown about the garden like black and white leaves until the rain soddened them at last and the wind hurled them into corners and under the clumps of dead chrysanthemum stalks that had never been cut down. Driven indoors again with no papers to arrange, the women scrubbed and polished the floors and furniture and washed the pictures and the windows. In that large house, built more than a hundred years before for a more spacious family than had ever lived in it, there were rooms which had never been used and some which had never been opened for twenty years. The women flung open their windows and the rain blew in on the mice-chimbled floor-boards, the old travelling-trunks, the piles of faded and forgotten church magazines, the rotting sunshades, the disused croquet sets, the piles of half-rotten apples laid out on sheets of *The Times* to dry for that winter and even the winter before. The women worked with a great show of noise and hustle, tiring themselves out in an unconscious effort to efface the effect and the memory of death.

Finally it was done: all the rooms had been cleaned and aired, the last of the big heavy foot-worn carpets had been turned and re-laid, the clumsy mahogany furniture had been polished and set back in its original places, as though it had never been moved. And suddenly there was nothing to do. The wet January days, which had seemed so short, began to seem very long, and the house, which had seemed so bustling and alive, began to recapture the air of silence and death.

Like a veneer, the lively effect of clearing-up the house began to wear off, leaving a drab under-surface of realities, a troublesome sense of loss, a dread of loneliness and bills and formalities. There was a will. The rector had left a little over a hundred and fifty pounds. With the books and the furniture, it was to come to Rose; so that there would, perhaps, after the sale, be two hundred and fifty pounds.

She realized that it was nothing. It might last her, with care, with extreme, bitter care, for five years — no more than a day out of the life which lay before her. To supplement it she might do a little private teaching. She would see: she would have to see. The house would no longer be hers; there would, of course, be another rector. These things seemed to her a cruel complication of realities, a kind of equation she had never been brought up to solve.

But one thing she saw, instantly. The servant must go. And having sacked her she felt at once an insufferable loneliness. Parishioners called in the afternoons and she called in return on them, but after darkness she sat there, in the vast house, absolutely alone, with nothing to think of except herself and her dead father, her mind fretted by its own fears and its half-imagined fears. She was driven to bed at nine o'clock and then eight and even earlier, with the Bible from which her father had taught her to read a passage every night since childhood. Upset one evening and going up to bed early to cry herself to sleep she woke, half through the night, to remember that she had forgotten, for the first time, for as long as she could remember, to read that passage. She went downstairs with a candle to find her Bible. As she came back the candle-light fell on something white lying in the passage, by the front door. She picked it up, a letter.

It was a note from Abrahams, asking her if she could not go up to tea on the following day. Inexplicably she felt offended. The very tone and language of the letter seemed offensive: 'What about coming to tea one day, say to-morrow (Thursday). Should like to discuss question of memorial to Reverend. Need not reply. Will send car.'

It was so common, so detestable that she felt quite suddenly enraged.

In the morning, trying to forget the letter, she succeeded only in recalling its words and renewing her own annoyance. She went about in a state of prim, rigid vexation, the very attitude she would adopt if she were to meet Abrahams. But beneath it all she was inexplicably afraid of seeing him.

And quite suddenly she saw it differently. She would go: of course she would go. Not to go would seem childish, so discourteous. She was not sure that it was not even her duty to go.

So in the afternoon she was ready, in black except for the thin stitched lines of white on the back of her tight black gloves, when the car arrived. No sooner was she sitting silent, behind the chauffeur, than she wished she had not come.

As the car drove down the hill from the rectory, towards the village, and then up by the private road through the park, she stared out of the windows at the wet January landscape, noticing for the first time the red misty flush of elm and beech buds, and then, in the park, the first flicker of aconites, coldest yellow, uncurling in the winter grass. Farther up, under the shelter of the house and its yews, a few odd half-opened snowdrops, like frailest white toadstools, bloomed about the grass. The flowers, so early, filled her with a sense of comfort shot with flashes of envy.

In the house it was so warm that she could have fallen asleep. She and Abrahams sat by a huge fire of wood in the drawing-room, she with her hat and gloves still on, parochial fashion, the words 'I mustn't stay' rising from long foolish habit to her prim lips.

'Ah, make yourself at home,' said Abrahams, genially.

Dotted about the room, on tables and in the deep window sills, were bowls of blue and white hyacinths, whose fragrance she breathed with an unconscious show of deep pleasure, longingly.

Abrahams seemed pleased and was telling her how he had planted the bulbs himself and how much he had given

106

for them when tea arrived, the pot and jugs and tray of silver.

'After tea I'll show you round the conservatory,' said Abrahams. 'Interested in flowers, I know?'

'I am indeed,' she said.

She had withdrawn herself again, sitting stiff, straight up, on the edge of the chair.

'Take your things off,' Abrahams insisted, 'while I pour out. You'll be cold when you go out again.'

'Oh! I mustn't stay.'

'Be blowed. What's your hurry? Not such a lot to get back for, have you?'

She could have wept. There was a kind of forced geniality about his words which seemed to her brutal. They were full, too, of unconscious truth. She knew so very well that there was no hurry, that she had nothing to get back for. And she could have wept at her own hypocrisy and from the pain of his unconscious truth and brutality. But she removed her gloves instead, finger by finger, aloof and meticulous, folding and pressing them on her lap and then gently rubbing the blood back into her starved white fingers.

'You're cold,' said Abrahams. 'Why don't you come nearer the fire?'

'My hands are just a little chilled,' she told him. 'That's all.'

'Know what they say!' he laughed. 'Cold hands — warm heart.'

She was frigid. She tried to put into her silence an austere disapproval of that familiarity. It did not succeed. He had poured out tea and was handing the cup to her, not noticing either the austerity of her silence or her sudden confusion as she took the cup.

'You drink that — you'll feel a little warmer about the gills.'

'Thank you,' she said.

With the cup in her hands she tried to renew the old austere silence. But she needed the tea and she began to drink with tiny sips, cautiously, the thin scraggy guides of her neck tautening as she tried to swallow noiselessly. Abrahams drank also, stirring his tea briskly and then drinking with quick guzzling sips. Watching him, she forgot her resolution to be silent in her revulsion at the sound of his loud sipping and the sight of the tea-drips shining like spittle on the bristles of his greyish moustache.

She watched him, fascinated, until he put down his cup and wiped his tea-wet moustache with the back of his hand.

'Well now,' he said, 'about the Reverend.'

She wanted to protest, as always, against the use of that word. It was the very emblem of his familiar vulgarity. But it was useless. He went on quickly, before she could speak:

'I like to see a man have his due and — well, no use beating about the bush, Miss Vaughan. I should like to see a memorial put up to the Reverend. That's what. A stone or a window — anything, I don't care as long as it's for the church and is worthy of your father.'

He stopped abruptly. With her cup still in her hands, Miss Vaughan was crying, the thin half-checked tears falling soundlessly on her black dress and into her tea-cup.

He let her go on, without a word or a gesture. And vaguely she was aware of his silence as being a comfort to her, and her tears began to come more easily, without pain, giving her relief.

At last she could blow her nose and lift her head and glance sideways through the window, in the pretence that nothing had happened and in the hope also that he would act as though nothing had happened.

But he took her cup, and emptying the slops into the basin, said:

'Nothing like a good cry. I know what it is to lose someone.'

The words brought the tears stinging up to her eyes again, but she twisted her lips and kept silent. She felt sorry, then, not for herself but for him.

'I should — ' she began, but she could go no further.

'Don't worry,' he said. 'Drink your tea.'

She found herself obeying, drinking with confusion but with a strange and inexplicable sense of comfort.

'We can talk about it later,' he said.

She only nodded. Her eyes were red from crying and her voice hardly audible, and in her black clothes and black hat she looked old and pale, tired out.

He suddenly jumped up. 'I was going to show you the conservatory, wasn't I?'

The old prim austerity of manner came back to her as his voice resumed its turn of familiarity.

'Oh! no, I think I must go.'

But he took no notice and before she could protest they were through the hall, where she had once used the telephone, and through the glass doors leading to the conservatory, the damp warmth of the place and the breath of its flowers and ferns meeting them heavily and sweetly as they entered.

He was very proud of the place. He had fitted up electric lamps in the roof along the stages where the flowers stood and he began to switch the lights on and then off and then on again so that she could see the difference between the flower-colours and greenness in the raw January light and in the white lamp-brilliance. The scents of hyacinth and freesia were exotic, the colours of the waxy petals very pure and delicate. And unconsciously, for the first time, she lived for a few moments outside herself, delighting in the flowers, forgetting that attitude of parochial stiffness which she had worn for so long that it was almost like second nature. Abrahams, delighted also, gave one or two of his sudden heavy laughs and she laughed also almost without realizing it. Between the laughter she touched and breathed the flowers, all except the frail powdery pink and yellow primulas, cowslip-scented, which he would not let her touch.

'You don't want to be infected, do you?' he asked.

'With what?'

He told of the skin disease which the touch of the primula could give.

'Oh! that's just a story,' she cried.

'No, it's right.'

'Well! I don't care!' she cried. She buried her face in the pink candelabra of blossoms with a sensation of doing something very delicious and abandoned.

It was not until she was back, alone, in the silence of the rectory that the significance of her behaviour struck her fully, and at the thought of it she broke out in a perspiration of shame, her prim soul curling up within her with horror. Oh! she had been very stupid. It had all been very silly, very thoughtless. And memory only made it more vivid and painful.

She went to bed early, trying to forget it. But in the morning a messenger and a message arrived from Abrahams, the messenger with pots of pink hyacinth and primula, the message asking her if she would go to tea, and again discuss the memorial, on Sunday.

As she read the note and saw the flowers she went very weak.

'There is no answer,' she said.

She went about for the rest of the week in an agony of shame and indecision. Yet the answer had to be written. There was no help for it. It was her duty to write.

She delayed answering till Saturday and then wrote, fearfully, to say that she would endeavour to look in, if she might, after Sunday school. The word endeavour she felt, kept her at an austere distance. It made her answer negative of all emotion, saved her from new embarrassments.

In the park the aconites had opened back flat, vivid lemon, in the watery January sun, and higher up, under the yews there were myriad snowdrops among the stiff dark crocus leaves. And again, in spite of herself, she was envious.

She put on the old prim parochial attitude, sitting with her gloves on, as Abrahams talked of the memorial to her in the warm drawing-room. 'Yes, I see,' she would say, in agreement; or, 'I am not prepared to say,' in disagreement. It was as if she were stiffly resolved not to commit herself, again, either to tears or laughter.

'Well then,' said Abrahams, as she rose to go, 'you'll decide between the broken column and the stained window.'

'It is very kind of you.'

'The sooner we know the better. What if you come up again on Sunday?'

'Oh! I really don't know.'

She spoke as though terrified, as though to say 'Yes' and to come again were against all her most cherished principles of duty and propriety.

'You can send a note and tell me,' said Abrahams, 'when I send some more flowers.'

She fled, half-glad to be back in the rectory with its silence and damp book-odours and solitude.

But on the following Sunday she was half-glad to leave it again. The agony of the silence and solitude had begun to wear her thin and white, thinner and whiter even than before. To see the aconites, to sit in the warm drawing-room, to talk with a fellow-creature again — it was all a little intoxicating to her.

Then, quite suddenly without preparation, as they were having tea and talking of the memorial, deciding on the stained glass, Abrahams asked if she would marry him.

She sat silent, staring, her face absolutely blank in pained astonishment. Suddenly, as if to reassure her, Abrahams smiled. She turned upon him instantly with a voice of half-weeping protest:

'You're joking! You're joking.'

He rose and put his arm on her shoulder. 'No, no. I'm serious, I mean it.'

'I — I — I . . .' But she could not speak and he sat for a long time with his arm on her shoulder while she sat struggling with her tears and astonishment.

'Don't cry,' he said. 'Don't cry. All in good time.'

She wept openly. He reasoned with her a little afterwards, but it was that unexpected tenderness in his voice which finally decided her. She tried to reason against it all, but the recollection of that emotion always triumphed.

A week later she accepted. The question of love never touched her. She had long ago begun to teach herself that marriage and love were words which did not interest her.

111

She reasoned that it was not a question of love, but of duty, and she was secure in that.

They were married in the spring.

III

The rains of late winter continued desolately into spring, drenching the crocuses until they bent over like limp spent candles of orange and purple and white, weighing down the first greenish canary buds of the daffodils by the lake, along the low-lying land by the stream, the park was flooded, the young leaves of celandine struggling up, yellow-tipped, through the water, and Abrahams was worried because even when the rain ceased and the sun had attained its first spring-power, the water did not drain away. In his concern he would walk down to the stream every morning, testing the height of the water by the wooden stakes he had had driven in and marked, pacing up and down the grass, pausing often, to consider what might be done. He would come back to lunch with a frown on his face, impatient: he wanted the place right, and he must have it right, he would have it right. Rose would say nothing but 'Yes' or 'No' as his tone demanded, obedient to a half-conscious resolution never to assert herself, never to disagree, never to do anything which might bring them into a state of intimacy. She often committed a kind of sin against herself in order to keep up that negative serenity. If Abrahams suggested deepening the stream she too would say, 'I was thinking so myself', or if he changed his mind abruptly, thinking that he might raise the banks of the stream, she would change her mind also, saying, 'I feel sure it would be better'. But it was a sin of duty, the sin that she had practised so long with her father that it was already both a habit and a virtue. She was scarcely conscious of it. And if Abrahams asked, as he did very rarely, for her opinion, she would manage, by some remark like, 'Oh! it's quite beyond my poor brain', to excuse herself and at the same time flatter him. Whatever he did must be right.

So when the question of the floods and the stream worried Abrahams she was worried also, and going down to the stream with him one afternoon she stood or paced about the grass in a pretence of harassed thought, just as he did. At last, when Abrahams had walked far up the brook to survey from a fresh point, she sat down for a moment on the deer-smoothed bole of an elm and watched the flood water and the yellow hosts of celandine in the damp places beyond. The stream itself came down quietly and the spring air was so still that she could hear every drop of its gentle fall into the lake below. Then, quite suddenly, as she sat watching and listening, the whole problem of the flood seemed clear to her. Surely all that they had to do was to widen the stream and deepen its fall and make a new weir into the lake, so that the stream could take more water and take it faster.

She got up and called Abrahams, timidly, and when he came back to her she told him, repeating often 'I know it's quite silly and impossible'. He listened and walked down to the waterfall and then, looking upstream, considered it all. Standing still, she watched the sunlight on the flowers and the water again in a state of timid apprehension until he disturbed her with a shout of excitement:

'You've got it!' He was already hurrying upstream to her. 'Can't think why it didn't come to me before. Can't imagine for the life of me why I didn't think of it.' He was very excited.

'Oh! You would have thought of it,' she said.

'I don't know so much, I don't know so much,' he kept saying, as they hurried back to the house. 'You must have been thinking it all out on the quiet.'

'Oh! no, oh no,' she said. 'Only sometimes I used to notice that even when there was water still standing about there was only a trickle at the waterfall.'

'And I never noticed it,' he marvelled. 'And I never noticed it. You're a bit of a marvel.'

'Oh! no,' she deprecated. 'It's nothing, really it's nothing.'

Back at the house he telephoned to the drainage engineers; they would send over a man in the morning, early.

In the morning, soon after breakfast, a little flaphooded

car, mud-flecked and ramshackle, chattered up the drive, swishing the gravel recklessly. A young man alighted and rang the front door bell six times, with comic effect, and Abrahams, in his enthusiasm, answered the door himself, and a moment or two later the car started again and chattered away into the park. When it returned again to the house, just before one o'clock, Abrahams and the young man seemed to be hilarious.

'Rose,' said Abrahams as they came in to lunch. 'This is the engineer, Mr. Phillips.'

Hearing their laughter, she had put on something of the old prim austerity of manner, in unconscious disapprobation.

'How d'ye do, Mrs. Abrahams?' said Phillips, shaking hands; and catching in a flash the feeling of cool distance in her outstretched hand: 'I'll bet you wondered what the tide had washed up, didn't you, Mrs. Abrahams?'

'I did wonder,' she said, 'what all the laughter was about.'

'Oh! Mr. Phillips is a case,' said Abrahams. 'He's a fair caution. I haven't laughed so much for years.'

'Ah! but be careful,' said Phillips. He advanced, and tapping Abrahams' waistcoat, said with a mock seriousness that set Abrahams tittering again: 'Do you know, sir, that the valves of your heart are worn out? Yes sir, worn out. Absolutely finished. You may go pop any minute. Punctured.'

And as Abrahams wiped the tears of laughter from his eyes Rose smiled a small, half-stiff, half-indulgent smile with unparted lips.

At the lunch table Phillips was irrepressible. He was a rather small, fleshy man, with a cherubic face and little vivid eyes that shone and quivered like blue glass marbles, with ecstatic joviality. His face was the face of a true comedian. He was never still, never silent. His eyes travelled electrically everywhere, untiringly, in search of fresh jokes, jokes which, when they came, might have been in bad taste, but for some reason never were. Rose sat at first aloof and frigid, as though ready to freeze the first germ of indelicacy or blasphemy, but it never came. 'The wages of gin', said Phillips once, taking up his water to drink, 'is breath.' Her face stiffened, then, with its first and only sign of offence, a sign that was lost on both Phillips and Abrahams, laughing into their serviettes. After that she sat a little less strained and less upright, though still with a shadow of severity in her face, her smiles mere polite motions of her thin lips. Phillips saw this, and as though it were all a game in which she must keep her lips set and smiling while he tried to make her smile in spite of it, he began to direct his jokes at her. It flattered her subtly and gradually, in spite of herself, she felt warmer and more tolerant of him, and at last she broke out softly, 'Oh, Mr. Phillips, you're too bad!'

'You'll laugh, Mrs. Abrahams, you'll laugh if you're *not* careful,' cried Phillips. 'You'll laugh, as sure as my name's Napoleon. You will — I warn you. You'll laugh. Now, now! Smile, but don't laugh. Smile —' he threw his serviette over his head, like a photographer, his voice comically muffled — '*smile*, please. That's it — now hold it — the left hand clasped on the right — splendid — exquisite — how delighted *he* will be — enchanting! Hold it — one — moment — tchtk!'

He threw the serviette off his head, making gestures of mock despair. 'But you *laughed* — you *laughed*,' he cried.

'Oh dear,' she said, her face flushed and her eyes moist with confusion and laughter. 'And no wonder.'

'Ah! didn't I tell you he was a case!' cried Abrahams.

'Oh! how silly of me,' said Rose, wiping her eyes.

Phillips was still making them laugh, Rose still half against herself, when they went down to the lake in the afternoon. Rose was unprepared to go, but first Abrahams and then Phillips insisted, Abrahams saying:

'It's really my wife's idea — she first saw how it could be done.'

'Oh, no, really,' said Rose.

'Now, now, Mrs. Abrahams,' Phillips joked. 'Come, come. Don't be afraid. The big man will pull out the nasty tooth and then it will be all over.'

'Really you could do much better without me,' she said.

But she went with them, protesting a little out of politeness and biting her lips or twisting them in order to keep her laughter quite circumspect. By the lake the kingcups had opened wide, their yellow petals glistening as though varnished, and further up the slopes of grass, in the damp places, the first lady smocks trembled, tenderest mauve, still half shut, on fragile stems. In the hollow by the flood water the sun was quite hot, and Rose, sitting down on an elm-bole again, could hear spring in the silence, a silence broken only by the singing of larks, far up, and the trickling of the waterfall, both very sweet and soft, the water faintest, like an echo of the birds.

While she sat there, Abrahams and the engineer surveyed the stream, made notes, took measurements, and at intervals laughed a great deal. When they returned to her Abrahams was simmering with enthusiasm, like a boy — it could be done, the thing could be done, easily, just as she said it could!

'Not easily,' cried Phillips, serious for once. 'It will take time — all summer.'

'Time's nothing,' said Abrahams. 'Nor money. I want the thing done, that's all.'

Phillips returned to the house for tea. Abrahams had taken a fancy to him, there was more laughter, and at last Abrahams suggested that Phillips, instead of driving backwards and forwards from the town each day, should come and spend the summer at the house with them. It would be so much easier, so much more convenient. Phillips seemed to hesitate and then said:

'Could I fish in the lake?'

'Fish? You're not joking? You can fish, swim, row — do anything.'

'I should like to come then,' said Phillips.

Before the week was out he had brought over his belongings, and before the end of another week the work by the lake was in progress, a band of workmen arriving each morning in a lorry and Phillips driving down in his dilapidated car soon afterwards, to superintend. He rushed hither and thither all morning, electric, untiring, coming back to the house at noon to eat a hasty meal, flying off a joke or two, and then returning. Dumps of yellow clay and piles of pink brick and wooden shacks for the workmen appeared by the lake and became visible from the house through the half-leafed trees.

Every afternoon, if it were fine, Rose and Abrahams walked down to watch the work. She, while Abrahams talked with Phillips, sat on the elm-bole and watched the workmen digging out the pure yellow clay, like stiff cheese, as they deepened and widened the trench which later would be the new water-course. Farther up they had dammed the stream and only a thin trickle of water came down the trench, so that the waterfall was soundless and dry.

On the first evenings, when the dusk still fell early and a little cold, Abrahams and Phillips would go into the billiard room and the click of the billiard balls would be drowned by their boisterous laughter until Rose at last would join them, ostensibly to see if they needed anything but in reality to share that laughter.

And gradually it became an unconscious habit to go down to the lake each afternoon and into the billiard room each evening. It was not until the evenings became longer and warmer and the two men began to play a game of bowls on the lawn that it became a conscious thing, something to which she looked forward. Realizing it, she reproved herself at once, and she did not go down to watch the work for two afternoons. But first Phillips and then Abrahams noticed it and Phillips made gentle banter about it, half teasing. Strangely, she felt hurt, and the next afternoon she went down to watch the work again. But Phillips was not there. When Abrahams explained that he had gone off on business for the afternoon she felt a spasm of unexpected disappointment that was almost a shock.

It was already early June, and Phillips had gone into town, not on business, but to fetch his fishing-tackle. In the evening and again the next evening he was at the lake and she did not see him until late. Coming back on the second evening he carried an immense basket, covered with green reeds, staggering along with it like a man with a load of lead. The basket was for her — an offering. He went through mock solemnities. At last, when she removed the reeds it was to reveal a roach, pink and silver, no bigger than a sardine. It was all that the basket contained. At the joke Abrahams and Phillips went off into explosive laughter.

It was a laughter in which, inexplicably, she could not join. She felt hurt again, and again without knowing why. It was as if they were laughing at her, and she could not bear it. She reproached herself; it was so silly, such a trivial thing. What was she thinking about? What was coming over her? Yet the sense of injury remained.

For a day or two she felt a strange resentment against Phillips. She went down to the lake, but she hardly spoke to him, and in the evenings his laughter irritated her. And suddenly she closed up, as into a shell again, with all the old primness and straight-lipped austerity.

Phillips, as before, noticed it.

'Have I done anything to offend you?' he said, one afternoon by the stream.

'To offend me?' she said. 'Why should I be offended?'

But the very tone of her voice was offended. As soon as he had walked away she hurried over the bridge, past the lake, and took the old path up to the rectory. At the top of the slope she sat down, in the sunshine, to regain her breath and think and come to a decision about it all. When she got up again she had solved the problem with the old formula and was half-content. It was her duty to behave differently to him. She would make amends. She would apologize. It was her duty to apologize.

Yet the days went past and she never apologized. She began to avoid Phillips and then, having avoided him, would feel wretched. He, absorbed in his fishing, seemed to take not the faintest notice of her.

She half made up her mind that if he spoke to her again she would make the fishing an excuse for her behaviour.

He had begun to fish on Sundays. She objected to that. Yet, when he asked if she objected she said 'No', as if she had not the heart to rob him of that pleasure. And so he fished all day on Sundays, taking food with him, sitting lost in the reeds that grew taller and ranker as the summer richened to midsummer, and to the first arid days of July. Coming back in the evening there would be the same jocularity as ever, the same mocking play on something, the same roars of laughter from Abrahams. She sat aloof, as though it did not interest her. Then, after one intense cloudless blazing Sunday by the lake, Phillips returned in the evening without a single fish, not even a stickleback, not so much as an undergrown roach with which to play another joke on her.

For the first time since she had known him Phillips was silent, in absolute dejection. She could not resist the opportunity.

'Well,' she said, 'perhaps it will be a lesson to you.'

'A lesson? — What in?'

'A lesson not to abuse the sabbath.'

He burst into roars of laughter. 'So you think the fish know Sunday when it comes!' he said.

There was no derision either in his words or his laughter. But she was bitterly hurt again. Yet it comforted her to go about nursing that sense of injury secretly.

Then also she hoped that he would, perhaps, take notice of what she had said and not go to the lake on the following Sunday. It would mean that he had, once at least, taken her seriously.

But the next Sunday, when she came down to breakfast, he had already gone. Hard and aloof, she put on her white gloves and went to church with Abrahams. It was nothing, she must forget it, it meant nothing to her. But she was troubled and would not acknowledge it and by noon she had fretted herself into a strange state of misery which her denials only increased.

In the afternoon she could endure it no longer. She left Abrahams asleep and went out into the hot Sunday stillness, across the Terrace and down into the park. She had made up her mind: she would walk by the lake, he would see her, she would speak to him, there would be an end of it all.

As she walked along, in and out of the great tree shadows, she reasoned out what she would say. It seemed very simple: she would say that his violation of her dearest principles had hurt her. That was all. Not those very words, perhaps, but she would convey that. She would make him understand.

Before she was aware of it she was by the lake. Panic-stricken, she hurried along, looking straight ahead along the reed-fringed bank, never pausing once until she caught sight, on the opposite bank, of Phillips, in his shirt-sleeves, watching over his rod, the wet float flashing scarlet in the white sunlight. But she hurried along, terrified that he might see her or shout, never pausing even when she was out of sight.

Back at the house she was angry that he had not noticed her. She felt that he had seen her and then, purposely, with deliberate indifference, had ignored her. And then, illogically, she felt a moment of acute tenderness for him. Perhaps, after all, he had not seen her, had been too absorbed even to look up. She must not misjudge him. It was her duty not to misjudge him.

For some weeks she went about half-comforted and half-troubled by the renewal of that anger and tenderness, not understanding either. Then one morning, at breakfast, Phillips declared:

'Well, another week and you can turn on the new tap.'

She sat very straight in her chair, prim but intense.

'Then you will be leaving us?' she said.

'Yes — no more fishing on Sundays.'

She could not speak.

A week later the work of the lake was finished.

'Mrs. Abrahams ought to pull the lever,' suggested Phillips.

'Oh! no!' she said. 'Really no.'

'But that's only proper,' said Abrahams. 'It was your idea. Yes, you pull the lever. We must do it properly.'

'But I shouldn't be strong enough,' she protested desperately.

'You don't need to be,' said Phillips. 'I'll work it so that just a touch will be enough.'

'It's easy,' said Abrahams. 'Phillips will make it easy.'

She gave in. On the afternoon itself she walked down to the lake with Abrahams and Phillips. The first trees were turning yellow, a few leaves floated about the still lake, and the air was very quiet. An odd workman or two stood about and she felt very nervous. Phillips had arranged it so that she should raise a lever and that the old dam should collapse and release the water. It was very simple.

Everything was ready. Phillips and Abrahams and the workmen stood waiting. She lifted her hand to the lever and then, at the last moment, hesitated. Her hands were trembling.

'All you have to do is pull the lever,' said Phillips quietly. 'It's easy.'

The next moment she made an immense effort. She clenched the lever desperately and pulled it.

There was a sudden crash as the dam itself collapsed and then a roar, increasing rapidly, as the water tore down through the new channel, with Phillips and Abrahams running excitedly along the banks, to see the first leap of water into the lake, and then at last there was a sound of thunder as the water fell. The sound for a moment was terrific. She stood in suspense, startled. At her feet the water tore down the channel furiously, so that she went giddy from looking at it, and there was a shower of soft white spray as the torrent thundered into the lake. She had never believed that there could be so much water. She stood pale and motionless, with tears in her eyes, not knowing what to do.

The tears began to run down her cheeks. Afraid that the men might see her she suddenly turned away and began to walk away up the slope under the trees. She heard the voices of the men call after her but she did not turn. Her tears kept on and behind her the torrent of water roared with soft thunder. She began to hurry, trying to dry her tears as she did so, but fresh tears filled her eyes as fast as she wiped them away and the sound of the waterfall followed her persistently. She hurried on as though afraid of it and long after she could hear it no more, the echo of it, like a remembered emotion, thundered through her mind.

The next morning Phillips went away.

INNOCENCE

A CHILD had wandered from the security of his mother's potato-patch. The afternoon was a silent infinity of shimmering heat, but in the field beyond the garden the young grass had begun to grow sweet again after hay-time, making a cool lawn in the waste of July.

Nothing moved across the flat green face of the field except flickering butterflies electric with sunlight, scraps of turquoise and lemon, tortoiseshell and ivory, soft and light as flying flowers. The child regarded them with apathetic interest, his eyes vainly hunting them. Once he took off his broad white sun-hat and held it poised, but the shadow of it had scarcely fallen on the grass before there was a mocking flicker of yellow brilliance far away among the potato-flowers. He listlessly put on his hat again and solemnly advanced across the field, his hands deep in the pocket of his miniature trousers. The sun-hat, too large for him, made him look like a little old man walking across a vast bowling-green in meditation. The butterflies seemed no longer to interest him. It was too hot for him even to watch them.

At the far end of the field stood a house, half-hidden by a forest of flowerless lilacs and dim laurels and unpruned fruit-trees. The faded yellow blinds of the house were drawn against the sun and the doors stood shut and blistering, giving it a deserted air. The garden was a wilderness of trees and sweet-briar, untidy hollyhocks with shabby pink buttons just unfolding, blood-bright poppies that had sown themselves in thousands about the flower-beds and the paths and on the front door-step itself. The air seemed sleepy with poppy odour. The brilliant scarlet heads blazed like signals of danger.

As the child approached the house he began to walk with a curious nonchalance. He squinted at something on a most distant horizon and sometimes he appeared to be searching intently for something in the grass or the sky.

The house might not have existed. The child walked towards it with a serene and aimless innocence.

Nevertheless that innocence was suspicious, for he walked in a perfect line to a point where the garden fence had broken, making a gap large enough for a dog to squeeze through under cover of the lilacs and laurels. As he approached the gap his innocence became angelic. He stooped to pick a white clover-bloom. He sniffed it languidly, plucked another and sniffed that also. He wandered in beautiful rings in the grass, ostensibly searching. All the time his eyes were upon the house, wickedly furtive and longingly alert.

He presently sidled sleepily towards the gap. In his sleepiness he appeared to be not only innocent but blind. Nevertheless his eyes in one swift flicker took in the safe emptiness of the field behind him and of the garden ahead.

He vanished suddenly through the hedge with a flash of white, like a rabbit. He crawled through the mass of trees and briar on his hands and knees and finally emerged into open sunlight, blinking like a man stepping out of a gloomy jungle.

There he staggered to his feet and stopped. His eyes had lost their look of suspiciously angelic innocence. They were filled with caution and wonder, with guilt and pleasure. They gazed with a new unflickering intensity.

Before the child stretched a plantation of raspberries, row after row of green and red luxuriance. Seeing them, he had eyes for nothing else. He seemed for one moment paralysed by the crimson burden of the tall thick canes. At home, side by side with the potatoes, his mother also had a plantation of raspberries, ripe, thick and lovely as these.

To the child however the raspberries that his mother grew seemed suddenly despicable. Moreover she had forbidden him fearfully to touch them. The fruit before him was larger and more luscious than his mother's could ever be and as he caught all at once the strong fragrance of the fruit and leaves in the warm sun his mouth was tortured.

He plucked a raspberry. It melted swiftly in his mouth like snow. Once a great fish-net had covered the plantation, but the stakes had rotted away and the net had fallen into useless tangles among the canes. There was nothing to stop his progress into endless raspberry avenues. He walked at first furtively, stopping to listen, but the garden was silent and safe and deserted. Nothing but himself moved and presently he walked more boldly, rustling the leaves carelessly with his eager limbs.

All the time he ate. He ate as though in a race against time or light. At first he swallowed, one by one, berries that were like great crimson thimbles filled with blood. Tiring of their very magnificence he gathered smaller, sharper fruit and ate it by handfuls, tossing back his head and crimsoning his lips.

There came a moment when the taste of even the loveliest fruit seemed curiously dead. He paused and sighed heavily and licked his lips, drunk with fruit. It occurred to him to take off his hat.

He began to walk up and down the avenues, filling it. There was still no sound or movement in the garden except his own rustlings among the leaves. The juice of many raspberries began to stain the whiteness of his sun-hat. He did not notice it. He was drunk with forbidden bliss.

It happened suddenly that he came to the end of an avenue and there looked up. Beyond him stretched an open lawn, deserted and poppy-sown. He regarded it with the brazen indifference of reckless confidence. He plucked a raspberry and ate it with loud and careless smacking of his lips, as though to defy the last danger of the place.

He turned to pluck another and stopped. A pale object, like a menacing vision, had appeared over the raspberry canes behind him. It was a panama hat. He gazed at it for one second with giddy astonishment. It moved. His heart leapt. A second later the panama hat bore down upon him with noises of stentorian rage.

'By God, I'll skin you!'

The child fled. He darted down an avenue of canes with a wild terror in his heart, scratching himself and running blindly. All the time he was conscious of pursuit by the panama hat. He was terrorized by cries of rage and threats

125

of annihilation. He stumbled and dropped his hat and dared not stay to pick it up again.

Out in the field he paused for an agonized moment to take breath. Behind him a roar of rage was hurled like a cannon-shot from among the raspberries. Glancing back he saw his white sun-hat picked up and brandished angrily. He fled with frightened speed across the field.

The voice of the man pursued him. He dared not glance back. He ran with unresting desperation until he could pause behind his mother's fence with security again. But even there he could not rest. He was trembling and exhausted. Finally however he took a long breath and with a great effort nonchalantly strolled through the potatoes and by the rasp-berries towards the house, trying to look angelically at the sky.

It happened that as he came from behind his mother's raspberry canes she herself emerged from the house. She was a wide, powerful woman, with arms like clubs and a black suspicious gaze.

Seeing her, he stopped. That pause was fatal. She swooped down upon him instantly. He remembered in that moment all the warnings she had given him about her raspberries. How many times had she not warned him that if he laid a finger on them she would flay him? She bore down on him as the panama hat had borne down on him in the other garden. He wriggled futilely to escape but this time there was no escape. He made frantic signs of innocence.

'I'll learn you!' she shouted.

'I didn't — I never!' he moaned.

'Look at your mouth!' she cried.

She seized him mercilessly. His guilt was so vivid on his lips that she belaboured him until her arm whipped up and down like a threshing-flail.

The child, as he howled his innocence of a crime he had never committed, dismally observed across the field an approaching figure.

It was signalling terrible threats with a white hat.

SALLY GO ROUND THE MOON

I

PHOEBE BONNER stood watching the sunset over the roofs of London. She was frying a kipper over the gas-ring in one of the two rooms which the Bonners rented at the top story of Pope's Buildings, and though her eyes were fixed on the sunset her mind was far away. She was thinking of the country and the kind of sunset she had grown up to see there. The sunsets in London were mere obscure reflections of the lovely sunsets in the country, brilliant crimson seas of light and waves of phosphorescent gold and clouds of purple riding behind black pine trees.

She turned the kipper with a fork; the fat hissed and a rank odour filled the room. She was fifteen, a thin straight-haired girl with bright black eyes; her clothes were very tight and her body, having no room in them, pushed herself into sudden curves or angles, giving her an appearance of gawkiness. She had come to London from the country to look after her sister's children and to tidy and scrub the two rooms while her sister and her aunt went out to work. Her sister worked in a restaurant from eight in the morning till eight at night. Her aunt was a rag-woman. One corner of the room was piled up with the rags she had bought and could not sell. Sometimes, when alone, Phoebe turned them over; they stank uncleanly, the discarded clothes of a vast humanity, clothes in which people had worked and loved and had even died, and the living-room was poisoned with a half-sour, half-musty odour that even the smell of the kipper could not destroy.

The girl felt unutterably lonely. When the children had gone to school and her aunt and sister had gone to work no one ever troubled to climb to the top of Pope's Buildings, though she heard people moving about on the floor below, the whiz and treadling of a sewing-machine and the sound of angry voices. A tailor and his wife lived there and whenever the tailor's wife came in drunk he beat her unmercifully.

She in turn cried and swore and he banged her about until she could not stand. But there were days when she was quiet and sober and they sewed and pressed in silence, and the world of Pope's Buildings on those days seemed vast and empty.

She turned the kipper again and looked at the clock on the mantelpiece. It was a little after four o'clock. The sun was vanishing rapidly and the golden light was fading. She spread the cloth and laid cups and a teapot on the deal table. In a few moments Christopher would be home.

Christopher was her sister's husband and it was for him that she was frying the kipper. He came home and ate his tea with the children and herself, and she often ran downstairs and along to the fishmonger's at the corner and bought a kipper or some shrimps for his tea, giving both herself and him great pleasure.

Five minutes later, when she heard him ascending the stairs, she knew by the sound on the bare wooden stairs who was coming up: her aunt lumbered and paused continually for breath, her sister ran quickly and in jerks, the tailor's wife climbed laboriously one by one swearing to herself. She knew her sister's husband because of the absolute weariness of his step. He climbed like a man whose strength and courage were fading away.

She could hear his loud breathing as he climbed the last few stairs and when he came in his lips were hanging apart and he was breathing harshly through his mouth.

He came in and took off his black felt hat and sat down.

'Oh! dear,' he said.

He shut his eyes. His voice, his eyes and the way he rubbed his hand across his forehead all had the same weariness as his feet climbing the stairs.

'I'm sure you walk too far,' said the girl.

'I haven't walked at all I'm sure,' he protested.

'Come now— the tea's ready,' she said. 'I've been and got you a kipper.'

He shook his head.

'I couldn't eat it,' he said. 'I'm sorry,' he went on, opening his eyes, 'but I couldn't eat it.'

'Oh! I got it for you.'

He turned his head and looked at the kipper lying in the fat of the frying pan and he wanted to be sick.

'I'll try in a moment,' he said. 'When I've had a cup of tea.'

He sat up to the table and put down the book he was carrying, a book called *The Meaning of God*. He was a thin white-faced man, quite young, with sparse brown hair which was falling out at his temples, and vague blue eyes, and as he sat at the table his body trembled, and his face looked as though he had been frightened and shocked by an explosion and he would never recover his calmness again. His hands were fine and white and his lips almost feminine in their gentleness.

He drank some tea, and sat silent, and as he drank the girl looked at him.

'Any luck?' she asked.

He smiled quietly and shook his head. He had been trying to sell the book called *The Meaning of God*. He was studying divinity but having no money with which to take proper courses he was trying to study by himself. He studied in the public libraries and with books that he was able to borrow. A paper sometimes gave him books to review, books like *The Meaning of God*, and when he had written the review, often working himself sick over it by his conscientiousness, he tried to sell the book and buy another with the money. The books were hard to sell, however. No one, it seemed, had any use for books on God, which were so soon stale and obsolete, and no thought on God seemed to keep its truth for long. The bookshops were full of books on God which would never be read again.

Staring at him, the girl wondered what he did with himself all day, what he ate and what he thought.

'Do have the kipper,' she said.

He did not want the kipper but for some reason or other he said 'Yes' and he knew a moment later that he said it because he did not wish to disappoint her.

It was Friday and the children were staying late at school for a concert and would not be home till five. As Christopher tried to eat the kipper Phoebe talked to him. They often talked together; they talked of each other's lives, and one day he told her why he had married Ada, her sister.

'When I first came to London I used to go to that tea-shop and have my lunch. I always sat at the same table and Ada always served me and somehow we drifted into it.'

He could not explain it any differently. Day after day he had gone to the restaurant and had sat at the same table and nothing had happened. He ordered very little to eat and generally he read a book while he ate, and somehow he got into the habit of ordering the same thing day after day, because it was less trouble and because in that way he could manage his money better. He did not notice the waitress much until one day, she said: 'I don't think it's good for you.' He looked up astonished, 'What isn't?' he said. 'Eating the same thing day after day; why don't you let me bring you something else?' Seeing the sense of it he acquiesced and she brought him some fish instead of his bread and stew, and for the first time he took notice of her. She was dark and sharp-featured, and her skin, even though she powdered it, had an anaemic pallor that was almost transparent. In a day or two she not only brought him another change of food but a larger helping and she begged him not to leave her a tip any longer. She was not strikingly attractive but she touched him by her solicitude, and one day, feeling unspeakably lonely and having not a soul to talk to, he said: 'Do you mind if I wait for you this evening?' When she came out of the restaurant in the evening she said, 'Well, where are we going?' He simply shook his head and said, 'Where you like. I don't know. Let's walk somewhere,' and they walked along the Embankment, talking trivially, and then back through the streets towards Lincoln's Inn. It began to rain and they stood in a passage-way for shelter. The passage was narrow and a cat brushed by Ada's feet and she pressed herself close to Christopher. He had never loved a woman and he had no intention of loving Ada, but as he felt her close to him all kinds of sensations which he could not explain surged up in him. His throat felt tight, his blood throbbed hotly, his loneliness vanished and finally he put his arms about Ada and she kissed his awkward lips. 'I suppose you're out for all you can get,' she said. 'Like all the rest.' She touched his body, and she leaned with all her weight against him. It was utterly dark and

London was silent except for a distant murmur of traffic. 'All right,' she said. He had asked for nothing, but she said 'All right' as though she were surrendering herself to his desperate entreaty.

Afterwards he saw her again, and one evening when it snowed and he had no money for a theatre she asked him to go home with her.

He remembered boarding a tram with her and travelling into that part of London beyond Rosebery Avenue. It was Saturday evening, the tram was full of half-drunken cockney women, and the lurching of the tram and the smell of gin made him sick.

When he first saw Pope's Buildings in the darkness it looked to him a great black rectangle with a courtyard fenced off by iron railings, exactly like a prison. He remembered mounting the stairs, following Ada's dark form and the trail of her scent upwards and upwards until he panted and began to breathe through his mouth. He caught the stench of stale rags even before she opened the door and from that moment he wished himself dead, his stomach revolting at the two big rooms, the foul rags, and the old woman with her yellowing teeth and thick lips and foreign-looking face, who sat sorting them. There was a single comforting object in the room, a large brown teapot bearing in white letters the words 'God Bless Our Home', and whenever he felt sick or depressed he looked at the teapot and felt better.

When Ada asked him to go home with her a second time he made a desperate excuse and refused, feeling that he could endure hunger and bad food and loneliness but not the Bonners' two rooms and the stench of rags, but one evening a bitter wind, driving icy rain and sleet, came up from the mouth of the Thames and he felt every lash of it pierce through his coat to his bones as he waited for Ada to come out of the restaurant. He wanted to refuse to go to Pope's Buildings, but Ada was tired and when she said 'Come on; we've got a fire at least, whatever else we haven't got,' he consented.

The blackness of Pope's Buildings seemed worse than ever. It loomed above them like a monstrosity. Who could have built such a place? he wondered, and he felt that only a monster could have conceived and built it so like a prison.

But inside, perhaps because he had exaggerated his horror of it, the Bonners' two rooms seemed less terrible. The old woman was not at home. A bright fire was burning and he warmed his frozen hands and Ada made him some cocoa and the pile of rags smelt less rankly than before. He drank his cocoa slowly and felt tolerably happy.

The old woman came home, a little tipsy, about eleven o'clock. Her black hat and coat were sprinkled with frozen sleet.

'Awful night, awful, downright awful,' she muttered. 'Christ!'

Christopher winced at the blasphemy. He could not bear to hear the name of Christ spoken with derision.

'You'd better stay here for to-night,' said Ada to him.

'Oh! no, no, no,' he protested.

Later Ada went out and looked at the night and when she came back she was shivering violently.

'You're not going out in this,' she said. 'You can't! It's a blizzard.'

She did not heed his protests and she went into the second room and banged the pillows about and flapped the sheets.

'Course you'll stay,' said the old woman. 'Course you'll stay. Lor' lummy.'

He resigned himself and later he undressed quickly and knelt by the bed and said his prayers and then crept into bed and thought of God. Sometimes he suffered from insomnia, and the quiet thought of God often sent him to sleep. 'God is a spirit,' he repeated to himself, 'and they that worship Him must worship Him in spirit and in truth.' What quiet words and how beautiful! He stared at the cracked ceiling and forgot the dirty room and the rags and the old woman, and then shut his eyes.

He was aroused by the presence of someone against the bed. He stirred himself. It was Ada, getting into bed with him. He touched her nightgown and her thin breasts as she came beside him, his mind too drowsy for speech. In the morning he woke and saw her standing half-dressed, by the window, gaping. Her cheap green drawers and her little green corset that pushed her breasts into a false prominence and her white legs, covered with little unhealthy blue veins, all made her look frowzy and cheap and vulgar. She drew on her stockings and slipped on her skirt and powdered her face. She did not wash herself and from that moment he felt that he hated her. He could not think why he had endured her so long or even why he had endured her at all.

Now it was no use wondering. He ate Phoebe's kipper with the same nausea as he had once felt for Ada. To-morrow it would not matter. He was married to Ada and had already two children by her and probably, she told him, there would be another.

He drank his tea and Phoebe poured out another cup. He had been silent for some moments, thinking.

'You're so quiet,' she said. 'I'm sure you worry too much.'

'What should I worry about?'

'Are you lonely?' she said all at once.

'I suppose I am,' he confessed.

There was quietness about her words, and her way of speaking that made him make the confession.

'Did you see the sunset?' said the girl.

'I'm afraid I didn't notice it.'

She told him about the sunset and then about the sunsets in the village at home, and as she spoke a queer wistful look of entrancement came into his face. And while he caught the beauty of the country in winter and of the green and golden clouds floating at sunset behind the pines, he caught also the faint unhappiness of the girl's voice. She wanted to go back; she hated London. His heart ached for her, because he knew perfectly the feeling of her loneliness.

Later his two children came in, two girls of five and six. Their voices were shrill and they sent pains screeching through his head. In moments of extreme nervousness or distraction his head became a machine in which there was a cog-wheel that whistled and whined and grated louder than all the rest. The cog-wheel was immovable; like some diabolical invention it was fixed so that its jagged teeth could just touch his brain. Gradually, he felt, it would wear away his brain or irreparably damage it.

He was glad when the children had gone to bed. The children, with Phoebe and the old woman, slept in the second room. Ada and himself slept on a single bed which was collapsible, but which nearly always remained during the day just as they had slept in it, the sheets and blankets still tumbled and frowzy. People sat on the bed to tie up their boots and the chamber stood on the floor beneath it, un-emptied. He hated this bed. Once he had hated the old woman's rags, but the rags were at least movable. They changed and were sold, but the bed never changed. It remained fixed and absolute: it was the expression of all that was foul and terrible in his life, the things from which he could not escape, sordidness and vulgarity and littleness. The bed was so terrible to him that he had never yet knelt by it to pray. He prayed only when Ada had fallen asleep, or he prayed in the public libraries, in their strict silence, or he sat under the plane trees in Lincoln's Inn, and watched the pigeons and prayed there.

When the children had gone to bed he sat down at the bare deal table and put on his spectacles and began to mend his watches. He had started life as an apprentice to a watch-maker. The old woman bought up lots of second-hand and broken watches and he repaired them and she sold them again. Sometimes the tailor from below came up with his watch. 'It's like my old woman,' he said. 'It won't go until its insides is oiled.' Like this he earned a shilling or two and he could keep up his head with the knowledge that he was not utterly useless.

Phoebe sat looking at him as he dismantled a watch and laid out the works on a newspaper.

He was working on a little silver-and-blue lady's watch which needed cleaning. The old woman had bought it in a rag-market. He laid out the tiny sparkling wheels and cylinders and screws and one by one cleaned them scrupul-ously. It was the kind of work his hands were meant for, the work they did well. He no longer looked weak and irresolute

and useless. He took in the dignity of work, his hands moving
with certainty and grace.

Phoebe sat watching, absorbed and amazed. 'How do you
ever get it right again?' she said.

'Oh! it'll come right,' he said. It was the only thing in his
life of which he felt certain.

One of the children woke in the next room and cried for
a drink of water. The tap was out on the landing and while
she drew the water the girl heard the old woman lumbering
upstairs. There were nearly a hundred steps and she paused
for breath every five steps or so.

A few minutes later she came in. She was very fat; her
bosom and her stomach joined in a great ballooning bulge
and her hips were loose and dissolute. She threw down a
great bundle of rags on the floor and began coughing and
spitting. 'Christ Jesus!' she muttered. And suddenly she
roared at Christopher:

'You might come down and give us a bloomin' 'and, you
might! Yes, you! 'Ang abaht all day and don't do nuthin'!
Why the 'ell don't you come an' 'elp a poor ole gal? Christ.
You're a one, you are. You beat me.'

She heaved the rags aside and sat down. Christopher tried
to take no notice of her outburst but his hand trembled and
he dropped a watch-screw.

'Ada ain't comin' straight 'ome,' said the old woman.
'I ran against her in 'Olborn.'

'Why isn't she coming home?' said Christopher.

' 'Ow the 'ell do I know? She's off up west somewhere.
The gal wants to enjoy 'erself once in a while, don't she? Lor'
lummy. I should say so.'

Christopher said nothing but the works of the watch
seemed to tremble before his eyes. Phoebe came in from
the other room.

'I'd better get your supper, hadn't I?' she said to the old
woman.

'Give me a drop o' whisky, that's all I want, then I'm off
again meself.'

The whisky was kept in the cupboard by the fire-place.
The girl stood in a wicker-bottom chair and reached the

bottle and a glass. Stepping off the chair, she slipped and the glass flew out of her hands, smashing against the fender.

The old woman suddenly sprang up and flew at the girl and dealt her a blow across the face that sent her staggering.

'God 'elp us, what the devil's the matter with you?' she screeched. She advanced on the girl and lifted her arm menacingly. 'You stuck-up bitch, you might 'elp your old aunt up with her bundle. But you won't, will you, not if you can 'elp it? Not you, my lady. 'Ere, let me get my whisky before I does summat desperate. You make me sick!'

The agility and strength of her fat body was amazing as she climbed into the chair and found another glass and poured out her whisky.

'And after to-day,' she roared at the girl, 'you come to the market and meet me. I don't keep you for nothing.'

She drank the whisky, coughed and went out of the door. As she went down the stairs, she swore aloud to herself.

Christopher stood up. The girl was crying quietly.

He felt that he knew exactly how she felt, that she must cry and go on crying until the very spending of tears brought her comfort.

Helpless, he went on mending the watch, feeling wretched, and he rejoiced when the girl ceased sobbing and came and sat by the fire.

'You'll forget it in the morning,' he said to her.

She shook her head, certain in her misery that she would never forget.

An inspiration came to him and he jumped up and searched in his trunk under the bed and found his Bible. Without warning her, he opened it at random and began to read.

'For my thoughts,' he read, 'are not your thoughts, neither are your ways my ways, saith the Lord. For as the heavens are higher than the earth, so are my ways higher than your ways, and my thoughts than your thoughts. For as the rain cometh down, and the snow from heaven, and returneth not thither, but watereth the earth and maketh it bring forth and bud, that it may give seed to the sower, and bread to the eater: so shall my word be that goeth forth out of my mouth: it shall not return unto me void, but it shall accomplish that which I please, and it shall prosper in the thing whereto I sent it. For ye shall go out with joy and be led forth with peace: the mountains and the hills shall break forth before you in singing, and all the trees of the field shall clap their hands.'

Before he could read any further she began to cry again.

He shut his Bible and put his arm about her shoulder, which shook violently as she sobbed, feeling in every tremor of her body the misery of her loneliness. 'I want to go back home,' she managed to say. 'I can't stand it any longer. I hate it.'

He had brought out his Bible with the intention of talking to her about God and the importance of Belief in times of trouble and weariness, but now he knew that his words would be superfluous and that God would complicate it all. She was unhappy and lonely and she wanted to go back to the country again. Nothing could be clearer than that.

She lived in Rutland, a lovely miniature county, like a park. There were green hills that undulated gently among great woods and old stone farms, churches with graceful spires and great country mansions half-hidden by stately trees. Spring was coming and the blossom in the orchards would be tossed like white foam in the wind, the primroses would run across under the half-bare trees like a yellow flame. She had only to think of it to bring about a sensation of fresh misery and joy.

'Where is your bag?' he said. 'If you'll get your things ready I'll take you to the station on Sunday morning before Ada and your aunt are up. I'll manage it somehow.'

She looked at him thankfully, her eyes brilliant with the film of tears, and suddenly she put her lips on his, lightly and with girlish tenderness, and then drew away and smiled. Her lips were soft and smooth and they reminded him of tulip petals and her kiss had a kind of devout thankfulness even its brief lightness. He smiled awkwardly, hardly knowing what to do, and went on mending the watch.

11

In the morning Christopher walked about London, trying
to sell *The Meaning of God* again. The day was raw and cold
and a north-east wind seemed to be in wait behind corners
and in alley-ways and then leap out at him and slash him
icily. Sometimes instead of selling he tried to exchange the
book, but he was unsuccessful. The author of the book was
obscure and again no one seemed interested in God.

About noon he came back to Lincoln's Inn and sat down
on a seat and rested for a moment, and then went on to see
another bookseller. There was a bookshop off Theobald's
Road owned by a German named Karl whom he knew
slightly. His shop was like a rabbit-hutch, but in it were
stacked thousands of volumes and there at all times of the day
all kinds of people gathered, poets and revolutionists,
painters and actors, novelists and critics, crowding in the
doorway and in the passage-way and leaning against the
shelves of books inside the shop. They dressed fantastically or
shabbily, with scarlet neckties and old tweed coats and
emerald shirts; the less artistic they were the more fantastically they dressed, the lesser poets making no mistake about
the poetic flavour of their dress. The poets and artists who
were really poets and artists looked like ordinary men, clerks
or shop-assistants or insurance agents. They behaved
quietly. The lesser poets argued and raved, sneering at the
successful and talking like prophets.

Christopher walked along the street, facing the wind and
wondering if he would sell the book at the shop. Karl had
no use for books on God, but often he bought for kindness'
sake books which he despised and which he knew he would
never sell. With the money Christopher could buy a dinner.
That morning he had been forced to ask Ada for a little
money and there had been an argument. 'Do you think I
earn enough to keep you as well?' Ada had shouted. 'What
about you keeping me for a change?' The old woman had
joined in, her fat face quivering with indignation. 'You're
a bloody fine 'usband, you are!' she told him. 'Why the
bleeding 'ell don't you do something?'

He felt ashamed and humiliated. How could he explain to them that he was trying to do something? It was no use explaining. They thought him superfluous and useless and nothing could alter that. Perhaps he really was superfluous and useless? he thought wretchedly. If only he could sell the book he might feel that he had done something, however small, to justify himself.

He came to the bookshop and stood outside for a moment turning over the odd volumes and the old art-magazines displayed on the trays. Suddenly his heart stood still. Among the shilling volumes was a copy of *The Meaning of God*, still in its paper wrapper. He tried to go on turning over the volumes as though nothing had happened, but his hand trembled. Lifting the cover of an art magazine he let the pages flicker slowly from under his thumb. Suddenly he caught sight of a reproduction of Ingre's 'La Source'. A feeling of extraordinary restfulness came over him and he thought instantly of Phoebe. The loveliness of the young girl in the painting, the profound light and shyness of her large dark eyes, the sublime purity of her nakedness were all more beautiful than ever Phoebe could hope to be, but he saw in both faces the same eternal longing of youth for something it could not name, its mystery, the blissful ache of its melancholy and its happiness. Forgetting the book he had come to sell, he stood thinking of Phoebe, remembering that she had kissed him.

A moment later Karl suddenly rushed out of the shop with a pile of books which he set down on the open magazine.

'Good morning,' said Christopher.

'*Is* it a good-morning?' said Karl. He ran back into the shop rubbing his cold hands, for another pile of books.

Christopher followed him into the shop. There was no chance of his selling the book, but he would go in and look at the books and warm his hands by the bookseller's stove.

Karl was in a great hurry, setting out the last of his books for the day. He raced backwards and forwards, in and out of the shop, with immense energy. He was a tall powerfully built man, very dark, with a face of great strength and striking sensitiveness. He often boasted that he lived on nothing but his books and had no time to eat, feeding his body when it needed feeding. Once a day or once a week, it did not matter. Just as he had no time to eat he also had no time to rest. Something within him had been wound up, as in a clockwork doll, and would not run down. He had time and strength for every kind of person and every task. Obscure young poets brought him their first verses, which he printed, though he often despised them and always lost money on them. He gave away the books that he liked and sold only the books that he detested, having no creed but generosity — a wonderful eccentric generosity, full of warmth and administered with blasphemy and sometimes with the blindness of pure affection.

When Christopher went into the shop two other men were inside, talking loudly. George, an elderly man with a heavy grey face and grey hair, was talking to a little cockney with a cherubic face, named Albert. George was deaf and Albert was shouting at him with a piercing cockney voice.

' 'Ow's yer wife?' shouted Albert.

'I haven't read it,' said George, shaking his head.

'I said 'ow's yer wife?'

'I haven't read it, I said.'

'Gawd!' said Albert. 'I said, 'ows' your wife?'

'Eh?'

' 'Ow's your wife, I said!' shouted Albert.

Karl came running in. Going straight to George he said quietly, 'He wants to know how your wife is,' and George answered at once:

'Oh! yes, yes, she's fine.'

Karl hurried out with a pile of books and Albert went on:

'Bring her round some evening.'

'Eh!' said George.

'Bring her round some evening!'

'I liked it. Did you?'

'Gawd!' said Albert. 'I asked you to bring her round some evening!'

'Who?'

'Your wife!'

'What about her?'

140

'Jesus wept,' said Albert. 'And well he might! Bring her round . . .' he began to shout. 'Bring her round. . . .'

Christopher could endure it no longer. He walked out of the door. He stood for a moment looking at the books in the window. Karl vanished into the shop, taking no notice of him. Christopher wanted to ask him as a special favour if he would buy *The Meaning of God*, but first his pride and then the fear of refusal prevented him. Turning over the pages of the art-magazine he gazed at 'La Source', thinking once more of Phoebe. Suddenly he went impulsively into the shop with the magazine in his hand.

'Will you exchange this book for this magazine?' he said to Karl.

Karl took the book.

'*The Meaning of God*?' he said, faintly derisive. 'What is the meaning of God?'

'Take it, take it, please,' urged Christopher.

'I don't want the bloody thing!'

'Oh, don't you? Can't you just for this time?' he pleaded. Karl's generosity triumphed.

'All right,' he said. 'I've got *The Meaning of God* all over the place now but I'll take it.'

'Thank you,' said Christopher. 'Thank you so much.'

As he turned to go out of the shop, carrying the magazine under his arm, Albert was shouting to George:

'Jesus Christ! I said bring your wife round some evening!'

Christopher hurried away out of reach of the voice. There was a curious feeling of exultation in his heart and he walked quickly. What was coming over him? Crossing the street he went through a passage into Lincoln's Inn, his favourite spot in all London, and sat down and gazed at 'La Source' again. Tears came into his eyes suddenly because of the great beauty of the picture. He felt ridiculously happy as he looked at the dark brimming eyes of the young girl, her beautiful breasts; the heavenly whiteness of her skin. The only woman he had ever seen undressed was Ada; her limbs were hard and her skin yellowish and her breasts had never blossomed, even for her children, and they too were hard and yellow. She only nauseated him. He had no desire to see Phoebe's body, content to feel in his imagination that she was like the young girl in 'La Source'.

Great clouds were flocking over from the sea, like immense grey geese flying southward, and suddenly he shut the book and gazed at them, gazing in a state of dreamy stupidity, not knowing what to do with happiness now that it had come to him.

Presently, too excited to sit still any longer, he got up and wandered down to the Embankment and walked along by the river. The water was chopped to small fierce waves by the wind; the smoke from tugs was snatched up and torn to shreds; gulls planed and swooped and breasted the grey waves, screaming mournfully. Young girls came hurrying along the pavement under the plane trees, leaving shops and offices. Trams lurched along and stopped and people clambered aboard and were wafted away. Over the Port of London itself a young moon rode along pale and transparent, appearing and vanishing again, whenever the clouds broke, like a far-off seagull lost among the geese of the clouds.

He stopped at a coffee-stall and bought himself a cup of tea and some biscuits. The stall-tender was a big fat man, in his shirt sleeves. A third man in dungarees came up and bought himself a sandwich and a cup of coffee. It was warm under the flap of the stall, with a smell of coffee and new meat pies, and the two men talked about the Government. 'There ain't enough work to go round — not if you argue till Doomsday. It'll never come right again.'

Christopher wanted to shout at them exultantly.

'What do I care about government? What does it matter? All my life I've never done anything better than mend watches and review books that nobody reads, and now I'm going to do something that is worth doing.'

He walked on again. The young girls hurrying away out of London all seemed like Phoebe! He looked at them wistfully and now and then he stopped and leaned on the stone parapet by the river and looked at 'La Source' again, thinking in the morning he was to take her to the station. She was to be snatched from his life. Her father, a big labouring man, had married a second time and there were eight other children, and probably he would belt her for going home, but he would keep her there simply because he could not raise the train-fare to send her back again.

He walked about till evening and then as darkness was falling he went back to Pope's Buildings.

He sat down as on the previous day and had tea with Phoebe and the children.

'Any luck?' she asked.

'Yes, I sold it,' he lied.

'Oh! I am glad.'

When the children had gone to bed Phoebe found her bag and together they packed her belongings. 'Oh! I shan't sleep,' she said. 'I know I shan't.' He took the bag downstairs and left it with the caretaker, who had a room on the ground floor. They could call for it as they passed in the morning.

When he came back Phoebe was turning over the pages of the art-magazine, which he had thrown in a chair, and as he shut the door she came upon the picture of 'La Source'. She stared at it, confused and embarrassed. Before she could shut the book he asked:

'Do you like that?'

'Oh! I don't know,' she said.

'I think it's very wonderful,' he said.

'It's just a girl.'

'That's not all,' he said. It's the significance of it — the meaning.'

'Why she is spilling the water?'

He tried to explain it.

'That's the whole meaning of it — the spring of life. She's overflowing with youth and life. She's careless — she doesn't know how precious her youth is. She just lets it spill.'

'I don't see it. Why does she let it spill?'

'That's the point of it — the spring of life spilling and wasting.'

'Why couldn't she hold the vase upright and not spill the water?'

'It wouldn't have meant anything.'

'Why wouldn't it?'

He went on trying to explain but she could not understand. Neither did she see, as he did, that she herself was like the young girl.

Later, when the old woman came home, a little drunk and talkative, he took out the watch he had begun to clean the previous evening and laid out the works on a sheet of newspaper.

'I saw Ada with a bloke,' said the old woman. 'Serves you right; serves you damn well right.'

He said nothing. What did it matter? And he went on cleaning the watch-works, happy in his silence.

III

On Sunday mornings Ada and the old woman did not wake till twelve o'clock, and when they at last got up they shuffled from one room to the other, half dressed, their hair frowzy and uncombed, the old woman's uncorseted body rolling from side to side grossly and flabbily as she searched for the hairpins her shaking fingers let fall in trying to pin up her hair. She always over-drank on Saturday nights and in the morning her drink-sodden face and her bleary leaden eyes were full of a sombre hatred for the world and for Christopher especially. Ada, without her rouge and powder, but with the remnants of both still on her cracked lips and sallow skin, lay huddled under the bed-clothes, half-asleep and muttering while Christopher and Phoebe got breakfast and sent the two children off at ten o'clock to a Salvation Army Sunday School at the end of the street.

The children always went into the bedroom to say 'Good morning' to the old woman before departing. It was her wish. And they would lean over the gross mound of flesh in the untidy bed and bid her 'Good-bye' and she would stir from her heavy-eyed stupor and say with a kind of bleary sanctimoniousness:

'Gawd bless you. Be good children, sing nicely. That's right! Gawd bless you, my dears, Gawd bless you!'

Christopher woke early. The first thing he remembered

was that Ada, somewhere in the middle of the night, had crawled over him as he lay in bed and had sunk down with an exhausted sigh into her place against the wall. It must have been two o'clock. Her coming not only woke him but set the bed-springs creaking with little sounds which sounded to him louder and more horrible than ever in the dead of night. By her clumsy movements and her grim and uncertain mutterings he realized that she too must be drunk. Sickened, he felt that another night in the same bed with her would drive him mad. Then he remembered Phoebe. He suddenly got out of bed and put on his jacket over his night-shirt. Everywhere was silent and he walked about the room in his bare feet and then he put on his stockings. Again and again he thought of the morning; he saw the train hissing on the platform at King's Cross and he saw it rushing northward through the flat country of eastern England. The thought of it all made him feel wretched and lonely, and suddenly he knelt down impulsively against the big leather arm-chair in the corner and prayed silently with his hands drawn over his face until he had exhausted his words and he could go on praying only through sheer desperation and unhappiness, his words no longer meaning anything. When he rose from his knees he felt chastened and his mind was clearer and he took off his stockings again, intending to get back into bed and try to sleep once more, but suddenly he found himself opening the door of the other room, where Phoebe and the children and the old woman slept. He opened the door impulsively by doing it with a kind of defiance against himself. In the bedroom the green blinds were drawn and it was pitch dark, but he knew the room so well he walked straight to the bed where Phoebe was asleep with the two children. The air was heavy with the silence of sleep. Phoebe, a dark image against the pillow, was sleeping on the edge of the bed and the children were huddled against the wall. All the beds in the Bonners' two rooms were pushed against the wall. Christopher stood and listened a moment and then impulsively he stooped and kissed the girl. Except for their warmth her lips might have been dead; there was no response from them. He took one look at her pale face, hesitated and then left the room himself. He walked about the other room for a long time, the thought of getting back into the bed which he hated so much bringing all his unbalancedness back again. When he crept back into bed again he was shivering and his feet were icily cold. He could not get warm again and they were still cold when he woke.

He woke at ten minutes past seven. The morning was cloudy, with a sickly yellow sunrise which was reflected in the windows, all with blinds still drawn, in the houses opposite. He put on the hands of the clock to half-past seven and set the kettle to boil on the gas-ring and washed himself at the sink. As he was washing he heard Phoebe moving about and then the children. The youngest child came out to fetch a jug of water for washing.

'Don't make a noise,' he entreated her as he gave her the water.

The train departed at half-past ten. He had put on the hands of the clock by twenty minutes in order to send away the children early. Phoebe would take the children downstairs, wait for him and he would follow.

Phoebe came out of the bedroom with the children, and they all sat down to the breakfast table. The children chattered, but Phoebe and Christopher hardly spoke. Ada stirred uneasily in bed in the corner, fighting wakefulness.

At ten o'clock it all happened as they proposed it should. At the back of his mind Christopher cherished a weak hope that something unexpected would happen to prevent it all, but event followed event implacably and smoothly: Ada did not wake, the children asked no questions, and as the clocks were striking a quarter to ten over London he and Phoebe walked away from Pope's Buildings, meeting no one in the silent streets except milkmen and Sunday-paper men and children running to Sunday school. The streets of Clerkenwell were dim and frowzy and littered with orange peel and fried-fish papers which floated sleepily along the pavements, the jaded relics of humanity's Saturday night. The time seemed to pass quickly, seeming to record itself not in hours and minutes but in streets and houses, every street and every house exactly like its neighbour, drab and soulless; in the houses, which were the minutes, dwelt crowded people, which were seconds, the seconds were part of the minute and the minute part of the hour, and the hour merely a fraction of time and eternity.

Before Christopher was aware of it, and while he was still thinking gloomily of the streets, they arrived at King's Cross. Life was beginning to move there, and in the station with people hurrying and waiting on the platforms, and trains waiting to depart, he felt less depressed. There was some meaning in life again; people were going away; people were setting out on adventurous journeys; there was a sense of freedom and escape.

He looked up the train on the indicator. 'Platform four.' He looked at Phoebe and smiled. 'You wait at the barrier while I get your ticket,' he told her.

'Here, let me give you the money,' she called.

'No, no! That's all right. Really, that's all right.'

Running to the booking-office he made himself short of breath and he was panting hard and his heart was beating with wild thumps as he asked for the ticket. This was his moment and his triumph. He put down the money, snatched the ticket from the pigeon-hole and ran off again.

'Now here's your ticket,' he said. 'You have it and I'll get myself a platform ticket.'

They entered the platform a minute later. His depressing thoughts had vanished and he felt joyfully defiant and triumphant. Then suddenly he glanced at Phoebe. Great white tears, like stormy raindrops, were running down her cheeks. He wanted to say something but all that he had wanted to say to her for the last two days surged up in him, and the words became confused, keeping him silent. She took out her handkerchief and blew her nose in order to cover up her wretchedness. He wrenched open a carriage door and she got in and he settled her bag on the rack for her.

He got out of the carriage and shut the door. They looked at each other in silence, she with the tears still glistening on her cheeks and lashes.

At the end of the train a whistle shrieked and unexpectedly the girl spoke quietly.

'I understand about the girl with the pitcher,' she said. He saw that she was crying again. 'You know — the girl all undressed, with the pitcher. I know what you were trying to tell me.' Another whistle blew and there was a flash of green.

What had he tried to tell her? He tried desperately to remember. She was weeping freely, when he said, 'What do you mean?' She only shook her head wretchedly, too full to speak, and a moment later the train began to move and he simply stood still, without a word of farewell, feeling too stupefied and unhappy even to wave his hand.

He left the station and went out into the streets. What had he tried to tell her? His head began to feel heavy and the cog-wheel began to rasp slightly but implacably against the edge of his brain. He tried to think clearly and intelligently, but his mind would not respond, and time began to manifest itself again in streets which were hours and houses which were minutes, and people like himself which were the merest fractions in time and eternity.

He walked back to Pope's Buildings, intending to find 'La Source' and look at it again and recall his own words about it.

A group of children were playing in the courtyard, four little girls swinging from a rope tied to a lamp-post, singing a song he remembered singing himself as a child:

> 'Sally go round the moon
> Sally go round the stars.'

He crossed the courtyard as they raised their voices and swung more joyfully to the rest of the song:

> 'Sally go round the chimney pot
> On a Sunday afternoon.'

Suddenly something, he did not know what, made him stop. Why should he go up? Why should he ever go back? Why should he spend another night in that awful bed beside which he could not pray and in which he had been so unhappy?

He turned and walked out of the courtyard, the children's

voices following him, the sound of their song diminishing as his resolution strengthened.

'Sally go round the moon,' they sang, fainter and fainter.

He began to walk more quickly, never looking behind, walking as though he did not care where he went or how or why.

THE BROTHERS

THE two men, with their grey, weather-blistered motor-van, arrived at the wood towards the end of August. There had been no rain for many weeks. The wood had been cleared the previous spring, to the last sapling, and where the sawmill had stood a dozen high yellowish pyramids of sawdust were dotted among the disused wooden workmen's shacks, the piles of empty petrol cans and the odds and ends of rusting machinery that the timber company had never fetched away. The riding, once a quiet and shady cantering ground for horses, had been ploughed by the wheels of lumber-carriages and tractors from end to end, and the summer had baked the slush of April to iron. In places the furrows had been filled with hazel-faggots, cut green in spring and thrown down in the ruts of slush, where they had become crushed and withered to tinder. The men drove their motor-van as far as the piles of sawdust and left it there. It was impossible to go further. As far as they could see the big wood was like a battlefield, a desolation of fallen tree-tops lying splintered and interlocked impassably with each other, with clumps of willow-herb and seeded foxglove struggling up between, pink and brown, on long weak stems. The wood-earth was cracked and burned grey by drought, the leaves on the skeleton tops of the felled oak trees brown and brittle as scorched paper, the primrose-clumps dotted among the dead timber like rosettes of yellow rag.

The men were brothers. They were each dressed in shirts of oily blue check, with black trousers and black knotted neck mufflers. But except for this they might have been strangers, they were so unlike each other. The elder, Marko, was a big man, about thirty-five, six feet tall, horse-limbed but sluggish of movement, with thick black curly hair that straightened itself over his low forehead; there was power and defiance in the way he shot out his spittle or put his little finger to his black-haired ear and screwed it savagely, a primitive power, at once aggressive and unconscious. He spoke frequently

with a kind of sneering annoyance, and never without some
growl or murmur of malevolence, as though nothing in the
world were right for him. He seemed to live in a state of
unnecessary aggression towards his brother, a mere youth,
thin and slight, with black eyes that were weak and a little
shifty, and a restless fervour about his movements and his
pallid face. 'I don't wanna be here all my bloody life if you
do!' he would say a dozen times a day, as though blaming
the younger man for the drought, the heat, the chaos of the
wood, for everything. The younger man took it all with a
kind of fearful serenity, in silence, without even a look of
protest or a spit of defiance.

'Never get the bloody wood ready the rate you're going on,
never see the money back. Shift your bloody self.'

They had come to clear the timber that was left. They
were half-gipsies, dealers in old-iron, rags, horses, firewood,
anything to be picked up cheap and sold for quick profit.
And Marko had made a bargain with the manager of the
timber company, whereby for next to nothing they might
have as much wood as they could clear and saw in a month.
In October they would set off, in the motor-van, and run
from town to town and sell the logs. There was money in it.
It all depended on how hard they worked, how much wood
they sawed before October. After that it was easy. Now,
while the wood was dry, and the days still long, they must
slave like madmen, hardly stopping to eat.

At first they brought the wood to the van, spending one
day dragging out the tree boughs with ropes and the next
sawing them with a cross-cut saw. The first days of rope and
saw blistered their hands and the blisters split with a salty
pain, leaving raw spots that would not heal. The saw-handle
became like hot iron and the spray of sawdust intolerably
parching. The dust seemed to get down to the lungs of the
younger man, setting him coughing in dry raking fits which
exhausted him but which had no effect on the insistence of
his brother's perpetual torment. Were they going to saw
the blasted wood or weren't they? Either they'd got to do
better than this or jack up. No good going on like this.
If one could do it the other could. Half a minute? — Christ!

nothing but half a minute. How many more half minutes? He would squat there in a derisive attitude of waiting, spitting rankly on his hands, the very sweat on his dark face expressive of his coarse strength, while the young man licked his dust-dry lips and tried to conceal or lessen his desperate panting for breath, his face pale with pain, his hands resting on his knees, white and strengthless, until at last the elder man, impatient of it, would mutter his black snarl and seize the saw-handle and pull it in motion, his brother's hand mechanically catching at it and pulling also, falling into the old automatic motion stupidly.

At the end of the fourth day Joe, the younger man, had an idea. It was he who drove the motor-van, and in the evenings, as he tinkered with the engine, cleaning the plugs, trying to correct some tapping in the engine, he seemed to shake off the weariness of the day and come to life.

He was alone when he had the idea that they might run a circular saw off the back wheel of the van. His brother had gone off into the wood on the prowl. There were no longer any keepers, but the life of the wood remained — foxes taking refuge in the impassable ruin of boughs, an odd pheasant, a wood-pigeon roosting in a surviving hazel-clump, a swarm of rabbits. Very often the men heard the high squeal of the stoat-bitten rabbit and could, by running towards the sound, scare the stoat and find the rabbit before the blood-sucking had begun. If there were no rabbit by evening, Marko prowled round, lingering till darkness very often for the chance of a roosting pheasant, while Joe tinkered with the motor engine and replenished the cooking fire. They had their last meal in the dusk, by the fire, and then slept in the van.

Across the road from the wood stood a solitary house, new-looking, of bright red brick, occupied by a thin stooping man who limped across to the wood to watch the two men sawing and to talk with them. He was an ex-soldier and limped from a wound in the leg and from time to time he would roll up his trousers and display the wound-scar, recounting the story. But the two brothers were unimpressed. They dragged in boughs, sawed them and added to the dry yellow stack of billets as though he did not exist. Only in this did they resemble each other, in their derision, unconscious and unspoken, of the outsider. They could convey that derision in a spit which left behind it a scornful silence, but derision and spit and scorn were all lost on the thin man, who would go on talking to them in a Cockneyish voice of whining familiarity, sucking at a cigarette and between the sentences, oblivious.

'Daresay you wouldn't believe it. But there's a bullet in my leg yet. You can't see it now. It seems to disappear in dry weather and then show again when it rains. Soon as it rains again I'll show it you. See? This leg's like a weather-glass. The bullet begins to show when there's rain about. What do you think of that?'

They would make no answer: only the silence or spit of contempt. But once the elder brother remarked: 'You can give us the tip when it's going to rain, then, eh?' and thereafter the man came across the road each evening, smoking the perpetual stained fag-end, and turned up his trousers. There was never a sign of the bullet and the parching heat continued, the leaves of the remaining hazels curling and shrivelling, the thistles and willow-herb making a transparent silken storm of seed which floated over the scorched wood, never ceasing, in the blazing sunshine.

The man appeared, as usual, limping up the riding by the sawdust heaps, as the younger man sat by the van pondering over the new idea of the circular saw, working out the mechanics of it in his mind, deriding himself gently for not having thought of it sooner.

Hearing the footsteps, he glanced up. For the first time he was glad to see the limping man. He could hardly close his fingers for the pain of the broken blisters made by the rope and the cross-saw.

Seeing him by the van, pondering, as if in dejection, the man began: 'Look as if you've lost something . . .'

But Joe interrupted quickly: 'D'ye know anybody what's got a circular saw? To sell or hire, don't matter. We can pay. I've been thinking how we could run one off the motor.'

'Circular saw?' the man repeated. 'I've got a circular saw myself. The timber chaps left it — they used to draw water from my well and they sort of left the saw — ' he seemed to become embarrassed, the tentative note in his voice an excuse in itself. 'It wants fitting up, that's all. It's a good saw.'

'D'ye want to sell it? Can I have a look at it?'

'Yes, you can look at it.'

'Now?'

'Now if you like — it's across at my place, in a shed.'

The gipsy began to walk away eagerly, the ex-soldier limping after him, and ten minutes later they returned, with the gipsy carrying the circular saw wrapped up in sacks.

'Then if you can fit it up,' the limping man was saying, 'you'll borrow it and let me have enough wood for winter for the hire of it. That's it, is it?'

'Ah,' said the gipsy, absently. He was gazing at the sun-baked ground, lost in thought.

'You'll want a running belt,' said the man.

The gipsy was down on his knees, gazing beneath the van. Intent on the saw and the motor, he was transformed, his actions full of a fervent vitality, his mind entranced by its new idea, the limping man forgotten.

'All right, all right,' he said once, looking up and seeing him still there, 'we can fix it.' When he looked up again the man was limping away by the heaps of sawdust.

By noon the following day he had fixed up the saw, the first high mournful whanging moan of the steel in the wood making strange reverberations among the dead trees. The weather was still unchanged, cloudless and oppressive, the heat striking back intolerably from the shadeless earth and the scattered sawdust. He had worked at the saw since daylight, moving the van to more level ground, jacking up the axle, worried alternately by the difficulties of the problem and by the attitude of his brother, who by spits and monosyllables and half-spoken words conveyed his contempt for the scheme, halting each time he made a journey from the wood with his load of boughs or logs, which he roped together and dragged behind him. Yet he never openly opposed the scheme; he offered no argument against it, only the half-glance or half-word of ridicule, softly bitter and provoking.

And strangely enough, at noon, when the saw was finished and whining in motion, he accepted it. Yet the old deprecating infuriating half-murmur of contempt was still there.

'Just about hangs together, don't it? Might do. Might try it.'

He looked it over, feeling the vibration of the saw on the wooden framework, watching the driving-belt. The younger brother, worried at first by the problem of the belt and the saw-frame, had searched among the odds and ends of machinery by the workmen's huts and had found the old saw-frame and some lengths of broken belt which he had riveted together. And now he was so proud of the work which had sweated him into a state of weariness that as before the derision of his brother was lost on him. His idea had been conceived, the work done. Nothing else seemed to matter.

Tired, he switched off the engine, the saw sighed to still-ness, and he turned to look in the van for something to eat. But the voice of Marko arrested him:

'Ah, what yer switching off for? Go on, switch it on again. I want to try it.'

Joe, leaning across the driving wheel, obediently started up the engine again. A moment later, with a loaf in his hands, he heard the whanging moan of saw cutting into wood. Sitting down on the earth, he watched his brother testing the saw with log after log while he himself ate the bread with lumps of cold bacon.

When he had finished eating he got up, ready to take his brother's place. But the chance did not come. Deliberate, arrogant, Marko never moved from the saw. He fed it with a kind of contemptuous zest, as though ridiculing it, yet keeping the young man from working it. At his feet the pile of sawn yellowish logs was growing quickly. He held the wood to the saw with immense strength, never pausing or relaxing, as implacable and powerful as the saw itself.

Soon, too, the heap of uncut boughs began to dwindle. The younger man sidled about, watching the saw, the motor, and his brother by turns, ill at ease, fidgeting, eager for his turn at the saw. But Marko never relaxed.

Finally came a sudden shout above the clatter and whine of the saw and the motor:

'Get some bloody wood along, can't you? — go on, quick! Go on!'

The brother hesitated, half-stubborn, half-afraid, and Marko raised the billet in his hand as if to hurl it.

'Want me to knock your bleeding head off?'

There was a moment's pause, like a flicker of defiance, but in another moment the boy was walking towards the wood with the rope in his hands.

The whine of the saw continued all afternoon, with melancholy echoes. The ex-soldier limped across the road to watch and smoke the eternal fag-end and offer approval: 'That's better beer, eh?' while Marko fed the saw with the boughs that Joe dragged in from the wood. The heap of billets and the pale pyramid of sawdust grew wonderfully.

It was the same on the following day, and all through the next. The saw ran unceasingly, Marko working it, Joe dragging in the boughs, the ex-soldier looking on, the piles of billets and dust growing rapidly. For ten minutes, on the second day, the saw broke down and Joe hurried down the riding, dragging the faggot of boughs, to put it right. Then the racket and whine went on again, breaking harshly the strange stillness that had come down over the wood in the pause. The still sunshine and the drought continued also. 'The old bullet'll die of thirst if this keeps on,' said the ex-soldier, but the brothers offered no remark. They scarcely spoke, now, to each other. When the saw had been repaired Marko offered not a single word of approval or satisfaction; and Joe said nothing. He walked back to the wood with the rope in silence, as if he no longer cared.

The following evening, the third of working the new saw, a cart and pony drove unexpectedly down the road and up the riding, swaying and pitching over the sun-baked wheel-ruts, halting just beyond the motor-van before the men were aware of it, the sound of its coming drowned under the rattle and moan of the saw.

In the cart was a woman, black-haired, youngish, hatless, with a white shawl crossed gipsy-fashion over her pink blouse.

She stood up in the cart and throwing the reins on the horse's back shouted at the men. The racket of the saw drowned her voice so that they did not hear.

'Hey-up! Hey-up!' she called again.

It was the boy who heard and noticed her first.

'Marko, Marko,' he said quickly. 'It's the wife.'

He went to the van to shut off the engine, Marko threw down the billet he had sawn, and together they walked towards the cart. The woman was climbing down from the cart.

'Ye never told us,' muttered Marko.

'How could I tell you?' she flashed. 'How was I to let you know? I been all over the damn place.'

'All right, all right,' he muttered. 'You're here now.'

The flash of antagonism, their only greeting, died down quickly again. They exchanged another word or two, of commonplace things, the younger brother throwing in an odd remark, and then the woman began to unharness the pony and the men went back to the saw, as though nothing had happened.

The men worked on in the warm evening, the woman busy about the fire, watching them sometimes, with her hands on her hips, her strong, big-boned face shrewd even in its pre-occupation, her eyes alert even in their immobility, the trembling ear-rings under the thick black loops of hair giving her a flashy air, half-beautiful. At first she was too occupied to notice much, to see anything more than Marko at the saw and Joe dragging the loads of boughs down the riding. There was nothing significant in that, but she wondered idly once or twice about the saw, wondering where they had picked it up, how they had made it work, and she was faintly astonished at the stack of billets.

But suddenly, standing idle, she sensed it all in a flash. Coming in once from the wood Joe threw down the rope and put one hand to his mouth and licked the palm, slowly and luxuriously, so that she saw instantly the pain and relief in his face. And in a moment she half-divined that the idea of the saw was his. He alone had the machine-sense. Marko could never have done it. A second later, still not quite sure, she walked across to Marko, watching him, to ask carelessly:

'Whose idea was it — the saw?'

'Joe's,' said Marko. 'He fixed it up.' His voice was flat, expressionless.

She said no more. But in the evening, when the saw was silent and they sat round the fire, eating, she looked at Joe's hands and saw the great crimson blisters, kept raw by the rope and boughs, that would not heal.

'What's the matter with your hands?' she said.

'What's up with his hands?' mocked Marko. 'What's up with them?'

Joe curled up his hands and would not show them and was silent.

But Marko extended his palms, with a sort of aggressive contempt. They also were scarred with red skinless patches.

'Poor Marko's hands,' he muttered.

The derision was directed through her to the boy. She tried to neutralize it at once by a flash in return.

'Yes, yes,' she said bitterly. 'Poor Marko's hands. Poor Marko.'

Joe said nothing. He had heard them quarrel often enough. And the derision he accepted with meekness, too weak to sustain even the thought of anger and retaliation.

In the morning the woman spoke to Joe, alone.

'Why don't you work the saw?'

'Marko works it.'

'I never asked you that. I said why don't you work it?'

'I don't know.'

'Don't you want to work it then?'

'I don't care.'

She gave it up, shrugging her shoulders:

'Well, you know best.'

But all through the morning, as she peeled potatoes and

cooked and washed out the men's oily blue-check shirts, she kept an eye on him. It was necessary, now, for Joe to go farther and farther back into the wood for timber, so that the journeys were longer and the saw often ate through one load of boughs long before another arrived. It meant that the saw must run empty or be shut off, and that Marko must wait empty-handed, furious. When the boy arrived at last the hot spit of that fury met him.

'Why the hell don' you shift yourself! I don' wanna be here all winter! Shift yourself!'

And never a word or gesture of retaliation from the boy. She marvelled at his silence and filled each time with anger and disgust.

In the afternoon, after his first journey into the wood, she said carelessly:

'I'll give a hand with that wood.'

She followed Joe up the riding and into the wood, through the ruin of dead boughs and withered thistlestalks and white-feathered willow-herb, along the path his constant journeys had made through the parched undergrowth. They gathered a load of oak boughs together, not speaking much, and Joe dragged it out of the wood while she prepared another load. Expectantly, she listened to Marko's voice, and a little later she heard it, deriding the boy, with half-direct, taunting words because he had allowed her to help him.

She was furious now also.

'I should think you're going to stand that, I should think so,' she said when Joe returned.

'It's all right,' he said.

'All right, all right,' she whispered bitterly. 'All right when he talks to you like that? Your own brother? I should think so.'

'I'm used to it.'

'Used to it! Used to it!' she half raised her hands. 'He don't talk to me like it, I see. You're hopeless.'

But she would not let him rest. Whenever they were alone together she urged him to retaliate, to show his spirit, to defy Marko. 'I can see myself letting him say the things he

says to you, I'm sure. Do something, boy. Do something.'
And she would argue, rationally, too.

'Didn't you fit the saw up? Wasn't it your idea? You're
his brother, ain't you? You're as good as he is? If it hadn't
been for you we shouldn't have been nowhere. Nowhere.
Ay! I tell you boy, I tell you, you're a fool, you're a fool!'

She kept on in this way all afternoon, lugging savagely
at the boughs as she spoke and so giving a strange compulsion
and strength to her words. At last he began to take notice,
half-agreeing, half-seeing the reason of her words, and
catching as it were the reflected fire of her passionate
indignation. He'd half a mind to do something. He could
see now. He'd half a mind . . .

'That's it, do something. Show him you don't stand that.'

But he did nothing. He would work himself up, nervously,
tensely, in order to offer a word or a gesture of defiance to
his brother, but the act itself was too much for him.

'I'll do it — just give me a chance, that's all. I'll do it!'

Half-detesting, half-pitying his weakness, she continued
to work him up, a sense of right impelling her at first, then a
curious illogical, fitful desire to witness a crisis between them.
Her own passion for Marko was dried up. She no longer
cared, neither one way or another. She satisfied something
in herself as she whipped the boy into a state of vengeance.

'Go on. The longer you let it go on the longer it will.'

By the evening he had worked himself into a strange
state of revengeful anger, an agitation that had about it also
the trembling terror of cowardice. He'd do something,
he'd do something all right, he'd do something. She was a
little afraid. Where he had been too weak to urge himself
to anger he was likewise too weak to sustain the sudden fury
she had whipped up in him. His white sweaty face was burnt
up with fatigue and anger, his hands were quivering, he
did not know what to do with the fury that had leapt up,
volatile and terrible, within him!

She calmed him down a little:

'Don't get excited. He'll notice. Wait till he gives you
the chance. Calm down a bit.' Her voice, touched with
pity, soothed him.

In the evening, as they sat about the fire, eating, the ex-soldier limped over the road and up the riding, to talk with them.

'The old bullet's showed up,' he told them. 'Might be a storm.' He rolled up his trousers and showed his thin, pallid hairy leg, with the faint bluish shadow of what might have been the bullet under the flesh!

'Clear the air,' said Marko.

The woman looked at him quickly as he spoke. He was half-glancing at his brother, significantly, darkly. She wondered if he suspected. But the boy, staring at the ground, brooding with his own anger, had noticed nothing.

The ex-soldier limped home early. The bullet hurt him very much, and the sky, filling with darkish oppressive heat-clouds, seemed to promise the storm too. The air was still and tense.

'It'll blow over,' said the woman, trying to speak casually.

'I ain't so sure,' said Marko. 'I'll have a look at the nag, anyway.'

He rose abruptly and began to walk away, towards the road, where they had tethered the nag on the parched road-grass. Instantly, as he turned his back, the boy leapt up behind him, silent, wild with passion, with a long billet in his hand. Before the woman could speak, he took one step forward, raising his arm, and stood poised as if to bring down the billet madly, with all his force on the head of his brother. His arm actually lowered. His face was watery with sweat and white in its fury. He became for one moment filled with the diabolical strength of pure cowardice.

And suddenly it left him. His arm dropped, his body seemed to go cold with weakness, and in a second or two his brother was down the riding, out of reach.

The woman, afraid, angry, began to whisper furiously:

'God, what d'ye think you're doing. What made you do that? God, he'd smash you! He'd smash you!'

He took no notice.

'I shall do it, I shall do it,' he said, tensely.

'You're a fool!' she cried. She was afraid; she no longer pitied him. 'Ah! you're a fool. He'll smash you, I tell you, he'll smash you.'

'Leave me alone!' the boy cried. 'Leave me alone, I tell you!'

He began to walk away, still clenching the billet, the force of his fury and hatred flowing back through his weak body again, inflaming his white face and eyes with its frenzy. As he retreated towards the wood she threw up her arms with a gesture of fatalistic abandonment:

'Well, you do it! she whispered. 'You do it. I'm finished. You do it. I ain't responsible. I'm finished.'

BEAUTY'S DAUGHTERS

It was a small two-storied farm-house built of brick the colour of sheep-reddle, with a wired-in yard of wooden cow-hovels roofed with corrugated iron that shone white hot in the straight afternoon sunlight. It stood quite solitary on the rise of land, and without a sign of life; the yard empty even of chickens; the surrounding fields, divided up into set rectangles by fences of wire, empty of cattle; the treeless grass scorched brown under the fierce heat, and the sky empty of birds. As I went up the hedgeless cart-track of summer-baked mud towards the house I looked down at my shoes. They were covered with soft red dust, ironstone dust, the colour of the land all about me. Even the pasture was coloured red; the red dust seemed to be choking the thin brown grass. And then when I looked up again it seemed as if years of wind had blown a bombardment of dust against the house and that the bricks, and even the woodwork, had absorbed it. Beyond the red house the fields continued in bare undulations, scorched up, almost grassless, and beyond the land the sky was a fiery blue without a shred of cloud. Nothing stirred and nothing seemed to be happening in the stillness of afternoon sunlight.

Then when I reached the turn in the track that led into the farmyard I saw a movement beyond the house: the flap of a shirt-sleeve. A man was digging potatoes in a wired-in patch of ground between the house and a line of damson trees. Then as I began to walk across the yard I saw that the house door was open, with splashes of white hen-dung fresh on the threshold.

Then, looking at the man in the potato patch again, I saw something else. A red puff of dust, like the puff of a miniature cannon, rose up every time he dug. And as I went closer I could see the dust, like a red blight, on the dark potato leaves, and on the man's boots, and on his black-green trousers.

I reached the wire and stood there, looking at the man digging. He did not see me. He was a tallish man, dark

163

and very thin: thin straight body, and thinner splayed-out
legs, like a split hay-rake. I could not see his face: only his
thin back curved and straightened with each lifting of
potatoes.

Then I spoke. 'Could I get something to drink here?'
I said. 'Some tea?'

He looked up and round at once: though not at me, but
at the house. Even then he did not see me. He stared at
the house for a moment and then put his fork in the earth.

'Could I get something to drink?' I said.

He looked up again: but this time at me, startled, with
astonishment. He stared hard, with a half-flicker of recogni-
tion in his eyes, as though he could not believe I were a
stranger. His eyes were very brown: there was a mild, almost
sweet look in them, inoffensive, almost childish. Then he
saw that he did not know me, and the sweet mildness shot
away and left him blank and uneasy.

I tried to reassure him: 'I only want a drink,' I said. 'Tea
or something, or water.'

'I'll ask her,' he said.

His voice was so subdued that I scarcely heard him.
And in a moment he was walking away across the potato
patch and then across the yard and so into the house.

As I stood waiting for him I leaned back on the fence-
wire and looked at the sun-scorched yard and the house.
At once I saw why there was so little sign of life about the
farm: the dog, a shepherd, lay asleep in the shade of a muck-
cart, and the hens, ten or a dozen of them, all raw-necked,
were huddled together in the thin shadow of a haystack, in
scratched-out nests of dust and hay-seed, half asleep. And
besides the man they seemed to be the only living things
about the place. Under the still heat it seemed deserted and
dead.

Then suddenly it came to life. A girl came half-running
out of the house to the yard-pump, with a water-bucket in
her hands. She did not see me. She was a heavy, big-
breasted girl, about thirty. She had nothing on but a white
under-skirt and white skirt-top: no shoes or stockings or hat
or corsets, so that I could see the coarse dirt-shiny soles of

her feet as she ran, her black curl-pinned hair, and the great unsupported breasts flopping heavily under the thin skirt-top.

She hung the bucket on the pump-spout and began to work the handle. I could hear the pump sucking air in the short intervals between each motion of the squeaking handle. The water seemed a long time coming up, and finally after working the handle madly the girl desisted for a moment, out of breath. I could hear her muttering, and I could see even at that distance the sweat shining yellow on her coarse-fleshed face. Then after a moment she began to work the handle again; and again the pump sucked air and nothing happened, and once more she gave it up.

But this time her anger broke out in a shout.

'Dad! Dad!' She bawled as if he were on the opposite field-slopes. 'Dad! Christ Almighty. Where are you? Where the hell are you? Dad!'

Nothing happened. She began to pump again, the pump sucking air as before, she swearing. Every time she lifted her arm I could see the thick sweat-matted hair black under her arm-pits. In anger her face was sullen, passionate, the dark eyebrows close together. But there was one thing about her that was different.

I did not see it until I began to walk across the yard towards her. She had begun to push back her thick hair away from her face, and as I came nearer I saw that she had lovely ears: small, lovely, soft-curved ears that shone very white against her black hair.

Then as I was looking at them and thinking that at any moment she must see me, she stopped pumping again and put her hand on the pump-head and drew herself up and looked down the shaft.

'The bloody pump's dry!' she shouted. The pump-shaft magnified the words, so that they rang out hollow and heavy and more blatant.

And they must have reached the house. For suddenly the man reappeared, half-running. 'All right, May, I'm coming,' he said. He kept repeating the words as he hurried across the yard to the pump.

'About time!' she shouted.

'What's up?'

'The bloody pump's dry.'

'All right, leave it to me. I'll see to it, May. I'll do it.'
He spoke in a half-frightened voice, apologetically. 'All
right, May, I'll do it. Leave it to me.'

'I tell y' it's dry!'

'All right, all right. I knowed it were running low.'

'But I wanna git washed!'

'All right, May, all right.'

He stood by the pump, tiptoed and looked down the shaft.
'If we could git some water down it'd suck up,' he said.

'Well, git some, then, git some. Quick.'

'Ain't no water near 'n Red Link,' he said.

'Christ.' She stood furious, clicking her tongue madly.
'And we wanna go out.' Then suddenly she seized the
bucket. 'Christ. Give us the damn bucket. Come here.
I'll wash in milk.'

She took the bucket, and turned, and started to run
back into the house. And turning, she saw me.

At once a miracle happened. By that time I was standing
only seven or eight yards away from her, in a direct line
between her and the house, so that she had to come past me.
And seeing me standing there, looking at her, she was
transformed. She shook back her hair with a gesture of
almost timid quickness, a sudden and quite absurd act of
modesty, as though she were scared at the sight of me. Then
she put her free arm flat across her breasts so as to cover
them. Then she set her lips straight and drew in her breath
and held herself almost primly. And she was looking at the
ground until the moment of going past me.

She looked up for a fraction of a second as she went past.
And she spoke.

'Good afternoon.' It was a soft, ladylike, quite genteel
'Good afternoon', and the voice was so unlike the voice that
had bawled across the yard that I was too astonished to
speak. And she went on into the house.

The man was working the pump-handle in a series of quick
motions, trying to suck up the water, as I reached him.

166

But the sinker was still sucking dry and he gave it up when
he saw me come.

'That's about the last on it,' he said. 'We're praying for
rain.'

Then he remembered:

'Oh!' he said, 'she says it's all right. She'll put you up.'

For a moment I didn't say anything. I was tired, but I
hadn't asked if they could put me up. Then I tried speaking
very quietly, with my face half turned away.

'I asked about a drink,' I said.

The man gave no answer. Then I remembered that I
must have been ten or twelve yards from him when I first
spoke. And looking at his face I saw that it was a deaf face:
it had the soft, touching, half-stupid look of quiet vacancy
that the faces of the deaf have. It was responsible for the look
of blank fear and the sweet mild expression in the dark eyes.
It explained why he had come so slowly in answer to the
girl and why he had misunderstood me.

And when I spoke again I raised my voice a little:

'All right,' I said. 'Thank you.'

'She's gitten the room ready now.'

'All right. But can I have a drink?'

'Ain't no water,' he said, 'only milk. You don't fancy that,
I expect?'

'Anything,' I said.

'I'll git it.'

He began to walk across the yard. Looking after him, I
saw something white moving at one of the bedroom windows.
It was a girl: not the girl I had already seen, but another.
She was combing her hair and watching me: combing the
hair straight through, then tossing it back and then looking
at the comb, all the time pretending she did not see me.
Then she vanished behind the curtain, abruptly, as though
she had been pulled there. And in her place I could see a
woman: a big florid woman, like an older and fatter replica
of the girl I had already seen. She took one look at me and
vanished.

Before I could see who appeared in her place the man was
calling from the door:

'I never thought. Come in. I never thought about you
standing out there in the sun.'

I followed him into the house, through the front door and
along the red-brick passage. The white and grey splashes of
hen-dung became mixed with bluish-white splashes of milk
as I went farther into the house, the trail following the bend
of the passage, and finally at the foot of the stairs a great star-
splash of milk lay on the bricks.

Just beyond the stairs the man stopped, his hand on a
door-knob. 'You make y'self at home in here,' he said.
'She'll be down in a minute.'

He opened the door and I just had time to see a deal
table covered with dirty dinner crocks before the man
hastily shut it again.

'Huh!' he said.

He walked across the passage at once and opened another
door. They were old-fashioned varnished doors, with comb-
grained patterns and knots of sepia and gold. And for a
moment, when the man pushed it, the second door stuck, as
though the varnish had liquefied in the heat. Then it opened
all of a sudden. And the man burst in.

'Better come in here,' he said.

Going in, I met the stale summer odour of the shut-up
room coming out with a rush. It was stifling. Half-stupefied
flies were crawling up the closed windows and on the
varnished wall-paper and the oil-smoked ceiling and the pier-
glass standing on the green plush-draped mantelpiece.

'She'll be down in a minute,' the man said. The words
were like a chant of reassurance. I put my rucksack down
on the oil-clothed floor. 'All right,' I said again, but he
left the room hurriedly, without having heard. When he
had gone I sat down and stared at the gramophone.

I could not help staring at it. Standing in the centre of
the table, surrounded by black piles of records, its horn was
like some great yawning ship's ventilator in blue and gold.
Looking at it, I wondered and waited. Nobody came.
Then I listened; and I could hear the clatter of crockery and
then the bump of feet in the rooms above. Every now and
then the bumps would increase, shaking the glass in the

brass oil-lamp hanging from the ceiling. But still nobody came. And the room was intolerable. I began to separate the stale odours: odours of sunstale air and sour milk and hens and then the softer odours of stale cigarette smoke and women's scent and women's clothes. At last I got up and walked round the room, looking at the cheap pictures on the walls and the tea-caddies on the cheap sideboard, all the stale paraphernalia of the farm-house front-room, seeing nothing to interest me until I came back to the gramophone and the pier-glass again.

Then I saw that the pier-glass frame was filled with all sorts of gilded and silver-lettered cards of invitation, stuck one above another: 'The Committee of the Oakwood Tennis Club request the pleasure of the company of Mrs. and Miss Rita and Miss May Thompson, at a Dance'; 'Lord and Lady St. John of Dean request the pleasure of the company of Mrs. and Miss Rita and Miss May Thompson, at the Servants' Ball'; 'Mrs. and Miss Rita and Miss May Thompson are cordially invited to . . .'

I was still reading the cards when the bumping began upstairs again. Suddenly it grew louder and nearer, and a second or two later the door opened and Mrs. Thompson came in.

'Good afternoon,' she said. 'Do please excuse me.'

It was the same ladylike, put-on voice with which the daughter had murmured her almost timid 'Good afternoon' as she hurried past me into the house. And the mother was like the daughter: the same florid body, with the big breasts, the heavy-fleshed passionate face, the black rope-thick hair. An odour of flesh and violets rushed in with her, half driving away the sun-staleness of the room. And she was dressed all in white: white shoes and stockings and a dress of white silk that stretched skin-tight over her big breasts and hips, leaving her arms bare to the shoulders. She was an imposing woman, and there was no doubt that once she had been a beauty. Now she looked like a fat white pigeon.

'That's all right,' I said.

'I'll take you up to see your room,' she said.

She opened the door and I followed her across the milk-

169

splashed passage and up the oil-clothed stairs, carrying my rucksack. Going up behind her I could see nothing but her fat white back and her tight-clothed heavy hams straining and quivering with the exertion of climbing. It was only when she turned the bend in the stairs at the top that I could see her face; and I saw then that she had the same little, soft-shaped white ears as the daughter.

A minute later we stood in the bedroom. White bed, white wash-stand, blue ivy growing on white wall-paper: it seemed all right.

'It's all right,' I said. 'But what I want most is a drink. Some tea.'

'I'll do my best,' she said. 'But the water is running out. We're praying for rain.'

I thought for a moment of asking her when she prayed for rain, and how, and how often, but she went on:

'How long will you stay?'

'I shall be away to-morrow morning,' I said. 'Early.'

'The room will be eight-and-six,' she said.

She kept fingering the silver locket-chain where it touched her breast.

'What does that include?' I said.

'Everything.'

'It's more than I wanted to pay.'

'It includes everything.'

I stood in thought. What did she mean by everything?

'It includes a good supper and a good breakfast,' she said.

'And tea?'

She hesitated. Then:

'Yes, and tea.'

'All right,' I said.

I dropped my rucksack on the floor. She still stood waiting. All the time she was the lady, speaking with that put-on aristocratic voice that nevertheless had something in it faintly hostile. And still the lady, but a little more hostile than before, she said:

'Could I ask you to pay for the room in advance?'

'It isn't usual.'

She smiled by merely pressing her lips together, so that

170

they widened a little, but without opening. All the time she kept up the ladylike fingering of the locket on her bare breast.

'I don't know you,' she said.

'You don't think I shall run off without paying?' I said.

'Oh! no. Not that.'

Then what? I said nothing. It was a deadlock. And there we stood: she the ladylike white pigeon, fingering her locket, I looking straight at her, for some reason uneasy, not speaking only because I did not know what to say.

And then the door opened. It burst open abruptly and the young daughter was in the room before either the mother or I could move.

'Rita!'

'I'm sorry, mother.'

'What do you want coming into the gentleman's room?'

'Nothing.'

'Don't be so silly. What do you want? Haven't I brought you up better than that?'

'A handkerchief.'

'Where do you keep them?'

'In the second drawer, mother.'

The mother strutted across the room to the chest of drawers and opened the second drawer. While she was finding the handkerchief I took one look at the girl. She seemed about nineteen, and as she stood there, with her bright red dress and black hair showing up against the white bedroom door, the hair curled back away from her small white ears, I thought she looked lovely. Later she would run to fat, acquire the same grossness as her sister and mother, but now she was delightful, her sallow face plump but delicate, her breasts firm and sweet as oranges, her naked arms smooth and pinky white, like barked willow. And there was a kind of sulky hauteur about her, only half-conscious, a kind of natural immobile contempt, as if to say, 'Damn you, who do you think you are? Who are you staring at?'

In another moment the mother was hustling her out of the room. 'Now you know better than that in future. Here's your handkerchief,' and so on. I could hear them going downstairs, the mother's voice purposely raised in reprimand so that I could hear it.

And the mother did not come back. I began to unpack my things, and then, all of a sudden, I heard the long ripping shriek of a car hooter. After the first long shriek there were two or three shorter jerked hoots, and then a longer one, and then the short ones again.

I went to the window and looked out. The car was standing down on the road, at the end of the cart-track. Two men were in it: one was sitting in the driving seat pressing the hooter-button, the second was standing up. He was whistling with his fingers in his mouth. The man sitting down had his hair cut with long side-linings that came low down on his cheeks. Every now and then the other would cease whistling and shout something and wave his hand. They were wearing straw-hats.

In about another minute the three women, the two daughters first, and then the mother, floundering behind, began to run across the farmyard and down the cart-track. They were dressed up to the nines, flashily, and as they ran the man on the hooter played short excited notes of encouragement. The mother, floundering behind, very soon ceased running and began to walk. She was still walking down the cart-track long after the two girls had reached the car and were sitting inside, laughing with the men at the sight of her floundering and stumbling in her white high-heeled shoes down the wheel-rough track.

Finally, the men ceased hooting and calling and began to clap her, as though she were coming in from a race. They were all hilarious and friendly by the time she reached the car, and when the car began to move down the road I could see her sitting on the knees of the man behind, laughing and giggling with her head thrown back and her mouth opened like a fat contralto.

It was strangely silent when the car had gone. The farm seemed to recapture abruptly the deadness of the hot afternoon. I could feel the silence of the house and the fields about it: a scorching August silence, without winds or birds.

I went downstairs at last to find the tea the woman had promised me.

The house was deserted. A cup and saucer and a plate had been laid on the front room table by the gramophone, but there was no teapot and no milk or sugar.

I went outside to look for Thompson. The yard was deserted too. I called once, but no one answered.

And then suddenly I saw Thompson. He was coming over the brow of the nearest field, carrying two water-buckets on a sway-tree. He began to quicken his pace a little when he saw me and he was spilling the water rapidly over his legs and boots when he came into the yard.

'Ain't y'ad no tea?' he said.

'No,' I said.

'They gone?'

I told him they must have been going as he came across the field. Hadn't he seen them? He was silent. Already he had set down the buckets by the pump; now he picked them up again and began to walk towards the house, motioning me with his head to follow him.

In the house Thompson boiled the kettle and I got some tea about half-past six. He scarcely spoke to me while he was getting the tea. Dumb embarrassment seemed to govern all his movements, and I scarcely spoke myself, partly because I could see he was troubled, partly because I was afraid always of his not hearing me.

The sunlight was going rapidly, but it was still hot and more than ever silent when I went out into the farmyard again. Thompson was still carrying water. He was filling a wooden cattle tub that stood by the kitchen door. He must have made by that time half a dozen journeys with the sway-tree, and the tub held less than a foot of water.

'If you'd got another yoke and the buckets,' I said, 'I could give you a hand.'

'You rest,' he said.

'I'm rested. I haven't come far.'

'What d'ye call far?'

'Twenty miles.'

He stared at me. I could see that he thought it a great distance, that I had come from somewhere beyond his world.

'Go on,' I said, 'let me help.'

'You couldn't manage the yoke,' he said. 'You rest.'

'I learnt to carry a sway-tree,' I said, 'when I was so little the buckets dragged along the ground.'

'Ah?'

He stood a moment longer, considering. Then he seemed to accept me.

'You take this,' he said. He set the sway-tree across the buckets. 'I'll git another.'

So we began to make the journeys across the fields together, to fetch the water. The spring came out of the hillside beyond the brow of the first fenced-in field, and the earth was so red that the water seemed, at first sight, to gush out like watery blood. But in the buckets it was wonderfully clear, like ice. We went on making the journeys for more than an hour. It was a short journey, simply past the potato patch and across the field and half-way down the hill, but it seemed long sometimes because, from first to last, Thompson never spoke a word. He just walked and stared at the sky. Then when he did speak it was to repeat himself, like someone nervous. 'How far did you say you come? How far did you say you come?' And then I would tell him again, raising my voice a little for fear he had not heard. 'Twenty miles.' And once I said, 'Twenty miles. From Langford up through Dean and Nassingham.'

'Nassingham?' he said at once. 'You come through Nassingham?'

'Yes.'

'That's where I were married,' he said. 'That's where she comes from.'

Gradually, after that, he talked a little more, but still repetitively, as though nervous of himself or me.

'What's it like now, Nassingham? What's it like? Changed, I expect. I ain't been down there for ten year. I reckon it's bigger?'

Then he would stop talking of the town, and talk of the

174

weather. At the spring or by the cattle-tub, after we had set the buckets down, we always stood for a moment and looked at the cloudless sky, a dark tawny yellowish-blue at the horizon edge. Then as we made more journeys it seemed to grow hotter and more oppressive. I could feel the sweat running in warm trickles down my back. And finally Thompson said:

'Might be some thunder about. God, we ain't had a drop for three weeks, not for three weeks.'

It was after eight o'clock before we made the last journey and the water-tub was full. I was hungry, and glad when Thompson said:

'She say anything about your supper?'

'Yes. We arranged it,' I said. But I knew that whatever supper I had he would have to get. And I went on: 'I'll have mine when you have yours. That's all right.'

'I'm going to have mine now. You sit and rest. I'll call you.'

Half an hour later we sat together in the kitchen and ate fried eggs and thick fat bacon and drank big cups of strong tea. Thompson hardly spoke and I was relieved when it was over and we went outside again.

'I got to shut the chicken up,' he said.

After we had shut the chicken house we sat outside the front-door, Thompson on a sawing-horse, I squatting on the doorstep. With the falling dusk odd owls were beginning to cry across the silent fields, the only sound in the hot air. There was no wind: the only trees, the old damson trees beyond the potatoes, drooped their scorched leaves, half-dead, in a stillness that was almost ominous. The world seemed in suspense. It seemed as if the thunder must come up with the darkness.

We sat there for a long time, keeping up a kind of vigil while the twilight thickened and deepened, our eyes fixed alternately on the sky and the darkening fields.

'It ain't been so bad as this since I bin here,' Thompson said. 'Never had to carry water afore. They reckon it were as bad nineteen-'leven, but that were a year afore I come. But I never remember it as bad.'

Once I asked him how large the farm was, and he said:

'Near enough eighty acres. Pretty near all grass. It gits a-top on me. I only got a man and a boy.'

'You've got your daughters,' I said.

That began it. It was as though the remark had touched a hidden spring in him. He almost turned on me:

'What good d'ye think they are? Eh? What good d'ye think they are?'

I couldn't answer. He answered for me.

'Nothing! Not a damn thing. *You* see how it is, don't you? Anybody can see how it is! You can see, can't you?'

'Yes.'

'You know why she put you up?'

'No.'

'That's her idea — wants to make a damn boarding-house of the place. Tennis court. Tables in th' orchard. She was a servant in a boarding-house before she married me — down in Nassingham. That's how I met her.'

'Would it pay?' I said.

'Eh? Would it what?' Then the echo of the word seemed to reach him. 'Pay? That's all she thinks about. Money, Pay. Money to throw about. And she's bringing the gals up like it too — money, tearing about, men, drink, everything. They used to be nice kids. Now look at em.'

He would go on like this for several minutes, talking in his soft husky voice, almost to himself, pouring out to me all the grievances pent up in him by time and solitude. And then suddenly he would break off, as though too exhausted and disgusted to go on, or as though he were uncertain of my confidence. After the nervous sound of his voice the silence seemed profounder than ever, the air more oppressive and hushed. Every moment it seemed that the thunder must come, but the air never stirred and the silence was never broken except by Thompson's voice going on in bitter complaint again.

'They gone off somewhere to-night. Dancing. A booze-up somewhere. I shan't see them gals till four o'clock to-morrow afternoon. They'll stop a-bed all day. What d'ye think of that? That's a nice damn thing, ain't it?'

'Why don't you do something?' I said.

He was silent. I thought for a moment that perhaps he hadn't heard me, and I repeated the words. But he still kept silent. He sat staring at the ground, in thought, dejected.

And finally when he did speak he said:

'What could I do?'

I didn't know what to say to him. What could he do?

'I tried all ways,' he said. 'She never lets me speak to 'em. I don't have to say half a word before she's down on me. As if they never belonged to me.'

So, gradually, from what he said and from what he didn't say, I began to see that somewhere there was a fundamental weakness in him: a lack of aggression, of spirit or vindictiveness, something hard to define, a little crack of gentleness running right across his nature. All his anger and bitterness was shadowy: shadowed over by his affection for the two girls. Underneath he was heart-broken. Whenever he spoke of the daughters that unconscious tenderness for them asserted itself, softening his voice and his rage.

'I told her she wanted to make street women on 'em,' he said, 'tarts, and she's done it. That's what she's done. And she's as bad. Worse. I don't know what I shall do. But one o' these days I shall do summat. I shall do summat. I waited long enough.' He was trembling.

We sat up till nearly midnight. There was no sign of rain. Long after I was in bed I was woken up by the sound of voices under the window.

'Don't be silly. You can't come up.' It was the younger daughter's voice. 'You can't.'

'Why not?'

'He's there. I told you. A boarder.'

'Boarder. Huh. Can't I come in at all? Rita! Rita!'

Then silence; and then softly again, 'Rita, Rita!' until the words changed to mere whispers and the whispers at last to silence.

In the morning it was six o'clock by the kitchen clock when I came downstairs. The kitchen door was open, but the place seemed deserted. I waited about in the kitchen for a time, but no one came, and finally I went into the front room, wondering if breakfast had been laid there for me.

There was no breakfast. Gramophone records lay strewn about the table and the room was sour. And suddenly I saw the girl, Rita, lying asleep, still in the red dress, on the sofa under the window.

I went out again and into the kitchen, and then I noticed a teapot standing on the dresser and by it a cup with dregs in it. The pot was warm, and I found myself a cup and poured out the tea and then drank it standing up, staring out of the window at the sunshine on the yard outside. The air was as hot as ever and beyond the yard the scorched fields stretched out parched and dewless, the sky beyond them as clear as glass.

Finally, when I had finished the tea I put eight-and-six on the table and went outside. The Sunday morning world seemed empty except for Thompson's hens pecking round a stack of early wheat. I waited about for a time but nothing happened, and at last I began to walk away.

Then, half-way down the cart-track, I saw Thompson. He was standing in the field across which we had journeyed with the water. He was standing on the brow of the field, quite still, staring away from me, towards the sun. I called him. 'Hi! Mister Thompson.' Nothing happened. He did not move. Then I called again. 'Thompson. Hi! Mister Thompson.' But still nothing happened. Then I realized that he could not hear me, and at last I began to walk on, slowly, turning at intervals and watching him in case he should turn too.

And when, far down the road, I turned and looked back, he was still standing there. He stood with a slight droop of the shoulders, like someone partly in dejection and partly in hope, his eyes fixed on the distance, as though he were waiting for something: for the chance of a cloud, for rain, for something altogether beyond his control and perhaps beyond his understanding.

CUT AND COME AGAIN

THE man cutting the hedge between the roadside and the field of winter wheat was quite young and slight. But he was wearing gloves: large hedger's gloves, having deep gauntlets scarred and ripped by thorns of bramble and haw, and for some reason they gave him an appearance of greater age and muscularity. The hedge, old and wild, branched high up with great trunks of ash and hawthorn dwarfed and thickened and misshapen by long confinement with each other. And the young man was laying it: half-splitting the boughs at the foot and bending them prostrate and staking them into a new order. He worked slowly, but with concentration, rather fiercely, and almost at times with anger. In the mild February air the sweat broke out on his fair skin abundantly, renewing itself as soon as he had wiped it away. He would take off his right glove repeatedly in order to wipe his face with his hand; and once he dropped it and it lay on the ground like a flat dry pancake of cow-dung. He picked it up, swore, and flapped it across his knee with exclamations of anger that were really against himself.

Then, at intervals, he stood still and looked down the road. It was almost noon, the sun was quite high, and the road, seen across the new prostrate hedge and in the quiet sunshine, would surprise him. It gave him a fresh sense of space; it was part of a new world, vanishing to a new horizon.

And he seemed to be angry even with that. He stared always as though expecting to see someone, but the road remained empty. And he would vent his anger at that emptiness on the hedge, slashing the hawthorn trunks almost clean through, hooking out the brambles viciously with the point of the bill, his quick sweat filling the wrinkles that ran across his forehead like ploughed furrows.

Then, at last, as he paused to wipe off the sweat and look down the road again, he saw someone coming. It was a young woman. He had no sooner sighted her than he was slashing the hedge again, with great deliberate blows of concentration, in an energetic pantomime of indifference.

In another moment or two the girl was quite near. He behaved as though he did not see her, as though he did not want to see her. But every now and then, furtively, with a kind of cross-glance, he would watch her. And each time she was walking as though he did not exist, looking at the wide winter fields of bare earth and corn stretching away in the sunshine.

Then he was angry again at her display of indifference. And automatically he increased his own. So that as she came nearer he kept up a pretence that she was going farther away; and she in turn walked as though she wanted to make the pretence a reality.

But suddenly he was aware of her standing there, close to him, in the grass, beyond the barricade of bushes he had thrown down. She was younger even than he was; and her gloves of thin creamy cotton, in contrast to his own, made her look still younger. She was very dark, her black hair only half-covered by her red woollen hat, her lips very small and tight, so that she seemed to be for ever biting them.

He looked up quickly, saw the basket she was carrying, and then looked away again. For a moment he did not know what to do with this pose of preoccupied indifference. He felt a fool. And then suddenly he dropped it. He muttered to her:

'Thought it looked like you.'

She did not speak. She was staring at the bushes. They formed a barricade so that she could not pass.

"I'll move 'em,' he said.

'You needn't bother yourself!'

She was already walking along the grass again, towards the gate into the field. He threw down the bill-hook, furious. Then he picked it up again and stood helpless against his sudden anger. He heard the gate click, and then the girl's feet in the dry hedge-grass. Slowly he took off his gloves, his anger evaporating, the sense of foolish embarrassment coming back again.

Then, for the first time, as the girl halted and set the basket on the ground, he looked full at her, but sullenly.

'What's the matter?' he said.

'Nothing.'

The word was like a bubble: very light and airy and careless. He broke it abruptly, almost savagely:

'I wonder you come at all.'

'I wonder.'

The sudden retaliation, quicker even than his own, silenced him. He picked up the basket, lifted the napkin, looked in, and then stared at the girl again.

'Had yourn?'

'No.'

'Better stop.'

'I don't want none.'

As he sat down, under the hedge that was still uncut, with the basket on his knees, she was looking across the wheatfield as though fascinated by some object afar off.

'Stand up there like somebody half-sharp,' he muttered.

'I can go!' she flashed.

He seemed not to hear.

'You don't want me!' she said.

'Who said so? Who said so?'

'Well . . .'

'I never said so. When did I say so? When did I say it?'

He waited for an answer; and when she said nothing it was almost a triumph for him; as though his words were irrefutable.

'You don't want *me*,' he said. 'That's what it is. That's the drift on it.'

Once again she said nothing. But now her face had lost its look of mock preoccupation, and was in pain, filled with thoughts and miseries too complex for her to express. When she did not answer again he took out the knife from the basket and then the food: the bread and cheese and onion and meat.

He sat for a moment waiting, as though for her. Then he began to eat, sullenly, staring at the food, not really tasting it. He tried to think of something to say. Then while he was still thinking she came and sat down. And they sat for a moment or two in silence, waiting for each other to speak, but as though at peace with one another, in the warm half-spring, half-winter sunshine under the shelter of the great hedge.

'Better have a mite o' summat,' he said.

'I don't want nothing.'

'All right. Be different.'

The silent antagonism renewed itself. He ate heavily. Looking up, he saw her staring at the earth, lost in reflection. And unable to tell what she was thinking, he was troubled. She looked as though she wanted to let it pass, to forget it. He wanted to thrash it out, get to the bottom of it, find the reason of it all. And he challenged her:

'We allus going on like this?'

She seemed indifferent.

'I don't know.'

'Don't you want me?'

'What do you think I married you for?'

'Ah, start that again. I thought we had all that out last night.'

They were silent again, waiting for each other to speak. He started to peel the onion, the dry sun-brown outer skin crackling like scorched paper. Then she spoke quite quietly:

'You want too much,' she said.

'Who does? Who does?' He was consumed with a fresh flame of anger. 'Prove it, prove it.'

'I don't want to prove it. It don't need to be proved. You're jealous as well.'

'That's it, you see, that's it. You say things and can't prove 'em. Jealous. My God!'

'You know you want too much. Look at last night.'

'What about last night?'

'Just because you couldn't have ——.'

'A trifle. That's all. A bloody trifle.'

'It hurt, any way.'

That silenced him; but he kept up the pose of arrogance, his mouth stubborn, as he peeled and sliced the onion.

'You know,' she said, 'we shall never get on. Not like that. Not if you don't give way, sometimes. We've only been

182

married five minutes. We shall be everlasting at logger-
heads.'

He kept his eyes lowered; they were beginning to smart,
sharply, with the juice from the onion. And he did not
speak.

'You lose your temper over nothing. Don't you? You
said it yourself.'

He was still sullen and silent, and would not look up at
her. And now the pain in his eyes was blinding, as though
he were weeping tears of vinegar. He was too proud to wipe
them, and the smarting water ran down his cheeks.

Then she saw what was the matter with him. And
suddenly she laughed. She could not help it. In an instant
he swung out his hand blindly, to hit her. She lurched and
his hand struck her shoulder, and then he could see nothing
for the pain in his eyes, the tears running down his cheeks
like a child's. Then as he sat there trying to press the smartness from his eyes with his knuckled hands he became
aware that she was crying. They were real tears, bitter and
half-suppressed, and she let them fall into her cotton gloves.
Hearing her cry, he wanted to do something, but could not.
And they sat there together for five minutes, he weeping
with the stinging false onion tears and she in reality, until
at last he spoke:

'Shall we chuck it? Afore it's too late?'

'What? How do you mean?'

'Finish. You go and live with your mother.'

He did not mean it. He felt cold and numb. And it was
a relief to speak.

'All right,' she said.

He was staggered. Did she mean it? His heart gave a
great upward pound of fear.

'All right,' he said. And then he saw the fresh opportunity
for bitterness. 'I thought that'd suit you. Damned if I
didn't.'

'Is that what you think of me?' she said.

He was sullen and silent, not wanting to commit himself.
But she insisted:

'Is it? Is it?'

'You know what I think of you,' he said.

'What do you think? What do you?' The words flowed out quickly, with her tears, and bitterly. 'Tell me what you think. Tell me.'

He sat for a moment in a state of wretched embarrassment, staring heavily, sick of himself and the argument and even the sight of the field stretching out before him, until suddenly she was overcome by extreme tenderness for him.

'You do love me?' she said, 'don't you? don't you?'

'You know I do,' he said. 'You know that.'

He stretched out one hand and embraced her and they sat in a silence of retribution; at peace with one another, not thinking, only staring at the bright green wheat and feeling the sun tenderly warm on their hands.

Until at last he knew it must be time to start again.

'I s'll ha' to get on,' he said. 'No use.'

'All right. I'll get back.'

'You needn't. Walk round the field and seek for a primrose or two.'

'No. I'll get back.'

'Have it your own way.'

Almost, but not quite, the old antagonism broke out again. But she seemed played out, too weary to accept the challenge again, and the moment passed. He picked up his gloves and she began to pack up the basket, wrapping the half-eaten food in the napkin.

'Don't storm out without your dinner again, will you? It's a long drag up here.'

'All right.'

He drew on his gloves, and the old appearance of age and muscularity returned. He seemed much less volatile in the great scarred gloves, and more sure of himself. And she in turn seemed less troubled by him.

'It's a funny old hedge,' she said.

'Ah.'

'Looks as if it could never grow up again, the way you're laying it.'

'Ah, it'll grow up. And be as bad again as ever.'

They stood talking a little longer until, without a definite parting but only 'I'll be going I think now', she went through the field-gate and began to walk along the grass by the road-side. At first the tall uncut hedge cut her off from him, and when she appeared at last he was watching her in a stillness of expectation.

She smiled at him. 'Don't be late,' she said.

'All right. So long.'

As she began to walk away he attacked the hedge as though it were the cause of all their differences, a tangible barrier that cut them off from one another. She walked slowly and he could see her stopping now and then, by the hedgerow, to look for a chance primrose. He paused at intervals, waiting for her to turn, but whenever he paused she was engrossed in walking or searching for the flowers, and finally he could see her no longer.

And even then he would cease his attack on the hedge and still look after her, unsure about it all, lost in a conflict of doubt and tenderness and some curious inexpressible pain.

WAITING ROOM

My brother and I were at the hospital early, before nine o'clock. The waiting room, a high one-windowed room painted a dark green, was empty. And for some time we sat on the bench and did nothing but stare at the opposite wall. It was the bitterest day of the winter, the bitterest day I could ever remember, the streets black rivers of ice, the sky full of the bitterness of snow which seemed as if it would never fall. The fingers of my brother's broken arm had already gone dead, blue to the nails, with the great cold. He sat with the fingers of the other tightly clasped over the dead fingers, trying to warm them. It was all right, I kept thinking, we were first, we should be away in a few minutes. In some other part of the hospital a baby was crying. The fitful sounds echoed and re-echoed down the empty corridors. Then suddenly the sound ceased. We listened for it to start again, but nothing happened. The whole place seemed empty and deserted, as though all the inmates had died in the night.

'We could pinch the radium,' I said, 'and get away with it.'

When we laughed the sound seemed sacrilegious. So we sat in silence again, waiting. All we had to do was to get an X-ray photograph of the broken arm, have the papers signed, and depart. I sat there with the papers opened ready in my hand.

For a long time nothing happened. Then we heard another sound, a sound of sawing. I glanced at my brother, who looked a little scared as he listened.

'An operation,' I said.

'Shut up,' he said. 'There's someone coming.'

A moment later the door opened and in came a woman, followed by a man. They were working-class patients, the woman very small and thin as a whippet and about forty-five, the man much older and much bigger. He was like a prize-fighter gone to pieces. His hair and his face merged into each

other, the same sickly grey colour. Both he and the woman
sat down on the seat. The woman had a sort of sparrow's
face, one of those perky colourless faces which twitter
inquisitively and without rest.

'What are you in for?' she said to us.

'X-ray,' I said.

'Some hopes,' she said. 'You'll have to wait.' She spoke
with a kind of dismal pleasure. 'Everybody has to wait.
Don't we? You!' She turned and spoke to the man. 'Don't
we have to wait?'

'Eh?' he said. He lifted his hand to his ear.

'Don't we have to wait?'

'Hm.' I could tell he didn't hear.

'He can't hear,' she said to us pleasantly. 'He's stone deaf
in one ear, and now the other one's going.' She seemed quite
pleased about it all. 'But it's his legs he comes in for.' Knowing he could not hear, she did not trouble to lower her voice.
'He's filling up.' Her little face began to light up with acute
pleasure. 'Filling up. Water.'

'What's he in for?' I said.

'Massage. Electric.' I thought it seemed a curious treatment for dropsy, but I wasn't sure and I said nothing. 'That's
what I'm in for myself,' she said.

'Are your legs filling up?' I said.

She looked at me with a kind of pitying disapproval.
'What I've got,' she said, ' 'll never be cured.'

'Oh, they'll cure you,' I said.

'Never,' she said grimly. 'I know. I've had everything.
I know what they can do.'

She was trying to recite for us a list of all the diseases that
had ever attacked her, from pneumonia with complications
to floating kidney, when I felt the old man staring at me,
trying to catch my eye. And after a moment I looked at him
and he looked back at me, neither of us making a movement
or a sign, until finally he lowered the lid of one eye.

The woman was still talking when the door opened again,
and instead of the nurse I hoped to see another man came in.
He sat down on the bench with an immense sigh, said
'Good morning' to us breathlessly, and held one hand over

his heart. He looked for a moment as if he were about to collapse. He was extraordinarily fat, with a very red, puffy, cherubic face, and he looked more than anything else like a publican who had lost his memory and had strolled in upon us by mistake.

'Christ, ain't it cold?' he said.

'Cold?' said the little woman. 'You got no business to feel cold.'

'Me? Why?'

'Your fat keeps you warm.'

'I wish it did,' he said. 'But it don't. It ain't natural.'

'It *looks* natural.'

'Well, you don't *know*. I used to be as thin as you. Thinner. I was a walking hat-stand.' And then: 'Ain't they about yet?'

'Who?'

'The nurses.'

'Internal patients first,' she said. 'Then us. We can wait.'

He was silent, catching his breath in great wheezy blowing gasps. And as though in sympathy, we all sat silent, staring at each other, sizing each other up.

And then, after a minute or two, the door opened again.

A nurse entered. I got up and held out the papers. 'I have . . .' She lifted down the receiver of the wall-telephone hanging in the corner and began to hold a conversation in a high-toned, icy voice: 'We are ready for you, doctor. Yes'. She was very tall, dressed all in white, and had a note-book in her hand. She was impersonal, a real ice-maiden, with her head high-up and a touch-me-not expression frozen on her face. Red-Face made signs to me as I stood waiting for her to cease telephonong, mute signs of comradeship and masculine sympathy. We were all listening to what she was saying, and she knew it. And knowing it, she prolonged the conversation. 'But why should I? Well, if you like. Yes. That would be nice. I will. I know. It would be lovely.' Suddenly she hung up the receiver. 'I have . . .' I began to say, but she opened the door and in a moment was gone.

'She's nobody,' the little woman said.

'You'd better tell her so,' I said.

I sat down, and then after a minute the door opened again, and in came a stubby man wearing thick spectacles and an iron and a spring on one of his boots. He sat down next to me. He sat quietly for a few moments and then began to unlace his boots.

'Going to bed?' said the little woman.

'Bed!' he said. He was speaking to us all, in a voice of bitter weariness. 'I hope to Christ I never go to bed again.'

'Oh?'

'I been in bed a year!' he half shouted.

He took out a paper and began to read it savagely, in silence. I glanced over his shoulder. It was a journal of the fried-fish trade, and in it I could see advertisements for cod and Yarmouth herrings and fish-oil and ice. It was new to me.

'Is that a good paper?' I said.

He was savagely silent.

And gradually his silence seemed to affect us all. We sat staring and waiting. Through the highest unfrosted panes of the window I could just see the sky, greyish black and full of the snow that seemed too bitterly frozen ever to fall. And we sat there in silence for a long time, nothing happening, no one coming, as though no one knew or cared we were there.

And then suddenly four nurses came in at once. They flounced in at one door, marched stiffly through the waiting-room and out at the other door, a procession of ice-maidens, going by us as though we did not exist. The last of them was very tall, the tallest girl I had ever seen, and almost the thinnest. In her stiff white nurse's uniform she looked like some great carrot-shaped icicle. When she had vanished we all burst out laughing. The fat man as he laughed quivered like a red jelly. We had scarcely recovered before the door opened again and three other nurses came through, marching in procession, white and frigid, and disappearing like the other four.

'The seven virgins,' I said.

In, a second later, came a doctor. He followed the nurses. He had a kind of lamp, like a miner's head lamp, strapped to his head. We waited for him to go and then we burst out laughing again.

'It's an operation,' said the little woman.

'It looks as if it's going to be very pleasant for him,' I said.

'It *is* pleasant,' she said. 'I've had three and . . .'

But we were all laughing like a pack of fools; and for the first time she couldn't go on.

The laughter was only silenced by the opening of the door. It opened slowly this time, and a nurse began to come in, backwards. I got up at once, almost out of habit, to say something to her, and then I saw that she was wheeling a carriage stretcher backwards, so that she could open the doors as she went. On the stretcher lay a woman between fifty-five and sixty. I thought at first that she was dead, but then I noticed that her eyes, which were the same dead grey colour as her face, were wide open and that she was looking at us as she was wheeled through. She had no expression on her face except one of blank terror. As the nurse wheeled her into the other room, the rubber tyres of the stretcher soundless on the wooden floor, she kept her eyes desperately fixed on us who sat waiting. It was as though she felt that we were the last fellow creatures she would ever see.

The nurse wheeled her through and closed the door. For a minute or two we were chastened, sitting silent, listening. I believe we all expected the woman to cry out. But nothing happened, and finally the little woman said to me:

'Now's your chance. Catch her when she comes out.'

'All right,' I said.

And I sat waiting in alert readiness, as a reporter waits to catch a public man as he comes out of a meeting. And when the door opened at last I sprang up. The nurse was flummoxed, and for the first time I succeeded in saying something.

'I have come for an X-ray,' I said. I tried to speak nicely, with consideration for her, gently. 'I have the papers.'

She took the papers and looked at them without speaking.

'I should like to be able to go as soon as possible,' I said.

'A broken arm,' she said. She spoke as though I were a

horse. 'Which arm?' She looked from one of my arms to another.

'Oh, my brother's arm,' I said.

'I see,' she said. I ceased in that moment to be as important even as a horse. She spoke to me as though I were a candlestick or a bed-pan or something she saw and handled every day of her life, her pretty pink lips thinning and widening into a half-smile of contemptuous tolerance of me.

'You will have to wait,' she said to my brother.

'We have been waiting a long time,' I said.

She went out of the room. After that we sat and waited again, the conversation giving way to periods of silence and the silence to the arrival of other patients. More and more people began to come in, so that we had to squeeze up to each other on the benches. At last a mother and her daughter arrived, the daughter wasted by some kind of paralysis of the arms and shoulders, so that she walked as though she were carrying a terrific and invisible weight across her back. Red-Face got up and gave his seat to the two women. 'How is she?' said the little woman. The mother shook her head, secretly, without speaking, and the little woman kept her eyes on the girl, as though weighing up the symptoms of an affliction she herself had not yet had the fortune to contract, but as though she had hopes about it still. Once a nurse came in and telephoned again and then went out again. Hours seemed to pass and finally we caught the fragrance of the hospital dinners, and I could tell by the angle of the icy light that it was almost noon.

I could bear it no longer. I got up, opened the door through which the patients came, and went along the corridors. After a time, meeting no one, I came back again.

'The other door,' said the little woman. 'Try the other door. They all go that way.'

I opened the other door and then stopped. The woman on the stretcher was lying in the half-darkened room, all alone. She was staring straight at me. The expression on her face had changed since I last saw her. She still had the same deathly grey colour, and her eyes still stared with desperation, but she had gone beyond terror into a kind of apathetic trance, almost childish, as though the interminable waiting had turned her mind. She stared at me without a change of that expression or a word and I stared back in return until I closed the door.

'Nobody there?' said the little woman, as I sat down.

'Nobody,' I said.

And we went on waiting.

LITTLE FISH

Every Saturday morning, Osborn, the schoolmaster, and Eric, his only son, walked down into the town to buy fish for midday dinner. The Osborns had eaten fish, some sort of fish, for this same meal on this same day for fifteen years. Osborn himself knew the calory values of cod and plaice as he knew the multiplication tables, and he believed in the value of fish almost as much as he believed in the value of himself. He was a small, perky, jumpy man, dressed in black coat and black bowler hat and white hard collar: a magpie with pince-nez. The boy too wore glasses. They were over-large for him, the lenses thick and gold-rimmed; so that his eyes had a round shiny look of magnified vacancy and fear.

'Hands out of pockets. Hands out. Hands out. Ha-nds ou-t!'

As they walked along Osborn snapped out abrupt commands, as though he were addressing an invisible class. He used a kind of verbal whip on the boy. Years of habit made him chip off the ends of his sentences, snap, clip, his lips like scissors: 'Where you're going, where you're going! Before you leap. Many more times have I to say it, many more times? Hands out, hands out.' The boy was silent, his terror of his father expressed in speechlessness. Each time he was commanded he took his hands out of his pockets, but somehow they crept back again, like fish sliding back into water. They were thin white frozen hands. He could not feel the ends of his fingers for the frost. The wind came in gusts of ice along the street, cutting and whipping up harsh storms of frozen dust from the skin of black ice on the pavements.

'Cross! Take care. Be safe than sorry.'

They crossed the street. The wind cut them crossways and the boy thrust his hands into his pockets and held himself rigid against the force of it and then remembered and took his hands out of his pockets in fear. He was carrying a yellow straw fish-basket; the wind flapped it harshly against his bare pink legs. And his father walked fast, with nipping jaunty steps, a little pompous, and the boy was always trotting behind, the bag flapping.

And finally at the fishmonger's he hung behind even further, standing on the threshold of the shop while his father went in. The open-fronted shop was an ice-house, the white fish cut out of gleaming snow. And his hands crept back into his pockets while his father catechized and snapped in the shop.

'Well, what have you got, what've you got? Anything any good? Eh?'

'Nice hake, sir.'

'Hake. Hake? What are the sprats? How much?'

Sprats were cheap and Osborn spoke as though he were saying: 'Well, the square root of forty-nine, how much, what is it, how much? Quickly, quickly. Can't wait all day!'

And as the fishmonger weighed the sprats Osborn watched him, critically, with professional superciliousness, as though he were doing an arithmetical exercise. He stood ready to pounce on the slightest mistake. The fishmonger weighed and wrapped the little fish in silence, subdued, his expression frozen up.

'Boy! Eric! Quickly, quickly. Quick-ly!'

The boy came forward with the bag, trying to open it as he came, blundering, his fingers frozen.

'Blunderbuss!'

Osborn seized the bag, snapped it sharply open like his own lips, and the fishmonger dumped in the little silvery fish. The boy stood with the bag at his side, meekly, his thick glasses reflecting the white shop and the frozen fish so that his eyes looked sightless. Then Osborn paid the bill and the boy followed him out of the shop into the street.

'Not cold?'

'A bit.'

'No business. Move. Circulation. Keep up with me.'

The boy, not speaking, tried to keep up with his father, but immediately his father seemed to walk faster, purposely. And as the boy hurried the fish bumped against his legs, bump, bump, like a lump of ice.

And suddenly his teeth chattered, involuntarily, against his will. He could not help it. And his father heard it. It seemed to startle him out of himself for a moment, into an accidental moment of humanity.

'Better get something to drink.'

Osborn stopped, looking up and down the street.

'Cross.'

They crossed, Osborn in front, the boy trotting.

And in a moment they were in the restaurant. The boy liked it. It was warm and steamy, there was a smell of tea. He sat with his elbows on the table, rubbing his hands.

'Elbows!'

The waitress arrived; and Osborn regarded her as the boy had seen him regard the infants' mistresses, as though she were a snail or something to be trodden on.

'Cocoa! For two. And hurry.'

And for a while after the waitress had gone and they sat waiting for her to return the boy kept his hands in his lap and rubbed them softly and furtively together. Then he became conscious of a steam condensing on his glasses, and he took them off and began to polish them slowly with his handkerchief. His eyes were very weak and the glasses had made sore lines of red on his cheeks and the bridge of his nose. And without his glasses the world, the restaurant, was strangely restricted and softened: a warm steamy world, vague and soothing.

He was still cleaning his glasses, holding them up to the light, squinting, when the waitress arrived with the cocoa. She set down the cups and Osborn watched her in silence until she went away.

Then all of a sudden he called her back. 'Miss!' She came, the full length of the restaurant.

'What's this, what's this?' The girl stood still, flushing. 'Well, what is it? I'm asking you.'

'It's some cocoa hasn't melted sir.'

'Take it back.'

'It'll be all right, sir. It'll melt all right. It'll ——.'

'Take it back! Change it!'

Osborn's voice was raised in command, as though he had

momentarily forgotten himself and thought the restaurant were the class-room. He half-rose from his seat and shouted. The whole restaurant listened and watched in surprise, the waitress alone moving as she walked away with the spilling cocoa. And the boy, suspended too in the act of cleaning his glasses, sat in a state of meek embarrassment. He was embarrassed for his father, and yet afraid, and he could hardly look at him. Osborn sat blinking through his pince-nez in anger, in aggressive outrage, as though he owned the restaurant. Then the boy dropped his handkerchief under the table; and stooping to pick it up, he could smell the sprats in the straw bag. In the warm restaurant the smell was faintly unpleasant. Then when he had picked up his handkerchief he put on his glasses again, blinking constantly. Osborn was trembling with impatience and outrage. His face was set in harsh domination. And the boy more than ever was afraid to speak or move. For five years he had seen his father behaving like that, glaring, snapping, terrifying everyone in spasms of half-theatrical anger of which he never questioned the justice, of which no one in fact ever questioned the justice. His father was always right. No one had ever dared to say his father was not right. He himself said so, and what his father said was axiom and proof in one.

And then as they sat there, and before the waitress had returned, the boy saw a change come over the face of his father. The anger in his face began to evaporate. It was gradually replaced by restlessness. He kept blinking across the restaurant through his pince-nez with little furtive glances of apprehension.

'Eric. Hold yourself up. Straight. And look straight across the restaurant. Do you see the man in the big grey overcoat? The big man in the corner?'

'Yes.'

'That's Mr. Wyndham. Chairman of the county education committee. Don't stare.'

The boy looked down at the table.

'He's a big man in the educational world. Sit up. Round shouldered. Round shouldered. He may come over and speak. It's very probable he may come over.'

196

The waitress brought back the cocoa. But Osborn scarcely noticed her and he began to stir the cocoa mechanically, not looking at it. He was looking instead across the restaurant, on the chance of catching the eye of the man in the big overcoat. The chairman of education was drinking tea and reading the morning paper, engrossed. The little schoolmaster watched all his movements. What was he in town for? What was in the wind? Little fears kept crossing his mind and in turn expressed themselves in his face. Ah! But what if he should come over? That would be a great honour. A great moment. Every time the big man turned over his newspaper Osborn coughed or spoke more loudly to his son. But the big man never noticed. And Osborn would go on staring and stirring his cocoa and wondering. What if he should recognize him? What if he should notice, condescend to come over?

And the boy, silently drinking his cocoa and watching his father through his polished glasses, could not help seeing the change in his father. The anger had vanished completely from his face, together with all the old domineering, perky, pompous air. His father seemed to have gone like a piece of cold toast, soft and flabby. His face was filled with an increasing and almost pathetic desire to be noticed, to attract the attention of the big man in the corner.

But time passed, and nothing happened. And gradually the boy and his father emptied their cups and it was time to go.

'Now then, cap straight. And hold yourself up. And be ready to raise your cap when we go out. Bound to notice us. Be ready to raise your cap.'

Osborn paid the waitress and the boy stood ready with the fish-bag.

'Hold the bag unobtrusively. Put it in your left hand. Left, left! And be ready to raise your cap with your right.'

Together they began to walk through the restaurant towards the door, Osborn sharply watching the big man in the corner, the boy trotting behind, and watching too. As they reached the door the big man suddenly turned over his newspaper with a great rustling, and in a moment Osborn raised his bowler hat and the boy snatched off his cap.

Unnoticed by the big man, they passed out in obsequious silence. Outside the wind whipped up little ice storms. And suddenly in a spasm of anger and disappointment Osborn began to walk very fast down the street, bobbing and jerking like a marionette, snapping at intervals for the boy to keep up with him as though he were a little dog in disgrace.

And the boy trotted along in habitual fear and obedience. His glasses were quite clear now. And every now and then he would look up at his father and blink rather sharply, in wonder, as though through the new clarity of the glasses he could see something about his father he had never seen before.

THE HOUSE WITH THE APRICOT

THE sun was setting behind me as I came over the hill, my body itching and clammy from the sweat of the long day's walking. I was looking for a place to sleep and from the crest of the hill I could see the village lying below me, half in and half out of the slanting sunlight, a drift of stone cottages fringing a thin trout stream, and a squat-towered church with a still weathercock catching the full gold of the evening light. Beyond it the hills continued again, folding and unfolding into the northern distance, yellow with corn, drab-green with sun-scorched pasture, and behind the church, high up, a binder was still working in a square of wheat, its white sails flickering like a child's windmill and the machine prattling like an old loom, the sound flat and wooden in the still air.

The road went down the hill steeply, narrow between the two grass banks which rose up sheerly, crowned on either side with woods that had been thinned a year or two before. In the open spaces left between the thin young ash-trees there were pink lakes of willow-herb as soft and delicate as drifts of early campion. All day, growing finer and richer as the hills grew higher and wilder, the flowers had been a delight. Wherever I walked there were blue multitudes of harebells, lemon drifts of rock-rose and cinquefoil, scabious which paled and darkened from place to place, butter-yellow mulleins and wild blue geraniums and always thyme in the full sweetness of its flowering.

I went down the hill and turned at the bottom to look back. Against the summer-darkness of the woods the patches of willow-herb stood out like countries on a map, territories of loveliest pink like the pink of an evening sky.

Later I walked about the village, looking for somewhere to sleep. It was one of those villages that have an inn and a public-house. At the inn the beds were full and at the public-house there were no beds, and I wandered about disconsolately, at a loss, wondering if I should go on.

At the street corner, deliberating, I stood and looked at an old stone house across the street. Over the front wall of the house grew an apricot, an old tree, beautifully and carefully trained, the branches steered and twisted strictly between the windows so that the light should not be kept out. It was a fine tree and I went across the street to look at it more closely. After looking at it a moment or two I saw something which interested me more than the tree, a card in the window, a correspondence card printed with neat letters: 'GUESTS'. It looked as though someone had been ashamed to put it there.

I opened the gate, went into the front garden and knocked at the door. There was no answer. I noticed an iron-bell-pull and I pulled it but the bell did not ring and I knocked again. There was dead silence in the house. I gave it up.

Walking away to the gate I heard a sudden voice in the house.

'Angela! Angela! Angela!'

After a brief silence, during which I went back to the door, it came again, louder:

'Angela! Don't you hear? Angela! Angela!'

It was a frightened voice, the voice of a man old and quavering. I listened. There were footsteps in the house. They too were old and afraid. They hurried fretfully away, were dead, and then seemed to return again, lighter and quicker, like the footsteps of another person.

A woman opened the door. Her hands were agitated.

'It's all right,' she said. 'It's all right.' She put her hands behind her back when she saw me looking at them.

'I thought you might have a room,' I said.

'For you? — just you alone?' she asked. She spoke quickly, in a half-whisper.

'Yes,' I said.

'All right.' She smiled softly, timidly, without opening her lips. 'Yes, it will be all right.'

She stood back from the door, opening it wider as she did so. 'Thank you,' I said. I walked into the house, and she shut the door quietly behind me, as quietly as though she were afraid of waking a sleeper.

'I will show you the room,' she said.

Out of the dark hall I followed her upstairs, slipping my knapsack from my shoulders and carrying it in my hand. With only a momentary glimpse of her face as she turned the angles in the stairs it was hard for me to say how old she was, but her body was slim and supple and though she moved always with a strange quietness, as silent as a bird on grass, her steps were light and vital. She was rather tall and straight and she was wearing a loose summer dress of light pink, the very colour of the willow-herb on the hill sides as it would be in a week or two, when the sun had bleached it. I remember it had some vague pattern of leaves and flowers on it, a little prim, and that it had faded and that its lightness contrasted vividly with the darkness of the twisting staircase. It contrasted even more with her black hair, which was brushed a little severely, so that it lay smooth and straight, showing the shape of her head beautifully. Evidently her hair was very long, for at the back it was coiled up intricately, like a nest of black snakes, and low down on her neck it grew into a mass of tiny curls like jet black tendrils. Always, as I followed her, I was trying to guess how old she could be, and it was her hair which made me think at last that she was still young, not more than thirty-three or four, ten years younger than she had looked when she opened the door to me and hid her agitated hands.

She took me finally along a landing, up another short flight of stairs and to a door which she opened without a sound. I felt her watching me as I looked at the room and touched the cool bed-sheets with my hand.

Didn't I like it? she wondered. Her voice was distant and shy.

Oh! Yes. I liked it. It was very nice. I would take it.

For how long? she wondered. It would help her if she knew.

I didn't know. It depended. Would it do if I told her in the morning?

That would do. It was only that she must get extra food if I were staying long, and to-morrow was Sunday.

In that case I would stay, I told her.

It was very nice of me. The village was so small and isolated. And she would kill a fowl if she knew I were staying. She could go and kill it now if I would excuse her. Oh, no, it was no trouble.

The window of the room overlooked the garden and I could see white bee-hives at the far end of it beyond groups of fruit-trees and stone terraces for flowers. It looked cool and restful, and as though divining my thoughts she went to the door.

There would be something ready to eat in half an hour, she told me. And would I mind — she wondered if I would mind very much taking my meals with them? There were only two of them. It would be easier. But of course if I objected.

All the time while talking to me she had seemed shy and nervous, and now she became agitated again, folding and unfolding her hands and hiding them with embarrassment, the colour rising up into her throat and flushing her face very slightly pink, no deeper than the colour of her dress.

It would be all right, I told her. And about the food itself — I wasn't particular about that either.

It was very nice of me, it was very considerate.

I didn't answer: the agitation of her hands and the flickering embarrassment of her eyes had begun to trouble me and I wanted her to go. And suddenly, after saying that she would ring the bell downstairs when supper was ready, she went, and she went so silently, without the noise of a footfall, without a breath, that I could hardly believe she had moved from outside the door, and I opened it and looked out to satisfy myself. The passage was empty.

But before I had time to shut the door again I heard her voice, below.

'It's a young man — a guest, that's all. No no. Not him at all. Nothing like Abie at all. No, I won't! In half an hour. Can't you sit still and close your eyes till then? No, no, it's not him. In a little while you'll see for yourself.'

Her voice had the same low softness as when she had spoken to me, but it had lost its accent of embarrassment and now there was something faintly peremptory in it, something firm but gentle, and at the very end it seemed tired. I shut the door.

It was a fine room she had given me. As I changed my clothes I kept looking round it in wonder — in wonder at the bed of pale old mahogany with its green silk spread and the lace on the pillow-slips, at the heavy green curtains with long tassel-ropes at the window, at the chairs and the chest-of-drawers and a writing-desk in one corner, all of mahogany and all old and beautiful. There was a strange half-sweet, half-musty smell about the room that for a long time I couldn't define. It was not until the bell rang for supper and I went downstairs and breathed it again that I knew it. It was the smell of prosperity.

Down in the hall it seemed stronger than ever. It was a rich and pungent odour that must have been flowing for countless years out of the fine wood of the long clocks and chests and chairs, the dark velvet curtains and the old silent carpets of which the house was full. It was the house of some-one who had had no need to display cards in the window that asked for guests, a house of tradition and beauty, the kind of house which a man does not throw open to strangers. It was full of the peace and sweet seclusion of prosperity. Why then the card in the window and why the agitation of the woman to please me, as though her life and livelihood depended on me and on the coming of people like me?

She met me in the hall, her hands folding and unfolding with the old agitation still.

'Supper is ready. Will you come this way?'

'I ought to tell you my name,' I began, and when I had told her she said:

'Oh! Yes, yes. And ours, Jefferson.'

A moment later she turned away hurriedly and I followed her down the hall and into the dining-room.

It was a long room, with a long mahogany dining-table that shone black in the summer dusk standing in the centre of it. Three places were laid for supper, and at one of these places, his white hands resting on the edge of the table as though he were saying a silent grace and his eyes straining at the bowl of white and purple stocks standing in the centre of the glass and silver, sat an old man. I discovered a moment later that his hands were not at rest, but were crumbling

with a kind of methodical inanity a piece of bread, crumbling
it by the tiniest movement of the tips of his forefingers into
fine white crumbs that were like bird-seed. Beyond that
infinitesimal movement of his fingers he sat as though he
were praying or asleep. He did not even lift his head at our
arrival.

But the woman was at his side immediately, shaking him
gently, insisting softly:

'You mustn't crumble your bread. No, no. You mustn't
do that.'

'Birds,' he muttered. 'You know I feed them every morning.'

'But it's evening. Now then. You mustn't.'

He caught sight of me at that moment and began to get up
out of his chair, uncertainly. As I went forward the woman
said, 'This is my father,' and he held out his hand and I took
it. Although the air was still warm and oppressive after the
long hot day his hand was bone-cold, making me start with
its almost death-coldness as I touched it.

'Good morning,' he said.

Partly from embarrassment and partly because as soon as
he had spoken the woman looked at me with that half-
desperate, half-smiling look of someone craving indulgence
or understanding for someone else, I said nothing, and the old
man slipped back into his chair, his hands fell listlessly to his
lap, and we began the meal with him sitting like that, staring
at the flowers again, the idiot-apathy of his body more painful and difficult to bear than the silence of the woman herself, who could hide her suffering of mind by silence no more
than she could hide the agitation of her hands by putting
them behind her back. I could not look at either of them
directly and all I could do was sometimes to glance at them
furtively and away again, taking in all I needed of their silent
painfulness of expression in a flicker of an eyelid. Between
those glances, which were always against my will, dragged
from me by the sheer force of silence, I stared at the food,
the reflections swimming like silver light in the black mahogany of the table. The food was delicious: veal, tender and
soft as butter, and a potato-salad, and bread that had been

made, I thought, of full-meal flour, and baked in a faggot-oven, in the old way. The food and the table were all in keeping with the luxury of the bedrooms, the staircase and hall, and after having eaten my meals under haystacks and hedgerows and in inns where they had no more imagination than tea and eggs-and-bacon from morning till night, I sat and ate in wonder, uneasy only because I could not fathom the luxury and the silence of it. And finally when I had begun to think that that silence would never be broken, the old man leaned across the table, took the earthenware water-pitcher in his bony hands, held it poised over my glass and said:

'Let me give you some wine?'

'Thank you.'

'And you, Angela?'

Slowly, with distressing, trembling slowness, he poured out the water into the three glasses, and as he poured it he seemed also to pour away his idiocy and weakness. When it was all over he sat back in his chair and gazed at me for the first time with consciousness, strength and complete intelligence. It was as though a miracle had been worked in him by the pouring of that water.

'You must have come a long way,' he said. His voice was normal, strong, unfaltering. And the change in him wrought a change in the woman too. She sat with bright eyes, her face flooded with the light of relief.

'Which way did you come?' she said. 'Over the hill, from the Roman villa?'

'Yes.'

'Then you saw some flowers?'

I told her about them, how I had followed them all day, up and up from the valleys, of the constancy of the harebells and wild scabious, which had blossomed everywhere, of the thickening of the flowers and the coming of the rock-roses as I climbed higher and higher, and finally of that hill, from which I had seen the village, with its festival of blossom on the banks of the roadside and the willow-herb thick as corn.

'Did you see the anemone, the mauve one?' said the old man. 'It's called pasque-flower by some people.'

'But not in summer, father,' said the woman. 'He wouldn't see it now. It's over long ago. That would be in the spring.'

'Yes, yes. But has he ever seen it?' He turned to me, making a cup of his frail hands. 'That shape, and pale mauve, like the scabious. Beautiful, a beautiful thing. You've seen it?'

'In gardens,' I said.

'But not wild, not wild? Up on the hills it grows so much smaller. It's so frail and so aristocratic. The Romans brought it over — they could make a dye from it. And wherever the Romans have been there's a chance that you'll find it.'

He began to talk rapidly, a little excited, but now always with control of his words and actions and with the light of understanding in his eyes, and he went on to tell me that it was the pasque-flower, the little wild mauve anemone, that he loved better than all English flowers, and how in the spring I might find it up there, on the hillsides, beyond the woods through which I had come that day.

'You must come and see us again then,' he said. 'You must come and I will take you up there.'

They were both a little excited by my love of flowers and as we sat eating the fresh raspberries and cream that the woman had fetched while the old man was talking, I excited them even more by saying that in the morning I thought of climbing the hills again and searching for rare species, for orchids perhaps and new campanulas. I asked them the way they thought I should go.

'He must go up behind the woods, mustn't he, Angela? He'll find orchids there all right,' said the old man.

'Oh, no, you're mixing it up, father. He'd find anemones there, but —' and she turned to me — 'if you want orchids you must go the other way. And campanulas too.'

She began to give me directions but I was confused, not knowing the place, and at last she saw it and said:

'If you've finished we could go out into the garden and I'd show you the roads going up the hill.'

We left the old man at the table, staring again. Out in the garden it was between light and twilight. The formal terraces of white stone rising up from the house to reach the final level of the fruit-trees stood out with strange whiteness. The scent of the day-blooming flowers, carnations and late pinks and stocks, had begun to mingle with the heavy exotic fragrance of the evening-scented things, tobacco-plants and night-scented stocks and evening primroses. We climbed the terraces. The beds were neat and formal and she told me how she had built the terraces and steps with her own hands, using the stone of an old barn that had collapsed in a blizzard. Where the barn had stood she now grew roses, in a square raised-up bed edged with a little wall of stone, all that was left of the barn and its foundations. On the highest terrace she had planted a long bed of pink and blood-coloured carnations and she wanted to take slips of them but she hardly knew how and asked me if I knew. I bent down and tore off a grey shoot and slit the stem with my pen-knife and found a pebble no larger than a grain of wheat and slipped it in the cut I had made.

That was the right way, I told her.

She laughed. And must she go searching about on her hands and knees for the tiny pebble every time?

It was the right way, I said.

Again she laughed. It might be right but she had no patience to do it. She trusted to luck. If a thing died it died, if it lived it lived. But she had no patience.

I would do it for her, I offered, in the morning, after I had been up to the hills, if she would let me.

It was very kind. She went up the last of the terrace steps hastily, as though she suddenly wanted to have done with it all.

I followed slowly, wondering, not knowing until I had caught up with her that she was embarrassed, almost frightened by what I had said. Her face was flushed, foolishly like a girl's. I said nothing and we went in under the fruit-trees, in silence, in a conscious, strained silence of common embarrassment.

At the highest point of the long garden stood a walnut tree, and reaching it she paused and looked back over the house and pointed out the road to me lying like a piece of dirty string on the opposite hills.

I was to go up there, as far as I could see the road now, and then turn off to the right, across the bare hill. In the hollow was a farm-house, where the road branched. I was to go left by the house.

As she was speaking, I picked off a walnut-leaf and crushed it in my fingers, smelling the strange walnut-sweet fragrance. She stood very straight, with one arm outstretched pointing to the hills, her head uplifted. In that moment she looked extremely young, her face very pale now in the twilight against her black hair, and her breast curving out strong and clear, as she stood so straight and lifted her arm.

Back in the house I had made up my mind about her. She cleared away the supper things and brought in the lamp and set it on the bare black table. Just as we had left him, the old man sat there, staring, back in the old mood of half-idiocy.

She brought some sewing and sat at the corner of the table, her face in the half-light, her hands in the full glow of the lamp, she herself silent and absorbed in the work. With my eyes half on her, half on her work-basket, a long beautiful basket of pale-yellow straw lined with rich green silk and with a hundred silk-lined compartments for her reels and needles and thimbles, I told myself over and over again that I knew all about her. It was so obvious, so easy to see I thought. All her life and her happiness had been tied by the old man. Without him she would have been eligible; the men would have run after her not only for the money but because she was good-looking; but no one would want the old man, the idiot, and she would simply go on living out her life until he died and all her chance for love and even her desire for it had gone. It was an old story; and what had at first seemed strange and mysterious was now just common. It was simply her destiny to sit there, sewing and waiting upon the chance guests that she took in to relieve the boredom of it, until he died, and then to sit there again, alone, until she herself died too.

She was sewing a length of lace round the collar of a dress of green velvet. It was a beautiful pale brown colour, as though dipped in coffee. I leaned forward to look at it.

Was it pillow lace? I wondered.

No, she didn't think so. She didn't know.

Had she ever seen them making it, with the pillow and the coloured bobbins?

No. She did not lift her head.

It was fascinating. She should learn to do it. I had always liked to see old women doing it.

She looked up at once, startled, a bright pin-light of pain in her eyes. Instantly I knew that I touched her, that I had drawn my finger harshly, as it were, over her heart at a tender place. She was not old, but it was the stupid unthinking inference in my words that had wounded her. After one moment of unconcealed pain her face brightened. All the time she had been a little distant with me, we had talked impersonally, but now she suddenly retreated even farther into herself. Her pain and her anger against me were too fresh and sharp to conceal, but presently they were withdrawn, leaving a blankness of silence that was worse than all reproach.

To my relief the old man stirred himself. He seemed to wake up from a sort of trance and presently he got up and went to a cabinet by the fireplace and took out an oblong box.

Putting the box on the table he asked me if I would be so kind as to play him a game of dominoes?

'It's years since I played,' I said.

'No matter. Threes and fives?'

'Just as you like.'

'And stakes? You would like to play for something?'

He had already opened the box and was fingering the dominoes. Before I could answer him I felt the woman looking at me and involuntarily I turned my head towards her. Her anger against me had vanished and she was shaking her head, beseechingly, frowning a little.

'I'll play for love,' I said.

There was something almost sinister about the glance he gave me as he began to spread out the dominoes on the table, each sharp flick of wood against wood a sound of disgust. We divided, I picked up a domino with each hand, he stretching out two thin white fingers of one hand and drawing his pieces sharply across the ice-smooth mahogany. In silence I set my dominoes in rows, making a triangle. With furtive glances at me, in which I could catch the half-sinister, half-childish glint of idiocy, he faced his own flat against the table, very slowly, as though memorizing every pip. I noticed also that he had kept the peg-board by his left hand; it was a beautiful board of some pale red wood inlaid with green and golden parallelograms and squares, and fine rings of jet about the peg-holes; the pegs themselves were of crimson and white ivory, very small and delicately carved like chessmen. He mistrusted every glance I made at him, the board and the dominoes. The quivering of his hands was pathetic.

When he saw that I had the double-nine his agitation nearly broke into tears, and cautiously, with fear, he lifted a dozen dominoes before he found the nine-blank. Having found it and played it his face broke into a strange slow smile, half-inane, half-cunning.

'I thought I remembered,' he said. 'I thought I remembered.'

All the time I could feel the woman watching us, looking up from her lace. I wondered if she also played dominoes with him and if she did how she endured, night after night, year after year, his suspicions and fears and imbecilities. I wanted to look round and catch the look in her eyes, but presently she put her work-case on the table and left the room. It was a warm, breathless night and I could hear her walking about in the garden, catching the sound of her dress as it brushed sometimes against an overdrooping bush or flower.

In a little while she came back, watched us for a moment, saw that I was losing and went away again. Then she came back and stood watching us for a moment and again retreated. She came back finally as the game was ending. I had let the old man win, and I heard her give a sigh, like someone who had waited for the passing of a crisis, as she saw him pegging himself home.

'Angela, my dear, I won! I've beaten our friend here. I've won. Angela, I've won. You see?' He was like a child.

'Yes.' She treated him like a child. 'All right. Now you must go to bed.'

'Another game, another game,' he entreated her.

'No!' She began to gather up the dominoes into stacks, as though she were counting up money, her lips tight and wintry against him and all his entreaties. She did not speak again and at last he slouched from the room like an awkward boy, muttering to himself about her.

When she had followed him I went out and walked in the garden. The warm summer half-darkness was drenched with the fragrance of evening-scented flowers, exquisite and intoxicating. It was very quiet. The sun seemed to have burnt up even the tiniest breath of air, leaving only a thick dusk of flower fragrance. The stone of the house-wall by the apricot was still warm to the touch. On the house, in the flower-beds and up in the orchard the leaves were black and motionless.

I was looking at the apricot-tree when I heard her footsteps coming. When she came round the corner of the house and saw me, she was startled. 'Oh, there you are!' There were times when her voice was girlish, with its sudden breathless timidity.

She had only come to ask me when I would like breakfast, she said. Her breath was agitated, as though she had been running to find me.

Would eight o'clock be too early for them? I wondered.

Oh, no. And would I like to have it in the garden?

It was very nice — but wasn't it a great trouble to her?

Oh, no, no. She would be up very early herself, and her father never came down till after ten.

Then I should like it very much, I said.

She stood silent, twisting her hands, more timid than ever, as though she wanted to ask me something embarrassing and difficult. But she didn't speak and at last I asked her about the apricot-tree.

It was very old, I said. Did it bear?

It had been planted, she thought, when the house had been built, in 1795. But it never bore anything. There had never been an apricot as far as she remembered.

211

I looked at the tree, up and down. It was a beautiful tree, strong and well-shaped, the thick branches making perfect candelabrum up the long wall of the house.

She watched me. It was pruned, she said. It wasn't that. It had been pruned and shaped every year she could remember.

Had it ever been root-pruned?

What was that? She didn't understand.

It was simple. It was only that the tree was making wood instead of flower-buds. There was a long tap-root which went straight down, too deep, and sucked up a richness from the earth which made the wood but not the blossom. It was the little surface-roots which mattered. The tap-root would have to be severed, so that the flow of sap would be checked, or it could be done by ringing the bark, by making a ring that did not meet by an inch or two about the trunk.

We went on talking for a long time about the tree. From the very first moment together we had talked as it were inarticulately, with a kind of distant embarrassment, impersonally. Her shyness was so conscious and painful that it was infectious. We never looked at each other. Now, in the summer darkness, we began to talk more easily. I often looked at her directly and she would return the look unquiveringly for perhaps half a minute and would let her glance flicker away again with only the faintest unsteadiness or embarrassment. Talking of the tree we grew almost intimate. She even raised her voice a little. Quite soon there were times when it sounded light and gay, the voice of a different woman. At last she broke off in the middle of a sentence, with abrupt anxiety, and looked up at the bedroom window. For a moment or two she listened acutely and then, aware of my looking and listening too, suddenly desisted.

'It's nothing,' she said in answer to my question. 'I was wondering about my father.' Her voice trembled a little with the old shyness, but she steadied it quickly. 'He's a little tiresome sometimes.' She paused, but I said nothing. 'I hope nothing annoyed you — I mean about supper or the dominoes?'

'Not at all. I enjoyed them both.'

'You saw me look at you? I mean when he wanted to play for money? I hope you understood?'

'Oh, yes.'

'And you didn't mind? You see . . .' she gave a sudden curious shrug of her shoulders, quick, a little impatient and with something bitter in its very brevity. It was a gesture at once of protest and resignation, at once stoical and cynical. It was scarcely perceptible and gone in a moment, but in it, I thought, was her whole life, the loneliness, and drabness of it, in the middle of luxury, the trial and suffering with the old man, the deadly dreariness of waiting for him to die, the bitter consciousness that it was growing more and more pointless. Like the apricot-tree, she was both rich and barren, strong and useless, and the old man, like the tap root, fed her with his riches but kept her starved of joy. A moment later the faintest smile crossed her face and vanished as quickly as the shrug of her shoulders had done. It was so secure and serene, as though she were deep in the preoccupation of some inner joy, that I began to feel that I had been mistaken about her.

In the morning she gave me my breakfast in the garden, on a patch of grass running along the highest terrace. The eggs were under a heavy silver cover and the coffee in a tall silver pot. There were little china dishes of quince jelly and white honey and lemon marmalade. It was all delicious. She had set the table full in the sunlight, so that silver and jelly and honey winked and gleamed with clean flashes of light.

As I sat down at the table she fluttered up the terrace. I could see she was nervous by the way she was folding and unfolding her hands.

Was it all right? She wanted to know. Had I got what I liked?

It was perfect, I said.

That was so nice of me. She was so glad. And had I slept well?

Very well. I didn't think I had even turned over.

She was so glad. I was sure I hadn't heard anything in the night?

Nothing. Not a sound.

Hurrying up the steps and across the lawn in the bright early sunlight she had looked tired and old and a little haggard, as though she had not slept well. As I spoke the look of relief in her face was startling. It rejuvenated her. She smiled again with that serene security which had surprised me in the half-darkness the night before. Remembering her words, 'Sometimes he is a little tiresome', I could guess at the reason for her tired face, but the smile was a mystery. It was as though something precious and comforting which she had forgotten had flashed across her mind again, startling her into joy. Without another word she went across the terrace and down the steps to the flower-beds, where I could not see her. But later I could hear the snip of her scissors at the flowers and the sound of her voice, almost girlish, singing tranquilly.

After breakfast I was walking upon the terraces, looking at her carnations, when she came up to find me, as timid as ever again, with a note in her hand.

If I were going upon the hills, she said, in the old timid voice, would I mind very much dropping in this note at the house, the farm-house she had told me about, where the road branched? There wouldn't be an answer and I needn't even wait to see anyone. I could just slip the note into the letter-box in the front door.

I took the note and promised to deliver it and before I departed she gave me a packet of sandwiches and some little yellow summering apples. I had told her that I should walk all day and not come back till evening.

'If you bring back any flowers,' she said in her calmer, natural voice, 'I'll show you how to press them and keep their natural colours.' And as I finally went off through the garden-gate she called, 'It's a lovely day for you'.

I thought there was relief in her voice and that perhaps she was glad to be rid of me. When I turned to shut the gate and say 'Good-bye' she had gone.

Down in the village and along the road winding gradually up to the hills beyond it there was a strange empty Sunday silence over everything. The earth was still fresh and sweet, though the sun was lifting up clear and hot, burning the dew away quickly except where the trees and the stone walls of the roadside threw wet shadows. In the sunlight the dewless campanulas were like little bells of blue transparent glass. The big wild geraniums were opened flat as blue pennies and the little yellow snapdragon spikes growing on the walls and in the sun-parched grass were as clear and pure as daffodils. As the road climbed up the flowers grew thicker and finer, the harebells more exquisite, their hair-stems frailer and finer and the colour of the flowers themselves changing from place to place like the blue of the sea. On the hills behind the village the willow-herb lay in vast patches, as soft as pink clouds between the dark young trees.

In a dip of the land before the hill climbed finally up I found the farm-house. I opened the iron gate and went across the deserted cow-yard. Nothing stirred.

The house itself looked empty. It was a large three-storied place of dark stone, early Victorian, with a blue slate roof and tall sash-windows set in regimental lines in the high flat walls, green with many damp-stains where the roof-spout had leaked. A strip of garden had once been laid out before the front door, but the wooden-palings had rotted and fallen and patches of nettle and sunflower had grown up and obliterated them. Rabbits had left their dung-tracks over what had once been the flower-beds and where nothing now bloomed except the rank sunflowers. The place was dead and rotten, and the silence of it alone lived on with something sinister and rotten about it also. The door had no letter-box and with the letter in my hand I hesitated. And wondering what to do I looked for the first time at the name, 'Mr. Abel Skinner', written in large, clear, candid hand-writing across the full width of the envelope. Finally I put the envelope under the door and walked away across the deserted yard and up the road again without having seen or heard a soul.

High up, on the bare sun-baked hillside, the morning was wonderful. The heat of the August sun was strong and naked, the stone walls of the cornfields already shadowless, the shadows of the trees gradually shrivelling also to black spots, the leaves above them drooped and motionless.

Half-way up the road I struck away across the bare downland, and climbed to the spine of the hill and walked westward along the ridge. Up the road, across the field, and along the crest of the hill itself, wherever I went, the harebells went with me, pure and ineffably lovely, as unstained and perfect as though it were the first morning of the world, the very beginning of flowers and light.

Below me was the farm-house and beyond it the village and farther beyond were the hills I had crossed the day before. The air was so clear and still that I could see a man, far off, walking in a half-mown oat-field with a white dog at his heels. I was watching him, feeling that he and I and the dog were alone in that vast expanse of sun-washed land when a voice hailed me, blustering:

'You know you're trespassing?'

I turned. Leaning on the field gate a man of forty-five or so, red, heavy-jawed, sullen, in dirty tweeds and a greasy felt hat, with a gun under his arm, was regarding me with exaggerated hostility, scowling, his loose red under-lip curled open, as though to frighten me. I looked at him in silence, trying to frame a reply in my mind.

'D'ye hear me?' he shouted, incensed. 'You're trespassing.'

I began to walk towards him. 'There's no law against trespassing,' I said.

'None o' your cheek!' He lifted his gun, as though to intimidate me. 'Who d'ye think you're talking to, eh? Eh?'

I didn't answer. He spat in sudden anger.

'I say who d'ye think you're talking to, eh?' he shouted. 'What the bleeding 'ell are you doing up here? Didn't you hear me say you were trespassing?'

I was angry. 'How do I know you're not trespassing yourself?' I said.

My words maddened him. I could see his temper colour his face an even darker, dirtier red as he climbed the gate and blundered across the grass, his body waddling a little on its slightly bowed legs, his long arms swinging loosely at

the knees, like an ape's. He was very tall but his shoulders
were weak and rounded, and as he came nearer I could see
his whole body trembling with a kind of nervous depravity.
He might have been drunk. His eyes, narrow and washed-
out, were servile and weak. He came towards me puffing out
his cheeks and snapping his jaw soundlessly open and shut.

We stood for a moment facing each other, I looking at
his face, he staring me up and down until at last he saw the
flowers in my hand.

'Flowers,' he sneered slowly.

'And what's that to do with you?'

'What's it to do with me?' he half shouted. 'What's it to
do with me, eh? I'll bloody well show you what's to do
with me. Any more of your bleeding cheek and I'll drop you
one! See? You clear off while your shoes are good.'

'I'll go when I'm ready.'

'You'll go when I tell you to! I own this bloody land.'

'How do I know that?'

'How do you know that? How do you know that, eh?
I'll bloody soon show you. Here, see that? Eh?' He held
out his gun. 'See that?'

He ran one finger along the breech of the gun and I saw
his name engraved in beautiful flowing letters on the steel.

'Read that!' he said. 'Abel Skinner. See? Well, that's
me.'

'Is that your house?' I pointed to the farm-house in the
hollow below us. I remembered his name on the envelope.

'My house and my land all the way up the hill. Satisfied?'

For a moment I hestiated about telling him of the note,
but finally I told him.

'Took a note?' he said. 'Took a note? Who from?'

'Miss Jefferson.'

'None o' your bloody sauce. What d'ye mean, eh?'

I began to explain, and as I was speaking a curious change
came over him. He quietened down. By degrees he concealed his anger with me. He lost his aggressiveness. But all
the time he kept looking at me uncertainly, in doubt as to
what attitude to adopt.

'Why didn't you tell me?' he muttered at last. 'Why

didn't you tell me?' His voice was half-apologetic, half-grousing.

'I put the note under the door,' I said. 'There didn't seem to be anyone about. Was that all right?'

'All right, all right,' he muttered.

'If you tell me where the footpath is I'll take it and go on.'

'Go on?' he said. 'Where you going?' It was the old half-menacing tone.

'I'm out for the day.'

'Well, you can't go on here. I don't allow it! I don't allow nobody up here. I got traps and things set. I don't want nobody interfering.'

'All right. I'll go back.'

He became half-apologetic in an instant again.

'That all right. That's all right.'

And then — 'It's bleeding hot. Drink wouldn't be in your line, would it?'

'Why not?'

'Better come down with me and have a wet at the house. You can come up again by the cart-track. It goes right along the hill there.'

I hesitated. I wanted to go straight on, alone, along the hot bare spine of the hill. He saw my hesitation.

'Too proud,' I heard him mutter.

Without a word I followed him down the hill.

We struck across the burnt grassland diagonally and climbed the fence into a field of barley and walked down the slope of the unploughed headland. Once he stopped and bent down and plucked off a barley ear and muttering something put the straw into his mouth. At the end of the headland he halted, took the straw out of his mouth, spat and remarked:

'Might cut it if the weather lasts.'

By the very tone of his voice, careless and a little cynical, I knew that he did not mean it. When I said nothing he looked at me cunningly, his mouth askew, half-smiling, and I felt that he knew that I knew. The field was a wilderness. Thistles and knapweed and great docks like sprays of burnt meadow-sweet had strangled and dwarfed the barley. The whitening stalks were thin and starved. If they were reaped the sheaves would stand no higher than a child.

He must have known what I was thinking. 'No bleeding money in corn nowadays.'

And later, as we went on, out of the barley-field and down a cart-track under a row of wych-elms: 'No bleeding money in anything.'

On a low branch of a wych-elm I saw a string of dead stoats, a few weasels, a jay or two and a line of magpies, quivering with white maggots and giving off a faint stench in the warm air.

'That's the trouble in this farm,' he said, pointing up. 'Pests. Alive with 'em. Time you're done contending with pests there's no time for nothing. The money I waste on shooting the damn things and laying traps! You wouldn't credit it. You wouldn't. You wouldn't credit it.'

Suddenly, in a spasm of anger, he stopped in the track, spat, lifted the gun to his shoulder, and blazed at the strung-up birds and animals. He shot in a frenzy of pleasure and hatred, his face flushed, his jaw working up and down with excitement. Now and then, as though he were actually killing them, he shouted up at the half-shattered carcasses: 'Go'n down, you sods; go'n down, you sods!' In the act of reloading his rifle he suddenly stopped, spat and swore with vague mutterings.

'Better leave 'em,' he said to me. 'Example — warning to the rest. Blast 'em!'

We walked on. He turned to me with sudden anger. 'And that's how it is in this farm. Fast as you slave some bleeding thing takes and puts its spoke in. I'm slaving day and night in this place, day and night, and never see nothing for it. Never see nothing for it. Never shall. Never have done.'

As he was raging we left the track through a gate and walked down the dry bare headland of the last field before the farm. Looking across the rough sun-baked acres of seeding dock and thistle and yellowing twitch I asked him if it were fallow.

'Foller?' he half-shouted. 'Foller! You'll get foller. That's winter cabbage! Winter bloody cabbage — that's what that should ha' been. And not a bleeding plant left, not a leaf!'

'Rabbits?' I said.

'You're right for once. Right for once, damn me if you ain't.'

'Why don't you wire in?' I said.

'Wire in?' he cried. 'You mean wire-netting? All round a fifteen-acre field? I should like. I should like.'

'Wouldn't it pay?'

'Pay?' he cried. 'Pay? Nothing pays on this place. If the rabbits didn't do it there'd be the flea and the caterpillar or some other damn thing. Even if I had the money to do it with it wouldn't pay. And I ain't got the money, so it's no use talking. No use talking.'

In his excitement and disgust he began to hurry and by the time we had reached the farm-yard his face was oily with sweat and his tongue was constantly licking his loose red lips. The farm-yard was still deserted and the hot sunlight pouring down on the dilapidated barns and wagons and the house itself seemed to intensify the silence and emptiness of the place.

At the front door he took a key from his pocket, snapped it in the lock and kicked the door open with his foot.

'Come in,' he said, stepping across the threshold.

'You've got your foot on the letter,' I said.

'Letter? What letter?' He looked down at his feet. 'Ah yes, yes. Damn it, damn it.' Stooping, he picked the letter up. His boot had left its dirty imprint across the handwriting. He wiped the envelope on his breeches.

'She said there was no answer,' I remarked.

In a flash he looked up at me, suspicious, and then, evidently reassured, muttered 'All right, all right. That's all right.'

A moment later I could see that he had changed again. As he invited me in for the second time his manner was subdued, apologetic, almost humble. He kept wiping the letter on his breeches, as though in contrition. He was a different man.

After the walk down the hillside in the hot sunshine the house struck damp and cool as a cellar. From the front door I followed him along the passage into a room at the back of the house. There was a damp, stale, shut-up odour about everything, an odour of rotting boards and wall-paper, of disuse and decay, with a whiff sometimes of sour milk and dung. In the room, bare-bricked like the passage, stood a dirty deal table, three or four broken chairs, a bureau littered with papers and half a candle stuck to the desk by its own crinkled grease. On the top of a great black cooking range, rusty and sour with old food-stains and patches of burnt grease where pots had boiled over, stood half a dozen black saucepans, a frying pan yellow inside with cold bacon-fat, and a big tea-pot with a rubber spout. On the hearth lay a hazel faggot and a bill-hook and a shovel of coal. The window looked on to the back farm-buildings. I could see a straw-stack and a cattle hovel, thatched with rushes, under which stood an old hay drag and a broken wagon painted blue, with the name *A. Skinner* in darker scrolled letters on the front board. Beyond the farm the hills rose up again, bare and parched in the strong sunlight.

Mr. Skinner spat into the empty fire-place of the range and then went to a cupboard in the wall by the window and opened it. He had hung his shot-gun carefully, almost reverently, on a gun-rack in the passage.

'Ah now,' he said. 'Ah now.' He licked his lips, from sheer force of habit, each time he spoke. 'Beer, cider, whisky, wine — what'd you like? What'd you like? Glass of whisky? I'm going to have a glass o' whisky.' He reached for a tumbler. 'Perhaps you'd rather have beer? Eh? I'm going to have a glass o' whisky.'

'Did you say wine?'

'Yes, anything, anything. Like a tot o' sherry? I'm going to have a glass o' whisky. You have what you like. You have what you like.'

He was already gulping down his whisky when I asked him to give me sherry. He set down his glass with a great 'Ah!' of fierce satisfaction. 'You'll have sherry? Half a minute, half a minute.' He finished his whisky, reached up to the cupboard for another tumbler, poured himself a fresh glass of whisky and then remembered the sherry and poured out that too.

'Not a tumblerful,' I said.

'Ah, go on, go on. You can drink it. Here.' He gave me the glass. 'Get that down you and come again.'

As I was sipping the sherry he seemed to remember something and after taking a hasty gulp at his whisky he went out of the room, excusing himself with his usual 'Half a minute, half a minute'. He came back with a cottage loaf in one hand and a piece of red cheese wrapped in grease-proof paper in the other. He laid the cheese and loaf on the bare table.

'I'm going to have a bite. Eh? What about you? I'm going to have a bite.'

'No, thanks.'

'Ah go on, go on. I'll find the bread knife.'

He began foraging about, looking in the table-drawer, in the top cupboard, even among the saucepans on the stove. Finally he opened the bottom doors of the cupboard. An avalanche of empty bottles was let loose and as they rolled over the floor he tried to kick them back, muttering angrily all the time. Disgusted and unable to find the bread knife he at last produced his shut-knife, a fine knife with a white lamb's-foot handle, three blades, a hoof-spike and a cork-screw, and began to slice up the bread and cheese, crudely, slashing at the loaf and chopping the cheese as though he hated the food, pushing a wedge of cheese on a doorstep of bread across the table to me at last, muttering with his mouth already full:

'Get that down you.' He strained at his bread and cheese, swallowed it, carved a second mouthful and tore at it ravenously. At frequent intervals, as he ate, he remembered his whisky and drank it like water, refilling his tumbler with one hand and gnawing cheese from the other. Taking a gulp of whisky once with his mouth still full of bread and cheese he suddenly choked and was seized by a fit of coughing, retching and hacking away until his face was muddily

purple and his eyes bloodshot and full of water. Pulling
his handkerchief out of his pocket in order to wipe his eyes
he pulled out the letter too. It fell to the floor and I bent
down and picked it up for him. Mechanically he wiped it on
his breeches.

'Better see what it says,' he muttered. 'Better see what it
says.'

He tore open the envelope, took a drink of whisky and
read the letter, sucking his wet lips soundlessly all the time.

'What time'll you be back — you know, up there?' he
asked me.

'Evening.'

'Tell her I'll come,' he said. 'That'll be all right. Tell her
I'll come. More whisky?' he inquired, the bottle poised
ready.

'Sherry,' I said. 'No, thanks.'

'Think I will.'

After pouring himself the whisky he looked at me with
unsteady watery eyes and asked:

'How d'ye get on up there? All right, eh? All right?'

'Very nicely.'

'What about the old man? Old bleeder's a nuisance.
Childish. Time he snuffed it.' He took a drink, quickly.
'Know what ruined him? Drink and gambling — turned
his mind.' He paused to eat.

'Play cards?' he asked suddenly.

'Not much.'

'Pity. Don't play at all?' A look of pathetic eagerness
came over his face; the corners of his mouth dropped.
'Might have had a game,' he said regretfully. 'Might have
had a game.' He made a final attempt at me: 'Sure you
don't play? Sure?'

I shook my head and he filled up his glass again, mournfully, and then held out the whisky bottle over mine.

'No more,' I said, holding my hand over the glass.

'Ah, come on! Come on!' he insisted heavily. He brushed
my hand unsteadily aside and proceeded to pour whisky into
the sherry, brimming the glass, spilling and slopping the
spirits over the table and my half-eaten slice of bread.

'Come on,' he kept saying, 'Come on.' And suddenly he banged down the bottle on the table and roared tremendously:

'Let 'em *all* come!'

He became seized with an extraordinary drunken vitality, waving his arms, standing up, dancing about the table, imploring me to help him stand on the table, swearing at me, shouting at me as though I were miles away, urging me to join in the words of a song which had only one verse but which never ended:

> Lift aloft! for I am coming
> In a donkey cart,
> The wheels are bent,
> The shafts are broken
> And the donkey wants to ——
> Lift aloft for I am coming!

When he grew tired of its ribald monotony he bellowed another:

> Rolling round the town
> Knocking people down!

And finally, lolling back in his chair, his eyes too thick with tears of drunkenness for him to see me across the table, he bellowed them together:

> Lift aloft! for I am coming
> Rolling round the town!
> In a donkey cart,
> Knocking people down!

'Why don' you sing?' he yelled at me.

'No piano,' I said.

'Pianer? Pianer? Who sha' no pianer? Front room!' he confided, staggering up. 'Front room. Beautiful pianer.'

He staggered out of the room into the passage and I heard him kick open a door. There were sudden tinkling discords and his thick voice above the voice of the cracked piano:

'Can you play? 'Cause I'm damned if I can. Where are you? Damn it, where are you?'

The thin discordant voice of the piano followed me
through the farm-yard and even up the hillside, dying away
at last to leave the hot noon as still as the early morning had
been before his voice had yelled at me across the hill. And
as I climbed up, skirting the barley-field to reach the sun-
scorched grass land of the hill-top at last, the harebells began
to follow me again, more and more exquisite as the hill itself
grew higher and the earth shallower and more scorched
under the August sun.

It was early evening when I came down the hill again,
by the road, the light of the dropping sun pouring horizon-
tally across the hills. In the hollow the village was already in
shadow, people were drifting up the street to church and in
the sultry evening air the parson's bell sounded sleepy and
slower than usual, as though the ringers were tired after the
heat of the day.

After I had tapped at the Jeffersons' door and no one had
answered I walked round the house into the garden.

Angela was sitting in a wicker long-chair, half-facing the
sunlight, on the highest terrace. She was alone and she was
sewing, her head bent deep over the work, but the moment
she heard me coming up the terrace steps she lifted her head
sharply and her tranquillity vanished. She began to flutter
like a bird disturbed on its nest.

So I had got back at last? She had just been wondering
about me. But wasn't I hungry? Couldn't she get something
for me?

It was all right. I would take a bath and wait till supper
was ready.

But I looked very tired. She did hope I hadn't walked all
day, in the heat, and without a hat?

As she was speaking she looked at my empty hands.

And the flowers? Hadn't I brought back a flower at all?

In the excitement I had left them at the farm-house, on
the whisky-slopped table, and I had gathered no more
except a sprig of honeysuckle which had died in my buttonhole.

They had withered, I told her.

We had fallen into the old way of speaking, impersonally,

curiously distant with one another. We had a way of looking past each other, missing each other's glances by a fine fraction, as we spoke.

Suddenly I remembered something.

I had delivered the note, I told her.

It was as if my words had suddenly ripped across the silly veil of all her hesitations and embarrassment.

'You delivered it? Oh, thank you so much,' she said. 'Oh, thank you!'

It was a new voice, clear and free at last of the old frightened restraint, untroubled by any self-conscious thought of me, and at the same instant a change came over her face, too. It became shining, almost exultant. It was the face of a young girl.

'So you found it all right?' she said, leaning forward in her chair, smiling vividly.

'Yes,' I said. 'And I saw him.' I saw her start with an almost painful tremor of joy. 'He said he would come.'

'Oh, what luck! How awfully nice of you to have brought an answer.'

'Not at all.'

'So you saw the farm?' she asked excitedly, and seeing me nod, went on at once, 'I half-hoped you would see him. And really that's why I sent you that way. The flowers are more wonderful up there. Did he say anything to you about flowers?'

Remembering his one utterance of the word itself I could only nod in reply.

'He did?' she exclaimed. 'I'm so glad. I really am delighted. He knows every flower on that hill-side — there isn't a flower he doesn't know. And he hates to see them picked. He hates it. He even hates people roaming about the field where they grow.'

'He told me that,' I said.

'That farm has been in his family for years. It's such a pity. Nowadays there is no money in corn and the grass so poor on those hills. It's so difficult to know what to do. He never had any luck. He needs fresh capital. A farm can simply eat money and show nothing for it.'

For an instant she ceased speaking, gave a half-sad, half-smiling glance at the house, and then confided in me:

'We must have patience and wait, that's all.'

I nodded in understanding and she went on talking in a voice that seemed to become more excited and girlish the longer she talked, and before I left her and went into the house to a bath and supper she had told me all about herself and Skinner and the farm. The only time her voice faltered and became embarrassed again was when she said:

'You see — well — I've known, we've known each other — we've been engaged a long time.' To make it easier she half lifted her left hand and showed me the ring on it that I in my stupidity had never noticed until that moment.

During all this I did not speak, but once or twice I smiled and nodded, as though to tell her I understood.

'Supper will be at half-past seven,' she reminded me as I went down the steps of the terrace.

When I went downstairs to the dining-room the old man was sitting in his place at the table again huddled up, crumbling his bread into crumbs like white suds on the dark table. He did not look up. Angela hearing my footsteps and obviously thinking Skinner was arriving, ran into the dining-room, her face radiant. Then, disappointed because he had not come, she began to shake the old man, excitedly impatient.

'No, no, you mustn't. You mustn't crumble your bread. Why don't you wait till we are ready? No, no!' She swept the bread crumbs off the table with one hand into the other. 'Now sit still.'

She hurried out. When she had gone the old man raised his eyes and looked at me, pathetically, his eyes imploring in their very vacancy.

A moment later there was a knock at the front door, and then a voice:

'May I come in?'

It was so unlike the voice of Skinner, the Skinner of that morning, that I was startled by Angela's voice at the dining-room door, saying:

'This is Mr. Skinner.' She was very excited, folding and

unfolding her hands and picking with absurd trembling hands at her dress. 'But of course, I forgot, you have met each other.'

'Good evening,' said Skinner.

We shook hands, and then Skinner shook hands with the old man, who half-faltered to his feet and said, in a low, penitential kind of voice, 'Good morning'.

'Good morning,' said Skinner. 'Nice morning!'

His voice and manner were extraordinary. He talked with a kind of clerical affability, half-sunny, half-jovial. He had dressed himself up in a suit of decent dark grey, with a gold watch-chain, a starched collar with butterfly-tips and white-spotted black tie pinned to his stiff shirt front with a gold horse-shoe pin. He had shaved, brushed back and oiled his hair so that it was sleekly black, and when Angela finally came in with a cold roast fowl on a large silver server and asked him to carve he took out a black spectacle-case from his inside breast-pocket and put on a pair of pince-nez before proceeding to slice up the fowl-breast into delicate white wafers. Peering over the spectacles at the fowl he looked somewhere between a nonconformist deacon and an auctioneer's clerk who drank on the quiet. All the time he behaved with a sort of respectable, restrained, Sunday-conscious cheerfulness. He carved beautifully. Once or twice he made little gestures or jokes, always beyond reproach, which made Angela titter. Finally when we were all served he took off his spectacles, laid them in the black case, tucked his serviette in his jacket and began to eat. He had carved himself a single slice off the breast.

Presently the old man stirred himself, seemed to shake off the idiot-apathy again, and reaching for the water-pitcher, said to me as on the previous evening:

'Let me give you a little wine?'

'Thank you.'

'And you, Angela?'

Trembling, he filled our glasses.

'And you?' he said to Skinner.

Skinner held out his glass. He was quite grave. Remembering the morning, I looked at him and he returned my look

with unflickering serenity, without a wink. He drank the
water in little sips, tasting it in his tongue, as though it were
actually wine, giving a long 'A-a-a-h!' of heavenly satisfaction
as he set down his glass.

Angela sat radiant and transfixed. Throughout the whole
meal her eyes never left his face and never lost that look of
abandoned adoration. Her naive intensity was almost
absurd. It was pathetic. She looked at him with the eyes of
a girl, with an adolescent earnestness and joy that had
something melancholy in it. She would have burst out crying
at a word and although she must have been nearly forty she
tittered sometimes like a school-girl into her handkerchief,
biting her lips and pressing the handkerchief hard against
her mouth to keep back the spilling laughter.

After supper when she had cleared the table and had gone
out into the kitchen the old man tottered to his feet, went to
the cabinet in the corner and brought out the dominoes and
the peg-board and spilled the dominoes on the table.

The clatter of them on the bare mahogany brought her
running from the kitchen.

'No, no!' she cried. She gathered up the dominoes with
exasperated hands. 'No! Not on Sunday. I won't have it.'
She put the peg-board with the dominoes back into the
cabinet. 'As soon as my back is turned! — really you are a
little tiresome!'

Skinner, who had been rubbing his hands expectantly
before her entry, intervened: 'It's all right. Just a bit of a
friendly, my love.'

'No, no,' she repeated. 'I won't have it. And you know
why. Let's go into the drawing-room.'

There was a piano in the drawing-room, an upright
grand of flower inlaid walnut, and after a time she sat down
at it and began playing, with her foot on the soft pedal,
Love divine, all loves excelling. She played it through twice,
swinging her shoulders backwards and forwards rhythmically
to the tune, revelling in it. After she had finished she found
a hymn-book in the piano-stool and played Bunyan's hymn
He who would valiant be and then *Oh, Love that will not let me go*.
Here and there she hummed a line and when she began to

play *Oh, Love that will not let me go* she broke into actual singing in a quavering soprano, but without articulating the words, singing only an exquisitely dreamy 'Ah!' all the time, as though she were afraid of the words. And to my astonishment Skinner began to hum the tune, with closed lips and half-closed eyes, and all through the remaining verses they sang a kind of broken duet without words, half the time out of tune, Skinner lying back in his chair with his eyes on the ceiling and she with her eyes no longer troubling about the keys or the hymn-book but fixed on him with a dreamy, passionate, foolish intensity of adoration. From that hymn they went on to others and finally I slipped out of the room as they were singing. As I went unnoticed out of the door I saw the old man staring at them with a sort of blank ferocity. It was as though he half-understood that they were waiting for him to die and hated them both for it.

When I came back again they were still singing, I did not go into the drawing-room, and upstairs in my room I could still hear their voices, but gradually there were longer pauses between the hymns, and at last silence.

I had asked to be called at six o'clock and the tap at my door woke me from a dream in which Skinner was sitting on his kitchen table, with a whisky bottle in one hand and a hymn-book in the other, singing with drunken sanctimoniousness while Angela played the piano in the front room of the farm-house:

> *Oh, Love that will not let me go*
> *In a donkey cart,*
> *I rest my weary soul in thee.*

Breakfast was laid for me in the garden, up on the terrace. At the edges of the pale-blue morning sky the dark orange rim of heat-mist was thinning and lifting: it was going to be hot. The scent of the evening flowers was still heavily sweet in the garden. The red and white tobacco-plant was still wide-open and bright.

Angela, in the pink summer frock that I liked, came up the terrace with my breakfast on a silver tray. I wanted to apologize for having left them alone without saying Good night but I did not know how to begin. She apologized to me instead. Her voice had taken on the old embarrassed tone.

She was sorry about last night — was sorry that they had been so carried away by the hymns and — she hoped I could understand how it was.

I understood, I told her.

She was so relieved.

It was nothing, I said.

When two people were — when they got carried away by something, by each other, it was so difficult to remember — to do what — to be polite.

She broke off, there was an embarrassed silence between us, and I poured out my coffee.

So I was really leaving them? she said at last.

Yes, but it had been charming, staying with them. And I hoped she would be happy.

She smiled at me in reply without a word.

And she wouldn't mind it, up there, all alone, at the farm?

She shook her head with smiling vehemence. The lonelier the better. Then they would be able to sing duets as long as they liked without fear of disturbing anybody.

We laughed together at the joke. Her laughter was full and rich with happiness.

It was a little after seven o'clock when I said 'Good-bye' to her. As she stood at the gate and shook hands with me and wished me a good journey she looked at me for one moment with shining eyes, with a radiant triumph that seemed almost too perfect. Did she know, after all, all about Skinner, and still pretend not to know? I never decided. She only waved her hand and kept smiling and waving as she watched me out of sight.

I walked through the village and up the road I had taken the previous day, skirting by the farm and taking the left-hand road to the hills. Under the trees the shadows were still wet with dew and in the sunlight the harebells glistened as though with rain. A binder stood in a half-reaped wheat-field still covered with its green tarpaulin. The farm was deserted. All across the hills there was a hush of summer and a pure brilliance of morning light.

THE PLOUGH

THE boy and the old man were ploughing the field that lay on the valley-slope. The plough was drawn by a single horse, an old bony chestnut. It was early March, but already the weather was beautiful, and it was like an April day. Great clouds of white and grey and stormy blue kept sailing in endless flocks across the bright sky from the west, into the face of the morning sun. The cloud-shadows, travelling at a great pace down the sloping field, vanished and then reappeared on the other side of the valley, racing across the brown and green of the planted and unplanted fields. There was a feeling everywhere of new light, which created in turn a feeling of new life. The light was visible even in the turned land, which lay divided into regular stripes of shadow and light at every furrow. The earth, a dark clay, turned up in long sections which shone in the sun like steel, only a little duller in tone than the ploughshare itself.

The slope of the field made ploughing awkward. It meant that whenever the plough went down the hill the man had to hold the plough-lines taut and keep up a constant backward pull on the handles; and that when the plough came up the slope he had to keep up an endless shout at the single horse and lash his back with the loosened lines in order to make him go at all.

At the end of each upward journey the man and the boy paused to wind the horse. 'Lug the guts out on him. Wind a minute.' Blowing with great gasps the horse would stand with his head down, half-broken, staring at the earth, while the man rested on the plough-handles and the boy stood and carved new spirals in an ash-stick.

The man, half-broken like the horse, would sit silent, staring at the earth or scratching his whitish hair. But the boy would talk.

'Ain't it about time we lit on a skylark's?'

'We'll light o' one. Don't whittle. It's early yet.'

Or he would bring up an old question. In other fields
he had seen men at plough with two, three and sometimes
four horses. Tremendous teams.

'Why don't we plough with more horses 'n one?'

'Ain't got no more. That's why.'

At the lower end of the field they would pause again, but
more briefly. Under the hedge, already breaking its buds,
the sun was burning.

'It's that hot,' the boy said, 'I'll ha' me jacket off.'

'Do no such thing! Only March, and stripping — you
keep it on. D'ye hear?' The old man glanced up at the vivid
spaces of sky, wonderfully blue, between the running clouds.
'Don't like it. It's too bright to last. We s'll ha' wet jackets
afore dinner.'

Like this, struggling up the hill, then resting, then half-
running down the hill and resting again, they went on
turning up the land. As the morning went on the clouds
began to grow thicker, the white clouds giving way to grey
and purple, until the distances of sky seemed to be filled
with sombre mountains. The intervals of sunshine grew less,
so that the fresh lines of yellow coltsfoot flowers, turned up
by the plough and pressed down between the furrows, no
longer withered like those turned up in the earlier day.
And very shortly it was not the shadows of clouds that ran
over the sunny fields, but patches of sunlight, brief travelling
islands of softest yellow, that ran over a land that was in
the shadow of unending clouds.

About eleven o'clock the wind freshened, quite cold, and
rain suddenly began to fall in driving streaks across the
fields. It was spring rain, sudden and bitter. In a moment
it seemed like winter again, the distant land dark and
desolate, the furrows wet and dead.

The old man and the boy half-ran across the upper headland to shelter in the bush-hovel that stood by the gate of the
field. As they stood under the hovel, listening to the rain on
the bush-roof, they heard the sound of wheels on the road
outside, and a moment later a thin long-nosed man, wearing
fawn gaiters, a check cap and a white smock, came running
into the hovel out of the rain.

He shook the rain-drops off his cap and kept saying in aristocratic tones: 'Demn it. The bladdy weather,' and the old man kept speaking of him as Milk, while the boy sat in a corner, on an old harrow, taking no part in the conversation, but only watching and listening.

A moment or two later there were footsteps outside the hovel again, and in came a second man, a roadman, a large, horse-limbed man holding a sack round his shoulders like a cape. He moved with powerful languor, regarding the milkman with extreme contempt. He seemed almost to fill the hovel and he lounged and swaggered here and there as though it were his privilege to fill it.

'The bladdy weather,' the milkman said.

'We want it,' said the big man. It was like a challenge.

'Who does?'

'We do. Joe and me. More rain, less work. Ain't that it, Joe?'

'That's it,' said the old man.

'Be demned,' Milk said. 'It hinders my work.'

'Get up earlier,' said the big man. 'Poor old Milk. All behind, like the cow's tail.'

The milkman was silent, but his face was curiously white, as though he were raging inwardly. It looked for a moment as though there must be a quarrel. And from the corner the boy watched in fascination, half hoping there would be.

Then, just as it seemed as if there would be a quarrel, the big man spoke again.

'Heard about Wag?' he said. 'Wag Thompson.'

'About Wag?' said the old man.

'He's dead.'

'Dead?' said Milk. 'Dead? I see him this morning.'

'You won't see him no more,' said the big man. 'He's dead.'

The old man stared across the field, into the rain, half-vacantly, looking as though he did not know what to say or think, as though it were too strange and sudden to believe.

'It's right,' the big man said. 'He's dead.'

'How?'

'All of a pop. Dropped down.'

234

The men were silent, staring at the rain. It was still raining very fast outside and clay-coloured pools were beginning to form in the furrows. But strangely the larks were still singing. The men could hear them above the level hiss of the rain.

'It whacks me,' the old man said. 'Strong man like Wag.'

'That's it,' Milk said. 'He was too strong. Too strong and fat.'

'Fat?' said the big man. 'No fatter'n me. Not so fat.'

'His face was too red. Too high-coloured.'

'It's a licker,' said the big man.

He took a snuff-box from his waistcoat pocket, flicked it open, and handed it first to the old man, then to Milk. In silence they took pinches of the snuff and then he took a pinch, the sweetish smell of the spilt snuff filling the hovel.

'Rare boy for snuff,' said the big man. 'Old Wag.'

'Boy. I like that,' Milk said. 'Must have been sixty.'

'Over.'

For almost the first time the old man spoke.

'Wag was sixty-five,' he said. 'We went plough together. Boys, riding the for'ardest.'

He broke off suddenly, drawn back into memory. It was still raining very fast but the men seemed to have forgotten it. It was as though they could think of nothing but the dead man.

'Ever see Wag a-fishing?' the big man said. 'Beautiful!'

'Times,' said the old man. 'He was a don hand. A masterpiece. I bin with him. Shooting too. When we were kids once we shot a pike. It lay on the top o' the water and Wag let go at it. Young pike. I can see it now.'

'And mushrooms,' Milk said. 'You'd always see him with mushrooms.'

'He could smell mushrooms. Made his living at it,' said the big man. 'That and fishing, and singing.'

'He *could* sing,' said the old man. 'Ever hear him sing *On the Boat that First took me Over?*

'I thought every minit
'We should go slap up agin it.'

235

The old man broke off, tried to remember the rest of the words, but failed, and there was silence again.

In the corner the boy listened. And gradually, in his mind, he began to form a picture of a man he had never known, and had never even seen. It was like a process of dream creation. Wag took shape in his mind slowly, but with the clarity of life. The boy began to feel attached to him. And as the image increased and deepened itself he felt as though he had known Wag, the plump, red-faced, mild-hearted man, the fisherman, the snuff-taker and the singer, all his life. It affected him profoundly. He sat in a state of wonder. Until suddenly he could bear it no longer. He burst into tears. And the men, startled by the sound of them, gazed at him with profound astonishment.

'Damned if that ain't a licker,' the big man said.

'What's up with you? What're crying for?'

'Something frit him.'

'What was it? Something fright you? What're you crying for?'

'Nothing.'

'What you think o' that? Nothing.'

'Whose boy is it?'

'Emma's. My daughter's. Here, what're you crying for?'

'Nothing.'

'He's tender-hearted. That's how kids are.'

'Here, come, dry up. We've had enough rain a'ready. Come, come.'

And gradually, after a few tears, the boy stopped crying. Looking up through the film of his tears he saw that the rain was lessening too. The storm-clouds had travelled across the valley.

Milk and the big man got up and went outside.

'Blue sky,' said Milk.

'Yes, and you better get on. Folks'll get milk for supper.'

Milk went through the gate and out into the road and a moment later the big man said 'So long' and followed him.

Patches of blue sky were drifting up and widening and flecks of sunlight were beginning to travel over the land as the man and the boy went back to the plough. In the clay-coloured pools along the furrows the reflection of the new light broke and flickered here and there into a dull silver, almost as light as the rain-washed ploughshare. The turned-up coltsfoot flowers that had withered on the ridges had begun to come up again after the rain, the earth gave up a rich fresh smell and the larks were rising higher towards the sunlight.

The man took hold of the plough handles. 'Come on, get up there, on, get up.' And the plough started forward, the horse slower and the share stiffer on the wet land.

Walking by the horse's head, on the unploughed earth, the boy had forgotten the dead man. Skylarks kept twittering up from among the coltsfoots and he kept marking the point of their rising with his eyes, thinking of nothing but the nests he might find.

But all the time the man kept his eyes on the far distance of cloud and sunlight, as though he were lost in the memory of his dead friend.

And the plough seemed almost to travel of its own accord.

JONAH AND BRUNO

SLOWLY Jonah rested his elbows on the high teacher's desk, first one and then with the same deliberation the other, tucking his white cuffs into his jacket sleeves at the same time. He looked at the class dangerously. It was the second lesson of the morning, but the windows of the class-room were north and south, so that we had no sun, a half-glass partition on the eastern side cutting us off from Miss Salt and standard five. We could see Miss Salt's iron-coloured hair, done up in a magnificent dome, if she moved across her room towards us, and in silent intervals we could hear her voice in haughty command, 'Pens *down*, fold *arms*, sit *straight!*' and the scuffle of obedience in answer. And sometimes Jonah or Miss Salt would write pencil notes to each other on the torn-out pages of exercise books and then hold them flat on the glass for each other to read, Miss Salt's neck reddening, Jonah's mouth leering up to one side under his stiff whitish moustache.

'India is the central peninsula of southern Asia.' Jonah began to articulate the words slowly and significantly, his grey eyes transfixing us. We sat still, forty of us, two to a desk, in a paralysis of attention. Jonah was about fifty, his flesh the colour of pork, a greyish white, his knuckles standing out almost like white raw bone under the drawn skin, his almost fleshless nose thin and very long, with a faint twist in it, a perpetual sneer of contempt at us. 'Extensive irrigation is practised. The crops include wheat, maize, cotton, coffee, tea, rice . . .'

'Pudden,' whispered Bruno.

'Opium poppy, spices, sugar-cane and so on. There are large tracts of jungle.' Jonah went on without a pause or change of his voice.

Bruno sat next to me, in the same narrow desk. He had hair like a lion, yellow, with tawnier streaks in it. As always, it needed cutting; it hung over his collar in fierce little curls of yellow which flopped down like a mane over his thick-skinned face whenever he bent over the desk. It was his hair that gave Bruno the untamed look as he sat sullenly listening to Jonah, his lips pouched.

'Precious metals are found in the provinces of Burma and Assam. There are mines of coal, iron, manganese ore, copper . . .'

'Nob,' Bruno said. He spoke out of the corner of his mouth, so that we could just hear. 'Copper nob.'

We sat tense, half-laughing inside ourselves, watching Jonah. There was no sign. He went on reciting, the tops of his fingers pressed together, forming a cage of bone. 'Tin and other metals. Then we come to one of the most important assets of India, its forests. Its forests — ' He paused for a moment. 'Its forests — ' He waited, spoke slightly louder. 'Its forests — ' His lips pressed themselves into the formation of a smile. 'If God had intended our friend Clarke to look out of the back of his head he would have given him eyes there.' Nobby came round like a shot, the blood in his face. Jonah relaxed his lips. 'Now that our friend Clarke is listening — its forests.' His hands slowly unformed and then formed the cage again. 'Characteristic trees are teak, sandalwood, ebony, rubber . . .'

'Soles,' Bruno whispered.

'Bamboo, deodar, and the banyan tree.' He finished speaking, made a pause. And then suddenly, like an unexpected shot:

'Did I hear you say something, Bruno?'

'Nosir.'

'It is curious, as I think I have remarked before, how my ears deceive me. I thought you spoke.'

'Nosir.'

'Curious. What are the trees of India forests, Bruno?'

'Teak, sandalwood, ebony, rubber, bamboo, deodar and the banyan tree.' Bruno spoke fast, producing the words in a mechanical strip, like a tape machine. His head was up, bold and sullen, his yellow hair flung back.

'One other tree, I think, Bruno.'

'Nosir.'

'I think so, Bruno.'

'Nosir.'

Jonah did not speak. He sat looking at Bruno, his fingers lightly caged, an expression of ironical sweetness on his face, his eyes like stone. The class, caught up in a new tension of fear and expectation, sat as still as tightened wire.

Suddenly Jonah spoke again. 'My mistake,' he sneered. Almost simultaneously he got up quickly, went to the window behind the desk and shut it.

It was the fatal sign; we knew it at once. When he turned back to us from the window the sweetish look had already vanished from Jonah's face, and the irony was also beginning to vanish, melted by a rush of anger. And now when Jonah was standing, upright, away from the desk, we realized how tall he was. He stood stiff and thin and ungiving, like a post of iron.

'I give you one more chance, Bruno,' he said dangerously. Bruno was silent.

'Very well. Stand up!'

Bruno sat motionless. His gaze had lowered a little now; it was more sullen; the tawny lion hair hung half down in his eyes.

'Stand up!'

There was no movement that Jonah could see; but underneath the desk I could see a movement of Bruno's hands, as they tightened on the seat of the desk.

An instant later Jonah was down on him. He came in long strides of fury down the gangway between the desks. His face was like bone, quite bloodless, his neck-muscles hard in anger against his come-to-Jesus collar. And now for the first time his voice was lifted:

'Will you stand up!' he shouted.

Bruno, staring now at the desk, never stirred. And suddenly Jonah seized him. He caught him at the back of the neck, by the collar of his jacket, and in one single movement of fury half-lifted him off the seat. The desk lid, caught by Bruno's body, flapped open and shut again like a shot. 'Stand up!' Jonah shouted. 'Stand up, can't you? Stand up!' I felt the desk lifting bodily at each of Jonah's shouts. By this time Bruno had locked his feet round the iron stays of the desk and his fingers were like iron clamps on the seat

240

and Jonah could not move him. The desk went up and down
with a dull clanging of wood and iron, like some stubborn
animal that Bruno was riding and trying to tame. And all
the time Bruno's hands were so clenched and his feet so
locked that Jonah could not move him. His jacket was
wrenched half-way up his back, so that I could see his shirt,
but each time he came down on the seat again, locking his
feet tighter.

Then all at once Jonah hit him. He struck him full across
one ear, knocking his head to one side like an Aunt Sally,
and then across the other, knocking his head back again.
He hit with furious frenzy, flat-handed, and Bruno, caught
unawares, half-raised his hands in terror. It was all that
Jonah wanted. In another second he had Bruno on his feet
and in another, before Bruno could make the effort to struggle
back to the desk, he struck him again.

It was a sort of half-blow. It caught Bruno on the back
of the neck and sent him staggering down the gangway and
out into the open space in the class-front, towards Jonah's
desk and the blackboard. In a second Jonah was after him.
We sat tense, in an excitement of fear and hatred. Bruno
staggered back against the teacher's desk and then out again
as Jonah came down the gangway, his hair more than ever
lion-like, flopping down into his eyes so that he had to shake
it back again. Jonah strode down between the desks and
went for him, his hand outstretched. He caught Bruno by
the hand, half-twisting it, swinging him out. The cane was
hung on a peg behind the blackboard and Bruno knew it,
so that when Jonah swung him one way he tried to swing
with a furious effort the other. But Jonah had him. He
could do nothing. Jonah kept swinging him outward and
then round and so nearer and nearer the blackboard, the
boy's face puckered with the pain of it.

And gradually Jonah fetched him round until he stood
within arm's reach of the blackboard and then of the cane
hanging on the wall behind it. He held Bruno like iron
with one hand and then whipped the cane off the wall with
the other, the spidery arm flickering up and down and then
in a flash across Bruno's shoulders.

'Now stand up! Stand up! Straight! And hold out your hand. Hold it out!'

And Bruno stood still. He was half-looking at Jonah, glancing up. We waited, tense.

'Hold out your hand! Hold it out! Hold it out.'

Slowly Bruno held it out. The cane went up. Something even more tense than our own hatred flared up in Jonah's face, an almost demoniacal look of fury. It increased as the cane quivered and began to descend.

It flamed up into frenzy, as the cane lashed down. The cane was like lightning, but Bruno's hand, whipped back, was quicker, and the cane whistled in the empty air like a whip.

Somehow Jonah controlled himself. He said nothing. He held the cane back, as to an oncoming animal. He was very quiet. There was something dangerous in it. And suddenly he seized Bruno's hand from behind his back and wrenched it out. Bruno knuckled it. Jonah held the cane high over his head and then, without warning, and with Bruno's hand still clenched, he brought down the cane with mad force, like a guillotine.

Bruno had no chance. He tried to tear back his hand, but Jonah had it and he crashed down the cane on the clenched knuckles with terrific power. And then, before Bruno could realize it, it went up and crashed down again, and then again.

It was going up for the fourth time when Bruno, half-weeping with rage and terror, kicked with all his force at Jonah's shins. It was a sickening sound. The bone seemed to ring hollow and Jonah went very white, a curious stark whiteness, with the pure sickness of rage and agony.

In another moment he dropped the cane and went for Bruno with blind madness, hitting him full across the ear with an open-hand blow that sent him staggering against the blackboard. We heard the sickening crash of Bruno's head and then the slithering of the blackboard itself as it came off the pegs and clattered on the block floor and then the rattle of the easel as Bruno pushed it back against the iron radiator like a man pushing back a crowd in a street fight.

Then Jonah hit Bruno again, and then again. Bruno was

on the ground, kicking. Jonah lugged him up and then half knocked him down again. Bruno got up with the tears pouring down his face and his breath fluttering wildly, kicking Jonah's shins again with all his might. Then Jonah seized the cane and hit him with that, across the shoulders and arms and even across the legs and wherever he could. The boy fell down again and Jonah seized him again by the coat collar and wrenched him up. Then Bruno tried the old trick, locking his arms about the iron stays of the front desk, and Jonah for a moment could not move him, until suddenly he seized hold of Bruno with both hands, front and back, and shook him, trying to break him free.

In another moment he stood straight up, with a sound of pain. We saw the blood start out on his hand where Bruno had bitten him and we saw it shaken off in little spatters of crimson as he rushed at Bruno to tear him away from the desk, seizing hold of Bruno's jacket with both hands.

Finally we heard the sound of Bruno's jacket ripping down the seam. We saw the cloth hanging loose and the dirty grey lining pouring through the rent. Bruno scrambled up wildly, in hysteria, crying in thick blubbers of hatred and terror, going for Jonah as a half-defeated boxer goes for another in a last hope of victory, punching his body with his hands.

And for a moment Jonah looked defeated. He stood with the momentary limpness of a man who half-mistrusts himself and his own rage. And while he stood there, limp, panting a little, the blood running down his hand, Bruno kicked him again.

In a moment it was all over. He suddenly descended on Bruno with the terrorizing swiftness of a new rage. Bruno seeing it, started towards the door. Jonah was after him, picking up the cane as he went, bringing it down madly on Bruno's shoulders as he struggled with the door and finally opened it, and went half-whimpering and half-wailing down the corridor beyond.

Jonah vanished in the corridor too. We were standing up in a moment, on the forms and half on the desks, gabbling with excitement.

Suddenly there was a tattoo on the partition. We stood paralysed. It was Miss Salt, with an odd scared look on her greyish face, tapping on the glass.

She stood watching over us until Jonah came back. He came into the class-room alone, his hair wild, the blood smeared now on both hands.

He took one look at us.

'Class — sit!'

We sat.

Presently Jonah too sat down. This time he did not cage his fingers and he forgot to tuck back the cuffs of his shirt into his sleeves. He was trembling. We could see the trembling slightly in his hands and hear it distinctly in his voice:

'The Hindus are the result of a mixing of Aryans and Aborigines . . .'

In the afternoon Jonah was not there after the bell had gone and Bruno's desk was empty. For a quarter of an hour Miss Salt kept watch on us through the partition door.

Finally Jonah came in. His face was whiter than we had ever seen it, almost as white as the bandage on his hand, and he seemed so preoccupied that he forgot to shut the class-room door behind him.

In another moment we saw why he had forgotten to shut it. Bruno came in.

And then, after Bruno, someone else: a soldier, a little fellow with stocky legs, a drooping yellow moustache and rather round bland eyes. He held Bruno's torn coat in his hands, and standing at the door, he spoke to Bruno as he walked to his seat.

'Y' know what I told you. If he lays half a finger on you, come and tell me.' He looked at Jonah. 'And you know what I told you as well, y'big sod!'

He went out without another word. All that afternoon and for almost another week Jonah did not even look at Bruno. And we in turn, like Bruno, could scarcely look at Jonah, and only then with fear in our hearts.

THE BATH

As we struggled with our bags up the little German road in the August heat, leaving the camp of English soldiers-of-occupation in the valley to the left of us, we were all wondering if there would be a bath at the end of the journey. And when was the end of the journey? We must have asked that question of Karl a thousand times. 'Soon,' he would say carelessly, 'soon'. But we were afraid of mentioning the bath, for at heart we all felt that we were going into some lost and legendary German world so isolated and primitive that baths would be as unknown as Englishmen.

It was beautiful country, lost and peaceful. The roadside was starred with many stiff blue chicory flowers and milk-yellow snapdragons and scarlet poppies, the flowers drifting thinly back into hedgeless crops of potatoes and ripening wheat and rye that had old pear-trees planted among them in wide lines, the lines gapped here and there where a tree had died. Along the road-side there were again lines of pear-trees, with odd apple-trees interplanted, and the same breaks where a tree had gone. Beyond the crops of corn and potatoes, the land rose gently, always a pale sand-colour, to the vineyards that gleamed a strange bluish-green in the straight sunlight. To the left was the valley with its broad river flowing between the many-coloured crops, and the English soldiers' tents grouped by the water like chance mushrooms. The road climbed continually, always farther and farther away from that river where we might have bathed and on towards the vineyards that we never quite seemed to reach.

'Where is this village, Karl? How much farther? Can't we stop and rest? Let's stop and get some beer. Karl, let's stop.'

But it made no difference to Karl. He and I walked in front, setting the pace, with chicory flowers stuck in our buttonholes, while Wayford and Thomas came behind us,

245

together, and after them the two brothers Williams. It was the Williams, the one like a little rosy pig and the other like some thin provincial photographer dressed to photograph a funeral, who wanted to rest continually. It seemed that they had once spent a week in Paris and had drunk champagne there; and now it gave them a sort of melancholy amusement to compare the boulevards with the little German road winding up to the vineyards, and the champagne with the lager. But Karl was deaf. The country was his native land, the little road with the poppies and chicory flowers had not changed since his childhood, and he was the prodigal returning after many years.

So he led us implacably on in that August heat until, very late in the afternoon, we came to his native village, a lost and beautiful place, full of old white houses with green jalousies and great courtyards shut off from the narrow shadowy streets by tall wooden doors, a forgotten place, as legendary as we had half-imagined it, lying up there between the forests and the vineyards like a village out of some old German fairy tale.

When we arrived there was great excitement, a sort of explosive excitement, all the fat German fräuleins who were Karl's sisters or aunts or cousins popping off shrieks and cackles of hysterical laughter, and the heavy German men booming thunderously in their round bellies and slapping themselves and Karl on the back in their immense joy. When we were introduced there was a great shaking of hands and a babbling of voices and a running hither and thither, together with all the pantomimic signs with hands and eyes and lips that pass between men who do not speak each other's language. And over and above it all, hysterically and incredulously:

'Karl! Karl! Karl! Karl!'

From that moment our visit became a kind of festival. Day and night there was an incessant pouring of wine and coffee in that old farmhouse with the great courtyard, a babbling arrival and departure of visitors, a cracking and frizzling of a thousand eggs over the great wood fire in the dark and lofty kitchen. We lived for three days the luxurious

and pampered life of a conquering army under the roofs of a
conquered people. In the mornings we lazed about the
courtyard in the hot sunshine, and in the afternoon walked
up to the vineyards to watch the peasants thinning and spray-
ing the vines for the last time; or we strolled off into the
forest, the breathless pine forest that shut us off from the
outer world, and then came back to photograph the peasants
cutting the patches of wheat and rye with ancient reapers
drawn by even more ancient oxen. We could go where we
liked and do what we liked and drink what we liked. We
were the English, which seemed to mean that we were the
favoured, the elect. Wherever we went in that village some
old man or woman or child or young girl would come out to
speak and laugh with us and make all the eternal pantomimic
signs of gladness and friendship. If we were tired we could
walk into the nearest house and sit there and rest; and there
would be wine and coffee, talk and laughter, and diffident
respect and a sense of quivering happiness. Everywhere there
was that feeling of relief and joy that comes between two
people who have quarrelled and are friends again, and want
only to forget their bitterness.

But there was no bath. And perhaps because of the bath,
or perhaps because the elder brother Williams had chased a
litter of pigs out of the courtyard with a broomstick, we
began to notice a subtle change of feeling towards us on the
third day.

We were still welcome; and there was still the same flow
of wine and coffee, and still the same air of great respect for
us. But now we began to sense the faintest air of suspicion,
of unrest, as though we had stayed too long. We began to
notice that the peasants would spy on us from half-curtained
windows as we walked along the streets. We noticed that the
women gossiping in two's and three's became silent as we
passed.

'Let's go to Berlin,' the Williams kept saying. 'We could
at least get a bath there. Let's get away from this hole.'

'Go,' said Karl. 'Do what you like.'

But they were reluctant. Perhaps the fare was too much?
We saw them counting their money in corners.

Then, next day, Williams the elder made a great shine over some cream at lunch.

'This isn't cream,' he whispered.

'Then what the hell is it?' said Karl.

'It's tinned milk.'

Karl sat furious, too hurt and angry to speak articulately. But at last he turned to me:

'Is it cream? You tell them. You're from the country. You tell them. Is it cream or not?'

'It's lovely cream,' I said.

'It's tinned milk!' said the elder Williams excitedly. 'Any fool can tell you that. It's tinned milk, I tell you!'

Across the table the peasants were watching the scene, suspicious. We were their guests. They must have detected the note of dissatisfaction in Williams' uplifted voice. Karl was miserable and furious.

'At least wait till we get outside!' he whispered. 'At least do that.'

The meal was finished in silence, in a silence of suspicion and unhappiness.

Afterwards, in the courtyard, it all broke out again:

'We're off to Berlin!' the Williams shouted.

'And good riddance!' shouted Karl.

'What time is there a train?'

'Find out.'

'We can't speak the language.'

'Learn it.'

They went indoors at last to pack their bags, furious. Coming downstairs again they stood in the courtyard and pored over their little red pocket dictionary in silence, anxious, but independent.

Karl, quieter now, went to them:

'You know the nearest station is four miles off?' he said.

'We can walk,' they said.

'It's a branch line.'

'We know that.'

'Hadn't you better wait? It's seventeen hours to Berlin.'

'We're going to Paris.'

Karl gave it up. Standing on the far side of the courtyard,

THE BATH

I could see the peasants standing unrestfully at doors and windows, watching the scene. They must have sensed the cause of the quarrel, that they and their food and their ways were no longer good enough for us, and the air was tense.

It was a wretched situation. Again Karl tried to make it easier:

'Wait till to-morrow. We'll all go then. We'll all go on to Berlin in the morning.'

'We're going to Paris,' said the Williams fervently.

'Wherever you're going, there's no train till four o'clock.'

They condescended to wait, sitting on their bags by the doorstep in the sunshine, so that every peasant going in or out of the house had to step over them. The atmosphere grew more tense and wretched.

Karl had vanished. But suddenly, ten minutes later, he came running back into the courtyard:

'A bath!' he was shouting. 'A bath! We can have a bath.'

The Williams tried to look uninterested.

'Schmidt, the richest farmer in the village, invites us all to his house to-night,' said Karl, 'to have a bath.'

'All of us?'

'All of us. It's a new bath. It's never been used. He's invited us over to use it for the first time. He's the only man for fifty miles round who has a bath. It's a great honour.'

We were at once excited. The mosquitoes had been devilish, the heat and sweat of the days very trying and for a long time we had ached for a bath. Moreover, the news seemed suddenly to dispel the air of suspicion created by the quarrel. Everyone began to act more freely. Only the Williams continued to sit on their suitcases in the courtyard, dismally waiting for the time when they should depart.

But at eight o'clock that evening, when we set off towards the house of Herr Schmidt, for the bath, together with all the girls and women who are Karl's sisters or aunts or cousins, and all their fat husbands or sweethearts, we noticed that the Williams were still with us. They walked a little sheepishly, behind us or apart from us, and the peasants never spoke to them.

The bath of Herr Schmidt was already a legend. Karl

249

translated for us the peasants' ecstasies, and now and then a man would stop and throw out his fat arms to indicate the size of the bath of Herr Schmidt, the colossal wonder of the countryside. Karl's sister Maria was very fat, and once her father paused and urged us to look upon her.

'So!' There was great laughter. 'So!' he said again, as though to indicate that even Maria would be lost when she sat in that bath. Even Herr Schmidt, too, would be lost. Even Herr Schmidt! There was still great laughter.

When we arrived at Herr Schimdt's house, a big farmhouse set in a spacious courtyard, just as the summer dusk was falling, Herr Schmidt himself stood in the doorway, waiting to receive us. Seeing him, we saw at once the reason for the peasants' laughter and the bath's immensity. Herr Schmidt stood on his threshold like the traditional innkeeper in a German opera, so fat that he could scarcely waddle forward to greet us, his laughter so rich and powerful that it rumbled like operatic thunder.

He was in a state of great excitement, greeting us with a thousand explosive invitations to enter the house, laughing mightily whenever he spoke, waving his arms, bowing, shaking our hands with his immense obese paws until we were pained and weary.

'Ender. Pliz go in!' he shouted delightedly. 'Ender!'

We all followed him into the house and he bowed us into the drawing-room. 'Ender. Pliz come in.' It was a great honour, a great honour. He was overwhelmed, overjoyed to have us bathe with him. He could think of no greater honour. And were we in the War? We were too young? Yes? But he, Herr Schmidt, was in the War, and was wounded. Ah! but let us not talk about it. It was all over, all finished. Let us not talk about it. 'Ender! Pliz come in. Pliz come in!'

He rushed away excitedly, excusing himself elaborately. Left in the drawing-room we all became conscious of a strange thing.

The drawing-room was like a boiler house. The heat was terrific, a thick steaming heat that had condensed on the walls and on the pictures and the old polished furniture. As we sat there the memory of the sultry summer evening outside seemed cool and delicious. And now and then we heard strange squeaks and guttural rumblings overhead and about us, like the sound of water bubbling hotly in hidden pipes, and at intervals the sound increased to a great stuttering grunt, as though the pipes must burst.

But Herr Schmidt, carrying many bottles of hock under his arms, came puffing in to reassure us. Had we heard anything? Anything we might hear was just the bath water. It was just beginning to get hot. Beginning! We sat in a mute sweat of alarm at that word. Only a little while and the water would be hot and the bath would be ready. Until then, we must have a little wine. Yes? Herr Schmidt brandished the bottles excitedly.

We were too hot to speak. Herr Schmidt uncorked the bottles loudly and poured out the pale green wine. We sat about weakly, too limp from that steamy heat to talk or move. All the time the subterranean squeaks and grumblings went on in the pipes about us, like the grunting of a litter of pigs, and each time there was some louder and more ominous growling Herr Schmidt would laugh with stentorian excitement, proud as a father at the chucklings of a new baby, drowning the sound of the boiling water with his own enormous voice.

During all this the Williams sat in silent discomfort, bathed in uneasy sweat. They never spoke, and the peasants sat apart from them, as though remembering the quarrel and its causes.

All the time the room grew hotter and the growlings in the pipes more alarming. When we felt that we could bear it no longer, Herr Schmidt rushed out of the room and back again and shouted that the bath was ready.

'Who'll go first?' said Karl.

But Herr Schmidt was not ready. First we must view the bath. It was, after all, unique, a virgin among baths, and ours were to be the first bodies to enter it. So with the peasants eyeing us enviously we all trooped out after Herr Schmidt to the bathroom.

'Ender! Pliz come in. Pliz ender!'

He bowed us into the bathroom. Inside, the heat was

infernal, and there, with an immense ten-foot stove of flowered tiles built against it, was the wonder, the virgin bath. We gazed in awe. It seemed to us that that bath could have held an elephant, or that a man might have used it with saftey as a boat on the high seas.

Herr Schmidt was almost hysterical with joy at our silent wonder. He dusted the tiniest flecks of dirt off the white porcelain and turned on the tap with a flourish, letting out a volcanic stream of hissing water that set all the pipes in the house growling ominously again.

We murmured in admiration, and Herr Schmidt thundered his laughter.

Ten minutes later I was standing in the bath, the water burning my feet like acid. We had drawn lots for the bath and I was first. But the water was so hot that I could not bear it and the water in the cold tap had grown lukewarm from the violent heat of the stove. I washed myself tenderly and got out of the bath quickly and went back to the drawing-room.

And one by one the rest took their baths and came out quickly, as though they had been through fire. It happened that the Williams had drawn the last places, and by the time they went into the bathroom the grumblings and squeakings in the pipes were already dying away.

'How was it?' we said when they appeared. They had gone in together to scrub each other down. 'Was it too hot?'

'It was beautiful,' they said.

They were radiant.

'Could you get down in it?' we asked. None of us had been able to sit in that infernal water.

'It was grand,' was all they could say. 'It was worth waiting for. It was perfect.'

They were smiling, their faces pink from the fresh warm water. And as they sat down to drink the wine that Herr Schmidt had poured out for them they seemed like different men. The bath seemed to have washed away their sulkiness and misery, their air of condescension, the memory of all their petty grievances. It was so plain in their faces that even the peasants could see it.

THE BATH

We stayed in Herr Schmidt's house all that evening. The wine and the coffee flowed endlessly again, there was good German food, and Herr Schmidt sang songs for us. We also sang songs in return and danced heavily round the room, clumping our feet, with the German women. Even the Williams danced, and all the old feeling of suspicion, and all the deeper feeling that our countries had once been enemies, vanished completely. It was as if the bath had washed them away.

We did not leave till early morning and perhaps because of the wine there seemed to be many more of us to go home than there had been to come. The night was very still and soundless; a big summer moon half-way to setting, a warm gold, in the clear and colourless sky, the corn white in the moonlight, the old pear-trees among it as still as the distant forest and the hills.

As we walked down the road we linked arms with the peasants, making a chain across the road. The girls rested their soft heads on our shoulders, and we all sang at the tops of our voices, not knowing quite what we were singing, in the common language of joy.

HARVEST MOON

THE barley-field lay white in the full moonlight, cleared of its crop except for a cluster of shocks standing like dwarf tents under an old hawthorn hedge. The cart was making its last journey. The moon, rising fast and growing whiter every moment, was turning the black mare to roan with its radiance, and the men's pitchforks to silver. For miles the land lay visible, quiet and stark, not even the shadow of a bird flickering across it and its windless silence broken only by the clack of cart-wheels in the stubble-ruts and the voices of the two children urging on and stopping the horse.

Alexander was nine and the girl, Cathy, was fourteen. The boy had the bridle in his right hand, his fingers boldly close to the mare's wet mouth. The girl, dark-haired, tall for her age and too big for her tight cotton dress, was holding the bridle also, in her left hand, though there was no need for it. Up on the cart the boy's uncle was loading the sheaves that the girl's father picked and tossed lightly up to him with a single flick of his fork. The girl, tall enough to rest her head against the mare's neck, would sometimes hold the bridle in both hands, her fingers casually stretched under the mare's silky mouth, as though by accident, to touch the boy's fingers. Impatient of it, he would snatch at the bridle, half to frighten the horse and half to frighten her into taking her hand away, and if the horse started on he would seize the chance of a swagger and would lug at the bridle and would lift his voice in manful anger:

'Whoa! damn you. Stan' still.'

'Here! What the nation you saying?' His uncle would growl the reprimand. 'By God, if your father heard that talk.'

'Stan' still,' the boy would say as though in soft correction of himself. 'Stan' still, mare, stan' still.'

Then he would walk round to the back of the cart ostensibly to see if the load were sitting right but in reality to see if his bow, made of green willow, and his arrows, made of

254

horned wheat-straws tipped with soft-pithed stems of young elder, were still where he had hidden them secretly in a slot above the cart-springs.

'Alexander,' the girl would say entreatingly as she followed him. 'Alexander.'

The boy in disgust would go back to the mare, and the girl, following, would hold the bridle again and caress the mare's nose, murmuring softly.

Suddenly, as they were loading the last of the sheaves by the hedge-side, the men shouted: 'A leveret! After it, boy! After it! A leveret!'

In the bright moonlight the leveret was clearly visible leaping across the stubble and then doubling to hide in the few remaining shocks. The boy let go the horse's bridle and a second later was hunting the young hare between the barley shocks, urged on and taunted by the men: 'After it, after it! Ah! you ain't quick enough. There it is, after it! Ah! you lost it.'

When the leveret disappeared the boy stopped, at a loss.

'It went in the last shock,' said Cathy.

She had followed him in the hunt, and now she followed him as he ran to the shock and began swishing it and beating it with his hands and rustling the sheaves in order to scare the leveret. Then when he began to unbuild the shock she also helped to throw the sheaves aside, and at last the leveret bolted again, scurrying wildly across the moonlit stubble for the hedge.

'In the ditch!' the men called. 'You'll have him. He'll skulk! You'll have him.'

Alexander, tearing across the stubble, flung himself into the ditch. He heard the soft rustle of the girl's dress slipping into the dry grass behind him, and a moment later she was beside him, panting quietly.

'You go that way,' he said.

'He went your way,' she said.

'Listen!' he whispered. 'Listen!'

In the ditch there was the faintest rustling. They lay still together, the girl touching him.

'Behind you!' he shouted. 'Behind you!'

Springing up, he scrambled past the girl and ran back up the ditch, kicking the dry grasses with both feet as he ran. There was a mad scuttling as the leveret broke loose again, and struggled among the dead thorn stumps of the hedge to make its wild escape into the field beyond. Flinging himself down in a last attempt to catch it, Alexander lay deep among the dry grasses in an attitude of listening and watching. There was no sound except the girl's breathing as she too lay listening. But in the blaze of the moonlight the stubble, seen from the ditch, seemed like a vast white plain with the barley-sheaves like an encampment of tents upon it and the loaded cart like a covered wagon being unhitched for the night.

The girl had crept along the ditch to lie beside him and for the first time he was glad that she was so near.

'We're Indians,' he whispered.

Without speaking she lay very close to him and put one hand across his shoulders, but he was so absorbed in watching the plain, the tents and the wagon in the moonlight that he was hardly aware of it.

'Don't move,' he said. 'They mustn't see us. Don't move.'

'Let's stay here,' she said.

'Be quiet! They'll hear us.'

They lay very quiet and motionless together, watching and listening, the girl so chose to him that her long hair touched his face and her soft stockinged legs his own. He felt a fine intensity of excitement, as though he were really an Indian stalking the white tents of a strange enemy. The girl, too, seemed to be excited and before long he could feel her trembling.

'You're frightened,' he accused her softly.

'A bit,' she said.

Rustling her hand in the grass she found one of his and held it. Her fingers were hot and quivering.

'Alexander,' she began.

But at that moment he became aware of a calamity. He, an Indian, had left his bow and arrows in their secret hiding-place by the cartsprings; and since the men were his enemies and the barley-sheaves the enemy tents he must recover them. Without heeding the girl, except to silence her with a soft 'sssh!' he squirmed up from the ditch and began to draw himself along the sun-baked stubble towards the cart, scratching his bare flesh on the stubble and thistles and the harsh dockstems without heeding the pain. Now and then he would squirm and swerve in his course and slip snaking back into the ditch, the girl following him all the time as surely as though she were obeying his commands. Out on the stubble, in the radiance of the high moon, the faces of the two men loading the last sheaves were as clear as though it were a midsummer day. Whenever the cart and the men halted, the field was hushed and the boy lay motionless in these silent pauses, not even breathing.

At last only two shocks remained to be loaded, and the boy, unseen, had crept level with the cart, with the girl close behind him. In another moment, as soon as the sheaves had been loaded and the cart was going up the field, he would break from hiding and capture the bow and arrows and the wagon and be triumphant.

'Alexander,' the girl entreated in a loud whisper. Her hand was trembling more than ever as she touched him and her face was so warm and soft as she pressed it to his that he felt impatient and embarrassed.

'We're Indians,' he reminded her savagely.

'I don't want to be an Indian,' she said.

He silenced her with a whisper of abrupt scorn. He was an Indian, a man, powerful. Why couldn't she keep quiet? Why was she trembling all the time?

'You're only a squaw,' he said. 'Keep quiet.'

With that devastating flash of scorn he dismissed her and in another moment forgot her. Out on the prairie, in the moonlight, his enemies had taken up their tents. It was the critical moment. He crouched on his toes and on one knee, like a runner. He saw the load-rope tossed high and wriggle like a stricken snake above the cart in the moonlight. Then he heard the tinkle of hooks as the rope was fastened and the men's repeated 'Get up, get up' to the horse and at last the clack of wheels as the cart moved off across the empty field.

It was his moment. 'Alexander,' the girl was saying. 'Don't let's be Indians.' Her hand was softly warm and quivering on his neck and she was leaning her face to his as though to be kissed.

He shook her off with a gesture and a growl of impatience. A moment later he was fleeing across the stubble at a stooping run, an Indian. The two men, his enemies, were walking by the mare's head, oblivious of him. But he hardly heeded them and he forgot the girl in his excitement at reaching the cart and finding his bow and arrows in the secrecy of its black shadow.

He rested his arrow on his bow-string in readiness to shoot. Then he had another thought. The load, being the last, was only half a load. He would climb up and lie there, on top of it, invincible and unseen.

Tucking his arrows in his shirt and holding his bow in his teeth and catching the load-rope, he pulled himself up, the barley-stubs jabbing and scratching at his face, and in a second or two he lay triumphant on the white sheaves in the white moonlight.

Fixing an arrow again, he looked back down the field. Cathy was walking up the stubble, ten yards behind the cart. He had forgotten her. And now, with his face pressed close over a sheaf edge, he called to her in a whisper, an Indian whisper, of excited entreaty:

'Come on, come on!'

But she walked as though she saw neither him nor the cart, her face tense with distant pride.

'Come on,' he insisted. 'You're my squaw. Come on.'

But now she was rustling her feet in the stubble and staring down at them with intent indifference. Why did she look like that? What was the matter with her? He called again, 'Cathy, Cathy, come on.' Couldn't she hear him? 'It's grand up here,' he called softly. 'It's grand. Come on.'

In the bright moonlight he could see the set stillnesss of proud indifference on her face grow more intense. He couldn't understand it. He thought again that perhaps she couldn't hear. And he gave one more whisper of entreaty and then, half-lying on his back, shot a straw arrow in the air towards her, hoping it would curve short and drop at her feet and make her understand.

Sitting up, he saw the arrow, pale yellow, dropping towards the girl in the moonlight. It fell very near her, but she neither looked nor paused and the look of injury and pride on her face seemed to have turned to anger.

He lay back on the sheaves, his body flat and his head in a rough sweet nest of barley-ears. Pulling the bow hard he shot an arrow straight into the moonlight, and then another and another, watching them soar and curve and fall like lightless rockets.

At last he lay and listened. Nothing had happened. There was no sound. He listened for the girl, but she did not come. He gave it up. It was beyond him. And almost arrogantly he freed another arrow into the sky and watched and listened for its fall, shrugging his shoulders a little when nothing happened. In another moment, forgetting the girl and half-forgetting he was an Indian, he lay back in the fragrant barley with a sense of great elation, very happy.

Far above him the sky seemed to be travelling backwards into space and the moon was so bright that it outshone the stars.

THE PINK CART

Across the stubble rain was spitting in the wind from the north-east, thin and icy, the drops hissing in the hot white ashes of the bush-fires we had been feeding since morning. The afternoon was darkening early and we were raking the last half-burnt twigs of haw and blackberry together. The black fire-dried twigs would spurtle up with little running yellow flames with a sound like the hiss of the rain spitting on the hot ashes, and the smoke, bluish-white, would soar up in quick spirals and dart away and poise itself in wreaths and dart off again and vanish wildly. The wind was freezing; it drove the heat of the fire away and snarled out the flames and herded the dead leaves together in the hedge-bottom with the wild sound of driving hail.

Walking across the stackyard to fetch a handful of potatoes from the copper-house to roast in the hot embers I was out of it for a moment, but coming back, the wind struck across the bare field furiously, lashing my face with the ice-rain. Down the fields and across the flooded valley ragged flocks of sea-gulls driven down from the coast by winter weather were drifting and struggling in the gale or resting on the darkening fields and the wind-whitened floods about the river.

My grandfather, leaning on his fork, was staring at something far down the road when I came back to the fires.

'What's that a-coming up the hill?' he said to me.

It was the sort of question that does not need an answer. He was long-sighted and must have seen as clearly as I did every detail of the green and scarlet caravan and the black horse with flecks of cream on its nose and fetlocks struggling up the hill against the storm.

With the fork across his shoulder he went slowly to the gate of the field and leaning on it stared at the approaching caravan. His hair, wind-ruffled like a hen's feathers, shone frozen-white in the gloomy air.

'I reckon it's Joe,' he called to me.

Before I had put the last of the potatoes into the fire he was out on the road, waiting for the caravan to come up. I followed him, and when the van drew up at the gate I could see the green and crimson paint glistening as though frosted with the fine wind-driven rain. A woman was driving the horse, and a low cart, painted bright pink, was hitched on behind the van itself. The woman was thin and dark, with melancholy black eyes and a yellowish wrinkled face, and she was dressed in a maroon-coloured skirt and a faded yellow blouse and a man's old brown buttonless overcoat. She had long green pear-shaped ear-rings that swung heavily against her neck when she moved. Crouching back half inside the van, she was driving with one hand, out of the rain.

'Goin' let us leave the little cart?' she began to recite. 'Goin' let us leave it, ain't you?' She spoke in the low half-whining melancholy gipsy sing-song.

'Ain't Joe there?' said my grandfather. 'How long d'ye want to leave it?'

'Don' know, don' know,' she half-chanted. 'All winter, ver' like, all winter.'

'Ain't Joe there?'

'He's here; yes, Joe's here.'

'I want to see him. Tell him I want to see him.'

The woman hooked the reins to the brass door-handle and disappeared into the van. The wind seemed more bitter than ever as we waited. It shook the van with great gusts and tore wildly at the horse's mane. There were voices in the van, and at last the woman appeared again.

'Joe's coming,' she said.

The wind half-gusted away the words. She stood back into the shelter of the van again, and out of the caravan, dwarfing her with his great height, stooped a giant of a gipsy dressed in snuff-brown corduroys with a black muffler tied in a loose bow about his neck and little gold ear-rings grown stiff into the flesh of his black-haired ears. Staring with curious dark vacancy he groped his way down the steps of the van like a man coming out of long darkness into naked sunlight. He stumbled a little as his feet touched the ground, and walking towards us he held his hands out before him, his head uplifted a fraction, his eyes black and dead.

The thumb of my grandfather's left hand was double. He had been born with it, and after sixty years it was earth-roughened and seamed as the knobbed end of an old stick. As the gipsy came forward he held out the double thumb for the groping hands to grasp.

'Know who 'tis?' he said. 'Know who 'tis now? Know th' old thumb, eh? You know?'

The gipsy fondled the thumb blindly in his hands and cried out:

'It's Lukey, it's Lukey! I knewed yer, Lukey. I knewed th' old thumb. Bless yer, Lukey, bless yer, Lukey boy, know y'are, Lukey. Goin' let us leave the little cart, ain't yer? I know y'are, Lukey, bless yer, I know y'are.'

'Wheer you winterin'?' said my grandfather.

'Up north, Lukey, t'other side o' nowhere. An' we're late goin'. Oughta been there a month ago, Lukey.'

'We oughta be pushing on,' droned the woman. 'We'll never get nowhere.'

'Why ain't you winterin' here?' said my grandfather.

'Goin' up north to take the gal, Lukey. She's been bad — bad, bless yer, Lukey. Goin' back to Drusilla's people — more call for the baskets up there, Lukey boy, and better for the gal, but we'll be this way in the spring, bless yer. Goin' let us leave the little cart till then, ain't yer, Lukey, ain't yer?'

'You know you can leave it.'

'Good, Lukey, good.' The dark blind eyes were suddenly restless. 'Who's here, Lukey? Who is it beside yer? I can feel 'em, Lukey. Who is it?'

'It's only the boy, Joe.'

'Bless yer, boy, bless yer. I could feel yer there. Can y' on-hook the cart, Lukey?'

From the door of the caravan came the woman's sad recital:

'We ought to be pushin' on. We'll never get nowhere, never.'

Going to the rear of the van my grandfather and I un-hitched the cart, and with him in the shafts, pulling, and I pushing the tail-board, we ran it over the grass and through the gate and across the stack-yard to the bush-hovel by the stable. The gipsy followed us for a yard or two, saying:

'Good, Lukey, bless yer. We'll stop a minute with yer.'

As we were pushing the pink cart under the hovel I heard him calling to the woman to get down from the van and then her droning melancholy answer:

'We'll never get nowhere, never. We ought . . .'

But the low muttering of her voice became mixed and carried away by the whine of the wind.

A moment or two later, looking up towards the gate, I saw her leading the gipsy into the yard. She was muttering dismally about the delay, her head bent low against the rain. Behind her came an unexpected figure, a girl of my own age, about fourteen or fifteen, with a thin yellow shawl draped round her shoulders. She came across the muddy yard slowly, the wind seizing the shawl and half-hurling it from her grasp and making her stagger. She was thin and delicate and there was something more than the mere gipsy sallowness in the pallor of her face. Coming into the shelter of the stacks she stopped a moment, her mouth parted a little, her body fighting in agitation for breath, her face turned weakly away from the wind. Presently she came towards the hovel where we had put the cart and where we were standing, my grandfather, the blind gipsy, the woman and I, in shelter from the storm. Only I watched her come: the woman was moaning about the delay and my grandfather was absorbed in talking to the gipsy who could not see.

'Lukey, boy, same as for the horse last time,' the gipsy was saying. 'You keep it, won't yer, Lukey, and if we don't come back it's yourn for keeps, but if we do come back I'll pay yer, Lukey — pay yer, Lukey, boy, I will. You know that, Lukey, don't you?'

The girl came into the hovel silently and sat down on an orange box in a corner. She sat down as though she were ready to die at that moment, the shawl slipping from her shoulders and rippling into a yellow heap on the dry earth floor. She was too weak to stoop and pick it up. There was death in her face. I sat watching her until the voice of my grandfather disturbed me:

'Better look at yer taters, boy. And bring us one if they're done.'

Going across the yard and along by the hedge to the fires I was haunted and moved by the look on her face. The potatoes were baked, the skins blackened, and I rolled them into my handkerchief and went back to the yard.

'Gie one to Joe,' said my grandfather. 'Roast taters!' he half-shouted to Joe.

There were six potatoes and I gave one each to the blind gipsy and the woman and my grandfather. Seizing hers with ravenous fingers the woman split the skin hastily so that the white snowy flesh spilled over her fingers and down her dress. Afterwards she sucked the crumbs off her fingers and picked them off her dress and then crammed the black skin of the potato into her mouth, smacking her lips and staring at me with wild hunger until I gave her another.

'Lukey, boy; Lukey, boy,' the gipsy was saying, 'they're good, the taters, Lukey. Got another for us, I'll bet, Lukey, ain't yer?'

'Gie Joe another,' said my grandfather.

'Good boy, good boy,' said the gipsy. 'Bless yer. You'll be lucky. I know you will. Bless yer.'

The woman watched me desperately as I took the other potato across to the girl in the corner. The girl had picked up her shawl and her body was at last tranquil, though her hands as they held the shawl were knotted tight across her breast.

'Starlina don' want no potato, boy,' the woman began. 'Starlina, you don' want no potato, do you? Give it to me, boy, I'll eat it. Give it to me. Starlina wouldn't eat it if you gave it to her. It's a waste to give it her I tell you, I tell you.'

The words were muttered in a low recital, in the flowing half-soliloquizing gipsy sing-song, and they broke off as I gave the last potato to the girl, who took it in both hands and said nothing. Leaning against the wall of the hovel I watched her warming her hands on the hot potato, never troubling to eat it, and gradually the warmth of the potato seemed to find its way into her blood, putting life into her face, banishing the old deathly look completely, and leaving only a kind of fragile quietness in her body and a deep tranquillity in her eyes as they rested softly on the rainy fields and the wind-driven gulls flashing white in the afternoon darkness. Presently the old grey she-cat came across the stack-yard and into the hovel out of the rain, and the girl called to her in a whisper and the cat leapt up and sat in her lap. 'Starlina, if you don' want the potato, don' have it. Don' you want it?' recited the woman; but the girl, absorbed in running her fingers softly down the back of the cat, took no notice. I could see the pleasure the cat gave to her in the way she smoothed it with a slow prolonged caress from its head to the curling tip of its tail, and I could hear the pleasure in her voice as she kept saying: 'You're lovely, you're lovely,' with her head lowered to speak.

Sitting there, at rest, comforting herself with the slow rhythm of stroking the cat, she also looked lovely. Some-times as she glanced up from the cat and over the fields at the sea-gulls again the tired, languid grace of her up-lifted head was painful in its loveliness. Turning her head from the fields to the cat again she caught me looking full at her once, and we looked at each other for a second or two without moving. Her black gipsy eyes shone with sick brilliance that was like the light of a restless passion.

The woman went on muttering about the potato and the cold and the delay, her voice a mournful accompaniment to the voice of the blind gipsy telling my grandfather a long tale about a horse. 'A white horse, Lukey boy, white as milk. We had him in the little cart, we did, in this 'ere same cart as you're a keeping, Lukey, and we painted the cart pink, colour as the gal wanted it, Lukey, we did. She loves that little cart. It's hers by right, Lukey, and all.' My grandfather also broke in with a tale about a white horse he had once had, and the two stories about white horses became intermingled with the moaning voice of the woman and the freezing whine of the wind.

The girl and I alone sat silent. We looked across at each other sometimes and then at the seagulls and then at each other again as though we wanted to speak, but we never did. All the time she stroked the cat, and I could see the blissful pleasure in her face as the cat curled its tail in her slow hand. Sometimes as she bent over the cat her hair fell down in black tangles over her face and in the sudden jerks of her head as she tossed it back again, and in the gold flash of her earrings I would catch for an instant the flash of her own spirit and the spirit of her race before sickness and poverty had degraded them, wild, careless, proud, passionate-blooded.

Suddenly she broke into an awful fit of coughing. When it came upon her she tried to stand up, but she only staggered forward a little and half-fell. The cat jumped away in alarm, and the potato bumped to the ground, and I saw the woman snatch it up as she darted forward to the girl.

'Starlina, Starlina,' she wailed.

She began cramming the potato into her mouth and trying to coax the girl upright at the same time. Suddenly there was a brief spurt of blood, and the gipsy let out a wild gipsy-wail as the bright scarlet splashed her hands and the girl's yellow shawl.

It was all over in a moment, and as though she felt better the girl staggered to her feet. As she leaned against the woman she looked at me. Her face was full of a dazed bewilderment that was terrible.

A moment later the woman and my grandfather were half-carrying her away. 'Starlina, Starlina!' the woman kept moaning as they went. It was raining faster and the wind seemed to be wilder, and half-way across the yard the girl staggered and my grandfather picked her up in his arms and carried her the rest of the way to the van out on the road, the woman running on behind, moaning and wailing, with the scarlet-splashed shawl that the wind had torn off the girl's shoulders.

'Boy, boy,' said the gipsy to me, groping with his hands, 'where are you, boy? Gimme yer hand, boy. That's right. Bless you, boy, bless you.'

I led him across the yard, and to the van. 'Good boy,' he kept saying to me. 'Bless yer.' His hands were trembling. My grandfather was coming out of the caravan as we reached the road, and from inside came the voice of the woman complaining over the girl.

'Where are ye, Lukey boy?' said the gipsy. 'Ah, here y'are, here y'are. Give us yer hand, Lukey, bless yer. Let's feel th'old thumb, Lukey. Bless yer, boy, bless yer till we see ye again.'

The voice of the woman came wailing that they ought to be getting on, and finally the gipsy climbed up into the caravan and as the horse struggled forward against the wind his last words were:

'We'll see yer in the spring, Lukey. We'll be back for the cart in the spring.'

We stood for a moment watching the van swaying slowly along the road against the storm, and the rain came in invisible bitter gusts and the sky was a desolation of storm-darkness deepening into the darkness of evening. Over the fields the seagulls, no longer visible, were screeching with wilder and wilder cries against the storm.

As we went back in the rain to the yard I kept thinking of the girl, enchanted and haunted by the memory of her as she sat stroking the cat and by the half-terror of death in her face as she stood with the blood still on her lips and looked at me. From the yard we watched the caravan struggling along the wind-lashed road and as it vanished out of sight I kept thinking of the gipsy's words:

'We'll be seeing ye in the spring, Lukey. We'll be back for the cart in the spring.'

But we never saw them again.

CLOUDBURST

HE woke long before daylight, all hot, in fear of having overslept. The small bedroom was stifling, the candle warm to his touch before he put the match to it. 'Hey,' he said gently. 'Missus. Nell. Missus, rousle up,' and with a kind of dreamy start she woke, the sweat of sleep still on her.

'Can't you lay still?' she said. 'You bin rootlin' about all night. Turn over and lay still.'

'No,' he said. 'Rousle up. It's time we were out. We got that field to mow. That barley.'

Then slowly she realized it. Work, corn. The field. Harvest. Then she realized the heat too, felt it no longer as part of sleep, but as an oppression in reality. The air seemed to drip sweat on her. The candle was like a little furnace. She pushed it away with what was already a tired hand.

Simultaneously her husband got out of bed. He looked, in the candlelight, excessively dwarfed and thin, an old man of bronze bone. Dressed, with blue shirt, leather belt and corduroys, salt-haired, he stood tired, heavy with sleep, dumb. She shut her eyes.

When she opened them again he had gone. Struggling, she got out of bed also, pulled on her clothes clumsily, smoothed her hair. The heat was wet, thunderous. It dripped continually down on her. Then, as she went downstairs with the candle in her hands, it burned up into her face. She was about sixty, very thin, straight-bosomed, and faintly sun-burnt, a stalk of human grass. Downstairs, on the kitchen table, another candle was burning. She set her own beside it. In the better light she saw the time by the alarm on the shelf: four o'clock. Four o'clock, twelve o'clock, four o'clock, five o'clock, eight o'clock, ten o'clock, dark, moonlight. How long was the day to be? She was not thinking. Her mind went round with the clock, stupidly. Like that, not really awake, she poured out tea. Then she cut bread, buttered it, sat down at last. Eating and drinking, she looked

268

out of the window. She saw, then, that there were changes in the sky, far distant appearances of creamy golden light, like the unearthly reflections of the candlelight.

'It's gittin' light,' the man said. 'Look slippy.'

Still eating, he got up.

'You all of itch?' she said.

'We gotta be all of itch,' he said. 'I don't like it. It's too hot by half. We get a storm on that barley we're done.'

She said nothing. She knew it: useless to deny it. So she got up, still eating too, and began to prepare food for the day: bread, cold meat, cheese, tea in a can. When that was ready she was ready. She had not washed. She put the victual-bag on her shoulders, locked the house, and went out.

Outside it was almost daylight. The heat steamed. There was a great dew on the roadside grass, a heavy silvering that wetted her big lace-up boots to the sweat-browned tips of the uppers. She walked quickly. By the time she was well out on the road it was light enough to see the colours of the August flowers, red and purple of poppy and knapweed, and then, more distantly, the blue of her husband's shirt as he opened the gate of the barley field.

Then, in the great stillness, long before she had reached the gate, she heard the sound of stone on scythe. It cut the drowsy air in steel discords. It was like the starting up of a rasping engine.

By the time it had ceased she was at the field gate. It was so light, now, that the barley, about five acres of it, was visible like a clean blanket of white, still, rippleless. It stood perfect, flanked by a long patch of scorched-up potatoes on the one side, by roots on the other. And somehow, so white and flawless, it also seemed vast. She could not help standing for a moment, to stare at it.

As she stood there, two things happened. The man began to mow and, almost simultaneously, far away, across distant acres of cut and uncut corn, the sun came up. It was like the sudden opening of a brass eye above the lid of earth.

It was hot from that moment. She rolled up the sleeves of her blouse. The man mowed a swathe, the first trashy thistle-thick swathe on the edge of the cart track. She

269

took straws from it, quickly and instinctively, combed them straight with her hands, held the ears bunched, tied the first bond, laid it on the earth at last. Barley bonds were awkward. The straw was short, needing to be locked. Wet with dew, it slipped in her hands. So early in the morning, sluggish, stiff, she could not catch the rhythm of the thing. The straws were like steel. She could not twist them. Her own hands were spiritless lumps of bone.

Then the first swathe was finished and another begun. She began to rake, foot under the gathering sheaf, rake light on the straw. Already the world was golden, great-shadowed. But with eyes on the barley and the earth, she hardly noticed it. She was watching how the sheaves would work out: how many to a swathe. At the end of the swathe she looked, but did not count. Some instinct told her that it was fair; that, later, it might be good. Secure in that, she began to go back, bonding the sheaves. For all her age and her sluggishness, she was quick, expert. She worked without premeditation, rapidly. Sheaves began to lie in rows, then in avenues. The stubble took on a new pattern, a great cross-knotting of sheaves, with the fringe of the untied swathe spread out at one end. All the time the man mowed with her own lack of premeditation, her own unconscious fluency. The scythe went sweetly through the barley with the sound of prolonged kissing, the stone swept the steel with ringing discords. They were the only sounds in an empty world.

Then, as the day crept up to seven, heat and silence were one, both intense. There was no breath of wind, only a vast sultriness of wet heat, ominous even so early with a gigantic promise of far thunder. The sun was brassy. The big-cracked earth came up at the touch of rake and feet in small puffs of greyish powder. There was a great sweetness of barley ears, of straw warmed in the sun.

Then, at eight, the man made a sign. His scythe was already on the ground and the woman, seeing it, put down her rake. He began to walk, a moment later, towards her. She got the victual bag as he approached; and in a moment, and afterwards for about five minutes, they ate and, between mouthfuls of bread and cold bacon, talked.

'I ain't on it,' the man said. 'I don't like it. It seems all of a boil everywheres.'

'You won't stop it,' she said, 'if it does come.'

'It'll come all right. Th' only thing is, we gotta git that barley down afore it does. That's all.'

He was on his feet. She followed him, still eating. 'If this ain't the best bit o' barley we ever had I ain't sharp. We oughta git some pork offa this. This'll make pigs.'

He was off across the stubble before she could think of anything to say. She swallowed her food, tied the victual bag, laid it under a sheaf, followed him.

And now it was hotter than ever. The dew was drying rapidly, the freshness evaporating. The sun stung her on neck and chest and eyes. She felt in it not only the heat of the moment but the promise of the blaze of noon and the bitter scorching of afternoon. The sky was deeply blue, far off, stainless. It was like some great blue burning glass; only, low down, on the horizon, was there any kind of blemish in it: a dark smokiness, tawnily hot, the promise of thunder.

As they worked on, all morning, up to noon, the promise swelled and sweltered into a threat. The heat never cleared. It dripped on them in invisible spots. The man took off his shirt. And the woman, sweat-blinded, would look up to see his back bathed in veins of molten gold.

At noon they ate again, squatting in the hedge-shadow. The day burned white, the barley a flat sheet of unquench-able white flame, the sheaves like smouldering torches, the beards like smoke. Even under the hedge there was a great sweating oppressiveness, without relief, the sun blinding beyond the black tip of shadow. They ate in silence, hardly speaking. They lay and rested with eyes shut. The heat rained on them through the hedge and the shadow. Sweat came out on them in great waves.

They were almost glad to get up and move again, to feel the slight wind made by their own movements, to feel exertion shake off its own sweat.

'We gotta git on,' the man would say. 'I don't like it at all. We gotta git on.'

They worked on mechanically. Heat and barley almost

effaced them. They moved like two figures of desperate clockwork. They kept up a changeless rhythm, he mowing, she bonding, which gradually the afternoon forged into iron monotony. Once the woman, looking back, tried to count the rows of sheaves. Her mind fainted. She counted, lost count. The sheaves seemed to dance and quiver as the heat itself danced and quivered over the lip of earth and the hedge. Two, four, six, eight. Twice four are eight, twice eight are barley. All barley. Barley for pigs. Pigs, barley, pigs, barley. Winter, pigs, pork, money. Twice two are pig, twice pig are sixteen. Her mind evolved a series of crazy multiplications. Constant heat and barley and motion made her drunk. Knowing that the barley meant so much, she reached a point, in the middle afternoon, where it and herself and all the world seemed to mean nothing at all.

And about that time there was a shout:

'Hey! You seen that?'

She lifted her eyes. The man was shouting, pointing. Far out, to the south, a vast cloud, tawny and blue, had sprung up out of nowhere.

'It's coming!' he shouted.

'Very like it'll blow over,' she called. 'It looks a long way off.'

'Not it! It's coming. I know. I felt it all day.'

And she knew. Five minutes later, as she looked up again, the cloud had risen up like a tower. It seemed to stand almost over them, an immense dome of strange white and darkness, against a thunderous background of iron and smoke. It was coming. She saw, even as she stood and watched, a great change in the wind currents, a sudden ominous rolling forward of cloud.

'Hey!' She turned. The shout startled her. 'Drop that. We'll git set up. We'll set up and be on the safe side.'

He came half running over the sheaves to her. He stopped only to pick up a sheaf in each arm. Dropping her rake, she picked up sheaves too. They met, humped the sheaves together, clawed up others, finished the first shock, went on.

'If we git set up it won't hurt so bad,' he kept saying. 'If we git set up —'

He did not finish. There was no need to finish. They had only one purpose: to set up, to make sure, to save. They lumped sheaves together clumsily, running to snatch them up. Not looking or caring, they made a line of shocks that was crazy.

Every now and then, looking up, they saw changes in the approach and form of cloud that were staggering. The sky was suddenly more than half cloud, a great hemisphere of shifting blue and smoke, of silent revolutions of thunderous wind. The sun was not quite hidden. The field was a strange world of stark corn-whiteness and emerald and tawny sunlight.

Then, abruptly, they became conscious that the sun was hidden. The world was instantly stranger, the colours more vivid, the air deathly. There was something like fear in the air, a shadowiness of terror. All the time they were running about the stubble, seizing white sheaves, like two ants hurrying their eggs to safety.

Suddenly the thunder came, the first split and rattle of it over the near fields. It seemed to shake them. The woman stood still. The man got angry:

'Here, here, here! Claw 'em up. Claw 'em up. We got no time to stan' an' gape.'

'That thunder frit me,' she said.

Almost before she had spoken it cracked again, rolling above their heads almost before the lightning had died. She looked instinctively up. The sky was chaotic, awful. The clouds were like the black smoke of some colossal fire. She ran with sheaves in her hands, still half looking up. The barley was dazzling, beautifully white. Suddenly a great silken shuddering and rustling shook the standing beards. It went across the field in a great wave, died in a tremendous stillness. They themselves were the only moving things on earth.

Suddenly a spot of rain hit the woman's hand like a warm bullet and the thunder cracked terrifically even as she lifted one hand to wipe the rain off the other. She stood stock still and a scorch of lightning split the sky before she could move again.

'You run!' the man shouted. 'Git in shelter. Go on! Git in shelter.'

'I'm all right. I —'

'Run!'

She turned and she saw the rain coming. It was coming out of the south, across the already dark fields, like a running curtain. She heard the sound of it, a great rising hissing. In a second, even as she started to run, it was on her, a smashing deluge of white thunder rain that drowned and blinded her.

She ran crazily across the stubble for the hedge and lay, at last, under the big hawthorns. The world was flooded, the barley washed out. She called feebly across the stubble at the figure of the man still staggering about with his puny sheaves, but rain and thunder annihilated her words as they almost annihilated him.

He came at last, a figure of water, a man saved from drowning, his clothes tragically comic. He stood under the hedge and stared. The stubble was flooded, great corn-coloured pools widening and joining and churned up by wind and rain. The nearest growing barley, just visible, was flattened like a mat. The shocks were like roofs torn apart from an earthquake.

'It's a cloud bust, it's a cloud bust,' he kept saying. 'I never see nothing like it. It's a cloud bust. We're done.'

Gradually, between themselves and the shocks, a pool widened into a small lake, with sprouts of stubble coming through it like reeds. They stood as though on an island, in desolation. It rained, all the time, with fury, the thunder turning and returning, the lightning scorching the storm-darkened air with savage prongs of gold. The sheaves became like skirted bodies, floating.

It was almost an hour before there was any brightening of sky, a full hour before there was any lessening of rain. But at last the man could walk out, boot-deep in water, and stand in the waste of flood and straw and look about him.

In a moment the woman slopped out too, and they stood still.

It was then that the man saw the victual-bag, shipwrecked as it were against the sheaf where the woman had left it, tea-

274

can adrift, bread and meat spewed out and swollen with rain.

'Whyn't you look after things?' he shouted. 'Whyn't you—'

His anger was impotent, useless. It was anger in reality not against her, but against the storm, the ruin. She picked up the victual-bag. Water flowed out of it as out of a net, all over her sodden skirt and legs. She shook it. It hung in her hands like lead.

'That was a good bag! Whyn't you—' The ruin of the bag seemed to hurt him more than anything else. Then his anger squibbed and died, damped out. 'Oh! I don' know! What's the good? What's the use? Oh! I don' know. Look at it. A good bag.'

She clung to the bag, as though in fact it had become precious. They stood and looked out on the waste of flooded water and drowned sheaves. They stood impotent. The man could think of nothing to do and nothing to say but, 'It was a cloud bust. Didn't I tell you? Didn't I say so?' which came finally to mean nothing too.

At last he waded and slopped across the stubble and found his scythe. He could not dry it. It dripped silver. The woman waited, clutching the useless bag in her hands.

Then, after another look at the field, they slushed out of the gate and down the road and away, clutching scythe and bag, like two figures setting out on a pilgrimage to nowhere at all.

ITALIAN HAIRCUT

I was in a great hurry. I went up the steps to the barber's saloon two at a time. The stairs were iron-tipped and had blue lettered tin plates on every rise: haircutting, shaving, shampoo, saloon, haircutting, and so on, the letters chipped by countless shoe-toes.

'A haircut,' I said.

From the moment I got upstairs I didn't like the place. The saloon was small, boxed-in, cheap. It smelt fiercely of old men and brilliantine. There were bottles all over its cupboards and shelves and wash-basins, pink, lavender, vitriol, green, jaundiced colours, all a little sinister. The whole place was dirty. I didn't like the barber either. He was dirty. It was not his fault: he was sallow, greasy-haired, thick-lipped, a sort of dago.

'You like it long?' he said, 'or short?'

'Medium.'

'Ver' good.'

He was Italian. I didn't like him at all. He didn't seem to like me either. He wrapped the sheet round my neck like a shroud, ramming it into my collar, tight. We might have been enemies. We were alone in the place. And what with the stink of old men, and the dirt, and the odd-looking bottles and his own surly down-look eyes I didn't like it at all. I wanted to get out.

'Just as quick as you can,' I said. 'I've an appointment.'

He didn't say anything. He began working the scissors, without hurrying. He pressed my head forward, suddenly, very hard: so that I was like a man with his head on an invisible chopping block. And with my head down I could see a razor on the rim of the wash-basin. It was open.

Then all at once he stopped clipping. I lifted my head, and we looked at each other in the glass. He was catching hold of my hair, running his fingers through it, making it stand up. He was a big man. He could have lifted me clean out of the chair. I have very light hair and when it stands up I look silly. With his derisive yellow fingers he made it stand straight up, like a comedian's.

'Look at your hair,' he said.

'What about it?'

'My dear sir, only look at it. It's going white. You're losing it.'

'It's a little dry,' I said. 'Certainly.'

'Dry? You use anythink on it?'

'No.'

'It's coming out. You're losing it. Look here, see.' Almost tender now, his derisiveness gone, he wafted my hair about again. ' 'Fore long you be bald. How old are you? Thirty-three? Thirty-four?'

'Thirty.'

'Oh, dear! Oh, my God!' He took his hand off my head and put it on his own. It was a good gesture, Italian, over-dramatic. 'Thirty? Look at me. Look at my hair. Seexty-five. That's what I am. Seexty-five. And as black as — but you can see it. You can see for yourself.'

'Yes.'

'And you, look at you. A young man. And such nice hair. Such lovely hair. Don't you care about it?'

'It's worry,' I said.

'Worry? Who said so? It's not worry. It's nerves. Starvation. You live on your nerves and your hair comes out.'

'I work hard,' I said.

'Work? What work? Pardon, but what work do you do?' I told him. He changed at once.

'Books? That so? Interesting. Books? My daughter write books.'

'Yes?'

'Yes! She writes books all her life. She write her first book when she was twelve. It was a beautiful book, a sensation. She got seventy-five pounds for it.'

'Good.'

'Everybody wanted her to write for them. Everybody. She was the craze. She wrote an essay for the gas company. A beautiful essay. The most beautiful essay a child ever wrote. For the gas company.'

'Good.'

'Success everywhere. She could of been famous. And you — what about you? You published anythink?'

'Some books.'

'Oh! Thass encouraging? Encourage you to go on? You make a name for yourself?'

'I may do.'

'You make a name for yourself,' he said, 'and then have hair like this? It's awful shame. Dreadful. Now if you was interested — perhaps you don' care, I don' know — if you was interested I could make your hair look different before you left this shop.'

'You could? How?'

'Wid my treatment.'

I didn't say anything. He clipped my hair a bit, ruffed it, pushed my head about, made a great show of indifference.

'Maybe you ain't interested?'

'What sort of treatment is it?'

'Special. A secret.'

He clipped.

'Of course if you ain't interested.'

'Tell me what you do,' I said.

'Maybe you ain't interested,' he said. 'I don' know. It make no difference. I'm only here to oblige. I ain't the boss. I don't get nothing out of it. In the summer I work in Brighton. Twenty pound a week. I don't get nothing out of the treatment. I ain't the boss.'

He took up the razor.

'Maybe you ain't interested?'

'I want to know what you're going to do.' Just then I wanted to know very much what he was going to do.

He flickered the razor. I didn't like it at all.

'It's electric. Electric must pass through my body. And then I massage wid ointment. Wid special stuff.'

'And how much?'

'Maybe you ain't interested. I don' know. Five an' six. You don' want to be bald, do you?'

'And how long does it take?'

All the time he was flashing the razor.

'Five minute.'

'You're sure?'

'Sure. Five minute. A young man like you, going white. At thirty. You don' want to be white, do you?'

'I've got an appointment,' I said.

'It won't take five minute. Sure. You won't regret it. You don' want to be bald, do you?'

'All right,' I said. 'I'll have it.'

'Good. Thass fine.' He went dashing round the screen, out of sight. I heard him tramping about. He came back with great alacrity, carrying a box. It had long lines of flex running out of it, and switches on it, like some antique wireless set. He plugged in. The box was black, a little sinister. I didn't like it at all.

'Jus' take your feet off the iron,' he said. I took my feet off the footrest. 'Jus' in case,' he said. He had become extraordinarily cheerful. 'You don't want to be contacted? Just hold that.' It was a kind of handle, of ebonite. I held it under the sheet, with the wires connected.

'Does it hurt?' I said.

'Hurt? No. A little. Not much. A bit of tickling. Thass all.'

'It's safe, isn't it?'

'Oh! It's O.K. If anybody's going to be electrocuted it's me. Oh! You won't regret it. You don't want to be bald, do you?'

He suddenly switched on and attacked me. His fingers danced on my head like springs. My scalp jumped with pins and needles. He attacked me until the sweat stood like grease on his face.

'Yes, my daughter write books. Wonderful. After she write for the gas company she could do anything. It don't hurt? You're all right? You won't regret it. And then I made her give it up. Altogether. She could of written for anybody. She write wonderful stuff. Stories, essays. Anything. She got genius.'

'Why did you make her give it up?'

'You know what they done? It don't hurt? Them editors? You know what they done? What I find out?'

'What?'

'The lousy —— they sent her scarves. Bits of ribbon. Anythink. Trinkets. I ain't a fool. The child was sitting up all night — writing that beautiful stuff. And all they sent her was scarves. I would of been a fool, wouldn' I, to of let her go on?'

He was still massaging, the electricity dancing on my head like springs.

'You know I'm right, ain't I? Ain't that what they do? Send scarves. There ain't no money in it. Kipling perhaps, people like that — it's all right. But for people like you and my daughter it's different. Thass right? You know it is, don' you?'

'My hands have gone dead,' I told him.

'Gone dead? You don't feel well?' He rushed to the switch and cut off.

'It's all right. How much longer?'

'Five minute.'

He rushed about. My hair now stood up, as in a caricature of fear. I looked like a wild man. He came back with a hot towel, wrapped it round my head, and I sat like a potentate with white turban.

'You feel all right? One day you'll come back and thank me. You'll have beautiful hair one day.'

'Just after this?'

'Oh! no, no, no. You gotta persevere. I make you up some ointment, and some spirit. My own recipe. You put that on.'

'How much is that?'

'Ointment. Thass five an' six.'

He took off the towel. My head felt beautiful: fresh and yet on fire. He rushed away with the towel and came back with a bright blue bottle. He was shaking it.

'How much longer?' I said.

'Five minute. I just put this on.'

The bottle had 'chloroform' on it. I didn't like it at all. Suddenly he poured it on my head, and it was as though my hair had gone up in flame. The effect was terrific, a hot pain driving right down to the roots of my hair.

'You take a bottle of this,' he said. 'And the ointment. And persevere.'

'By God, how much is that?' I said.

'The spirit? Thass forty-two an' six.'

'I'll take the ointment.'

'You want both. I'll charge you ten shilling for the spirit.'

'No. I'll leave it.'

He became suddenly very nice, beaming, the real Italian, his voice sweet.

'Is it a question of cash?'

'Oh! no.'

'If it's a question of cash, don't let it worry you.'

'No, I won't take it.'

'I tell you what. I won't charge you for the ointment. You take the spirit and the ointment and you come in some other time.'

'No.'

'I tell you what. I won't charge you for the spirit. Only the ointment. Because I'm interested in you. You can't afford it, can you? I know. I don't care. I know, because of my daughter. The lousy —— sending her scarves! For that beautiful work. You needn't wonder I wouldn't let her go on? You see, I understand.'

'No. How much does it come to?'

'You mean? — you take the spirit?'

'No.'

'Take it if you like. I trust you. I ain't the boss. I don't care.'

'Only the ointment.'

'O.K. Thass twelve an' eightpence. Wid the haircut.'

I gave him thirteen shillings. He brushed my coat. 'One day you'll come back and thank me. You will. I ain't like one of them editors. Don't give nothing in return. Your hair looks better already. Beautiful. It'll be so thick and beautiful.'

'What time is it?' I said. 'How long have you been?'

'Five minutes.'

I rushed out.

It's no use. Somehow my hair is as bad as ever.

THE CAPTAIN

WHEN the Captain and the woman first took the cottage, they looked out for a boy. 'Just a kid to mow the grass and tidy up a bit,' the woman said. At the end of a week they found him. His name was Albert. He was sixteen, one of a large family. He had little black arrogant eyes and a cool way with him and some unconscious habit of looking not quite straight. He was talkative, always on the spot, and the woman liked him from the first. She was amused by his sauce, and he liked to talk to her, bring her little things. He told her of otters one day, five cubs in the river-bank, at the foot of the field beyond the garden, among the meadowsweet. He could bring one. The Captain was listening. 'You ever seen what a dog can do to an otter?' he said.

The Captain himself had a dog, a greyhound, the colour of a field-mouse. It was a sharp, dainty sensitive creature, and the Captain liked to lie under the apple trees, in the grass, and roll with it and nuzzle its mouth with his two hands and tease it into a pretence of anger. He liked the dog, the boy thought, almost more than the woman. The Captain was a heavy dark stiff browed man, about forty, with a way of answering people as though shaken out of an ugly dream. 'Huh! Eh? What? What? Huh?' The woman was rather common, with her fair loose hair drooping about and her flopping poppy-coloured pyjamas, but she was human, warm, with a sugary red-lipped little grin for the boy whenever she met him. At first the boy did not understand them, did not get the relationship. Then once he called her Mrs. Rolfe. 'Mrs. Rolfe! Ha! That's good. Oh, boy! Mrs. Rolfe. No, I'm just Miss Sydney. That's all. Plain Miss Sydney.'

All the week, from Monday to Friday, the boy would be alone, working in the garden, with only the dog for company, and the house locked up. All he had to do was to cut the lawn, trim the quick hedge flanking the lane, sweep the paths, weed the flowers, feed the dog. At first he could not get used

282

to it, with the cottage lying at the dead end of the lane and no one coming, the summer days hot and empty, the warm flowery stillness of the little garden almost deathly. He had been used to company. There was not enough to do. And sometimes, in the heat of the day, work finished, he went down in the rough grass among the hazels and beat about for snakes or the young rabbits that scratched under the wire-netting from the field. Bored with that, he would lie half in the potatoes, half in the shade of the empty hen-run, and go to sleep for a bit.

Then when the week-end came again he was excited. He was like a dog himself, joyful, eager to please. He nosed into the house, could not stop talking, followed the Captain and the woman about everywhere, like some little cocky terrier.

He brought the woman a snake. It was a little viper. He had it in a seed-box, with gauze stretched over it, and the snake kept darting up, striking, flicking the gauze. He brought it to the woman as she sat lounging in a deck-chair on the lawn, in her red pyjamas, by herself.

'Look,' he said. 'I got him for you. Look. I caught him.'

The woman saw the small darting head and shrieked. The Captain came running out of the house, hands clenched.

'What's up?' Then he saw the snake. 'Christ almighty, take that damn thing away! Take it away, damn you! Take it away!'

Afraid, the boy stood still, held the box tight, did not know what to do. Suddenly the Captain tore the box from his hands in a rush of passion and flung it away across the grass. The boy saw with small slantwise eyes the snake slithering out over the grass.

A sudden flat-handed blow stunned him for a moment. He could not see. The garden went black, surged to crimson and then went black again. On his right wrist the Captain wore a leather strap, with double buckles. It seemed as if the buckles had made hot prints of pain on the boy's cheek-bone. He stood dumb.

'I'll teach you to scare people. D'ye·hear? You hear me? Look. You see that?'

The Captain wore a leather belt round his waist. It was

heavy buckled. He took it off. He held it loose, like a flat whip.

'You see that? Well! Do you see it or don't you?'

'Yes, sir.'

'You see it. Good. Next time you'll not only see it but feel it. You understand that? You understand?'

'Leave him alone, George,' the woman said. 'That's enough. He knows. It's all right.'

'Leave him alone be damned. Bringing snakes. What next? What the hell?'

'All right. But let him go. He understands. You understand, don't you?'

'Yes, miss.'

'I just don't like snakes. They scare me.'

'Yes, miss.'

'And what goes for snakes goes for anything else,' the Captain said. 'See that?' He still held the belt. The boy had his eyes half on it and on the thick black-haired wrist. 'And now make yourself damn scarce! Quick!'

The boy went, humble, half watching.

'There's something about that damn kid I don't like,' the Captain said.

'You shouldn't have got the belt,' the woman said.

'Huh! Eh? What? What? Why not?'

'He's only a kid.'

'Kid be damned. Isn't he old enough to know?'

After that the boy was glad to be alone. It was a comfort, the empty week, the hot stillness, and nobody but himself and the dog among the sunflowers and hollyhocks. He liked the small drowsy world, the feeling of being shut off, of having no fear. He felt boxed-up but secure, like the creatures he caught. It had become quite a habit now, since he had so little else to do, to catch something and box it up, half for companionship, half to satisfy in himself some small demon of joy. So at one time he had another snake in a box gauzed over, two fragile lizards in another, a bank vole, reddish-tinted like a fox. He would lie and watch them at the bottom of the garden, in the shade behind the hen coop, out of the hot white edge of sunlight, teasing the snake with straws to make it strike, holding the little vole under his hand, half letting it go, then catching it again, like a cat. All the time he wanted an otter cub, but fear held him back: fear of the Captain, of what the dog might do. In consolation he caught a small rabbit; he fell on it in the grass and then kept it in the hen-coop, in the full blaze of sunlight, until it scratched a way out of the soft cake-floor of hen-muck.

Then the week-end came, and he let his creatures go. He was miserable. He watched the Captain, sheered away when he saw him coming. He scarcely spoke to the woman. She gave him her little sugary grins, but he no longer brought her anything.

She saw what was the matter with him. She caught him alone and said, kindly: 'How are your little otters? Do they grow much? Can they see yet?'

'They're all right,' he said.

'Funny, are they? Nice? You said you'd bring me one.' She gave him a little petulant smile.

He brightened. 'So I will,' he said. 'I will. I will. I'll get one. I can get one.'

He came with it the next day. It was Sunday, his day off. He had the little otter in a bird-cage. It lay in one corner, dead frightened, eyes like slate. It never moved. He came in by the back of the house. When he knocked at the door there was no answer. He waited, set the otter and cage down on the path by the fringes of catmint, and listened. Then he heard voices: the Captain's, the woman's, giggling.

The boy went across the lawn towards them, cage in hand. His mind was on one thing: the otter. He had to give it to the woman. She wanted it. She'd asked for it. He had to give it to her.

He got to within the shade of the tree before anything happened. Then the woman suddenly stopped laughing. 'Shut up, you fool. Shut up. There's someone here. It's the kid. Let me go, let me go.'

The Captain sat up, swivelling round on his heavy buttocks. 'Huh! Eh? What? What? Huh?'

Then he saw the boy. He leapt up in passion, stopped.

'What the blazes you got in that damned cage? Eh?'

'I got the otter, sir.'

'You got what? Didn't I tell you not to bring your damn pets here? Didn't I tell you?'

'It's all right, Goerge, it — '

'You know what I've a good mind to do to you, eh?' He took a step forward towards the boy, his two hands in his belt. 'Coming here, with your damn pets, disturbing people, Sunday afternoon. What the blazes you mean by it?'

The boy dropped the cage, stood frigid, paralysed.

'It's all right, George. I asked him. I — '

'Then you ought to know better. That damned thing can't live. It's a water animal. Don't you understand? You can't keep it. It'll die, in misery.'

'Well, I — ' She stood a little embarrassed, folding her arms, unfolding them, smoothing her white shoulder-straps over her white skin.

'Look at the damn thing,' the Captain said. He kicked the cage round, so that the woman could see the little otter, cringing, terrorized, almost dead, in the corner of the bird-splashed cage. 'Expect that to live? How can it? It's nearly dead already. It wants killing out of its misery. It — '

Suddenly he had an idea. He whistled, called once or twice 'Here! Here! Here!' and then whistled again. In a moment the dog came bounding out from the door-porch, in great leaps over the flowerbeds. He stood quivering by the Captain, in delicate agitation, waiting for a command.

'Down, Bounder, down. Down!' the Captain said. He turned to the boy. 'You've never seen what a dog can do to an otter, have you? Down, Bounder! Down! Eh? Have you?'

'No, sir.'

'All right.'

Suddenly the Captain bent down and unfastened the cage and took out the little otter and let it run across the grass. 'No, Bounder! No! Down, down!' The otter ran a little way, cramped, crouching. It ran and limped four or five yards. It was small and helpless. The dog stood quivering, watching, waiting for the word, his mouth trembling, in pain. Then the Captain shouted. The dog took an instant great

leap and was on the otter and it was all over. The otter hung
from the dog's mouth like a piece of sodden flannel, and
then the dog began to tear it to pieces, throwing it about,
ripping it in lust, until it was like a blood-soaked swab.

'Now you know what a dog does to an otter, eh? Don't
you? No mistake about that, was there?'

The boy could not speak.

'George, let him go home,' the woman said. 'You go home
now,' she said to the boy. 'You go — '

The boy turned to go, white-faced, his eyes half on the
woman, half on the dog playing with the bloody rag of the
dead otter.

'Wait a minute,' the Captain said. 'You understand this,
once and for all? You stop bringing things here. Stop it. We
don't want it. And now get out! And when we come next
week don't come here on Sunday afternoons, nosing. Behave
your damn self!'

The boy turned to go. In a rush of rage the Captain kicked
out at him, catching him on the flank of the buttocks. The
boy ran, hearing the Captain protest to the woman: 'It had
got to die, I tell you. How could it live? It's a water animal,
the little fool.'

In the morning the boy was back again early. The Captain
and the woman had gone. The garden was still, hot already,
the dew drying off.

The boy had a fixed idea. He had worked it out. Nothing
could stop it. In the mornings, when he arrived, his first job
was to feed the dog. That morning he did not feed it. He
let the dog out of the wash-house, where it slept, and the dog
bounded about the lawn, sniffing, cocking its leg, coming
back to be fed at last.

The boy did nothing. The dog watched him. When he
moved the dog followed him. Then, about 9 o'clock, he
took the dog down to the hen-coop. Already the sun was hot,
with a fierce July brassiness, the sky without cloud or wind.
The boy opened the hen-coop and put his hand on the floor
of hen-muck. It was hot. He looked up at the sky. The hen-
coop was full in the sun. For the whole day it would be in the
sun.

Then the boy called the dog. 'Bounder, Bounder! Rabbits! Look! Fetch'em, Bounder! Fetch'em, fetch'em!'

In an instant the dog tore into the hen-coop. The boy slammed the door. The dog tore round and round for a moment and then stood still. The boy bolted the coop door and went up the path.

When he came back, half an hour later, the dog was scratching frenziedly. The boy had not thought of that. So he rushed back to the toolhouse and came back with a hammer and a small axe. He began to cut short stakes out of bean-poles and hammer them into the ground all round the foot of the coop. The dog stopped scratching and watched him.

Then when the boy had finished, it began its frenzy of scratching again, clouding up grey dust, already terrorized. The boy watched for a moment. Then he got bricks and laid them in a single row alongside the stakes. He was quite calm. His mouth was set. He was sweating.

But he was still not satisfied. He went up to the toolhouse and came back with a spade. Then he chopped out heavy sods of rough grass and piled them over the bricks, hammering them firm down with the back of the spade, until he had built at last a kind of earthwork, heavy and tight, all round the foot of the wire.

Then he stood and looked at the dog. Every time he looked at the dog he hated it. Each time he remembered the otter, saw the bloody piece of flannel being ripped and slapped to bits. His hatred was double-edged. He hated the dog because of the Captain; he hated the Captain because of the dog.

All that day, at intervals of about an hour, he went and looked at the dog. At first it scratched madly. Then it tired. In the afternoon it did nothing. It lay huddled up, as the otter had done, in the corner of the coop. Then, towards the end of the day, it got back its strength. It stood up and howled, barking in fury. Whenever the boy went near it hurled itself about in a great bounding frenzy of rage and anguish.

All the time the boy did nothing. The next day he did nothing. In the morning, first thing, he was frightened that something had happened, that the dog might have escaped, might be waiting for him. But the dog was still there. He set up a howling when the boy approached. The boy looked at the sods and bricks and then went away.

All that day he did nothing. All morning the dog scratched and leapt about in a kind of indiarubber agony. Then in the heat of the afternoon he quietened again. He lay motionless, abject, tongue out. The boy looked at the tongue. He had an idea that it ought to turn black. He wanted it to turn black.

He wanted the dog to die, but also he wanted it to die slowly. By Wednesday the dog was sick. Heat had parched it, withered it, made an inexorable impression of misery on it. Lean always, it now had the look of a dog skeleton, with the grey skin drum-tight over its ribs. It held its tongue out for long intervals, panting deeply, right up from the heart, in agony. Then the tongue would go back, and the eyes would shine out with dark mournfulness, strangely sick. Then the panting would begin again.

The boy was satisfied. On Thursday he did not go too near the coop. He had some idea that, in time, before death, the dog would go mad. On Thursday he thought he saw the beginning of madness. The dog began to slobber a great deal, a sour yellow cream of saliva that dribbled down its lower lip and dried, in time, in the hot sun, into a flaky scab. By the end of that day the dog had lost all fight. It lay in supreme dejection. It no longer howled. When its tongue fell out, for brief, slow stabs of breath, the boy could see a curious rough muskiness on it, as though the dog had been eating the sun-dried dust of hen-muck. All the time his hatred never relaxed at all: hatred of the dog because of the Captain, of the Captain because of the dog, and all during Thursday he watched for the dog to show its first signs of madness and dying.

He wanted the dog to die on Friday: on Friday because it would leave him clear, free. He could drag the dog out and bury it and then go and not come back. To his way of thinking, it seemed simple. The Captain would be back on Saturday.

THE CAPTAIN

On Friday morning he hoped to find the dog dead. It was not dead. It still lay there, against the wire, eyes sick and open, waiting for him. The boy had a spasm of new hatred, really fear, because of the dog's toughness. Then suddenly he saw the tongue come out, slowly, in great pain. It was swollen, almost black. He jumped about, glad. It was black; it was mad. He knew, then, that it was almost the end.

Friday was not so hot. White clouds ballooned over and gave the dog a little rest from heat in the afternoon. By afternoon the boy was afraid. The dog still lay there, strangely still, the deep mad eyes almost closed, the mouth sour-flaked, the tongue terribly swollen. But it was alive, and he could do nothing. Once he got a goose-necked hoe and opened the coop door, holding it half open with his feet. He fixed the dog with his eye. If he could hit it once it would die. Then the dog stirred. And in a second he slammed the door shut with terror.

Then he had another idea. He made a loop with a piece of binder string and let the string down through the mesh of the coop-wire. He let it down slowly, until the loop was level with the dog's head. But the dog, mouth against the floor of the coop, would not stir, so that he could not slip the knot. He called it once, and for the first time, by its name, 'Bounder Bounder!' but it would not move.

Then he was frightened. He'd got to kill it. He'd got to finish it. Then he thought of something. He could give it food and poison the food. He could give it bread and rat poison, with water.

He ran up the path. Then he thought he heard something. He stopped and listened. He could hear the noise of a car, braking on the gravel and stopping. He stood paralysed, for about a minute, listening. Then he heard the woman's voice. He could not believe it. Then he heard it again. There was no mistaking it. She was laughing and he heard also, in a moment, the Captain's voice in answer.

The Captain. He could not move. After what seemed a great time he heard a shout. It was for him. It was the Captain, bellowing his name.

'Boy! Albert! Boy! Where the devil are you? Where are you? Boy!'

The voice moved him. He began to walk up the path, slowly, in terror, without intention. The dog, hearing the new voice, was making strange whimpering sounds in the coop behind. The boy half ran.

At the crest of the path he slowed down. He could hear footsteps. They were coming towards him. He raised his eyes, so that when the Captain came round the corner his eyes were fixed on him.

In the coop the dog was crying bitterly. And hearing it, the boy stood still.

THE LANDLADY

I

CORA INGRAM took in lodgers, when there were lodgers to take. Her husband played the cornet, which did not help much. Six weeks, no work.

It was summer. No work, no lodgers. No money, no fun. Cora listened all day for the front door. She knew the raps as a commissionaire knows faces. Insurance-man, sharp and bony. How long could they go on paying? Milkman, knock and open. Drink more milk? Baker, solid and respectful, a nice boy. Trade club, noon Saturdays, just as they were sitting down to dinner, comic, saucy. Rum-tiddley butter-scotch, brown-bread. Walk straight in. How long could they keep it up?

Cora was big, smart: too smart for the street. At forty, she still fancied herself. The street was an arid gully of houses all alike: two long window-pocked walls facing each other, white lips of doorsteps shining, grey lace curtains, grey blistered paintwork, once white. Cora by contrast was like some heavy flower, sulky, full-blown. She had fair thick hair which hung down in one brassy pigtail in the mornings. Her eyes were very small, little dark bone-button eyes that she kept buttoned up, as though trying to disguise her emotions. She smiled much, fetching, a little false, her heavy lips easily shining. She blossomed fleshly at the doorway to answer knocks.

The card in the window was beginning to fade in the sun: the board to yellow, the lettering to grey. Lodgers. Some hopes. In a street like this? Tired of it, she blamed Ingram. Ingram was tired too, but differently, and had no answer. He had worked a consol in a boot factory. The consol is a demon, a killer. At forty-five Ingram was worn out. With his fleshless face and peppery hair and a tired sprout of a moustache, he was tired, body and soul. He played, in the evenings, tired notes on his cornet. 'You and that damned cornet!' Cora would shout. 'Shut it! Shut it for God's sake afore I bust it. What good does that do?'

Then something happened. A knock. From the kitchen Cora could detect its difference. It had discretion in it, manners. None of the boniness of the insurance, the sauce of the trade club. Apron off, she blossomed at the doorway.

'Could I see the lady who lets rooms?'

A young man, about thirty, black hair, and with him a girl, about ten or eleven.

'I'm the lady,' Cora said.

'I'm looking for rooms,' the man said.

'You're looking for rooms. Just for yourself?'

'No, for the little girl, too.'

'Oh! For the little girl.' Expressionless, in polite negation, but thinking and meaning: 'Oh? That's different.'

The girl stood with still eyes, taking it in. She was dark, a little delicate. The man carried a suit-case. He was delicate himself, but the pale skin had fire under it. He had a way of looking sharply, magnetically about him.

'If you've got rooms perhaps we could look at them,' he said.

'Yes,' Cora said. She was hesitating. 'I don't know about the girl. I've never taken children.'

'She's a good girl,' the man said. 'She'll go to school. She could sleep in my room.'

'Well, come in. Put your suit-case down in the hall.'

So the man put down his suit-case and Cora said 'Come up', and they went upstairs, the girl last, to look at the bedroom. The girl took it all in with still eyes, never speaking.

'This is the room I was thinking of for you,' Cora said.

The man stared at it; brass bed, marble washstand, grey lino, texts. 'How much?' he said.

'It's a good room and I could let it any time for thirty shillings.'

'I can't do it,' the man said.

'That's with full board.'

'I couldn't do it. With the girl on top.'

He stood looking at Cora with his small fascinating eyes

dead still, almost supercilious. He looked straight at her, into her small buttoned eyes, in a way that made her feel queer, nettled. He seemed to sting her. The girl stood close up to him, proud. They were an irritating pair, aloof, just that bit different. They looked like accomplices. Ideas flashed on Cora: crime, *News of the World*, kidnapping, missing from home, abduction. And with them emotions: fear, excitement, affront. Classy folk. She looked at his hands. That was it, classy folks. The hands were white, seemed cut out of paper.

'Well?' she said. Then suddenly she realized how much she wanted a let. No money, no fun. No work, nothing. Ingram, that damned cornet. Well,' she said, 'how long will you be here? I could make it less for a long let.'

'How much less?'

Same supercilious tone, classy, as though she were muck. It nettled her.

'I dunno. It depends.' She was rattled. 'Well, I'd make it thirty-five shillings for you and the child.'

He smiled, not casually, or in acquiescence or triumph, but personally, straight at her, eye to eye. She saw, suddenly, a glint of wickedness in him, not *News of the World* wickedness, crime, kidnapping, but something sporty, devilish. She saw the classiness as skin deep, like a shop-walker's. She saw him human at last. His eyes held her briefly and fiercely. The dago. She had it now: he was the dago, the film-star sort, with his black sleek hair and side-lines and paper-white hands. And slowly, in reflection, she smirked back.

'That's all right?' she said.

'All right.'

He set down the suit-case. It was noon. Cora thought of dinner.

'I expect you'll eat with us,' she said. 'I couldn't let you have a separate sitting-room at that price.'

'That's all right. I'll be out all day. Ina'll help with odd jobs when she comes home from school. Yes, we'll eat with you, Mrs. ——?'

'Ingram,' she said.

'My name's Weston,' he said.

294

Cora went out and stood on the landing. She remembered dinner. Friday.

'I thought of fish-and-chips for to-day,' she said. 'They fry Friday dinner. Do you mind that?'

He looked at her with the dago-look, flashy, still faintly supercilious, nettling and attracting her at the same time.

'I don't mind anything,' he said.

He smiled. Cora went downstairs. All the time the child had not spoken.

11

'Widower, Mr. Weston?'

How many times had she tried to get that out of him? Wasn't it a fair question? Three weeks and she didn't know a damn thing about him. What did he travel in? Every morning out with that aluminium suit-case, all day, catching buses, tramping from door to door, selling something. Selling what? Three weeks and she didn't even know what he travelled in.

She had tried, more than once, to get a look inside that suit-case. Fancy, aluminium. He kept it in the room. She tried it one Sunday. It was locked. She dropped hints, gave him cues. 'That suit-case of yours is heavy, I know, Mr. Weston. Might be full of bombs.' But it was no good. Always the same, no answer, no giving anything away.

'Widower, Mr. Weston?' Always the same. He regarded her with simple inscrutability, with bare superciliousness, offering nothing except that occasional dago smile, one-sided, with the small magnetic eyes fixing her wickedly. She couldn't make him out, couldn't fathom him. A mystery. He had her beat.

Otherwise, no complaints. He paid up, Fridays, regular as clockwork. He ate anything. Never dainty. He was clean: clean to a point of faddiness. His black pin stripe trousers brushed every night, pressed every week. She had felt of the cloth of them: good stuff, thin now, but good stuff, classy. Had he come down in the world? She liked to think it:

romance, mystery, woman's cruelty, trying to forget. Tramping the country with the child, Sunday newspaper drama. But it was no use. She could not bottom him. And she was angered and fascinated, alternately. She wanted to be on terms with him, equal.

'If you ask me,' Ingram said, 'he's all show and nothing else.'

'Nobody asked you!'

'All right, all right. I only — '

'He does *work*, any rate! Shut up!'

Well, it was the first time she'd said that; but it was no use. She was nettled. She liked things straight. 'Widower, Mr. Weston?' Wasn't that straight? It wasn't a crime if your wife had died, was it? It was no use; it beat her.

Then the child. There was something funny about the child, something dark, stand-offish, classy. Ina: classy name, too classy. Cora didn't like it. The child had such set lips, set as though in excessive pride or wooden determination or arrogance or secrecy. Yet her eyes were fluid, soft, beautifully child-like, and would be set in long reflective stillnesses, day-dreaming. Cora didn't like that either. Give me a child who acts sharp, so you can tell what is in their minds.

At twelve, every day, the girl came home from school, hatless, black hair peacock-shining in the sun, to lay the table for half-past twelve dinner. She laid the knives and forks in silence. She moved silently with her rubber gym shoes on the lino, dainty as a cat.

Suddenly Cora saw in her a medium. There were days when Weston did not come back at dinner-time. Working on the far side of the town or in some other town, he took sandwiches, returning to eat hotted-up dinner at night. At times Ingram was away, looking for jobs, fed up, mooching about, bread and cheese in pocket. So there were days when Cora and the girl sat down to dinner alone, in a silence that for Cora was like the infuriating shrillness of a note out of pitch. Potatoes? Gravy? Words of necessity hit the note and killed it momentarily, but there was no conversation and no harmony.

Then Cora tried a different tack: she gave sweetness a trial. It was drawn-lipped sweetness, forced, a pointed too-niceness. 'You tell me, dear, if you've got any trouble. I know what it is, your age. You tell me, when the time comes.' She made false shots, in the dark. 'I know how it is. I know about your mother. Do you miss her?'

No answer. No answer! Only that damned brazen dreamy stare. Only that silent haughtiness, making her look a fool. She looked at the child with fury. So silent, so abnormally aloof, she maddened Cora past all bearing.

'Don't you know better than that? Not to speak when you're spoken to? Eh? Don't you know better than that, my lady?'

'Yes.'

Ah. Something at last. An answer. Very nice. I'm sure. Nice manners. That's classy folks for you.

'Little girls round here answer nicely. They speak when they're spoke to, chance what they do where you come from. Understand that?'

'Yes.'

'Well then, act as if you did. Who else is to correct you when your father isn't here if I don't?'

No answer, only the grim little lips, haughty, tightly shut.

'Where were you brought up?'

'I can't remember.'

Ah! Can't remember. The haughty, stuck up puss. Can't or don't want to? The saucy cat.

'You know what God does to little girls what tell lies?'

The small black eyes were dreamy, swimming in fear. Cora leaned across the untidy dinner-table, big soap-white arms locked over the vinegar-stained, gravy-sprinkled cloth. The girl was mute with unexpressed and inexpressible little terrors.

'Ah, so you don't know what He does, eh? You don't know? Well, I know. I know, my lady. I know. I was brought up to know. What does your father carry in that case?'

'Samples.'

That was quick enough. Too quick. Answer you back before you could wink.

'What samples?'

'I don't know.'

'And how long's he been carrying it? Doing this work?'

'A long time.'

'How long?'

'Ever since we were in Liverpool.'

'Liverpool. Liverpool, eh? Nice place.' She'd read about it. You couldn't open the *News of the World* without reading about it. So it was Liverpool. Well, perhaps not so classy after all.

'I want to know what he carries in that case.' Then, sweet suddenly, Cora smiled, cajoling, her mouth blossoming in the old easy way. 'It isn't my curiosity. I want to know. Because of the insurance. You see, if he carried something that easily catched fire, the insurance company would chelp. Supposing it was celluloid or something? I don't suppose it is celluloid?'

'I don't know. I —'

The damned brazen, stubborn puss! Wouldn't tell you nothing! You couldn't get to know nothing! Here in the house a month and she was no nearer than when she started.

She got up from the table in anger. She tossed her hair: a gesture of pride, smartness, almost a threat.

The girl sat mute. The threat became an actuality, fierce, delivered with upraised voice.

'I learn you, my girl! I learn you! By God if you were mine I'd limn the skin off your back. I'd learn you damn well whether to answer or not.'

She clattered knives and forks together on plates: an enraged clash of steel and platter that was like the echo of her maddened voice. She flounced out, plates in hand, into the little whitewashed kitchen. She stood trembling. She went outside, into the backyard. It was a mid July day of still, brazen sunlight. Buzzers were blowing and moaning for the afternoon shift, men diving past down the backyards. In the sooty little garden marigolds blazed starrily, butter-coloured, deep-gold, hot. She stood a moment to look at them, the cinder-path hot under her feet. She stood almost in a trance, trying to calm herself.

When at last she walked back into the house the girl had gone to school. Cora felt queer. What was it? She cleared the table, washed up, stared at the soft soda-diamonds dissolving in the water. What was it? Something got her goat: something about the girl, about Weston.

And then she had it, vaguely at first, intuitively, not certain. Something about him got her down: the way he looked at her, black-eyed, the dago, supercilious. He had her fascinated, like a cat. She had the thought of him playing about at the back of her mind all day, elusively.

Then, next day, she was at the girl again. They were at dinner, alone again. It was suet day, Thursday: lumps of boiled suet drowned in grey gravy, onion-faint, Cora's speciality, given to lodgers, take it or leave it, every Thursday, for years. The day was burning, the slate roofs like hot glass, and the girl looked at the suet, tried it softly, sickly, with barely opened lips, like some little black kitten, and then couldn't face it.

'Well, my lady? What's wrong with it?'

'I'm not hungry.'

'Been to school, nothing to eat since seven, and you're not hungry. You mean you don't want it?'

'No.'

'I tell you yes! You're too dainty, very dainty, my lady. Too dainty. That's what. Too damn dainty. It ain't good enough for you, is it? You had better food than that where you was brought up perhaps?'

'No.'

'Then where were you dragged up?' No manners, won't eat the food decent people eat. Stuck up, my God!'

The girl began to get up from the table, fear in her face.

'Where are you going?'

'Nowhere, I — '

'Then damn well sit down!'

The girl half-stood, paralysed. Cora rammed food into her mouth, wet suet, almost cold, the greasy stew slobbering down

299

her chin. She rammed it in fast, in a sort of angry pantomime, as though to show the girl, as an example.

Show her! She wants showing! By God I'd show her
something, manners, chelp, ignorance. Stare at you as
haughty as haughty. Look right through you, get you down.
Like her father. Dark, close. Too close. There was something in these people that defeated her.

'Didn't I tell you to sit down?' she shouted. 'Then sit down!
Whose house are you in? You ignorant little bitch!'

Suddenly she leaned across the table and hit the girl,
openhanded, across the face. The child reeled, went white,
stood still finally in a terror of paralysis. She saw nothing,
did not understand. Her head sang with pain, she could not
speak. She made motions of feeble humility with her hands,
small motions of defeat and fear.

'Now we'll see if that'll learn you! See if that'll learn you
any different.' Cora shouted with excessive elation, with
triumph she did not feel. 'And if that don't learn you we'll
see what will. We'll see what will!'

III

A week later Ingram got a job, in the next town, five miles
off, so that he was off by cycle before seven every morning
and not back before six at night. The hot days took it out
of him, leaving him limp, more tired than ever, lacking
energy even for the cornet.

Weston left later, was home earlier. The heat did not seem
to touch him. He came in with the same saucy supercilious
look in the evenings as he left with in the mornings, always
smart, always the shining-haired dago.

Then things got slack: holidays, people not at home, other
things on their minds. He began to come home for tea, at
four, to lie on the sofa and smoke aloof cigarettes, with that
half haughty, half likeable air that had Cora mystified and
beaten. And he would lie there and look at her, brazenly,
with black winey eyes and a sort of sleepy fascination, while
she laid tea. Until, sometimes, he had her in torture. He

seemed to know, also, that he had her in torment, and he kept it up, cat with mouse, for the sheer luxury of it, smiling to himself, tasting the devilry of it.

All that time Cora hated the girl. Dinner was a daily bout of silence, antagonism; Cora, driven wild by the child's mystery and inscrutability, by something she could not name or get hold of, by some thing unchildlike, uncanny. They kept it up darkly, bitterly, for weeks, until the child's soul was tied up inextricably, in knots of terror and pain, until Cora's only release from anger was to hit her again.

'And one of these fine days I'll shut you up until you *do* know better. I don't care who you are or what you are. I'll learn you, begod!'

And still she was no nearer about anything: who they were, what Weston sold, where they had come from. 'Widower, Mr. Weston?' Unanswered, she had given up that question at last. She hated it. She always had known about her lodgers. She hated not knowing. And so she spilled her revenge on the girl, in hot bursts of fluid anger, hitting her, threatening, angered most because there was no protest, so that she had to imagine protests and whip up her impotent rage against something the child had not done or said but which only she herself had imagined.

Then Weston came home very early one day, mid-afternoon. She was washing herself in the kitchen, blouse off, thin shoulder-straps loose. Weston came in with the old superciliousness and looked at her. He looked at her shoulders. They were handsome, heavy shoulders, the flesh pure white. Her chest flowered into heavy breasts. Her arms were powerful and fine. He looked at them openly.

'Oh, sorry,' he said. 'Sorry.'

'You're home early,' she said.

'Nothing doing. I think I'll go up and lie on the bed.'

'Shall I bring you a cup of tea?' she said.

'Just as you like,' he said. He smiled in his slow, winey-eyed fashion. 'Just as you like.'

She took up the tea in about twenty minutes. She knocked on the bedroom door. She was quivering. The tea squabbed over. 'Come in,' he said. He was lying on the bed, hands clasped behind his neck. She stood at the lower bedrail, leaning against it. He looked at her for about a minute, the smile on his face. Slowly she smiled back.

'Well,' he said, 'how can I drink it if you hold it over there?'

She took the tea to the bed-side.

'Put it on the table,' he said.

She set the cup and saucer on the table. Suddenly he pulled her down, across the bed, hands spanning her breasts, his mouth against her neck. She turned, struggled a bit, and then lay down beside him. He kissed her and began to take her almost immediately; and she knew, suddenly, that there were a lot of things she no longer cared about, which no longer mattered: Weston and the girl, who they were, where they had come from, what he sold. Lying there, with him, in the small hot bedroom, in the summer afternoon stillness, she knew she had what she wanted. She had all the solutions at last.

It was past four when she went downstairs again. She felt elated, clarified, a new woman. The necessity for knowing things, the anger at not knowing things, had both been destroyed. It was all right at last. No more trouble, no more anger. It was all right at last.

As she came into the kitchen the girl came in from school. Cora stood smiling. The girl did not come in. She stood at the doorway in unbelief, not moving.

'Come in,' Cora said. She was smiling, continually without a break. 'Come on in. Well, why don't you come in?'

The child moved at last and came in. She did not speak. Cora tittered. The girl's face showed no response. It was hard with the crystallization of many emotions: fear, hatred, unbelief and some proud dumb notion of revenge.

THE PALACE

THE Palace stood high up, a landmark in bleak yellow brick, overlooking the roof of London. In March long avenues of almond trees blossomed on the cinder terraces above the race-course. Fred Lemon and his wife lived on the very top of the place. They had three rooms from which the view would have been wonderful if there had been any windows. In reality there was no view, except of the sky, seen through a thick green sky-light as though from the bottom of an aquarium. Lemon was caretaker. The air in the rooms seemed in some way dead, to be made up of an unchangeable formula of burning gas and cabbage and the odour of pink disinfectant that Lemon sprinkled down on the stairs and after concerts and dances in the big amusement hall. From the Lemons' rooms it was a hundred and fifty-three steps down to the ground floor, and another fifty-seven from the terraces down by the race-course to the gates and the tram-stop outside, and somehow, for a year or two, Mrs. Lemon had got into the habit of not going out.

Mrs. Lemon was forty-eight. She was a thin, dark woman, with an unhappy yellow skin and straggly hair. From behind she looked attractive, still slim and quite a girl. She had lived up at the top of the Palace ever since Lemon had first had the job, for nearly thirty years. At first it had been very nice, exciting, more than wonderful. The Palace had just been rebuilt after a fire. Everything was very grand. The concert hall, with its vast gilt gas chandeliers and its gilt-breasted goddesses, would seat five thousand. Brass bands and military bands came to play at concerts. There was a feeling of prosperity and security, and to Mrs. Lemon of secrecy also, a feeling of being shut deliciously away. She was just eighteen then, and it was a thrilling privilege, living up there at the top of the grand building, all alone with Lemon, with her own plush green couch and her own aspidistra and her own pictures. What did it matter that there was no view? She felt she had other views, far grander and far lovelier than the famous view of London that people walked up to see from the main terrace. She felt that she cherished views down into the recesses of her own heart, where no one else could see, views into a future of infinite possible loveliness, where only she was going.

Fred Lemon was a man nearly ten years older than herself, a little man with rabbity hair rubbing off at the temples, and a way of sitting in his trousers as he walked. It was a good job: thirty shillings a week with free rooms and free gas and tips after the concerts and dances. She felt that it was very grand. They entertained a bit, had friends up, showed them over the Palace. Lemon would light the gases with a long taper as they went from room to room: dining-hall with accommodation for five hundred diners over-looking the race-course, to the main concert hall with the gilt-piped organ, and all the amusement galleries, and the long corridors with the penny-in-the-slots and the naughty peep-holes. The main hall alone had — she had almost forgotten just the number — but anyway more than ten thousand panes of glass in its windows and glass roof. And every night, when Lemon did his last round, she went with him, and they would stand in the vast empty hall and look up and see the stars beyond the black roof of glass and stare at them in a fixed wonder that for her was sometimes ecstatic. At times she went back up the stairs alone while Lemon went round to the kitchens and got a bagful of fish and chips for supper, two bags if there were any guests. Then he would run up all the hundred and fifty-three steps with them, so that she should have them hot. Then she would make tea or cocoa, and they were quite happy. Lemon never reckoned to take anything strong, and she hadn't started the whisky then.

It was only after the war that she had started the whisky. The war changed everything: the Palace, Lemon, herself. Lemon was called up, the Palace was turned suddenly into an internment camp, and she lived alone in the three rooms that already badly needed painting, and where the odours of gas and cabbage were already as stale and permanent as the aspidistra and the pictures. And for a time, cut off by the hundred and fifty-three steps, half-forgotten by the authorities, she read books and wrote letters to Lemon, looked into the future and hoped and waited.

At that time the Palace was very quiet. Sitting by herself, right at the top of the building, she could hear nothing: no brass bands, no rag-time, no rifles in the shooting galleries, nothing but the silence of three hundred enemy civilians imprisoned. She felt that it was alien, foreign to her. The same outside. When she slipped out to do her shopping the almond trees were there the same as ever, and the grandstands on the race-course, and the trams running by the park railings. But there was also a strange new feeling, a new element, the prisoners.

At first they were not allowed outside. She saw them only as she hurried along the terrace. They stood behind the big windows, and stared at her. They were mostly Germans, with a few Austrians. She always hurried past, looking straight ahead, seeing them only out of the corners of her eyes.

Then, in the summer, they were allowed outside. They began to dig up the race-course, each with his little plot, and the potatoes stretched in dark lines like spokes across the curving track. They were allowed to walk together. Restrictions relaxed a little. And released, they ceased to be silent. She heard them singing, in concert, in their own language, richly, the tenors breaking out with falsetto.

But what meant freedom for them meant a restriction for her. If she passed through the grounds and they too were in the grounds there might, the authorities thought, be contact. So she had to report her movements.

It was pure formality, nothing at all. At the main entrance there was an office, with a sliding frosted window, and whenever she went out she tapped on the window. It opened and a clerk's head appeared and she said: 'Mrs. Lemon. I am just going out.' And when she returned: 'Mrs. Lemon. I am back now.'

At first there was an English clerk only, a corporal with ginger moustaches and spectacles and a blue pencil behind his right ear. She got so used to him that one day she was astonished, almost frightened, to see the glass open and the Austrian's head appear and say:

'Yes?' The upward singing inflexion of the voice was very gentle.

'I am Mrs. Lemon,' she said hurriedly. 'I have to report. I am just going out.'

'Oh! yes. It's all right. I know about you.'

When she came back the Austrian's head, a dark and rather large head, with grey gentle eyes, appeared again.

'Oh! yes, Mrs. Lemon. It's all right.'

Subsequently she would see him every day, except on Sundays. The office was shut on Sundays and she could walk straight out. All down the stairs and along the corridors and even in the Palace grounds she could feel the sanctified Sunday air, somehow strained and curiously silent. At the entrance gates she took the tram and the penny ticket that would take her within five steps of the church. She climbed up to the upper deck and sat so that she faced backwards. The tram glided rapidly away, but for a long time she could still see the Palace, ugly and rather forlorn on the hill behind the barbed-wire fences and the young almonds and limes. On early winter evenings she would see the great gloomy mass of brick looming up sepulchrally from behind the bare trees and the house-tops as the tram swerved and glided away. She felt herself watching it each time with the same odd sensation: a completely empty heart.

From time to time Fred Lemon came home on leave. In uniform he looked more rabbity than ever. Mrs. Lemon did not notice it. As in the old days they had fried fish and chips together, but now Lemon had to go down two streets past the tram stop to the fish-shop, and the fish was cold by the time he got back. Mrs. Lemon did not notice that either.

But Lemon noticed something: 'The war's gettin' you down, Hilda. I can see it.'

'Who said so?'

'Yes, it is. And I'll tell you what. If I was you I'd get summat to do.'

'Me?'

'You was at Pitman's three months, wasn't you? You know shorthand.'

'I *did*.'

'Well, you still do. Shorthand's like riding a bike. Once you can you always can.'

'Oh, I don't know, Fred.'

'You'll be getting morbid howdyedo, or whatever it is.'

Lemon went down and spoke to the corporal.

'The corporal's in the know. They's some big changes on. He'll keep his eyes open.'

In the late autumn, just before the second winter of the war, the Palace echoed with days of forlorn hammering. The office was being enlarged, and in a day or two the corporal stopped Mrs. Lemon on her way out. 'About the end of next week,' he finished. In a little over a week she was working in the office. There were two other women beside herself in the office, with the corporal and the Austrian. The Austrian had a desk by the pigeon-hole and Mrs. Lemon sat by the window. Every time the pigeon-hole opened something was startled within her and she looked up. She kept up her stare at the pigeon-hole until it shut again, so that each time, as the Austrian turned round, he would see her sitting there, in what seemed to be a state of transfixed fascination.

At first it was nothing more than that: sitting and staring, silence, a kind of day-dreamy wonder. All that she did was unconscious. Something kept her back: the war itself, her idea of patriotism, a lot of things. She did not stop to analyse them. All her emotions and reasons and even her desires went into staring. She did not really understand herself at all.

The Austrian did not understand it either. He was a foreigner, but not a stranger. He had lived in London for fifteen years. He was a barber and, at the outbreak of war, had just set up for himself off the Brompton Road. It was a rather select quarter and, like Mrs. Lemon, he had visions. The war smashed them. He had been engaged to an English girl in Fulham. The war had smashed that too.

Thus, in a sense, he was on common ground with Mrs.

Lemon. The war, from different angles, had struck them down.

Towards the end of the winter Mrs. Lemon began to make tea in the office, about four o'clock every afternoon. The Austrian was very thin, his natural dark pallor had begun to look unnatural. Mrs. Lemon felt tired too. She was oppressed by a lack of escape. She had become, in a sense, a prisoner herself. The Palace held her tight. Regulations were difficult; she needed special permits in order to go out at night, and in a general way she never went out after dark, except perhaps to church on Sunday. She sat upstairs, read a little, wrote letters, stared, waited. Lemon, home on Christmas leave, had bought a bottle of whisky, and about half the bottle was left. That winter she began a sip of whisky, with a little water, as a nightcap. She slept better. Then when she had finished the bottle, she bought another, drank it with rather less water, and more quickly.

She kept a medicine bottle of it down in the office. It was nice to have a little in the afternoon tea. Then one afternoon the Austrian saw her pouring it into the tea-cup.

'What is it? What are you doing?'

'It's brown milk,' she said.

'*Brown* milk?'

'You have some — it's nice, it'll do you good.'

'No, no. In tea?'

'It's nice. It'll do you good. You look run down.'

He smiled. 'Not in the regulations, you know.'

'A lot of things are not in the regulations. You have some. Please. With me.'

'All right.'

She poured the whisky into the cup, a mere sip, and then a little more for herself. The office overlooked the terraces. It was March, the days were lengthening, and here and there the almond trees were out, blowing in the wind like balloons of pink lace.

'I'm going to have a garden,' the Austrian said.

'Oh!' She was quite startled. 'Why? When?'

'In April. In two weeks. In two weeks I will get my potatoes in.'

'Why?'

'I want to be out of here. Outside. I don't like it inside. Not in summer.'

'You won't be in the office, then?'

'Sometimes.'

'Not often?'

'I don't want to be.'

She began to understand herself. She knew, at once, for the first time, what was the matter with her. She made no effort to conceal it, from herself at least. That night she drank no whisky at all. She went out, walked about the streets, up and down, going nowhere. It was something which seemed to be quite purposeless but which had, for her, quite a definite and almost terrifying purpose. It was as though she were half-way up a precipice and had to decide for herself whether to climb up or down. That night she could have let go without a murmur, irrevocably.

In the morning the need for a decision had gone. There was now no going up or down. She knew, somehow, clearly, and very bitterly, that there was and never could be anything so definite. There was no getting out of it, no solution, no compromise. She was there, stretched out, between one thing and another. And she was broken up with the terror and knowledge of it.

The Austrian saw it. He took it that she was ill, run down. He did not connect it with himself until she said, quite as though it were some passionate concern of her own:

'You're not strong enough to do the garden. You're not strong enough!'

'But that's why I want to do it. To get strong. It is bad for me in here. I don't feel half alive. I want to do it.'

'Don't do it. I don't want you to do it.'

It was a kind of confession. She was so strung up that she could not have concealed it now if she had wanted to conceal it. And, for the first time, the Austrian was upset.

'You mustn't . . .' he did not know what to say, 'you can't . . .'

Then the corporal came in with order papers, and temporarily at least they were saved from themselves. She went back to her desk. She was in a state of stupid anguish.

She could not work. The sun on the papers, blinding white, created a blank of despair in her mind and when she wrote on a sheet of paper, 'I want to say something to you. Be on the east side stairs at 9 o'clock to-night,' she hardly knew what she was doing.

It was a stupid request, but anguish turned it for her into a reasonable one, imperative. There was never any question of his obeying it. When she put the note on his desk he looked up at once and shook his head violently. Even then she was quite certain that he would come.

At nine o'clock she waited in darkness on the stairs for almost an hour. The Palace was in darkness. It surrounded her sepulchrally. For the first time she hated it. She had nothing on but her underclothes and a dressing gown, and the cold and her worked-up feelings gradually set her shivering.

Finally she went back to her room. Her hatred turned from the Palace to the war, from the war to Lemon, from Lemon to the Austrian, and finally upon herself. She sat and drank a great deal of whisky.

In the morning she was in bad shape. Excessive whisky had produced in her something of the effect of excessive tears and excessive debauchery. She looked wild and ill. The Austrian was quite shocked. He wanted to do something for her. It was an almost polite solicitude, negative, foreign, meaning nothing to her.

'Are you all right?'

'I asked you to come. Why didn't you?'

'Regulations. You know. You know. This isn't a hotel. You want to get me shot?'

'I want you to come, that's all.'

'No, no, no.'

'Come to-night.'

'Oh! no. We're prisoners. It can't be done.'

'It's quite dark. No one can see.' She was speaking with a rising hysteria, still under the whisky. 'You must come. You must come. If you don't come I shall do something.'

'Mrs. Lemon! Please!'

That night, in the big living-room, she got a table, set a

chair on it and climbed up through the skylight. She was going to throw herself down to the terrace. She had reached a point of extreme distraction, a point where the wildest act seemed credible and right. It seemed quite right and natural that she should end her life there. The night was quite clear and dark and windy. It seemed a fitting end to her life that she should go off the roof of the place in which she had lived so much of it. She felt quite clear-headed, almost elated. In the sky the searchlights were playing and swinging about in great fans of light. She stood and clung to the skylight, bracing herself, almost ready, and watched them. They seemed like the beckoning signals from the other world.

Then, quite suddenly, she went far beyond the need for decisions and the necessity for sacrifice. Her nerves crumpled suddenly into a mass of entangled wool. She stood in a half-faint, cold shivers of hysteria running up her back, her mouth whimpering. It was all she could do to climb down through the skylight and lower herself on to the table without falling.

As she sat in the chair in the room below it was as though she had jumped off the Palace, not in a physical way, but mentally and spiritually. She felt that she had committed another kind of suicide, that the best of her, the sweet core of all her feelings, had gone off the roof into an eternal disaster.

The next morning the Austrian was not in the office. She showed no surprise, no distress at all. She did not ask either for him or about him. She worked on without feeling. In the afternoon the corporal said: 'Künsberg has good weather for his first day in the garden. I wonder if he'll miss his tea?' but she did not answer. The fact of the Austrian's departure evoked no feeling in her at all. It was as though the centre of feeling in her were irrevocably smashed. Her only sign of distress was that she drank her tea with a little more whisky than usual.

She worked on in the office all through the war. After the war Lemon came home to a strange Palace: deserted, filthy, a derelict prison whose prisoners had departed.

He did not like it at all. The Palace had been his pride.
He had kept it beautiful. Now the soul seemed to have gone
out of it. He did not understand it. He did not understand
Mrs. Lemon either. She seemed so strangely attached to the
Palace. She never went out. Drinking her whisky, she sat
in an unemotional stupor in the room with the skylight.

And often Lemon would say to her:

'It isn't right, Hilda. You shouldn't do it. Pull yourself
together. You never used to be like it. You'll be getting me
sacked. I don't know what's come over you, Hilda. It's not
right.'

She in turn would try to convey, by a look, a gesture, by
silence or a little more whisky, that it was not right at all.

COUNTRY CLASSICS

This popular series of quality paperbacks includes famous classics and forgotten masterpieces of writing about the countryside and rural subjects. The books are all produced in a 216 x 135mm format with beautiful colour covers. Selected titles are available in hardback.

Adventures Among Birds
W. H. Hudson

W. H. Hudson was one of the great field naturalists and ornithologists of the last century. In this book, he describes incidents and adventures watching birds across England, from wild geese in Norfolk to goldfinches in Dorset.

'This enchanting book is about the time before motorways and about the pure joy of having ears and eyes.'

EDWARD BLISHON,
Pick of the Paperbacks,
Radio 4

Paperback £3.95
Hardback £8.95

A Cotswold Village
J. Arthur Gibbs

One of the most beautiful and detailed portraits of the English countryside ever written, Gibbs describes rural life at the end of the last century when the Cotswolds were one of the most primitive and old-fashioned districts of England.

'Genial and amusing.

ALEX HAMILTON,
Guardian

Paperback £3.95
Hardback £8.95

The Country House-Wife's Garden
William Lawson

The first book ever written on gardening for women, a delightful pot-pourri of hints and gardening lore written in the seventeenth century by a Yorkshire parson. A perfect gift for the gardener.

Introduced by Rosemary Verey.

'This is an enchanting book.'

ALAN MELVILLE, Popular Gardening

Paperback £2.50
Hardback £4.95

The Essential Gilbert White of Selborne

The first popular selection from all of White's writings. A perfect introduction for the newcomer to White and Selborne.

Illustrated with wood engravings by Eric Ravilious.

Paperback £4.95
Hardback £8.95
384pp

Gypsy Folk Tales
John Sampson (Ed.)

Nothing brings us closer to the spirit of Romany life than these strange, haunting tales of poor country folk, beggars and travellers in a land of giants and dragons, great mansions, hovels, enchanted castles, witchcraft and magic.

'His great collections of folk-tales are treasure-houses of quaint expressions and beautiful turns of phrase.'

WALTER STARKIE

Paperback only £3.50

Life in a Devon Village
Henry Williamson

An enchanting memoir of village life in the Twenties. A companion volume to *Village Tales*.

'A welcome reprint ... Williamson is still our best nature writer since Richard Jefferies.'

BRIAN JACKMAN, The Sunday Times

Paperback £3.95
Hardback £8.95

Memoirs of a Surrey Labourer
George Bourne

'There's writing for you.'   HENRY WILLIAMSON

Paperback only £4.95

The Old Farm
Thomas Hennell

A fascinating record of traditional farms and farming methods, it presents a vivid portrait of old-fashioned country life and lore, from the dialects of the shepherds to cider-making, straw-plaiting and charcoal-burning, from weather-forecasting to mole-catching.

Paperback only £3.95

Sweet Thames Run Softly
Robert Gibbings

The story of a summer journey by rowing boat from the source of the Thames to London. Illustrated throughout with the author's own wood engravings.

'For the soul's refreshment read and keep this book. It is wise, kindly and full of lovely things.'

Sunday Times

'An intoxicating book, almost Edwardian in spirit.'
ANDREW LANGLEY, Daily Telegraph

'An enchanting experience ... there is only one other in the compendium of Thames literature which is deserving of inclusion in the same class — the immortal Three Men in a Boat.'

SENEX, Oxford Times

Paperback only £3.95

Tales of Old Ireland
James Berry

From a great tradition of storytelling in West Ireland, these are tales of poor communities living in a bleak and beautiful countryside against a background of man-hunts, smuggling, murders, wakes, rebellion and starvation.

'A marvellous book, readable, amusing and educative.'

Hibernia

Paperback only £3.95

ORDER FORM

COUNTRY CLASSICS

		Hardback	*Paperback*
——	ADVENTURES AMONG BIRDS	£8.95	£3.95
——	A COTSWOLD VILLAGE	£8.95	£3.95
——	THE COUNTRY HOUSE-WIFE'S GARDEN		£2.50
——	THE ESSENTIAL GILBERT WHITE	£8.95	£4.95
——	GYPSY FOLK TALES	—	£3.50
——	LIFE IN A DEVON VILLAGE	£8.95	£3.95
——	MEMOIRS OF A SURREY LABOURER	—	£4.95
——	THE OLD FARM	—	£3.95
——	SWEET THAMES RUN SOFTLY	—	£3.95
——	TALES OF OLD IRELAND	—	£3.95

If you cannot find these titles in your bookshop, they can be obtained directly from the publisher. Indicate the number of copies required and fill in the form below (in block letters please):

NAME ....

ADDRESS ....

....

....

Send to CS Department, Robinson Publishing, 11 Shepherd House, 5 Shepherd Street, London W1Y 7LD. Please enclose cheque or postal order to the value of the cover price plus:
70p for the first book plus 15p per copy for each additional book ordered to a maximum charge of £2.20. Applicable in U.K. only.
EIRE: Please write to Irish Bookhandling Ltd., North Richmond Industrial Estate, Dublin 1.
While every effort is made to keep prices low, it is sometimes necessary to increase prices at short notice. Robinson Publishing reserve the right to show on covers, and charge, new retail prices which may differ from those advertised in the text or elsewhere.